"You don't read this book, you pull it on like Athena's helmet, as it grabs you by the collar for a flying trip through Oxford."
–**David Hannula**, *Omlet, Prynce of Fynnland*, **playwright**

IF YOU'VE EVER LUSTED after an Oxford education, here it is.

Diane Quinnell's irresistible summer voyage leaps into the confluence of two monolithic educational philosophies: Smith College, largest of America's mighty Seven Sisters where Quinnell earned her art degree, and venerable Oxford, hot-wired and vital with its formidable tribe of intellectual warriors. It is 1996 and Salman Rushdie materializes there too, braving the *fatwa* that threatens his life. And there is romance of the cerebral kind, as well as Bollywood musicals, a swami with a wicked sense of humor, and art, learning and debating, men and women, twilight in the garden, more art – and a spectacular theft, whose discovery and recovery are all orchestrated by Quinnell, who is more of a huntress than she lets on.

Advance praise for RD McHattie's

Oxford Vindaloo

"*Oxford Vindaloo* is a charming collision between old world and new, east and west, technology and tradition, vaudeville and academia, age and youth, eccentricity and desperate normalcy. It's also my favorite recipe for curried shoes."
–**Howard Jay Patterson, M.E.M.**
(a.k.a. Ivan Fyodorovich Karamazov, C.P.K.)
founder emeritus of *The Flying Karamazov Brothers*

REMEMBER THAT ARTY FRIEND from school?

Join her in some of the adventures you always suspected she would have and in some you never would have dreamed of, all in a story that's sometimes heartrending, often hilarious and always compelling.

Returning to Denver
by RD McHattie

"Part coming of age, part mystery – this book delivers on many levels. Diane's search for answers in the Denver Art Museum sparks a quest for self-definition and a broader exploration of the meaning of success: an introspective and intriguing read."
–Dr. Kristyn Gorton, Department of Theatre,
Film and TV, University of York, UK

"Vividly drawn characters! Arch social satire! Thousands of well-focused details, cultural allusions and wry remarks – all delivered by just plain good story telling that never loses the thread!"
–Jeanne Emrich, poet and President of Minnesota Branch,
National League of American Pen Women

"I knew Robyn back when she was an artist and singer. Now that she's a writer, I'll bet she's good at that too."
–Penn Jillette, *Penn & Teller*

Available through online booksellers
in paperback with local printing and shipping
in U.S.A., Canada and United Kingdom
—and now reissued for E-book.

Also by RD McHattie

Returning to Denver, A Diane Quinnell Story

Children's picture book by Robyn Dean

A Black Cat Named Smokey

Oxford Vindaloo

A Novel
RD McHattie

ZYXALON PRESS   MINNEAPOLIS

Excerpt from *The Moor's Last Sigh* by Salman Rushdie, published by Jonathan Cape. Reprinted with permission of The Random House Group Ltd.
Excerpt from *The Moor's Last Sigh* by Salman Rushdie. Copyright © 1995 by Salman Rushdie, reprinted electronically in the U.K. with permission of The Wylie Agency LLC.
Excerpts from *Jude the Obscure* by Thomas Hardy and *The Barrel-organ* by Alfred Noyes are reprinted here through Public Domain usage.

McVitie's is a food brand owned by United Biscuits Limited, registered offices at Hayes Park, Hayes End Road, Hayes, Middlesex UB4 8EE UK.
The Glenlivet is a brand name of Chivas Brothers Limited, registered offices at 111/113 Refrew Road, Paisley, Refrewshire PA12 4JS UK.
Guinness is a trademarked brand name owned by Guinness & Co., registered offices at St James's Gate, Dublin 8 Ireland.
Trivial Pursuit is a game brand name of Hasbro Inc., Pawtucket RI, U.S.A.

History assistance: Clare Hopkins, Archivist Trinity College Oxford
Editorial assistance: Dominique Jean Maugein, David Hannula, Greg Shea.
Cover and text tech executed by LinnellDesign.com

COVER ART: Needlepoint and drawing © 2011 by RD McHattie.

E-book conversion by Smith House Press.com

ZYXALON PRESS   MINNEAPOLIS

Introductory message

Oxford Vindaloo – a thoroughly entertaining and credible narrative which combines attention to the historical detail of Trinity College with an ability to convey the spirit of the place. I enjoyed it hugely and wish our summer visitor RD McHattie every success.

Sir Ivor Roberts
President
Trinity College Oxford

Oxford Vindaloo

Diane Quinnell's Summer Term

ARRIVE
London

DIANE QUINNELL LOOKED OUT upon the tidy street of shut-up shops, then penned her furious message on the postcard.

June 24. London: 5 AM – I am sitting on a bench in a typical London square. A lie. Typical London squares don't open until 7 AM. I am sitting on a bench in Belgravia, where three sidewalks come together in a triangle. To paraphrase **The Pirates of Penzance:** *'It is the very spot for homeless people' and I am one this morning. The others should pop out of the public lavatory cubical across the way at any moment.*

She flipped the card over. The rakish James Bond stared back, gun pressed against white dinner jacket. She drew spirals emanating from Bond's eyes. Next to his head she lettered carefully: *I HATE JET LAG,* encircled the words, made a line pointing to his mouth.

11

Next card: Queen Victoria, Empress of India.

June 24. London: 5 AM – My bed & breakfast two
blocks from here, like an authentic London square, will
also open at 7 AM. So said the nameplate on the door.
Like Christopher Robin, therefore, I have bump, bump,
bumped my rolling suitcase along the quaint cracks in
the quaint sidewalks from Victoria Station to the B&B
and now to here: a bench. I shall wait for 7 AM. Here I
shall stay. Here I shall probably expire from
malnutrition and jet lag. Did I mention, I hate jet lag?

She made herself as small as possible. Her suitcase tucked up next to her, her back turned in the least threatening direction, she waited. If this had been Denver, she could easily have found an all-night diner and ordered her own eggs and toast. Perhaps coming this far alone had been a mistake?

Expecting the worst, she sat up a bit straighter, ready to repel attackers. Surely in the next moment, pickpockets out of Dickens or the Baker Street Irregulars would emerge from behind every bush and phone box ready to strip her of her belongings. Funny how the calm morning did not translate to tranquility for her in this picturesque spot.

She tried to feel lucky. As they arrived at Victoria Station, the bus driver had pointed out the grassy area covered with sleeping bodies in sleeping bags accompanied by lumps of backpacks. 'Them that's missed their connections,' he had told her. She shook off the Doom of that sight, checked her wristwatch again.

LONDON 1996. Population seven million. Diane and the bus driver who drove the route into the city from Heathrow appeared to be the only two humans active this morning. In the dawn light and relative silence, the city had looked recognizable as the London that Diane had visited fifteen years earlier. Yet unfamiliar. Outside the airport, a shimmering video billboard screen changed messages three times as they drove by it. What next? wondered Diane. She hoped for no more freaky things straight out of *Bladerunner.*

Just after quarter past seven AM, she sauntered past newsstands and tobacconist stalls preparing to open for service. Killing time. Her room would be ready at ten – *just a short wait* – the desk had informed her after she had dutifully consumed her plate of runny beans and dead-looking tomato half.

She turned through a rack of postcards just outside a small shop, purchased a few of the city, then went looking for a park bench or café table from which to observe, reflect, write. Sort out this city. This trip. *"Killing the London Morning,"* she began another card, then stared into space for a long while.

Everything added together, the place felt backwards. Not just the cars on the wrong side of the street. More an all-encompassing disorientation, as if her innate sense of direction had gone on vacation as well, but flown away on the wrong plane. Now that she was here and on her own, this trip felt like a challenge far greater than imagined. *No wonder my mom thought I was nuts to get on a plane and go 1600 miles to New England for college,* Diane thought now, tapping into a parallel experience from her freshman year at Smith. But everyone flew, Diane had rationalized. Why not me? And now, in 1996, everyone flew everywhere. People took entire families – even toddlers – on vacations by air as if they were just climbing into their own cars in their own driveways, not jetting through thousands of miles of sky at 35,000 feet altitude. A flicker of her initial excitement returned – from how many hours ago? – then faded.

She watched a crowd forming outside Buckingham Palace with no interest in joining them.

*   *   *

She awakened groggy in the muggy, late afternoon, stood up a little taller, trying to stretch the kink out of her neck. She splashed some water on her face and went out.

Well-dressed people moved about on the sidewalks. Many chatted quietly on tiny, hand-held telephones. She guessed that's what they were. Certainly there weren't any in Denver. Nor in Boston where she had paused for a day before flying across the Atlantic. That Merry Olde England had a more high-tech gadget than America – land of luxury items and competitive consumers – struck her as bizarre. And with a rectangle of black plastic pressed to each ear, Londoners went about their business.

No one stepped into her way to bother her. That felt wonderful, in a way. She'd always disliked that part of visiting New York City, strangers continually trying to pull aside visitors. Here, rarely even one glanced her way. Instead of fostering a delicious sense of autonomy, however, the moment conjured her mother's voice saying with typical finality: *'You're on your own, Diane.'*

The afternoon napping had been brutal, exploding all myths of cooler, northern climes. The night in London remained hot. She propped her door open a shoe's width, just wide enough to invite a breeze but not visitors. She'd learned from her one night in Nice, never to leave a hotel room door open – big mistake – no matter how stifling the weather.

Just after four AM, she peeled herself off the smouldering sheets and sat in the window. Wide awake, she found the cards she'd bought and grabbed a pen.

Postcard: Marble grand piano, Highgate Cemetery.

> *June 25. London: 4 AM – My London adventure has not yet improved. I am sitting up for long hours now, listening to the basso-continuo down the hall. The barking-one on the other side of the partition (formerly called a wall) I am anxious to meet. Imagine being able to pick them out at breakfast in a few hours? This slow-paced symphony reminds me of those ill-advised trips to some relative's rustic cabin in the mountains, the one*

they were building with their own hands, where a great
sawing of logs fills the night air, and perhaps keeps
away the bears.

How had she ever gotten the idea to sit in this inferno of a room, listening to people snoring and call it an adventure, she asked herself. Oh yes. Senior year, the way Pamela and Faye had raved about this summer program at Oxford had convinced Diane that she must try it. Unfortunately, her poor career start put travel out of the question, yet she had refused to abandon her plan. Finally, Diane had given up on an art career and had begun teaching. A full time job that included summers off? Unbelievable. And so, at thirty-one – to England at last!

Most unexpectedly at that moment, a classic double-decker bus chugged past and for a moment, she – in her nightgown on her second story windowsill – was suspended at eye level with the sleepy passengers on its upper deck. One person managed a feeble wave. Diane chuckled for a moment at that incongruity, until the wake of diesel fumes followed. A distinctive smell for Diane, straight from her high school choir trip. This was definitely London. Wouldn't her old choir friend love to hear about this?

Postcard: Classic London red phone box.

Vaudeville's small hotel room joke left out the part
about the free tickets to the snoring symphony that is
performed all night. My room resembles more a closet or
a berth on a ship than a bedroom. But for this trip, I
thought it would be romantic to travel on my limited
budget as a fledgling school teacher. Perhaps, as in
Goodbye, Mr Chips, *I too will meet another history-*
loving traveler on the steps of whatever ancient place I
will visit with my Oxford classmates.

And maybe, just maybe, it'll be cooler there, she smiled limply to herself.

* * *

Tuesday, wandering through Knightsbridge, Diane spotted Harrod's, a place that would probably get her into trouble, so many tempting things to buy. The money she had in her pocket needed to stay in her pocket, as much as possible. Six weeks of school lay before her, and a week of vacation following.

So she continued down the street, and stumbled upon The Victoria & Albert Museum, a better match for her than Harrod's. Standing in front of the V&A, she knew the building by sight, having been driven past it several times on her choir trip, years earlier. Yet just like seeing the Louvre in Paris, when the voice on the coach loudspeaker always said, '*Just there, just now, but not stopping today,*' Diane had been kept from it. Today would be her day.

The turquoise blue banner snapped crisply announcing the V&A's special exhibit: *Textiles of William Morris.* Diane scooted inside and tagged along with a tour just forming, viewing the progression of tapestries and fabric swatches. She studied the charming miniature animals and repeating floral vines woven into beautiful cloth coverings and wall papers. The scope of Morris's designs impressed Diane the most. Endless variations on themes consumers loved, even to that day. Her lawyer friend Emily back in Denver had her entire classic home restored with newly reissued William Morris textiles and wall coverings that complemented the Mission Oak furniture so popular in that area. Diane stepped along past the slow-moving tour as her art history knowledge eclipsed the general information the guide was providing. Soon she was at the exit.

Once out in the hallway, Diane turned left instead of right, to step out of the crowd, but also with the hope of finding some secret corner of the V&A collection. Having worked at the Denver Art Museum, she knew that the most popular galleries were not necessarily the most interesting to her with her broad range of art interests. Therefore, continuing down an empty corridor and around a corner, she chose the next door. *The Cast Collection*, the plaque read. She pulled open the door and entered into a cavernously large, glass-ceilinged space crowded with marble sculptures and colossal chunks of architecture. The sun streamed in, bathing dazzling white upon the hundreds of huge items: classical pediment reliefs, tomb effigies, grand portico arches and figures all squeezed in upon each other. No one else was in the huge room. Was this a display or had she stumbled into some storage room?

She wandered about stunned as she started recognizing pieces. She had studied most of them in art history – and none of them belonged in this museum, nor in England. Why were they here? She returned to the doorway and looked for information. So, this was not a family named *Cast* – as it would have been in Denver – bestowing its collection; these were plaster reproductions, cast from the originals for use as academic teaching tools, the sign informed her. Unbelievable. And how exactly did someone cast the entire height of Trajan's Column? She wondered as she saw that the trunk-like forms that dominated the room, reached to the very ceiling vault. Wasn't that column over 200 feet high? Well, here it was in two pieces, side by side. Because the top half began on the floor, viewers could actually see at eye level a portion of the carved relief storyline that in Rome lies forbidden to close scrutiny, a hundred feet above the average pedestrian's head. Amazing! She studied the images of the Roman Trajan's triumphs, conquering and enlisting foreign nations into his powerful Empire, until she felt the strain in her neck from tipping her head back so long.

She took a few steps staring at the floor, and nearly bumped into Giovanni Pisano's elaborate church pulpit from Pisa. Diane walked in circles around it, agog. *Too bad I left my sketchbook back in my room*, she was saying to herself just as she caught a glimpse of a familiar figure out of the corner of her eye; she stood below it, incredulous. Michelangelo's *David* towered over her on its high platform, just as it would in Florence, the tiny stone thrower grown gigantic in marble, proportioned to accentuate his deed. Dee Quinnell – Diane's mother and biggest Michelangelo fan – would never believe this. Why hadn't she just packed a bag and come along?

Diane felt giddy with the discovery. She remained fixed in the lonely room until closing time.

In the evening of that first full day, standing on Chelsea Bridge over the Thames, her eyes followed a small boat flowing downstream with the current toward Greenwich. She'd walked what seemed like five times the distances she had expected everywhere she had headed, covertly studying her map, trying not to look like a tourist. Nearly five thousand miles west of here in Denver, she'd tacked the huge map of the London Underground onto her apartment wall to get familiar with the city's street names, orderly station stops, directions. Everything in a simple grid: subway trains east-and-west, buses north-and-south. She imagined great adventures, none of which included the burning feet that peeked out of her sandals right now. Yet hadn't she discovered Michelangelo's *David* and – even more unbelievable – the entire Column of Trajan? She still felt dumbfounded by that.

How nice it would be to catch someone's eye and tell them what I'm thinking, here in London. Her eyes sparkled for a moment. People continued past. That's when the boat she was watching faded from sight around the curve. With a small gasp, she suddenly realized where she had gone wrong. That easy-to-follow subway map had set everything into a simplified parallel universe, divorced from the realities of nature. No wonder she had been lost all day. Everyone in London must know the river executes a nice turn here and there. Everyone except Diane. She laughed out loud.

"Everything all right, Miss?" an elderly gentleman enquired.

"Oh yes! Fine, fine," Diane assured him as he nodded and continued on his way. *You are so self-amused, Diane,* she chided herself, but laughed a little longer before seeking a very late dinner.

ARRIVE
Trinity College, Oxford
by 4:30 PM, Thursday, June 27

THE RIDE TO OXFORD gave Diane time for expressing her adventures in classic-Diane fashion: more postcards. This one showed a rectangular room filled with paintings of exotic plants all packed frame-to-frame and to the ceiling, the wainscoting and display cases made up of every type of wood sample collected from the artist's world travels.

> *June 27. London –* 'Go down to Kew in lilac-time (it isn't far from London!)' *What a great advertising jingle! In Kew Gardens, I saw such wonders: the enormous glass plant house, a Royal Cottage, and the Marianne North Gallery which is a cottage of botanical paintings. Amazing, yes? All of those paled next to having been able to count the rivets on the Concorde jet overhead as it landed next door at the airport. Welcome to modern England.*

She watched the landscape whizzing past. The turnoff for Oxford taken, she looked into the bright afternoon sun, rising off her seat with anticipation of everything ahead of her.

"Are you sure this is it?" Diane surveyed the ornate canyon of spire-covered buildings that lined the High Street. Oxford, a honey-colored fortress. She glanced about for two seconds, looking for a sign or welcome banner. Not a one. Aren't people supposed to meet travelers, Diane wondered. The late afternoon light outlined the architectural details, slanting filigreed shadows down onto a scattering of cars, a truck, a random handful of people in the distance. Clearly no one was waiting for her. She cast a mournful look back at the motorcoach driver and remained standing on the coach's step.

"Oh, no. This isn't the Trinity front gate. That's just over on Broad Street," the driver said. "Just follow the lane between buildings there," he indicated with a gesture, "and it'll lead you straight there. Cheers!" The look that accompanied his farewell said, *Move along. I've a schedule to keep.*

Diane descended onto the cobblestones, lugging her suitcase behind her. The bus pulled away, the rear panel proclaiming: *Oxford Tube.* No wonder she had trouble finding it at Victoria Station. Diane had come to know through all of British literature that trains came into Victoria Station, not buses. And certainly not The Underground, their subway, which is also called The Tube. She mumbled to herself, still irritated at that mix up that had added to an already blistering hot day. Now she stood, deposited in the middle of nowhere. *Cheers, indeed.* She didn't feel at all like celebrating.

The towers and spires of Oxford stood sentinel as Diane decided how to proceed. Any quaint sign post with arrow, reading: Trinity? She took a deep breath and pulled her suitcase along behind her, putting on a bold face for the fortress-like town. After a hundred steps down an alleyway in the direction the driver had pointed to, the pedestrian way suddenly opened upon a wide, paved courtyard encircling a squat round building encased in tall thin windows. It might have been considered very beautiful on a different day with a different attitude. At the moment, in her own determination not to be lost, not to be in the wrong place and not to be late – it was already nearly five – Diane vented her frustration by shouldering past the magnificent building, unwilling to acknowledge its harmonious lines and singular situation. Marching in a straight line past a second round building, this one sporting a white cupola topped with a patina-colored roof, she emerged through a tall gate giving onto the next street and halted. She scanned left, then upward. Atop a row of stone columns, enormous bearded Roman heads glowered down at her. Who exactly could see them up there? she wondered, irritably, as she craned her neck to inspect them. To her right, she spotted the full figures of Roman matrons perched even higher up on a nearby building. Absurd! Was this city built for a race of giants? No. She recalled from art history: grand architecture was meant to intimidate visitors.

She studied the bearded heads again, their stern faces frozen in classical stone. Feeling their scrutiny, she scowled back. With a huff of scorn, she turned her back on all staring eyes and took a tentative step out into the thoroughfare.

Far down the block on the other side of the street, a tall young man with a clipboard stepped out from an ironwork gate, then performed some highly unexpected antics. Like Buster Keaton or Harold Lloyd doing a double-take, the young man glanced in her direction, then leaned in the opposite direction looking far down the street, scanned the arc between them in exaggerated slow-motion until he leaned far over in her direction. Finally, he raised his hand high over his head and waved at her. Diane scurried in his direction and soon came upon the tastefully proportioned sign on the tiny cottage: Trinity College.

The tall young man with the clipboard smiled hopefully. "Hello. Welcome. I'm Daniel Glasser, the program assistant. I was here last summer so ask me anything you're wondering about. You're going to love it here. Let me guess." He scanned his check list. "Estelle Giddons?" he asked with a quizzical look.

"Diane Quinnell," she said, liking this animated young man. A tuft of fuzzy hair wafting up in back added to his whimsical mannerisms.

Good natured. Bubbling. He exuded the best feelings.

"Excellent, Diane. You're one of the last to arrive." He checked off her name with a flourish.

"Yes. I had a little trouble finding the right bus, but then it was a quick trip." Diane felt again the windblown speed at which they had sailed through the countryside on the M-40. She unconsciously smoothed back her short dark hair and blew out a quick puff of breath, now that she felt free to relinquish the grip on her suitcase. Had the ride been only ninety minutes from Victoria Station? She had anticipated a day's journey. And worried every minute all the way.

"And here is your roommate, Natalie," Daniel said and called to a young woman approaching on foot. Diane now had a chance to look around. First impressions: Tranquil. Quiet. Green. Not another person in sight. No fanfare. No banner. Just the greeter and the elegant young woman who sauntered idly toward them along the gravel path.

"Nice to meet you, Diane," she elongated the name as if to make sure Diane noticed that she'd learned it already, before an introduction. "I'm Natalie." Flawless skin. Clear, calm eyes. The accent, definitely New York. She offered Diane her hand and looked into her eyes. Diane felt some familiar electricity pass between them. The electricity grew as her roommate retained Diane's hand with gentle firmness, and held her gaze. Challenging behavior, learned where? Diane wondered momentarily. New York, of course! But to establish what? She returned the eye contact for whatever ritual this young woman was conducting. Natalie scanned Diane's dark brown eyes, taking a reading, as it were. The intelligence of this young woman was apparent. Beautiful – and perhaps she knew it. Diane rather liked it, finally coming into the long-sought harbor, and now feeling moored to this steady individual, who neither fluttered nor broke into meaningless social chitchat. Very un-American, Diane smiled to herself. The experience lingered.

Diane, who would normally make a comic remark at this juncture, instead felt comfortable enough to simply pause and see where this first examination would lead. At that moment two thoughts struck her. The extending handshake. Cherise Vander-Lyden, the woman who Diane worked for briefly at the Denver Art Museum, had engaged in a similar ritual, an introduction that vacillated between challenging and thrilling. Diane repressed a shudder at that association and consciously chose to brush that shadow aside. The warmth and gentle pressure of Natalie's hand also made her wonder when the last time was that Diane had held hands with someone? Anyone?

Daniel stepped forward. Natalie gently relaxed her grip on Diane's hand, finally allowing it to escape. "Natalie is a graduate student as well, so we put you two together. But first you'll need all the official things. Let's just step into The Lodge. Just leave your bag there with the rest." He attached a tag on which he scribbled a number and letter. "The staff will bring it to your room. Come meet Mr Dickens, the Head Porter. This is Diane Quinnell. Sixteen-C, Mr Dickens," he addressed the uniformed guard.

The Porter nodded cordially to her, stepped up to the counter and handed her a wedge of plastic about the size of a fingernail clipper. "Here is your key. This opens all doors including the gate, plus operates the laundry." She looked at it with curiosity, though Daniel gave her little time for asking how exactly this flat rectangle did all of that.

"You'll check here for mail, announcements," Daniel continued. "The Lodge is also the gathering point for outings." He led her outside again to her roommate. "I have just one more to check in. Natalie, why don't you two head for the garden and meet everyone?" He smiled to them and stepped through the gate to scan Broad Street again.

"So, Diane," Natalie offered, "I'm not going to volunteer much information just now. Just let you absorb this place." Diane sensed a certain calculation in her roommate's simple declaration. Perhaps extending silent time for watching and forming opinions. Nevertheless, she appreciated skipping the usual formal dance. A refreshing beginning for a foreign, new world.

They followed the wide gravel path along the Broad Street palisade, and at the turn of the drive, continued toward a large stone building with a chunky clock tower, accompanied all the while by the crunching of their own footsteps. Striped towers in a completely different style soared above Trinity's rough stone wall to their left.

As they passed an ancient cedar tree, five fuzzy ducklings scurried their way, changed direction, then circulated near the tree just out of reach. "What a greeting!" she said to Natalie, who also stopped. Who could resist ducklings? With glee Diane lurched forward in pursuit.

It felt to Diane that at exactly the moment her foot landed on the grass, a gruff voice shouted, "Stay off the lawn, you!" She glanced up while obediently jumping backward off the grass, perceived the Porter motioning, and in the same instant, waved in assent to the authority of The Lodge. The ducklings peeped merrily. Her clownish act would have entertained anyone, especially her circus-arts friends back in Denver, Diane thought.

First day rules, strictly enforced. Training visitors for proper behavior within the walls of Trinity reminded her of another admonishing guard in her life. Reggie, head guard at the Denver Art Museum. He had also made sure to set the boundaries the first day she worked there. She wondered just now if Mr Dickens would also become the friend Reggie had, though at this moment, she could only giggle self-consciously and bow to his formidable rule-laying.

In the fray, Natalie had emitted a quiet chuckle. Diane sensed something calculated in it.

"Have you been watching the same act played out all day? I'm not the first to fall into this trap, am I?" Natalie's calm eyes slid sideways toward her, smiled slightly, and slid back.

Diane weighed the moment, and pressed her: "C'mon now. Weary travelers. Irresistible ducklings. The official admonishment." Natalie smiled quietly from where she remained on the gravel path observing but saying nothing. Seeing Natalie's composure, Diane laughed a little harder at the contrast they presented, then suddenly remembered a passage from an essay the seniors all read back in Denver. "Very much not the first!" she said to Natalie, then made quick arm gestures to the lawn and then the path. "Just what Virginia Woolf said in *A Room of One's Own*, when she visited Oxford, isn't it? They shouted at her too, as she stepped on the lawn." With furrowed brow, Diane admonished the invisible Ms Woolf once again.

"No *women* on the lawn, was more her point, I believe," Natalie quietly corrected her. "I'm writing my thesis on several aspects of her feminism. That's why I'm here."

"Ah," Diane replied simply and raised her eyebrows, wondering if Natalie had caught her mocking tone. Perhaps she had, as they both smiled silently, eyes twinkling.

Through an archway, they entered a small quadrangle. Their footsteps echoed quietly. Here the courtyard was filled with a raised bed, surrounded by a knee high concrete wall that enclosed not flowers, not a fountain, but rather an octagon of close-cropped turf. For what purpose one used a raised flat of grass, Diane could not guess, especially under the advisement that walking upon it was probably forbidden. A putting green? Croquet? If that wasn't absurd enough, upon it stood a workman pushing some weighty contraption.

"Rolling the turf," Natalie filled in, in a conspiratorial aside as they strolled past. The workman nodded cordially. Diane liked what she was seeing in her roommate, until her next comment, which struck Diane as just short of funny.

"Yes. Otherwise it might grow normally and they would have to mow it rather than clip it with hand shears." She shook her head melodramatically as though pitying the plight of all groundsmen and the dreadful inconveniences they must face from Nature each day. Just then, a burst of cheering from windows above punctuated their quiet progress. "World Cup," Natalie sniffed, looking up at the second floor windows. Diane grinned but remained silent, pretending she knew what that meant rather than appear more foolish than she already felt over the duckling escapade on the lawn.

They continued through another arch, then a short corridor that opened onto a large orderly quadrangle filled with people. Three sides of the courtyard were bordered by pale gold walls, three stories of tall windows above. Tall, narrow dark blue doors were set at regular intervals. The gathering spilled over into a garden beyond a bright blue iron fence.

"Yes. Sir Christopher Wren designed our building. How fascinating that we have such a ready supply of big names here." Natalie rolled her eyes slightly which made Diane wonder at her comment, but then her new roommate continued: "Each door is a staircase up to dorm rooms."

Diane couldn't take it all in. Sir Christopher Wren had designed her building? Diane looked over the heads of the students, the architecture suddenly more interesting to her than meeting people just now. A faded mural of crossed oars and heraldic shields caught her attention. Crew team winnings, she guessed, from early in the century. That must have been their last big heyday for it, according to the dates recorded above her: 1914 and 1915. Think of it; unseated for over eighty years now, yet still pleased to announce bygone success. They had crew teams at Smith as well, rowed by fanatical early risers willing to brave the frost at dawn down on the banks of the Connecticut River for practice. She had no idea if Smith won their races or not. Despite her mother's athletic inclinations, sports news always slipped past Diane unnoticed, except for this curious display. Everything different in England! Perhaps that explained it.

"Stairwell Sixteen, that's us," Natalie motioned to the last door closest to the garden, where clusters of tidily dressed students chatted with nervous energy in the warm afternoon. Diane noticed that the only two young men with ponytails had found each other and had gravitated toward a young woman with similar, long dark hair. She and Natalie each grabbed a glass of wine then joined a pair of new roommates, both wearing pearls. The redhead sported a wispy bob.

This farthest end of the quadrangle gave onto a great length of garden bordered by thick stone walls and a wide lawn that continued perhaps one hundred yards into the distance, Diane estimated, ending with a wide iron gated driveway. Busy with finals at the prep school where she tutored in Denver, Diane hadn't done much research on what awaited her at Oxford. This magnificent garden was completely unexpected, as well.

"Introductions," Natalie said, nudging Diane. "There's the College historian – the very tall woman – talking to William Clarence." Luckily Diane knew one official name, the program director, the name that all correspondence was addressed to and signed by. They made their way over to him.

"We are pleased to welcome you, Miss Quinnell – and Miss Hull – as graduate students." Dr Clarence shook her hand warmly.

"Dr Clarence, as I am stepping in here, I begin to realize all the details I know nothing about. First of all, how many are in this program? Are we all here?" Diane asked.

"The Trinity College population consists of approximately 300 undergraduates during regular term. During summer, we limit to seventy students." He arranged this program from the University of Massachusetts at Amherst, yet his accent was British. Another thing she hadn't known.

Seventy? There had been eighty in Emerson House, her dorm at Smith, alone. So few here? She'd thought only of her own interests when applying: good classes, an amazing experience and travel. Suddenly, she understood that she had been fortunate to get into such a tiny program. The situation felt familiar, however. When she had met the freshmen in her dorm, they all had twittered about how lucky they were to get into Smith. It was their life's dream, many of them said. One admitted how during that first day, she had expected to be tapped on the shoulder and told, *'I'm sorry. We've made a mistake. You'll have to go home.'* The entire group had burst into agreement at that point, which shocked Diane, whose arrival at Smith had been nearly random, by comparison. She laughed to herself again now, remembering her own road to Smith College. She'd seen the Smith bulletin on a table at the high school counselor's office, looked at the classes offered and sent an application. She hadn't even mentioned it to her parents; she just did it. The Quinnells – a family of handymen who congratulated themselves on being able to fix or build anything – had expected their daughter to follow their lead, take a steady job after high school, maybe as a cashier at a grocery store. Something concrete, dependable. They also had predicted that her artistic abilities would pay off in the chance to make signs here and there for the store, they were sure. That's how Diane's illustrator mother had gotten started, in a drug-store, making sales signs for displays. Diane had certainly thrown the proverbial wrench into their plans, by boarding that airplane for Massachusetts. The first Quinnell to go to college.

"And what is your acceptance rate?" she asked, making sure to use the proper term to give some dignity to her ignorance. Elevated by her august surroundings, the formality of the occasion made her keenly aware of her own quick decision, based on instinct instead of research. *'One of your best traits!'* several juggler friends back in Denver had told her affectionately, and dubbed her: *'The Amazing Diane: she who looks while leaping.'* She stood up a little straighter in the quadrangle at Trinity.

"Each year, we generally accept ninety-nine percent of those who apply," Dr Clarence said. "The group is surprisingly self-selecting. A student must have the interest, the nerve to apply and the grades to support the decision. It always works out well."

"Yes! I'm sure the mere concept of applying to Oxford is enough to frighten off the light-weights," Diane said, happy to agree heartily, having never really thought about that aspect before. She and Natalie stepped aside as an Asian couple introduced themselves and their daughter to the director. Diane smiled and bowed to the three, tried to imagine her own parents deciding to fly over to drop her off.

Natalie suggested another glass of wine. Once at the beverage table, she asked quietly: "Do you always so readily announce everything you don't know to your professors who are going to be grading you? Interesting approach."

"I learn a lot that way. And how do you know so much about this place already?"

"I am good at research," Natalie said quietly, then added, "and I arrived eight hours ahead of you. I scouted around."

"Ah," Diane said, pleased to have an insider confession from a New Yorker. Those weren't easy to come by, each one not wanting to give away the advantage. Lost in her own thoughts again, she looked around the courtyard, drew in a deep breath and let it out feeling satisfied. Good thing she had been bold enough to step forward. Compare this moment to ringing up groceries for the rest of one's life.

A hand tapped her on the arm just then. Daniel appeared by her side and winked. "Diane, have you met Professor Bede yet?"

Diane lifted her eyebrows in question. "No, I don't think so." She hoped he'd fill in the missing information. "She is – ?"

"Your Women's Literature teacher. Constance Bede. Can you pick her out? She used to be a Carmelite nun. Which one do you think she is?" His eyes danced mischievously.

"Really? I didn't know that." Certainly that would have stood out in the biography for her professor. Diane had nearly memorized the program information when applying. She hadn't thought about names recently, however, just the book titles she needed to read to be ready. Wrapping up the school year for the students she tutored, crowded in on her preparations to leave for London.

Now she scanned the groups and made a stab, based on Daniel's description, but wondering at the twinkle in his eye all the while. There must be a trick to this, but I'll play along, she thought. "Maybe that woman, across there, in the navy blue suit?" Diane chose the elderly, plainly dressed woman, figuring that the initial pursuit of simplicity probably stayed with a woman who had chosen to live in a convent, even after she had decided to leave it. Diane's mind flashed back to her own Confirmation at fourteen. At that time, she was sure that she wanted to join Mother Teresa's work. Piecing that together now gave her a laugh. Perhaps choosing to help dying people off the streets in Calcutta was Diane's first plan for avoiding the grocery store job her parents were grooming her for. She suppressed another laugh remembering the sensible voice on the phone that day. *'So, you speak Hindi?'* the nun at the New York office of Missionaries of Charity had asked her. That one practical question had foiled Diane's first escape plan.

"Ha! Good guess, but wrong." Daniel let out a little laugh and turned Diane's attention to the tall slim woman now speaking with the College historian. "That is Professor Bede! Not at all what you'd expect an ex-nun to look like, is she?"

Diane stood agape. Constance Bede was breathtaking. The silver threads of her soft hair flashed in the late afternoon sunlight, the short wisps played about her high cheekbones and tickled her dangling earrings. Perfect makeup accentuated her classic features, the enhancements convincingly natural. Upon her slim frame her silk shift rested, the color an arresting turquoise, yet lingering somewhere more subtly toward slate grey. Stylish. Elegant in its understatement. The breeze existed to tease her skirt hem into a graceful dance, revealing her tan ankles in an occasional, playful sigh. Beautiful yes, but the most captivating aspect was the intelligence in her eyes. As she spoke, she was attentive. Responsive. Endowed with a natural, relaxed smile. Lovely in all aspects. Gracious in manners as well, she noted, as Daniel introduced them and everything seemed to fall into some magical slow motion, as Diane grew completely content to worship this extraordinary being for all eternity.

At that moment, someone bumped Diane from behind. She immediately tried not to spill on anyone. Her wine glass, which she saw now as having been emptied already, advised her to curb her worshiping tendencies or make a very poor impression. Fortunately for Diane, the moment to pay homage to this divine entity was also cut short by a general calling together by the director. His welcoming comments included an introduction of the College historian, who spoke to them from her towering height.

"Hello everyone. I am Charlotte Ashcroft, the College Archivist. I am pleased to welcome you, the twenty-seventh group of American students, to Trinity College. We are now gathered in the Garden Quad, designed by Sir Christopher Wren and begun in the year 1668. If you will follow me, a short walking tour will take us to dinner." The group set off on a leisurely stroll into the gardens and around the grounds. "The Laundry Cottage to our right" she indicated, "The Wilderness to the left. Let us continue forward and all pause just ahead." The crowd ambled along and drew up in the College's Library Quad.

"Although its silhouette rarely alters, Oxford itself looks strikingly different today, when compared to even twenty years ago." She beckoned them through an archway under which Diane was sure Charlotte would need to duck. "Watch your heads," she instructed, much to Diane's gratification. "You see this portion of blackened wall? It has been left in its natural state for comparison. Seeing this, you now understand that until recent sand blasting city-wide, Oxford was a coal soot-encrusted place. The cleaning has greatly changed the appearance of the entire town. Sir Christopher Wren would be pleased indeed to see his buildings here, his Sheldonian Theatre – you can just glimpse the cupola there above our cottages fronting Broad Street – restored to the warmth of the natural honey-colored stone with which they were built."

With a sweep of her long arm, the College Archivist invited everyone to step around the corner, where a trellis covered in pink roses marked a door. "This is the President's Lodgings. Our President, Mr Merton Jeffreys, is away until August." The group now followed the gravel path by which Diane and Natalie had entered Trinity grounds. No ducklings in sight, Diane noted, wanting to ask everyone around her if they had seen them, but also not wanting to miss any of the history details. Perhaps the historian would illuminate them about the grassy enclosure through the next archway, Diane thought.

"The zigzag patterned buildings you see here along our wall belong to Balliol College, founded in 1263. The walls around most of the Colleges at Oxford University carry over from the monastic origins of each one. To be sure, friendly rivalry between Trinity and Balliol is a long-standing tradition. For the last several centuries, it has played out in competitive singing. During regular term, choir groups gather here and sing challenging songs over the wall. Balliol singers return fire, as it were, with equal gusto."

"Singing bouts over the wall. Very manly," Natalie spoke over Diane's shoulder, just as Diane noticed something unexpected glinting in the western sunlight.

"What is that? See, on top?" Diane said to Natalie, pointing. The gesture also caught Charlotte Ashcroft's eye.

"Ah, yes. I'm glad you noticed that. The walls are topped in the old manner, with broken glass set in. To keep the monastic students in, I believe. We maintain them as a part of our history."

Finally the group entered the courtyard of the mysterious octagon. Diane stayed close to the Archivist, waiting.

"Trinity, founded in 1555, was built on the ruins of what was Durham College that initially occupied this site in the Twelfth Century. This is therefore the Durham Quad. We will step for a brief moment into the present chapel, begun in the year 1691 on the foundations of the original. Note the painted ceiling by Paul Berchet as you..." Diane didn't hear the rest as she peeked into the chapel and exited immediately. Cool and damp, the scent of incense and wood polish struck her forcibly. Childhood. Required trips to confession, always at night, always smelling creepy, like this old chapel.

She sat down on the edge of the grassy octagonal enclosure to wait. Her stomach grumbled. She looked up to the clock tower, wondered when dinner would be served.

Perhaps this very spot was all that was left of the original grassy spot left by Durham College and its Twelfth Century monks, preserved for all to better contemplate history? She'd seen stranger things.

A patch of grass enclosed behind chainlink fencing in the median of a highway somewhere in Denver that the airport van driver had pointed out for tourists on the way downtown. '*Last piece of original prairie grass in the metro area,*' he had told everyone. Funny what people will decide is worth preserving, she thought now.

Finally, Charlotte returned to the Durham Quad where she next drew them all into a low-vaulted stone hallway. "Probably the most visited spot is Trinity's Jacobean Gothic Dining Hall of 1618, with its stained glass memorials and portrait gallery of dons and fellows gone by." She pushed open the enormous arched doors and beckoned them into a huge, magnificent banquet hall. The heavy wooden tables that formed parallel divisions leading to the head of the room were set with impeccable care for dinner. "You may now take your places for dinner."

The long benches groaned as everyone rushed to climb into their places at once. Diane found this amusing, the polite group abandoning nearly all reserve once food was mentioned. She plied her full shirt easily over the bench top and Natalie squeezed in next to her. Once settled, she found that her feet dangled inches off the floor. In that way, this grand institution had thought up one more way to dwarf this petite inhabitant. A moment later, Daniel Glasser slid in next to her. She noticed he didn't have the same issues for his long legs.

Gazing about at the massive portraits in elaborate carved frames, Diane locked onto a smallish painting directly above the Head Table. The only woman's portrait in the room she immediately recognized as belonging to the Tudor era, her degree in Art History told her. The square neckline, the kennel headdress and thin necklace, as seen in most portraits of King Henry VIII's wives, said: Tudor, but the dates were just wrong. Fifteen-fifty-five put the school's founding directly following Mary Tudor, or if the painting dated from the building of the Dining Hall – what was it again? Sometime after that. Jacobean, Charlotte had said. Diane couldn't quite remember the date itself. So, perhaps Diane was mistaken. She also realized how hungry she was.

Eating was definitely in order. Salads arrived. Conversations ceased. Diane continued to think about the painting. For Diane, art analysis was nearly automatic.

Courtly styles, she considered while she devoured her salad, were copied by everyone the moment they appeared at court. Perhaps a dire economy following the reign of Queen Mary Tudor would explain a carryover of styles? If you have a trunk full of clothes, you might as well wear them. She certainly saw old people clinging to fashions long gone, back in Denver. *'Plenty of wear left in that coat,'* they'd say. She looked down at her own full skirt, a treasured find from a thrift store back home. Did Audrey Hepburn still wear Fifties haute couture? she wondered. Is Audrey Hepburn still alive? She laughed quietly to herself, she was sure, until its echo returned to her from the high vault above her. Natalie glanced her way, but said nothing.

Diane turned to Daniel between bites. "Daniel, you said you were here last year. Who's that woman in that painting up there?"

"Foundress," he barked, rather garbled by a mouthful of bread. Diane wasn't sure what he had said, nor did he clarify after swallowing. No matter just now; she would ask Charlotte later.

"Do you think every evening meal will be like this?" She turned to Natalie as she daintily severed the tiny, arabesque-shaped molded butter pat on her personal butter dish and applied it to her third petit baguette, more delicious at that moment than any tasted before, she was sure. "I hope there's a lot more of these."

"Yes. I believe we have all been elevated to aristocratic heights for the summer," Natalie agreed with characteristic blandness.

*   *   *

Diane returned from the top of Staircase Sixteen to the common room of their suite and padded back to her bed chamber, all the while fixated on one minor complaint. She called to Natalie in her adjacent bedroom. "That was strange. The light in the bathroom wouldn't go on. I had to leave the door ajar to see. Not exactly what I want to be doing," she laughed.

"That's odd. I didn't have any trouble," Natalie called to her. "Nighty-night."

Diane landed on her bed, glad to be horizontal. And it is actually cool, she realized suddenly, amazed at how far off steamy London seemed. The midsummer twilight continued to light the western skies, filtering into the front room of their suite and through her bedroom doorway. Think of it: I am heading into my first night of sleeping under the auspices of Sir Christopher Wren, everything orderly. The bed turned down. A pile of folded towels ready for me, all the work of the Scouts, Natalie had told her.

"You know," Diane called out into the semidarkness, "this isn't bad. I hadn't really thought about it until now, but I was expecting these would be like the dorms at Princeton, where men have been allowed to live without women for two-hundred-fifty years. Have you seen those? They are completely trashed."

"That's an interesting observation, Diane," Natalie called back. "Sweet dreams."

Week ONE

Friday, June 28

FIRST THING FRIDAY MORNING, Diane giggled while watching her small bare feet pad upon the uneven wooden stairs that spiraled up to the single bathroom and shower at the top of her staircase. She pictured the shock for the three hundred year old wood, recoiling at the touch of a girl's bare feet now prancing upon these men-only steps. And in her nightgown! Such sacrilege!

On her way back she paused at the open window and looked out for the first time across countless roofs. The Trinity clock tower announced five AM. Diane studied the elaborately-draped female figures that balanced on the tower's four corners. Two backs turned toward her, two faced her. One's arm pointed east. The figure directly east of the pointing one seemed to be missing her right arm and therefore could not join in, greeting their old friend, Rosy-fingered Dawn. Diane let out a little laugh and ran to get her sketch book. As she sketched the skyline, the variety of styles began to differentiate themselves. The blocky Romanesque Trinity clock, two zigzag striped spires of Balliol next door. A fanciful weather cock atop an arched bell tower. And those were just the few in the foreground. Scores of others filled the view far into the misty morning. Better light was needed for detail, but even the brief outline pleased her. When had she had time to draw? Not for a long time. A brief flurry of soft quacking made its way to her as she closed her pad.

Curled up in bed with a stack of postcards, she listened to the light clip of raindrops on the leaves outside her window, and wrote.

Postcard: A very straight row of Buckingham Palace guards in red coats and tall furry hats.

June 28. Oxford: 6 AM – Upon arrival yesterday evening, a squadron of ducklings rushed forward to greet me, like the Disney version of my life at Oxford – until the Porter ordered me off the lawn! In this morning's stillness, I just heard a burst of quacking from the front quad echo over the 1668 architecture to the third floor window, high atop Staircase Sixteen. Trinity's tiny ambassadors must be welcoming the cooks as they arrive for breakfast shift. After runny baked beans in London, dare I hope for fragrant cinnamon rolls here?

Fragments of history from the College tour last night played through Diane's head as she accompanied Natalie to breakfast. Trinity. An intimate setting. Nowhere to get lost or feel disoriented. Homey. Safe, as it was, enclosed by high walls, the tranquil feeling perhaps enhanced by the gentle drizzle. England and rain: a classic combination Diane had only read about. Now the mist on her face felt fresh and invigorating as they followed a scattering of other sleepy students toward what she hoped would be a lovely breakfast. Ah wonderful! The prospect of hot tea and toast with all the never-seen-in-Denver European jams and marmalades. Perhaps peach! Her mouth watered at the thought.

At the end of the serving line, a matronly woman stood peering steadily at them. Diane took in the woman's name tag: Mrs Whappington. The name struck her as oddly familiar, enough to stop Diane from her usual habit of addressing the woman by name when she approached. A peculiar feeling crept up Diane's neck, as she bid the woman a simple, "Good morning."

"You haven't got your budgies on," the matronly woman announced, stone-faced.

The phrase made no sense to Diane. What does this woman want, Diane wondered, and why do I know that name? She paused to think about the two things at once, concerned yet distracted – and starving!

"You haven't got your budgies on," repeated Mrs Whappington.

"Budgies on?" asked Diane cautiously.

"Yes! Your *budgies*! You haven't got them on," the woman insisted, much louder this time.

Trying to understand her meaning felt like running up against a damp wall while blindfolded, everyone else looking on, sniggering. Diane tried to think quickly, formulate a guess, much like leaping forward into muck. Yet at leaping, Diane was a professional. Her mind raced to find a solution. Perhaps *budgies* meant 'parrots' if Monty Python's *Dead Parrot Sketch* represented anything in reality. Substituting *parrot*, however, made no sense in that sentence, not even in this British-speaking, albeit, foreign place. *'You haven't got your parrots on.'* That made for an absurd non-sequitur, though something akin to Tom Stoppard's work, perhaps, Diane reckoned. Was Mrs Whappington therefore playing a practical joke? That seemed unlikely from this serious-faced woman. Diane looked her over warily and concluded: probably not.

Parrot, hmm. With lightning speed, Diane dug deeper into her international-lexicon-of-a-brain for a flash of insight. She grabbed upon this: Considering that classic English umbrellas often had handles carved into a parrot's head – witness: *Mary Poppins* – perhaps *budgie* was a local word for umbrella? After all, *pram* ended up being the corruption of the word *perambulator*, or baby carriage as they called them in Denver. And in French, *umbrella* was some p-word that Diane couldn't precisely recall, sensing additional pressure from the line forming behind her. Wishing to move along, she seized upon the umbrella theory, since it was raining a bit. Diane volunteered hesitantly, "No, it wasn't raining hard so we've left them... ."

"No! Your BUDGIES! Oh! – Go through!" The exasperated woman

waved Diane and her roommate through to the Dining Hall with a look of contempt, as the next student stepped up.

"I think we've done something terribly wrong." Diane whispered over Natalie's shoulder, then heard the drama replayed behind them. She had correctly understood the *"You morons!"* part of Mrs Whappington's message.

"So what? Let's eat," Natalie concluded without concern.

"How about over here?" Diane suggested, leading Natalie to a long table just out of view of the vociferating Mrs Whappington. They climbed over a long wooden bench and settled down.

"Well, we certainly have not made friends with Mrs Whappington; that's clear." Diane laughed quietly to herself. "It's so funny how English-speaking people, all speaking English, can't even understand each other. Actually, it's one of my favorite things about traveling. Surprising absurdities."

Natalie dunked her tea bag in detached silence, evidently unaffected by the bungled exchange.

Diane plunged her spoon into the jam pot, still feeling a twinge of guilt. She sniffed the golden sludge – apricot? – and considered why. Making anyone's day more difficult always made her feel clumsy, but particularly more so when upsetting anyone who was placed in a position to serve her. Cooks, servers, custodians, bus drivers, groundsmen: she liked getting to know them personally, the invisible force that kept schools or business-places running. And, a good rapport with those who kept the keys, or fixed small broken items – or baked the fresh cinnamon rolls that Diane found so irresistible – never hurt her either.

"And that name!" Diane blurted. "Of course. Now I remember. Did you ever read that children's book, *Mrs Whappington's School of Manners*? I loved it. An old Victorian cat in her proper old lace cap who dispenses discipline with a decisive, fluffy paw. *Elbows on the table? Whap-Whap!* It was right on the tip of my tongue."

"Must have missed that one," Natalie mumbled, her green eyes staring off into the distance.

With her back to the serving area, Diane faced a wall full of stained glass windows extending up until they met the vaulted ceiling. Although she had looked about intently last evening, wanting to absorb every detail of the Jacobean Gothic hall, her attention had been preoccupied with introductions and first greetings among the tables of classmates at the opening banquet. She twisted around several times now on her bench to get a good look at everything. The portraits, the architecture, lay revealed in the morning light.

Over her shoulder just leaving Mrs Whappington's station, Diane recognized her Women's Literature professor with her breakfast tray. She caught Diane's eye.

"Good morning. May we join you?" Professor Constance Bede paused and surveyed the two with her deep set, languid eyes. A few steps behind her, an old gentleman also drew up, his dark brown eyes sparkling at the pair of them. His closely trimmed white beard hugged his jaw line but didn't hide the deep dimple in his cheek that gave him a boyish look. Fifty – or perhaps sixty-five? – his black eyebrows and long dark lashes masked his age. Perhaps he was from India or Pakistan, Diane judged by his ornately embroidered long jacket. She found herself smiling warmly back at him, hoping for an opportunity to compliment him on the jacket and let him know he could give it to her when he got tired of it. They looked about the same size.

Effortlessly, Professor Bede glided around to Natalie's side of the heavy table, the long skirt of her deep plum colored dress wafting to a resting place on the bench. The gentleman bowed and remained standing to Diane's left.

"Let me introduce Dr Chandra, our Edwardian scholar," Professor Bede said, systematically peeling a banana as she spoke. "I haven't mastered your names yet, I'm afraid. Natalie, I believe, and..." She paused and raised her shapely eyebrows slightly.

"Diane Quinnell," Diane filled in as Bede began mashing the banana onto her toast as if it were jam. Diane sat transfixed by an act

she had never witnessed, nor dreamed of, being performed on a piece
of innocent toast. Natalie sat up a bit straighter, but felt content to
chew her toast while merely nodding toward Chandra's extended
hand. Tearing her eyes away from her professor's breakfast ritual,
Diane turned and half-rose to meet the proffered hand of Dr Chandra.
"How do you do?" They both said.

"Very fine, thank you." He seated himself with quiet efficiency, his
dark eyes taking in all three women, then resting upon Diane. "What
a beautiful name, Diane. I am afraid it is also the name my parents
presented me with. Yes, I am also a Diane though spelled with
excessive detail to an extraneous amount of letters more than yours, I
am sure. Dyan-dara-wa-hara. You see? Seven syllables! Princely, yes,
but I have shortened it to D-y-a-n. Simple. Easy."

Diane enjoyed the musical rhythm of his voice, yet choose to
trump his clever compliment. "I usually have a tough time
remembering names, but yours, *I've got*," she smiled, then asked:
"Doesn't *chandra* mean *moon*, in Hindu... or Hindi? I don't know the
proper name for the language, I realize as I say it." She tried to recall
exactly the voice on the phone all those years ago.

"Hindu: that is me. Hindi: that is the language. But how
extraordinary! Yes, *chandra* does mean *moon*. How did you know that?"
He awarded her a big smile, his dimple deepening.

"Just one of those words I picked up while studying India or
Indian art history. Or maybe from the Beatles trip there?" She ventured
a guess. "I'm not sure. I go off on tangents when I'm interested in
something and end up collecting some off-beat stuff on the way.
Probably the reason I get invited to *Trivial Pursuit* parties, I think." She
tried a tiny taste of the jam. Peach.

"*Trivial Pursuit?*"

"A popular board game for people like me who collect a lot of
useless facts."

"Oh my, if you like word games, then I must introduce you to another. Perhaps you know the game *Hobson-Jobson?* We here have transformed it into a more casual word game we call *Bon Mot.* I'll introduce you, once I get settled with my newest students." He glanced at Natalie, studied Diane for another moment, then applied himself to his breakfast.

"What is that? *Hobson-Jobson?*" Diane asked.

"Ah! Words from India that are now in common use in English. *Veranda. Pyjama* are a few for instances."

"*Karma. Khaki. Vindaloo,*" Diane added to the list as Chandra nodded.

"Vindaloo?" Professor Bede cut in. "That is not in common use."

"Maybe not, but it's a delicious sauce with chicken, appears in a popular Ramones' song, and is in the *Scrabble* dictionary. I scored a pile of points with it on a triple word score space, Professor Bede," Diane turned to her with a smile.

"Please, call me Constance. We're all adults here, Diane." Bede leaned forward slightly and studied the bottom of her empty cup.

"That's what *I* thought!" Diane blurted, happy to hear it while having anticipated additional formality in this age-old setting. "You know, at Smith I figured we were all adults, too. So, I called my history professor 'Jim' one day during class; he corrected me immediately. I felt like an idiot! The other students ribbed me about it for weeks."

"Dyan," Constance smiled warmly, then bobbed her head toward Dr Chandra as she set down her cup, "Diane here is a writing tutor. I believe you told me that last night?" She nodded to Diane, then vanquished her single egg with a second piece of toast.

Diane nodded.

"No, really? Oh, and to think I have been mistaking you for an undergraduate, Diane. What brings you here to us? Perhaps our grand surroundings?" He motioned to the great expanse of walls and stained glass windows that encircled them.

"Yes, isn't the Hall lovely," Constance said somewhat mechanically. "Excuse me. Coffee is what I need most. Late night. Anyone?" She raised her eyebrows as she rose, then departed.

"Yes, though I haven't really had a chance to look around yet," Diane answered Chandra's question. "But I'd like to spend the entire morning just studying these walls." She gestured with a flourish. She took a moment to glance at Natalie as well, who seemed content to enjoy her own thoughts. "All this art is a real bonus. I am here, actually, to improve my credentials. I'd like to move up to a teaching position at the prep school I tutor at."

He studied her for a moment, then ventured: "But you are already a tutor?"

"I'm sorry. I don't follow you," Diane said.

"Oh yes, yes. That's right. I had forgotten. We use that term, *tutor*, to mean teacher, professor. Even *lecturer* means a full teaching position. Our word *don* signifies having risen to the top position. So, as a tutor, you are...?" he inquired.

"I'm an assistant, outside the classroom. Extra help for struggling students. Sometimes for enrichment, but believe me, I don't get much chance for that." Diane shook her head, once again amazed by the different meanings for common words.

"And what is your degree? Art history I believe you said."

"Yes. Fine art. Also one in graphic design." She paused, remembering that just a few years ago she gave up her search for a design position and took the tutoring job instead. "An art degree includes a lot of writing for the art history papers, though people usually only picture me covered with paint," Diane laughed.

"Oh, wonderful. Then you will surely become familiar with all our hosts here. That is what I like to call them." Dr Chandra again motioned toward the room full of paintings.

Dark oil portraits in heavy gilded frames lined the towering walls. The crown molding that capped the walls, Diane estimated, ran in a line about twenty feet above the floor. Yes, perhaps four levels of acrobat friends standing on each others shoulders could just grab that rail where the recessed lighting lay hidden. Above that, perhaps another six feet rolled as a half-shell upward into the murky dimness of misty morning light. A decorative motif she'd never seen before ran along the front and back walls, consisting of plaster or wooden urns of enormous size, sliced into equal halves for the wall, or into quarters for the corner positions, then affixed flat side to the wall. The urns repeated at regular intervals, sort of like a bannister, but for what? She couldn't imagine the origins of such a functionless piece of decoration. Perhaps the ceiling had at one time been painted with cherubs and what-not celestial beings motioning upward toward heaven? In that case, the fake bannister would serve to corral them in, if nothing else. Aside from the simple molded central sunburst, surely the white barrel vault bespoke an era that would not include a Baroque-ish view of heaven. Not like the chapel's painted ceiling that people were talking about as they came into the Quad last night. She smiled, feeling lucky to be spared the bare bottoms of pudgy cherubs served up with her morning tea and toast.

She lowered her gaze again to the level of the portrait paintings in their ornate frames. A quick survey yielded this summary: all single portraits, no groups or scenery. Not one still life. Approximately fifteen males plus the one female portrait at the head of the room centered above the Head Table. By morning light it was Anne Boleyn who looked back at her, Diane was convinced. The same Tudor kennel on her head, the same square-necked dress from the Hans Holbein portrait but especially that same necklace at the throat. All those hours researching costume designs for that friend at the Colorado Renaissance Festival paid off now.

Interestingly, while only a fraction of the size of the over-sized representations of the dons and fellows wearing voluminous robes, this woman's diminutive portrait was placed directly in the location of primary importance. Portrait of a former Royal? That made sense. The modest size symbolized a modest demeanor, perhaps? She chuckled. Queen Victoria also had been petite in statue, yet with no loss of commanding qualities.

Diane had forgotten what Daniel had called the woman in the painting. She turned back to Dr Chandra. "Who exactly are they all?"

"Oh! Former Fellows of the College, all the way back to its founding, I believe. That is nearly four hundred and fifty years of head-men. Many were notable scholars, others perhaps excellent drinking companions. The place is rich with history, which I am sure is no surprise to you or your friend here."

Natalie tolerated the general comment with a sideways look that said '*So what?*' and returned languidly to dunking multiple tea bags. Diane noted Professor Bede in the serving area, tipping back a quick cup of coffee, then returning with a refill.

Chandra laughed gently and glanced at a small digital clock he pulled from his breast pocket. "Ah. Time to begin. What is your first assignment, Diane?"

"I go straight to Thomas Hardy class at ten."

"Ah! With Dr Harding. Please enjoy it." Chandra rose, nodded to Natalie and Constance, who now collected her tray as well. "We're off!" he smiled at Diane. "Again. More later," he promised her.

* * *

Diane nearly vibrated with the thrill of her first class session at Oxford, the famous school. Even her mother had switched sides of the fence when Diane told her she was applying for a summer study program there. Of course, her two previous degrees – each a battle relying solely on her own devices to propel herself through – had softened the practical Quinnell family's resolve to condemn all forms of higher – expensive – education. But the name Oxford and its history had worked the charm.

Dr Nicholas A. Harding, the brass door marker read. Dr Harding's suite was on the second floor of the building next to her own. They shook hands and she chose a chair opposite him, glad to have arrived a few minutes early in order to get a good spot. The room was cozy, filled with books on old wooden shelving. An old clock on the mantelpiece. Two easy chairs, several wooden chairs and a well-worn chaise longue formed a little square around an old Persian rug. A reading lamp on each table gave the impression that scholarship was a twenty-four hour pursuit here. Harding himself fit the classic mold Diane associated with professors: baggy tweed jacket year round, neatly tied brown leather shoes. The only surprise: no tie, probably an acknowledgment that summer had arrived.

"Your application essay," he began immediately, "a lively piece. Most interesting, although I am not quite sure I am following the title: *I Was a Teenage Beowulf.* Could you elaborate on that, Miss Quinnell?" His heavy brows squeezed together forming a thatched roof over his reading glasses.

"Oh! I worked at a movie theater for many years and really enjoy film," she said casually, while adjusting a cushion, flipping open her notebook and bouncing around again to get comfortable. "I figured you'd know the reference to the classic Fifties horror film: *I was a Teenage Werewolf.* I liked skewing the title a bit for England, to convey my love of early British literature – and of course Hardy's dark subject matter mixed in really well. I just thought it was a good laugh." The silence grew thick as she waited for him to say something more. She glanced over her shoulder at the empty chairs. She wondered where the other students were.

"I see." He set down her folder suddenly and peeled off his reading glasses, studying her intently for a long moment. "What an extraordinary coincidence! I am a great fan of Hollywood movies. Though I haven't seen that particular film, I do now recall having heard the title. Yes, yes. Of course. Wonderful. You American students: so well-versed in movies. I look forward to any film insights into Thomas Hardy, Miss Quinnell. In fact, jumping right into our discussion of *Jude the Obscure*, I am looking forward to the release of Winterbottom's film, are you?"

"I'm not familiar with that name. A British production?"

"Oh, yes, yes. And Winterbottom read English at Balliol – right next door," he added when Diane didn't react.

"I'm a little out of the loop on films made abroad, out there in Denver. I don't tend to pick up popular movie magazines, so you've got me there."

Dr Harding began to bubble about the casting for *Jude*. That was the only term for it. As much as she enjoyed talking about film, Diane shifted uncomfortably in her seat and glanced at the clock. There they were, killing time, waiting for the rest of the students. She wondered how the others could be so lax in arriving. Diane's puzzled feelings grew as Dr Harding charged in with a string of enthusiastic questions involving plot structures and the Academy Awards.

"Shouldn't we be waiting for the others?" she finally managed to cut him off.

"One don, one student, Miss Quinnell," he smiled politely, then gestured casually with his glasses.

"You're joking?" Diane gaped at him.

"This is the Oxford tutorial tradition. Centuries old."

"Well! What do you know?" she said lamely, both puzzled and embarrassed for having been caught so completely unaware.

One professor, one student. The arrangement readily explained the superiority of the education one acquired at the venerable institution. And her analytical nature quickly grasped the ramifications: *You'd better be ready for class!* She felt a quick jolt of laughter at the comical results she pictured. Other unsuspecting students, caught off guard. No, it hit her like lightning as he now said: "Shall we jump directly into Jude Fawley's tragic origins?" She pictured all the other students who may not live through this trauma, discovering that they would not be able to hide in the back row any longer. And the composed Natalie. What a nice surprise for her. Diane wasn't sure why she found the thought rip-roaringly funny, but it definitely set her chuckling.

Dr Harding waited, intent. Nearly memorizing the advance materials from Trinity, she noted that their summer term was to be six weeks instead of the usual eight weeks, which meant the same amount of studies condensed into a shorter time frame. She hadn't imagined anything as challenging as this singular class arrangement, however, nor had she read anything about it in the Trinity Summer Session program application. How had she missed that?

"Yes, well of course there are other students," Dr Harding clarified, "but I meet with each of you privately. Then Tuesday evenings in town as a group. Hardy set many of his famous scenes in special nooks of this town, Miss Quinnell. Also, we'll all pile into a van for a full day driving on site visits. And the full day Hardy Hike, of course. Seventeen miles, if you're willing. I hope you brought good shoes for that."

Everyone else must just know the way things work here, she figured, once again aware of the vast array of everything she didn't know. Everyone knows how it works at Oxford, except me, *as usual*, she thought to herself. *'Figure it out, Diane,'* she heard her mother's voice in her head.

"Ah, me! Always the last to know!" She placed the back of her hand gently to her brow like a wilting Southern belle and held the pose for a moment, half to hide her embarrassment.

"Ah. You Americans! So amusing," Dr Harding chirped.

"Well, well. Lots more to learn," she admitted with a twinkling smile, recovering.

"Quite," said Professor Harding as Diane continued to ponder. "So, I will see you Fridays at ten and Tuesday evenings with the group, following dinner. We assemble at The Lodge at seven."

* * *

At two o'clock Diane reported to Professor Bede, just a door down and across the hall from Dr Harding's rooms. Another chaise longue occupied the center spot in Professor Bede's suite. Right out of a Napoleonic painting, Diane thought.

"Charming isn't it?" Professor Bede said as if reading her mind. "Do try it, if you like. Wherever you're comfortable." Diane circled the chaise and tucked herself into the raised corner, left elbow on the back rest, her feet dangling.

The professor settled her slim frame in the upholstered chair with broad armrests, the end table next to it stacked with note pads and books. "Chairs here are built for long hours of sitting, I'm afraid. I always cringe a bit as I sink in here wondering when I will fill out the rest of the chair. Previous tenants evidently have done so, judging by the permanent dent that the upholsterer couldn't quite get rid of. I'd ask for another, but perhaps some historical literary genius may rub off on me this way. I can always use insights, wherever they come from.

"Let's get to business. I have seven students this term, Diane. Each meet with me individually twice a week for an hour. For you that will be Fridays at two as today, and Thursdays at ten. No." She put an X through the number on her note pad. "Let me make that eleven. I tend to get a slow start on Thursdays after High Table dinners. So those are our sessions together. Then I like the group to have a more casual interaction, so on Mondays we shall gather at dinner in a sequestered corner of our own in the Dining Hall. A conversation over a meal is an excellent way to spur discussion and revelation. Dinner is also where I ply my students with wine. Helps people relax and speak more freely, I've found."

"A classic tradition," Diane added without thinking, then felt a little uncomfortable for interrupting.

"*In vino veritas*," Professor Bede said, nodding.

Diane quickly translated: "*Truth in wine.* That's very neatly put, Professor Bede, but I was thinking rather of the continued benefits of it, like The Clash's lyrics about wine loosening the tongue. You know. From their *London Calling* album."

"Quite." Professor Bede frowned. "And please, just *Constance* is fine, Diane."

Diane's nervousness surprised her. Speaking spontaneously while connecting ideas felt exciting, yet daunting, though Diane found Constance's current frown akin to the one she wore while smashing her banana onto her toast. It would take practice to gauge these Oxford dons. Diane shifted on the chaise longue. Perhaps sitting sideways on a chaise longue was not what it was designed for, though this perch certainly made Smith's central table classrooms into more of a business conference, not the mutual exchange that this setting suggested.

"These girls, I am finding, are particularly in need of loosening up. I tell you privately, having met some of the girls last night, it is a stiff, frightened group. But I shall transform them, with your aid. Obviously you are the widest-read in the group. I will rely on you to help me show them how it's done at first, until they find their footing and begin to speak up."

The compliment caught Diane off guard, especially as she felt she had already derailed the discussion by adding in the punk rock lyrics. But Constance's matter-of-fact delivery seemed merely a sensible request. Diane felt flattered nonetheless, and smiled a faint smile after her eyes had popped opened. Help an Oxford professor? She was just a high school tutor. Yet the exchange tripped something in her memory. The Smith alums in Denver often would say to prospective students: *At Smith, the class president, the newspaper editor, the head of every student organization is female. That reality gives a young woman a subconscious understanding to never question one's ability.*

Diane also felt a good deal bolder after four years in that single-sex environment.

Diane's new-graduate confidence had floundered, however, in the buffeting she received once back in Denver. It took her forever to find a good career as a tutor and that opportunity arrived in a Plan B sort of accident, when decent graphic arts positions proved unattainable. Maybe because she'd been raised without the myths and legends of what a Seven Sisters college can do for a person, Diane still needed reminding of the inherent advantages.

These thoughts of Smith recalled to her another part of her mission. An informal comparative study. She wanted to see firsthand how the education at Oxford – for centuries a university for men – compared to the education at Smith, one of the country's top women's colleges. In what ways would it be different here? Firmly in student mode, memories of her four years at Smith flooded back. Sitting with Professor Bede, she felt as giddy as any new freshman, full of energy, eager to please.

"Then twice – I hope we can squeeze it in – we will step out into town for dinner, once we have tired of the menu here." Professor Bede continued. "It will depend on our budgets. Call it a field trip if you like, though I hope conversation will circle around our readings, naturally."

Diane's mind flickered back and forth, comparing what she was hearing to what she had already experienced. See a Smith professor outside of class or the office? Not likely.

"So our session today is to get to know each other. I, of course, have your lovely answers to general academic questions." She lifted her reading glasses and Diane's application paper at the same time, then set them both in her lap once again. "I enjoyed your humorous essay. Refreshing after all the other timid ones. And now you have a chance to ask me whatever you wish. Within reason, of course," she laughed.

Diane smiled, not quite knowing where to dive in. Certainly not the nun story that Daniel had mentioned the night before. Constance must be asked about that at the start of every interview. As Diane fished about for something original, Professor Bede filled in the gap in an unexpected turn.

"Yes, I am working on a new novel, a sequel to the one you are reading for this class."

This new declaration made Diane feel as if she had just tripped into another hole. She didn't recall seeing Constance Bede's name on their book list. Diane usually skipped names in general, preferring to deal in personalities, instead. "Ah, very nice," she murmured slightly off balance. Her brain flashed around; she pulled out her reading list and pinpointed how this gap had occurred. "Speaking of our reading list, where do we find these three titles? I couldn't find them in Denver. Including yours." That's where she'd come up short.

"Oh yes, that's part of the learning. You must go looking for them." Constance smiled playfully.

"Yes! So much learning happens outside the books," Diane agreed, thinking of the vast experiences she gathered as she tagged along with friends to Boston or New York while at Smith, or made sure to join any visiting writers or performers at meals when they were housed in the guest rooms of Emerson House.

"You see then: the hunt is on. Find the feminist books and learn what work you must do to get them. They are not available every-where, mainstreamed – as are titles written by men. That alone should give our group some thought."

"Interesting," Diane agreed, thinking about what it must be like to write an excellent book, find a publisher for it and then have it practically hidden from the reading public. Writing anything took years of effort, she knew. She'd spent two summer breaks casually engaged in a project to write a novel herself. The end product – a finished manuscript – seemed to move farther and farther away from her, the deeper she got into the work of it. And yet, here before her sat a published author eager to answer questions about her craft. Diane considered her own journey.

At Smith, Diane had come to understand her best time for writing. As a freshman, she had lived boldly each day. So many activities to try! Then she had rushed to catch up, writing papers the night before they were due... with withering results. A classic approach to college, she was learning from her students back in Denver. Diane had been fortunate to shift gears in the spring of her sophomore year. Wide awake at dawn one morning for no apparent reason, yet feeling rested, she crawled out of bed, took up residence in the window seat and soon picked up her notebook. The pre-dawn silence and the transition to daylight were like a magical atmosphere. From there, her writing assignments were started sooner, grew more organized – and also became filled with light. No more dead-ends in dark, brooding thoughts or hurried, sarcastic conclusions. Yet only one professor had commented as her papers made a drastic turn that semester. *'When light replaces dreariness, you have made great advances toward understanding,'* he had written at the bottom of her paper, while others had scribbled only *'sig?'* or *'split infinite.'* She must remember to send him a card from Trinity, she decided right then.

Her recent writings had eclipsed that mark. She now filled her tales with light and humor. *Though the divorce is probably responsible for that,* she added to herself with a laugh, and posed the question for Professor Bede: "So, when do you like to write?"

"Oh, I am a late-night writer, I'm afraid. In the romantic tradition," Constance said. "I'd be murder on the candle allowance for any home if it were an earlier era. Actually it was my burning need to write that drove me out of the convent. You did know that I was a Carmelite nun for many years? Well, writing all night – writing anything, and anything at night, actually – was forbidden, of course, and with Matins service arriving at dawn each day, I was entirely unsuited for nunhood, yet there I was." She drifted off for a moment, with a sweet smile on her lips that Diane interpreted as amusement over the misguided chain of events that led her there. "So, my career as a writer had a very resistant sort of beginning. It drove me from the convent... and ruined my eyesight, causing a need for these horrible reading glasses." She gestured with the pair in her hand. "I found an antique lorgnette I use at theater events, otherwise I just drift off in a calming blur. Though I never take them to lectures. Perhaps I should," she admitted. "Some of my colleagues could put a rock to sleep." Her look said: *'You'll keep that to yourself, I'm sure.'*

Diane picked up on the thought. "At the theater. So you'll be joining us on the Royal Shakespeare events?" She pictured some good company on the bus ride, seated next to Professor Bede. Perhaps some incidental comments on the passing scenery. Local insights from a native. You can hardly purchase that as a tourist. *So lucky to be here,* she said to herself, patting the cushion next to her.

"This summer, I decided to use your outings as my time to write, so alas, no. I am skipping the theater portions – for a nobler cause. I have to produce some pages or my editor comes down upon my ears. Very noble." That this elegant woman, facile with droll asides, once chose the Spartan life of the convent intrigued Diane. Her beauty alone contradicted the austere choice, which triggered a different memory from her own girlhood, in that confusing year of her Confirmation. Professor Bede continued, however, drawing her attention away from any deeper reflection.

"Back to class basics. Your papers. The parameters for papers are unusual, yet meant to ingrain the classical experience upon our summer students. Everything is to be handwritten. Then all the other details are the same: write every other line, one inch margins. You know the drill. As you would expect."

"Handwritten? That'll be great!" Three years earlier, on the first day at Diane's tutoring job, they had presented her with her own laptop computer. Very exciting for someone who could never afford one of her own, on her sporadic pay from design work. The gift was a mixed blessing, however. "I still prefer writing by hand, so I'm going to love this."

"Wonderful. Though please don't take it so far as to buy a quill and ink bottle. I had a student last year who insisted on the thrill of authenticity. It resulted in ruining the library chair." Constance exchanged Diane's file folder for a book from the side table and applied her reading glasses to her nose. "Business concluded, I believe. Shall we begin with Angela Carter's book?"

* * *

After an hour, Diane emerged into the Garden Quad, dragged herself up Staircase Sixteen and folded onto the small couch in her suite. What a long day! and it was just three-thirty. Luckily it was Friday. No classes until Monday, unless a load of activities filled the weekend, she realized suddenly. Dreading what she would find stacked up for her, she grabbed the program itinerary and list of students, kicked off her shoes and propped her legs across the farther armrest. "Unbelievable!" she shouted to the empty room. "A quiet weekend to get acclimated? How humane!" She glanced at the students' names and their colleges: Duke. Johns Hopkins. Wesleyan. Smith. Smith. Smith. Vassar. Mount Holyoke. Columbia. UMass Amherst, of course. Natalie Hull: Barnard. Diane set the papers aside and closed her eyes, relieved. Not having to endure non-stop required activities when arriving? What a smart place this was! At Smith, there had not even been a moment to unpack – for five days. That Welcome Week had nearly killed her. She let out a grateful sigh and drifted off until she heard the electronic click in the door lock. Natalie.

"What a long day, eh?" Diane said from her comfortable spot.

"Yes," Natalie agreed, quietly set her books down on her desk and disappeared into her bedroom. "Wouldn't a nice cup of tea be wonderful right now?" she called out to Diane.

"Hey, it's Friday. They have tea at Smith on Fridays. What do you think?" Diane sat up as the tantalizing image appeared before her.

"They serve a coffee break at ten."

"They do?"

"Yes. And also tea at four, they told me. Shall we?" Natalie emerged wearing a very short dark gray dress. Diane splashed some water on her face and was ready.

"Did I ever tell you how glad I am that you're my roommate? You know everything."

Natalie replied with a completely straight face: "Yes. I'm not just pretty; I'm smart, as well."

A small laugh escaped Diane. At Smith, that phrase had been dubbed: The Equalizer.

Natalie regarded Diane sidelong through her thick eyelashes, as they walked side-by-side down the winding staircase and out into the Garden Quad. As they ambled toward the Dining Hall, Natalie asked: "Anyone waiting for you back home?"

"I was married for a few years."

With a quiet nod, Natalie took in the past tense of the statement. "Dating anyone now?"

"Nope!" Diane said with finality and perhaps too much verve, she realized after she said it. Dating again, after her marriage ended, had been some vague concept for Diane. Old, unattached friends had gotten back in touch immediately, then vanished. Yet, Diane found it strange to even think of dating, having gotten used to being unavailable for four years. The entire interim had led to a good deal of confusion. To cover her thoughts, she returned the question: "You?"

Natalie gave her a steady, quiet look. "Hmm. That's hard to say." She left the question up in the air as they entered the foyer to the Dining Hall.

Once there, the sole painting caught Diane's attention.

The joke of it leapt out at her. "Let me guess this title: *Five White Guys*. Let's see what the tag says. See? I was very close: *The Five Fellows*. Well, they certainly aren't *The Five Lasses*. Very different from all the paintings in the Hall. No wonder they keep this one out here." She glanced into the Hall and added, "Yes, the only modern one. Quite a leap from the robed crowd in the other room." She looked more carefully at the image for a moment.

Natalie frowned and looked serious. "Yes. The only portrait painting in the entire Hall by a woman. That's worth noting."

Natalie's combination of blasé demeanor and keen eye for detail continued to astonish Diane. Diane's sense of gender imbalance had stopped at noticing that the woman's portrait over the High Table was the only female in the room, but Natalie was right. Certainly this recent work was the sole canvas by a female hand. "Well, bravo for Rosa Martínez," Diane added, after glancing again at the nameplate on the frame, and rather cowed by Natalie's superior sense of authority.

"Brava," Natalie corrected her.

"Say, are you sure you only arrived yesterday?" Diane said in jest.

She took Diane gently by the shoulders and steered her inside the Hall. "Here we are. Tea as promised."

Here was exactly what Diane had pictured. Every scene in every single British book written before Queen Victoria died was about serving tea, wasn't it? That was a beautiful exaggeration, but it surely included Oscar Wilde and his delightful Cecily Cardew, Diane's favorite ingenue. Except for during The Restoration and The Enlightenment when coffeehouses were the rage, England was synonymous with popularizing Tea to the West.

Diane took a greedy bite of her big cookie after admiring the foreign imprint: McVitie's Digestive Biscuit. She chuckled under her breath as she chewed; the brand-name sounded like the medicinal remedy that came right before the spoonful of castor oil. The cookie proved no such punishment. "This has to be the most delicious cookie I've ever had!" she informed Natalie, whose idea of refreshment – a lemon wedge – was more stringent than Diane's. She crunched down the last of it and popped back to the plate for more. There she found that chocolate-covered McVitie's had replenished the plain variety. She returned to their bench and handed one to Natalie, saying, "You've got to try this." Diane didn't wait for approval to shove the new variety into her own mouth.

"Chocolate. That's an improvement." Natalie first sniffed then took a minuscule bite of the biscuit.

At nearly the same moment, Diane exclaimed: "Oh look! Latin!" She stood on tiptoe and tapped the phrase at the base of the stained glass window casing just behind Natalie, then read it aloud. "'UBI INIQUITUS VINCTUS EST.' *Where unfairness is vanquished*. Ha! I love it! And always five-words or less, have you noticed that? Very quotable. These Wise-Guys had excellent marketing editors."

The *So what?* look from breakfast reappeared on Natalie's face. Once she swallowed, however, she asked, "You know Latin? I didn't think anyone did anymore."

"Sure. I squeezed in five years of it during high school. There's no better class. Chanting declensions, conjugating verbs, translating adventure stories and silly love poetry. Latin's wonderful! Excuse me,

I just want to have a look around." She nearly skipped from window to window to see what treasures of wisdom were offered here, just above nose level.

Latin was the word of the day here at Trinity. Diane was just beginning to sense its ubiquitous presence. Epitaphs and dedications, words to the wise, advice to all who were willing to read and think. If you knew Latin, that is. No one studied Latin anymore, Natalie was right about that. It disappeared back in Denver the minute Diane had finished high school. They certainly didn't teach it at the prep school where she tutored now. In fact it wasn't offered at any of the private schools in Denver. It wasn't even required at Roman Catholic schools anymore. Which was an ironic statement of medieval proportion. For a thousand years only priests knew Latin. Now? Parallel moment in time, wasn't it? What a loss! Though no longer of vital importance – life and death – Diane began to see that Latin was woven into nearly every context in Oxford. Though now these messages read more like the secret language from a secret society.

She thought again about what she had learned from Professor Bede in class. *In vino veritas.* That was Latin. *Truth from wine.* Then I say: 'Like the punk song.' She scoffed quietly, self-amused. Only Diane Quinnell could have added that to a class discussion. She loved finding wisdom in unexpected places... or did she just like telling others odd stories?

She continued her circle at a camel's pace. Marvelous stretches of canvas, men in ecclesiastical robes, this one bright red – perhaps a cardinal – another man in long Restoration wig with an ornate walking stick, finally a brown clad monk holding a book of verse. One could easily chart the progress of history, the paintings growing more modern as they spread down the length of the room.

Now, at the Head Table. The center portrait: up close, it was Anne Boleyn. Diane nearly ran around the table to get up close to the wall where it hung just above her head. Craning her neck she could see much better the tight-fitting necklace on her bare throat, along with the

"B" that Holbein used to name Boleyn in oil paint. Diane wondered. Why would Anne Boleyn, King Henry VIII's second wife, accused of witchcraft and beheaded in infamy – why would she be preserved here in place of honor at an Oxford college dining hall? And what year had that historian said? Founded in 1555? Suddenly Diane was unsure of her grasp of the exact numbers.

The far wall held similar portraits as the opposite wall had, all of them wider than her arms stretched, the wall making up a sort of yearbook page with official dress codes for instructors and poses intact for properly recording the dignified individuals, who started to all look the same to Diane.

Absorbed in her circuit around the room, she suddenly remembered Natalie, abandoned. A glance over her shoulder showed a swarm of boys chatting with her roommate, who upon catching Diane's eye, raised her hand in adieu, and sauntered away from tea in their company.

Saturday, June 29

Awake, the room was already light. Finding Natalie's door open and bed turned down, awaiting Natalie, Diane wondered what to do first. She checked her watch: five o'clock. Breakfast wouldn't be served for hours. Loaded with energy and longing to see the morning dew on the gardens, she grabbed a book, stuffed several items in a pillowcase, then headed down the uneven wooden staircase. A load of laundry could run while she read in the library. Emerging from the tall double door of her staircase, she followed the steps the school historian had led them on their tour, through the garden, down a little path.

She investigated the flower beds up the path toward the Laundry Cottage. The generous swatches of flowers and foliage consisted of different varieties, not just a repetition of the main gardens that bordered the walls all along the wide lawn. The Trinity garden plan was magnificent. Dense, flowering areas alternated with simple colored foliage, lush growths contrasted with delicate items like this Yarrow patch before her. Even in this shady area, the fern specimens never turned to predictability. A delicate patch of Maidenhair fronds from Diane's part of the world spread forth their tiny shamrock-shaped leaflets.

So intent on reading botanical tags, Diane nearly stumbled over the half-hidden person who was tucked under the next large yew tree, asleep. He had that homeless color about him, that dusty beige that resulted from exposure to weather. Living under the sun tans the skin – any skin – and bleaches the hair, as well as the clothing. Add an even coating of dust and homeless people often turn to an earthy color resembling sandstone or paint from the pallet of Pieter Brueghel, whose peasants have gamboled in cloggy shoes on canvas for centuries. This tiny person before her, his hair turned wild and the beard gone to nature, looked like a movie makeup department's best effect for a tree gnome. He was well-covered by heavy canvas overalls, the kind auto mechanics wear. He'd certainly found a cozy, picturesque spot, safe behind the walls at Trinity. She concluded that sheltering a favorite homeless towns person was in keeping with a college that kept their own brood of ducklings near The Lodge.

Any other female alone at five in the morning might have felt startled, even frightened, by the random figure. Similar harmless sleeping forms lay peacefully tucked in pine needles, quietly snoring on the balmiest mornings in Wash Park, back at home in Denver. She knew most of them by name, though some friends discounted her claims as fanciful stories. Nevertheless, today at Trinity, she stepped quietly by and gave the figure little thought.

The aged wooden door of the Laundry Cottage opened soundlessly with the electronic key. It amused her to find ultra-modern machines along with everything one could possibly need – steam irons, steam pipes for hang-drying – all disguised by the crofter's cottage exterior. Everything ran on her electronic key. The key, however, produced no action with the washer, though three red bars in a row, like a dash-dash-dash, registered on the machine's display panel. Stopping short of thumping the machine a good hard thump to get it to work properly, Diane checked the connections one last time before seeking advice.

The Porter was ready to help. "Ah, Miss Quinnell. You must first load the key. Have you any notes with you? What, no purse?"

"Pound notes? Yes." She produced a carefully folded ten pound note from her pocket, thinking how odd it was that he didn't want coins. Everything in Denver, from soda machines to laundromats, used coins. "Emergency fund," she said, handing him the note. *For just such emergencies*, she added to herself.

"Just step over here. You insert your key here, then place the Queen facing up into the feeder. See?" Silently the bill disappeared, the red light blinked and the numerals 10.00 appeared on the display screen. A small '*wow*' escaped her. She'd seen her first bill feeder on a vending machine at the Denver airport when she left for London, but the system evidently hadn't been perfected yet. It spat out Diane's dollar no matter which direction she tried. People near her had said they had the same results. How this tiny plastic wedge opened every door and gate at a four hundred year old school, as well as maintained a student's account, seemed like science fiction.

"Oh, and that reminds me. Staircase Sixteen-C, weren't you?" The Porter disappeared into the next room for a moment. "You'll need this name badge for your breakfast. Sorry they weren't available yesterday. Caused a bit of a rumpus in Hall, we heard. Ah, well. No harm done." He handed Diane the troublesome 'budgie.' She smiled, pinning it on and chuckling once again over her own confusion with the English accent. "That ten should cover you nicely for plenty of laundry and breakfast as well. Reload here anytime. Also you can insert the key to check your balance anytime. Just always make sure the Queen is smiling up at you and you'll be set."

Diane smiled, thinking that last line could be a life philosophy here, couldn't it? She thanked Mr Dickens and returned to the laundry, noting that the resident homeless man had, in the interim, left his sleeping bower.

Arriving at the Trinity Library, she swung open the main door to the lobby, then used her electronic key to unlock the Library door itself. The scent of centuries of waxy furniture polish, dust and old leather bindings breathed from the walls that were covered with heavy shelving. A wooden staircase rose to a balcony loft on the left that ran half the length of the room. Above, books covered the entire wall nearly to the very high ceiling. Classic library ladders allowed access to those stacks. Evidently, centuries of scholars remained thin out of necessity, considering the narrowness of the staircase and upper walkway.

Diane walked the center aisle. Tall wooden shelves set like ribs, perpendicular to the large windows down the length of the room, created study areas between the rows, two wooden chairs at a narrow study table in each row. The windows themselves were huge. In

Denver an average window was set probably hip-high. Here, the Library windowsills began at chest level, then soared upward for another ten or fourteen feet, like everything else in Oxford, built in grand scale meant to dwarf mere humans. Well, it had worked for the ancient Egyptians. An excessive amount of door towered over her even at the simple entrance to Staircase Sixteen. In Denver, a standard door was six-feet eight-inches high, a number Diane's handyman family had drilled into her head.

Considering the beautiful, sunny morning, Diane felt free to let the morning air in. No danger climbing onto the sill here on the ground floor, she readily stepped up onto a chair seat, then onto the windowsill, as wide as a bench. Standing in the enormous window, the lower sash moved easily and continued up, up until her arms extended high above her head. She rose on tip-toe, still gripping the handles. A glorious six foot stretch of pure, open space. No screens! That alone was unheard of in her part of America. She filled her lungs with the fresh morning air.

Two hours later, Diane shifted her armful of clean, pressed laundry to her left arm and pulled the tiny knob intended to open her staircase door. Unfortunately, the turning ratio of the tall double door threw her off balance. She lost hold of the tiny knob and the door snapped shut again. These crazy Oxford doors! Either huge enough for an army of elephants to pass through, or this! This one, divided down the center therefore swung on two hinges. Was it designed to humble her by its narrowness? *'New homes feel inconvenient'* as her friend Miyoko had put it when she moved into her apartment in New York. Or perhaps Staircase Sixteen was just the place for a tall, stick-like Joey Ramone to live? Had Sir Christopher Wren pictured that? she giggled.

Once inside, Diane deposited her laundry and galloped back down the staircase, driven by visions of breakfast. Perhaps she would find Natalie there?

"Good morning, Diane," Dr Chandra entered the Garden Quad

Oxford Vindaloo

with a bounce in his step. His rooms were evidently in the same building as those of her dons, Dr Harding and Professor Bede. He greeted her as he emerged from his staircase door of the building perpendicular to Diane's.

"Good morning, Dr Chandra," she replied, falling easily into stride with him. She glanced up at the wall as they passed by the crew team mural.

He stopped and faced her. "No, no. You must call me Dyan as well. You see, that is the delightful part of the greeting. When I say *Diane*, you say *Dyan*. It will be fun," he gently prodded her.

His request to link them this way fit his boyish grin, though she wasn't sure she would like having to echo him at every meeting. She hated those kinds of rituals, like having to endure the same puns from comedian friends for years. When they shouted the Worcestershire sauce joke: *'You saucy worster!'* it was funny... the first ten times – maybe. Yet something playful in Chandra's simple manner disarmed her. She smiled obediently and said in sing-song, "Good morning, Dyan," trying not to feel as if she were auditioning for some children's show where everything played out sweetly.

"Thank you for indulging me. It is like a little joke of our own, don't you see? And I already know that you like word-play." They had taken only a few more steps toward breakfast when he stopped her again. "One moment. I see you noticing the crew team here. This wall is one of my favorite trivia items, and you said you collect trivia. And I must admit to having watched you standing under it for a good amount of time the afternoon you arrived, a most curious look on your face. What was it?"

Diane turned a similar, puzzled look at him now, she was sure. "Yes. I wondered if these weren't the peak of Trinity's rowing abilities. No recent wins, I wondered?"

"Ah, yes. Very observant. These winning teams have been pre-served to honor them and to remind us. The dates, you see? Very important: the First Eights of 1914 and 1915. The majority of these young men fell in The Great War. A touching sentiment," Dr Chandra trailed off, the conclusion only too clear to Diane. "I am always pleased to begin my day, thus reminded."

Diane nodded. "At Smith – my college – as a senior I crossed Elm Street each day to get to classes. You have no idea how often I had to stop for a funeral procession. It's a main street lined with churches," she explained.

He motioned for her to pass ahead of him through the wide doorway. They strolled through the cool air under the gothic stone arches and paused while Diane finished her thought. "My classmates went nuts having to wait, irritated they'd be late for class. Personally, I loved it. No way to rush ahead. You had to stop. You would be late for class, but so what? I really loved the way those moments put things into perspective." Over Chandra's shoulder, Diane found the center guy of *The Five White Guys* looking directly at her. She glanced at the others, smiled broadly, but kept her creative title to herself.

They crossed to the serving area. "You are very alert in the morning," he said, possibly commenting on her smile.

"I've been up for hours. I've already been to the Laundry Cottage twice, no three times," she began.

"So much laundry already? You must be a fashion maven."

"Nope! Just the opposite. I travel light so that means washing the few things more frequently," she answered off-handedly as she took her tray. "I've also been to The Lodge, the Library and discovered the College's resident homeless man, asleep under a tree."

He nodded, which she took as a confirmation that the man under the tree was an approved College fixture, as she had guessed. "That's a lot of territory to cover before breakfast, Diane. It seems you've been everywhere. Which reminds me, I did not get to ask you when we first met, but I have been wondering, have you ever been to India?"

"No, but I used to have a Himalayan cat," she answered without thinking, then turned to gauge his response. "Excuse me. A joke answer is pretty automatic for me. I have a lot of comedian friends. I didn't mean to sound flippant." She asked the server for an extra egg.

"Himalayan cat. Ah, you absorbed the experience through it, I suppose?" He laughed kindly, studying her and sliding his tray along behind hers.

"You stole my punch line!" She put on an astonished face. They both giggled. To Diane, this felt like permission to speak freely, but maybe not quite so freely for telling all the India stories right now. Maybe she would skip the part about her childhood plan to help Mother Teresa pull dying people off the streets of Calcutta. Too absurd to begin that way. She thought a moment longer, while noting how Chandra continued to beam at her with anticipation, she thought. There was plenty more she could tell him, that was for sure, but more breakfast choices preoccupied them for the moment.

At the end of the serving line, Diane proudly tapped her name tag for the cashier. "See, Mrs Whappington? I've got my budgie on." She handed over her electronic key.

"Yes, yes. I've got you now, Miss Quinnell. Some people have prepaid for breakfast, that's all. We check the budgies for the code, as much to keep students honest as our books straight." The woman inserted the key in the electronic pad before her, then handed it back to Diane. Mrs Whappington's domain appeared back in more manageable order this morning.

She held up her plastic key. "Aren't these amazing?" she said to Chandra and led him to the far end of a center table near the head of the room. Again, Diane found Dr Chandra beaming at her, so she continued where they had left off.

"So no, I've never been to India, but a lot of my dorm mates at college went to Kathmandu for spring break my freshman year. I guess it was the place to be that year. Funny, I had all pictured them flocking to Paris. Shows what I know!"

"And Kathmandu is not India either, Diane, though I think you are making a joke on the word 'cat' perhaps?"

"OK, besides my cat, my Big Sister was Hindu."

"Ah! You have a sister from India? From your father's first marriage perhaps?"

"Oh, no. I mean my Big Sister from college, the one they assign as a buddy so you have someone to help you when you first get there. She grew up in California, but her parents are from India. Her mother visited us often and she adopted me. So sweet! They included me in every visit – so I have learned a few small things about the Diwali Festival of Lights and decorative henna, dying your fingertips for your wedding and such. Oh! Maybe that's why I know the word *chandra* as moon: the white crescent moon that grows up at the base of the fingernails as the bridal henna grows out, that's also called a moon."

"Perhaps," he agreed, continuing to study her.

They both drew in a deep breath and spoke simultaneously: "And everyone leaves the newlyweds alone until the henna grows out completely." Chandra smiled sheepishly, she thought, and she felt a little foolish for speaking so freely about honeymooners to the old man – let alone in unison – yet that was part of the ritual for a bride dying her fingertips; it served as a timekeeper.

"Ah! That was lovely! And so you are familiar with Urdu poetry readings as well?" He eyed her, a deep dimple appearing beside his close cropped mustache. She raised her eyebrows slightly in question. He continued: "Everyone chants the last line together. Our poetry readings become nearly a competition, so eager are we to prove that we know the poem. Who can spit it out first?"

"Like a scramble to invent a punch line for a joke. My comedian friends back home wore me out that way, sometimes. Very competitive." Even though the word *Urdu* was new to her, she was struck with the familiarity of the ritual he described, the audience participation. "Isn't that interesting? I didn't know that at all. But people don't actually like doing that, do they? It sounds like stealing someone else's story ending."

"Oh no, no. It is a wonderful competition because we all have studied the classical poems as school children so it also brings back sweet memories of our earlier days. And the poems! Oh, especially the ghazals of Ghalib. Such delightful, twisting, surprise endings. Truly satisfying to speak them together with friends and family. A beautiful tradition I am sure you would enjoy."

At that moment Natalie passed by, nodded, but continued on to a farther corner, a charming little alcove under the far windows. It seemed odd she would sit by herself. Diane noted that she must have returned home to change. She was no longer in the short gray dress from yesterday at tea.

"I fear I am keeping you from your friends, Diane. I am monopolizing your company."

"No, not at all," she replied. Just then, she spotted a number of young men drifting over to join her roommate. Diane motioned for Chandra to take in that detail as well.

"I wonder where our other dons are this morning?" Chandra asked. They both looked around. "Well, I have you all to myself. Very fortunate for me. Left to my own devices. Oh, I don't mean to alarm you!" He said, suddenly apologetic, it seemed to Diane, but soon continued. "So, this is very interesting. Kathmandu. Paris. And what exotic location did you pursue for your school holidays, Diane? New York? How I have loved my visits to New York."

"No. I usually took the bus to Boston. That's two hours away. I stayed with a friend, slept on her floor, actually." Diane clearly remembered all the territory she'd covered there, exploring museums and historic sites, living on cheese and crackers for most of the time, never thinking twice about how pathetic that must have sounded to others traveling to exotic destinations.

"I am sure your adventures there were more adventurous than all your classmate friends in Kathmandu, combined."

"Actually, perhaps they were." Diane reflected, knowing he was right. Who else spent spring break in the park along The Charles, learning to juggle with crazy circus-arts friends? "I was lucky enough to have some theater friends who made sure I had free tickets for their stage shows at The Hasty Pudding in Cambridge, Massachusetts, each spring. They got so popular! Sometimes I'd have to watch from the lighting booth," she recalled. "That was fascinating, listening to all the tech cues over the headphones." She'd forgotten that detail until just that moment.

"You see? You are not the type to remain home and catch up on correspondence."

"Oh, yes I am! I did that one Thanksgiving at college. Locked myself in the guest room at a friend's house and wrote out my Christmas cards over the long weekend. I don't think she ever forgave me. She thought I'd be a good shopping companion. Wrong! And I would have always spent breaks that way, locked in the dorm, if they hadn't closed them all and made us leave. They turned us out like orphans; it always felt like that to me. Some of us at Smith didn't have elaborate plans or elaborate budgets for traveling. I would have happily stayed at school, found a quiet café corner and written letters all day. I did that, actually," she realized and sort of leapt up on her bench as she did. "My first October break, I went to New York to visit a friend, but New York City is so – assaultive, you know? I ended up coming straight back to Northampton just for some quiet time."

"So, just as I suspected. You are a natural born storyteller."

"I guess!" she agreed. She never planned it that way, but often found herself in the middle of stories, adding humorous details, seeing joke after joke once she got launched. Her juggler friends nicknamed her *The Amazing Diane* and hovered around her as if she were some rare, tropical bird. "Well, I have a lot of material to draw from, having all those friends in theater and comedy. They're all pretty amusing, doing the strangest stuff."

Diane stopped at that moment as she saw Mr Dickens pause inside the Hall. After a brief look about, he walked directly to the far alcove and presented Natalie with a flattened roll of paper that appeared bright white in the golden morning light. Natalie nodded pleasantly, Mr Dickens left without a word and the murmured conversation at that table continued without a glance at the delivered item.

"You most likely are an accomplished writer, as well," Dr Chandra was saying, focused on Diane's story and unaware of the scene playing out behind him.

"Well, perhaps, if postcards count," Diane added off-handedly, still watching Natalie's serene countenance. Diane looked squarely at Chandra again and sat up a little straighter. Had he said: *'an accomplished writer?'* She'd never been told that before by someone who knew writing and wasn't just trying to flatter her to pick her up. She had spent college navigating the criticism of professors and critiques from the other very exacting students. Never a direct compliment there. Here, it felt startling but good.

Natalie and company stood at that moment. The roll of papers rode by on Natalie's tray, as Dr Chandra was saying: "Comedy and theater. And also art history, I believe you said. Have you formed opinions of our painting here? I certainly have my favorite." *Let's see if it is also yours,* his eyes said.

"Actually, yes I do. It's why I wanted to sit up here near the High Table, near that woman's portrait. Who is she?"

"A president's wife, I believe."

Maybe that's who Daniel Glasser said she was, Diane said to herself, thinking back. "Well, I wonder if she isn't Anne Boleyn. That's what all the symbols say to me. I studied historical costumes to help a friend design some dresses to wear at a renaissance festival. There's a big one in Colorado."

"Pardon me: a *what* festival?" Chandra interrupted her.

"Renaissance festival. RENNN-a-saNNNce," she enunciated as he stared at her mouth forming the words.

His black eyebrows came together for a moment, then he said: "Forgive me. Go on. The context will make it clear to me as you continue. Your accent is, shall we say, different from mine." His eyes twinkled as he concentrated even more intently on her tale.

"Yes, the neckline – you see there? The square neckline is a classic renaissance type. You see it earliest in Italian paintings, say in the late Fourteen-Hundreds, then it shows up in The Netherlands, which brought the fashion here as Hans Holbein was called over to paint at Henry VIII's court."

"Ah! Eureka! The late Fourteen-Hundreds: Ree-NAY-sauce!" he shouted.

"Renée Sauce? What's that? Some new curry flavor? A French chef's specialty?" Diane flung back, completely confused.

"The rebirth of classicism in Europe. The Ree-NAY-sauce. R-e-n-a-s-c-e-n-c-e," he spelled out for her.

"That's how you spell it? You're kidding! And you pronounce it that way? It sounds ridiculous!"

"Ah. Ridiculous to you, my cowboy-girl, but here we practically invented the word." He gloated ponderously for a moment.

"As I was saying," Diane drew out the words with a comical frown, "look at that necklace. That's the giveaway. That's the same iconic "B" that Holbein used for Boleyn. I am sure I have discovered something."

"An excellent theory, Diane, and excellent detective work. I wish you were in my class. Let me see what you think of this. Come along. No, no. I'll get these." He consolidated their plates and trays bidding her follow him to the dish return in the foyer.

Diane followed obediently. "G'morning, Kent," she said through the window to the dish washer, as she watched Dr Chandra dump their wet tea bags onto the others that were already discoloring a roll of fax paper perched in the waste bin.

"The foyer corridor contains a spillover of portraits from the Hall." He led her to the portrait of *The Five Fellows*. "Let me introduce you to this one, the latest addition to the gallery."

"Who are these gents? They look pretty smart." Diane said, happy to learn more about the gray-haired men, three of whom wore dark-rimmed glasses. Three were seated in modern lounge chairs, two stood behind, leaning against the window frame. They looked affable but perhaps bored, Diane thought. Her semesters in drawing classes made her aware of how long a model must sit doing nothing while an artist sketched them. *The Five* looked comfortable in classic uniform: tweed jackets, leather patched elbows, neckties in place. Two held pipes. Exactly what Diane pictured when thinking of professors emeritus. Also, at ready on the low table before them, four drinking glasses filled with two fingers of amber liquid, one for each, to join the man on the right who already had his glass snugly in hand.

"These are, or were, our five most prominent Fellows. Perhaps you know Lord Clark, here? A noted art historian." Chandra pointed to the man on the far left.

"If you mean Kenneth Clark, yes. I didn't know he was a Lord."

"Oh, yes, though he was always just Ken to us." Chandra paused a moment quietly. "And the artist is quite famous, I believe, but I know nothing of modern artwork. She has captured the approachable natures of the men. The College is very happy with it, so they placed it here, front and center. Make sure everyone can admire what good fortune it was to have – who is it again?" He studied the signature, "Ah, yes. Rosa Martínez. A real coup in the art world, we are told."

Diane studied the composition further. Now that she was more familiar with the main Hall, she saw that these five were a complete departure from all the other scholars, cloaked and hatted in academic regalia, or perhaps just trying to keep warm as they sat very still reading all day? A grouping of men, as opposed to the single figure, oversized paintings in the other room, also a departure. The scale of the canvas was friendlier. You could embrace these men as friends, unlike the heroic proportions of Fellows from the old centuries. She looked again at the low table, spread with drinking glasses. "I like the way they all are having drinks. Very funny."

"Funny?"

"See here. Because it is in the foreground, closest to the viewer, this low table certainly holds more meaning than just conviviality." She started laughing. "I guess I would have thought that here at Oxford

University, *A is for Academics* but now I see that..."

"...*A is for Alcohol*, as well." They pointed and spoke simultaneously for the second time that morning.

"Ah, yes. Where would our thoughts wander if not for alcohol?" Chandra laughed.

Intrigued, Diane looked more carefully at the details. The low glasses, the amber liquid. "What is that they're drinking? Something special?"

"Oh yes. The Fellows drink the single malt Scotch whisky: The Glenlivet. See the label on the bottle? I always notice that detail, too, wondering when we humble senior tutors will have the budget for such delicacies." Dr Chandra chuckled and looked at her pleased, as though his favorite pupil had just asked all the right questions.

"Glenlivet. Sounds like something that goes straight to the liver, eh?" she laughed. "So this is your favorite, you say?"

"Yes, I like the human scale, the pleasant tones. Nothing dramatic. Very approachable."

As he smiled kindly at them, she understood that these were his old dead friends.

* * *

"Yes. Boswell's, the chemist, opposite," Mr Dickens told her succinctly when she stopped there to ask directions.

Diane put on a pleasant smile and thanked him. It would all explain itself on the way, she was sure. She had asked The Porter for the nearest drugstore. His first word: *Boswell's*, she guessed must be the name, though it sounded to her more like a name for a bookshop. This much she did know: *opposite*, meant across the street.

The fact that she hadn't understood his accent didn't give her permission to be saying, "Pardon me?" every other minute. That was just being pesky. Look how that had already worked out with Mrs Whappington. Don't burden people every moment with clueless tourist questions, Diane lectured herself. She had been raised to be self-reliant. She also had learned during her short-lived career as a graphic artist how annoying repeated questions could be. At the Denver Art Museum one day, she had stepped back to see how a sign she had made looked. There it was, sitting in the perfect spot to face the crowd as they arrived. The sign simply stated: *Lecture Room*. An arrow indicated the direction. While she chatted with the old guard for a few minutes, over a dozen people had entered, walked past the large sign and asked him, "Where is the lecture room?"

"Now you see the thrills I face everyday at my important job," Reggie, the old head guard had told her. She had laughed all day over the incident and held onto the lesson. The experience also brought new clarity to her sense of self-worth as a graphic artist: making signs in a world where few people read them. It had helped her in deciding to switch careers.

She stepped through Trinity's front gate out onto the sidewalk. Broad Street. The noontime traffic surprised her. The cars and pedestrians gave the empty town she had arrived in Thursday evening a new personality. She still felt wary toward the town and a bit rattled by her lost-sheep dilemma. She hoped *Boswell's, the chemist, opposite* would be just a few steps away.

So between motorcoaches, cars and bicycles, she crossed Broad Street, first to the row of cars parked at the centerline, then to the far sidewalk. She continued three steps to the left, joining the flow of the crowd, when she eyed the round theater front and frowning Roman heads of Thursday evening. No shops beyond. She sneered at the Romans and reversed directions. Now hugging the building fronts, she fell in step with the throng, pondering why *chemist* was the chosen term for druggist. She imagined that Brits would use *apothecary*, instead. Yes, like the character in *Romeo and Juliet*, an apothecary prepared medical prescriptions.

She regarded the shop fronts as she passed along them. Blackwell's, a music shop filled with shelves of scores and books. Morton's, sandwiches. OxFam, a clothing store. A soothing, orderly progression of souvenir shops. Then Dillon's, a bookshop led her nearly to the corner. And there was the sign: *Boswell's*. She stepped into the department store with pharmacy.

She swept through each aisle, seeing all the items, mostly in brands she recognized – which surprised her, having expected that England had their own brands of everything – but apparently they lacked what she needed: a simple face cloth.

Having covered the ground floor in one circuit, Diane came upon a short staircase. She stepped up one step and peeked at the jumble that said to her: SALES BINS. She had extensive experience with clearance sections hidden in back rooms. As a student of history, she knew that non-sellers of the past decades and telltale artifacts often provided revealing sociological commentary. This was treasure hunting at its finest. Plus everything was marked way, way down.

The cashier in cosmetics smiled quizzically as she watched Diane climb the short set of stairs.

She passed by quaint tourist items, such as the ashtray stamped with the spires of Oxford, with a small chip in the edge, until she had wedged her way to the back of the overstuffed cubby, where faded felt pendants draped down from the low ceiling to mark the back wall. Next to the wooden clothes pins, she examined the tea towels and small tablecloths in piles. Among the doilies, she found a wash cloth.

She clutched her prize and turned back toward the steps, upsetting a pile of fabrics, which she caught as they slid to the floor. Resettling them in more orderly fashion, she spotted it: a shoe box filled with old postcards. Eureka! She nearly yipped out loud. Exactly what she'd been hoping to find. Canned styles from long-gone eras spewed saccharine wishes for missed companions left at home. *Wishing you were here.* Oxford, *like nowhere else.* Past fads like *attack of the daisies* – from the psychedelic era – and sunflowers – to commemorate Van Gogh's masterpiece fetching millions on the auction block, she guessed. Here, a series of multiple-choice generic phrases. Real time savers for those touring twenty cities in eighteen days. Next came the era of kittens. An orange-striped kitten at Trafalgar Square. A fluffy white kitten at Westminster Abbey. What? None of kittens in the Chamber of Horrors at Madame Tussaud's, nor puppies sacrificed at Stonehenge? Diane laughed as the most absurd images came to mind. Great ideas for applying for creative director at that card company. Next: costumed teddy bears, the first one wearing an athletic polo sweater along the Thames, lifting a toast to the crew team, another in a scarlet riding habit outside a country estate. With relish, she pulled out the few that were just ridiculous enough to forgive the cuteness factor. Then, here in Oxford's sales bin shoe box, the young Queen Elizabeth II, enthroned on her coronation day looked lovelier and younger than Diane had ever seen her. While in London, card vendors had featured Fergie and Princess Diana, no longer the Princess of Wales. She felt a kinship toward the radiant young Elizabeth instead, a noble monarch, frozen in time, expected to hold up that enormous crown above her slender neck and hand-tinted shoulders.

Then she came upon the show-stopper: an old lord, all done up in tweeds, enjoying his copy of *The Times* on the couch with the family's African lion cub for company, seated next to him. She grabbed several, barely able to wait to send them to friends all across America.

She descended the six steps to mezzanine level and placed her items on the counter. The other clerk across at the cosmetics counter leaned obviously her way and sniffed. *Paltry purchases, just weird*, her wrinkled nose said. To which Diane replied by lifting her chin a bit higher and flashing a triumphant smile her way.

Diane stood on the corner outside of Boswell's and had a look around the intersection. Surveying in each direction by turn, but not taking one step out of sight of Trinity's front gate, she noted the divided thoroughfare – Magdalen Street – running north. More shops across. All looked somewhat the same to her. Partially hidden by the dense shade of old trees, a small graveyard lay in the median that divided the street. Beyond the low iron fence, Diane noted two lumpy figures. One slept with his head propped on a gravestone, the other curled up between headstones. That must be their spot. Getting to know every crack in the sidewalk and as many locals as she could meet was part of her plan for the summer. She'd learn their names sooner or later.

She faced the opposite direction now. Cornmarket Street stretched south. More churchy spires filled the nearer distance. She would investigate farther another day, sorry that she hadn't tucked a town map into her pocket in order to place a name on an edifice or two. Although less than an hour ago she stepped from Trinity still feeling edgy about this town, she felt now that she could possibly make friends with it.

Twenty-nine colleges – or was it thirty-two? – made up Oxford University. She wasn't sure of the number, but the thought opened up a reflection. She wasn't as completely lost as she had been during her first steps at college in New England. If nothing else, she knew now that a university designation meant a group of several colleges. A student from Yale had set her straight on that at the first Smith mixer in the fall – once she'd learned that *mixers* were cocktail parties.

"What *college*?" the young man in the crested jacket had answered her, looking affronted. "My *college* is The Wilson College of Law. That *college* is at Yale *University*."

"Ah, I see!" replied Diane, who lived to learn new things, and this was a fact for her trivia list if she had ever heard one. She knew Yale, of course – who hadn't heard of Yale? – but never having visited it, she asked with natural ease: "Yale. That's in Connecticut, isn't it?"

To this the young man replied with a stiff smile: "Excuse me, won't you? I see my cousin motioning to me. Goodbye."

She had watched one of Yale's finest follow his stage directions: *Cross to group of girls.*

Well! She thought, rather affronted herself. *That works as an excellent tactic for extricating oneself from snobby visitors. Just ask them: 'Where is Yale, anyway?'*

Along Broad Street, as motorcoaches and traffic picked up, Diane began feeling better acclimated. Therefore, she sauntered back toward the Trinity gate, impeded for a moment by the line of hungry tourists outside Morton's. A line implied a good item there; she made a mental note. The tangle gave her the moment to notice another sign: OxFam. Where has she heard that before? She decided to step inside the small shop and see if anything clicked.

Used clothing on hangers covered one wall; along the other, the counter with two clerks and the OxFam logo behind them. Then she recognized it. OxFam was the tag line at the end of a series of British television commercials she'd seen as part of the British Clio Awards. Three years running, she had sat through two hours of them in design class, in order to see the newest and best in advertising trends. Funny to travel all this distance for that small revelation: OxFam was the British equivalent of The Goodwill. Always room for more trivia!

Her self-congratulations were preempted by a wonderful discovery: excellent price tags on very interesting garments. This was the place for finding fun clothing. She could probably trade outfits often and look like she'd brought a huge wardrobe with her. Always a luxury to have some variety while living out of a suitcase. And right across the street from her gate.

Based on her outfit today – a Japanese-print silk bowling shirt and burnt-orange silk trousers – the clerks tentatively agreed to her plan, within reason. In her enthusiasm, she found herself showing the young Queen Elizabeth to the clerks who, Diane knew, could appreciate the value of retro. Elizabeth II produced an unimpressive response.

"OK, so you've seen that photo a million times, but what about this one?"

She snapped the lord and lion card onto the OxFam counter, and left the shop having made two new friends.

* * *

Long after dinner, Diane settled in for an evening of letter writing. Such busy days, new discoveries. So much to tell friends before the novelty wore off and life became routine. She began by adding an arrow pointing to her window on the photograph of Trinity's Garden Quad buildings.

June 29. Oxford – Life in England: Everything backwards, in more ways than you'd expect. Like these nutty light switches. I spent the first day in the dark. I had to leave the bathroom door ajar before I figured out that ON is DOWN on the wall switch, instead of UP. I thought all the light bulbs had burned out. And do you understand that all the pubs close at eleven?

Just after the Trinity clock tower chimed nine, Diane was pleased to hear the door lock click and find Natalie entering the suite. She went into her room and returned, brushing her hair. "Have you been out into the town much?" she asked pleasantly.

"Not really," Diane said, feeling cozy and growing accustomed to the love seat before the fire place. Yet she wondered with a twinge of envy where Natalie was getting herself off to. "I noticed that the roads wind and everything seems so twisting. Stone walls rising up everywhere. Little alleys. I barely found Trinity on Thursday." She winced inwardly at the emotional memory of Thursday evening: arriving frazzled, losing her way, encountering glaring Roman heads every time she stopped to get her bearings. "I'm very content right here." She patted the couch.

Natalie looked unconvinced and continued to study her with an intensity that made it clear she expected more of an answer. Diane parried: "I did get these postcards today at the drugstore. Check out this lord and his lion! A real scream, isn't it?"

"Really sweet," Natalie agreed, still waiting for more.

Diane tried to ignore Natalie's scrutiny, but finally shouted: "OK! Look: the architecture is sized to intimidate visitors; well, it works. I'm afraid I'll get lost."

"Yes. Go get lost!" Diane's roommate urged her. "Go wherever looks interesting, then hail a taxi and say: *Trinity Gate.* They'd bring you right back."

Diane blanched at the simple logic of it. "Have a cab bring me back? That's so smart."

"Nothing easier. Well, see you later." Natalie slid out the door.

Nothing easier, Diane repeated to herself, feeling profoundly foolish but also suddenly freed.

Natalie appeared again around the door. "Diane. Put your letter down and come to the Beer Cellar with me. It's Trinity's student center, below the Dining Hall. C'mon," she added as Diane balked slightly in her cozy spot. The motherly tone hit home with surprising effectiveness.

Everything in this country ran in its own mysterious ways, Diane observed. Earlier that week, when she had sought out a pub in London late in the evening, hoping to spend some time there adjusting to London time, she laughed out loud when the waiter had said: 'Last call, Miss. What'll it be?' Pubs closed at eleven o'clock sharp all over England? Impossibly strange.

Here was a chance to find out why. James the bartender in the Trinity College Beer Cellar set her straight on that account. "Eleven, yes that's right. Everyone needs to get home, get a good night's sleep so they are ready for work on the morrow. That's one thing that you Americans have not yet understood with all your discos open all night, aren't they? How do you manage it, I'd like to know. People have to work for a living here. That's right, isn't it Mags?"

"Right-o, James," confirmed Maggie, the pub keeper's wife and co-worker. "What will you have, my dear?"

"A pint of Guinness, please," Diane said and made herself comfortable on the stool at the corner of the counter, a good spot to chat with the two until they got too busy, whenever the rush happened here. When that happened, she would rejoin Natalie, maybe – if Diane started better liking the vibes those two burly boys were giving off. Natalie had introduced her to Brandon and Tucker when they arrived.

Diane found it most convenient to step away to the bar to order her beer at that time.

"Excuse me, Miss," James said to her. "That stool you're sitting on is reserved for Archie."

"Archie?"

"Yes. Archie's stool," nodded Maggie. "Any other is fine, just not that one, Love."

Diane was aware that regulars usually had special places that were theirs like ownership. She'd seen it in bars back in Denver, had it pointed out to her by natives even in the super-populated New York City. She figured that it was human nature that people like routine and therefore fall into comfortable habits. Alvin Toffler's *Future Shock* expounded upon the point, that the faster things change, the more people will cling to the familiar. Despite the exaggerated extrapolations Toffler used to augment his basic tenet – she chuckled again, just thinking of those – Diane had seen the *familiar* formula at work all through school. Diane, forever arriving early, made a study of watching students take seats. Certain students claimed the same chair each session. If someone took that chair first, their distress was often palpable. Diane noted the hostile body language, the jockeying uncomfortably around the area, circling, circling and finally landing in apparent discomfort in a different chair. On one occasion for an experiment, Diane decided to sit in a large football player's regular chair. He arrived. Without a word, he upended it, saying merely: '*My spot!*' She chuckled as she looked up at him from her new place on the floor. Luckily for Diane, that was his idea of flirting and he was good natured about it – but firm. No one was taking his chair.

"Go have a seat at a table, dear. I'll bring you your pint once it's settled."

Once it has settled, Diane repeated to herself. Another interesting practice, and surely one found only in England. She rose and slid a few coins across the counter.

"And there are rules that keep this pub open, and fine rules they are too. That includes no tipping, Miss." James waved away the coins.

"No tipping? Ridiculous. I've enjoyed talking with you."

"No matter, Miss. No tipping anyone who serves alcohol on this Island. You see, the Crown doesn't like any foolishness going on involving the accurate dispensing of spirits." He patted the one-shot pour gadget under one of the upturned bottles of golden liquids. She'd already watched him measuring out exact shots of liquor with the tidy contraption.

Now she commented on it to him: "That's interesting. In the US, they'll pour and pour. You never know how strong a drink will be."

"No such nonsense here, Miss. Keeping the customer happy but under control is our job here. Keep the younger people in check. Not proper for anyone to get in their cups here, among their friends and their dons and tutors. That's not what we're here for. And I'm proud to say, that doesn't often happen under our watch. So know your limit, my dear. That's my advice to all the new students." His manner was kindly, fatherly and easy to respect.

She wished she could preserve the beauty and simplicity of his statement and present it as graciously in a letter home to all the American campuses overrun with rowdy students.

About that time she noted some scratches on the wooden ledge at the bar counter. They looked like they'd been scribed there centuries before. She remembered seeing similar marks on a tour at Westminster Cathedral. "*School boys with pen knives have rendered this area off limits to visitors, I'm sorry to say,*" the guide had told them. Carving initials and the year, the newest of which had been 1729, had given Diane a lot to think about. Maybe troublesome students were nothing new. Undoubtedly, not all British students were perfectly behaved. Then she remembered reading about early universities and student revolts in her Middle Ages history class at Smith. Medieval students at the University of Paris could buy pre-written letters to make the obligatory writing home an easier task. Simply check all the boxes that apply: *In good health. Missing you. Send money.* Hadn't she just seen something like those, reiterated on postcards at Boswell's? There was really nothing new; perhaps that was it? Maybe students had ever been the same throughout the ages. Surely drink took its place in the traditions of educational institutions, along with mild property damage.

The heavy stone piers and low ceiling arches that formed the basement Beer Cellar made it clear that this student pub had been open for centuries. Even the petite Diane could touch the ceiling, would have to duck down at each pier or get a knock on the head. The rough mortar could do some fine damage to anyone's scalp.

As she considered her next move, her finger traced the scratched initials, wondering how old they were. Her gaze wandered to the stone wall next to her, as she contemplated how many other hands had touched these gouges, like the reliquaries in cathedrals across Europe. The whole College was filled with history. And James was right: *Not proper for anyone to get in their cups here.*

"That's very interesting," she said, turning back to James. She was surprised to turn and find the little homeless man atop Archie's private stool.

"Those marks are first thing on my list, come November." The bearded little man spoke while watching her hand. "I like to keep at the outdoor work while the weather is fine. Indoor marks must wait their turn."

Diane stared dumbfounded. Upright, the little man would have blended into a herd of shaggy Highland cattle.

"This is Archie, our stonemason." The bartender spoke. She caught the reverential tone.

"Were you who I saw under the tree in the garden this morning?" Diane asked, still puzzled.

"In the Wilderness along the Library? Yes. I sleep under the night sky when the weather is fine," Archie told her.

Nothing really odd about that, in beautiful weather. Lots of people she knew went into the mountain parks on weekends for that very privilege. Though she did wonder for a moment, remembering her immediate impression of Archie tucked under the tree by the Laundry Cottage.

Sitting on his bar stool now, he gave a different impression that brought to mind a neighbor who had lived across the hall from her in the motel-like building of tiny studio apartments on State Street in Denver. Often enough, she'd opened her door early in the morning and stepped across the neighbor sleeping on the carpet. His door just across from hers was usually ajar, with keys still hanging in the lock. A young man, too. He was a bartender at the local dive that lay along the edge of the transition between very different neighborhoods. The kind of place that offers up a mighty spread of deep-fried chicken wings, a twenty-pound block of cheese, with cheap crackers and a bucket of pickled herring along with dollar beers for an hour at five, then again before closing, in exchange for glasses dunked instead of washed. A person learned to order what came in bottles in a place like that. Every town in America must have had one. Diane always kind of liked the way the rebellious and drifting young university dropouts mingled with the weatherbeaten manual laborers there, all of them out of work, including Diane, until quite recently. It had the charming familiarity she felt comfortable with, a step along the path from her childhood spent in corner hardware stores with her dad and in smoky afternoons at the bowling alley with Dee, the child Diane fascinated by all the different shades of lipstick that ringed smouldering cigarettes perched between space-age aluminum zigzags, while Diane pressed the special plunger to make the spindle spin and drop the crushed butts into the ashy chamber below.

"And that's a hardy mug you've got there, my girl." Archie called her attention back to the moment. Her Guinness had arrived.

"Yes. Nothing like this creamy brew." She smiled, knowing that American men were always impressed when a female ordered beer, not wine, especially if it was a hearty black brew, not something 'light.'

"It's not the brew, it's the size. Ladies here drink half-pints. And you seem like a nice girl not wanting to make a wrong impression. Oh, don't misunderstand me; you can have twice as many, but it grates on us gents to see a slip-of-a-girl hefting such a weighty mug."

Diane let out an echoing laugh. "That's hilarious! And look!" she pulled back her sleeve and motioned for him to squeeze her solid forearm. "I bowl. I juggle. Plenty strong!" She laughed at the theatrical face he put on while performing a dainty squeeze.

"What do you know? An arm like that would well suit stone masonry." He grinned, politely impressed, or just flirting? Diane couldn't quite tell which.

"So, you lay brick?"

"No, not I. I build nothing. I repair, but in a special way to preserve the appearance of age. That's the craft of the stonemason. And dusty work it is, too. Another round here, James." He tapped the counter congenially.

"Here it is, Archie, and it is last call, so don't try to convince me that I missed you for that. There are rules that keep this pub open, and fine rules they are too." James repeated his mantra.

Diane had watched the exchange with fascination. The elfin stonemason grinned, nodded amiably, then continued his tale. "Every Oxford College has its own stonemason, to keep the walls and walkways exactly as you see them, exactly as they have been for – well, at least the last three hundred years." Neither boastful nor understating, Diane liked the way Archie described his job. It certainly explained his coveralls and the fine dust that was still in evidence in the crease above his eyebrows, despite the comb he had evidently run through his hair and beard before he made his entrance into the Beer Cellar. Nothing wrong with the remnants of hard work about a person, Diane knew, who had grown up with a mother who not only bowled, but who had made a hobby of woodworking. Thus Diane found sawdust quite endearing.

"To keep it looking old." She ruminated out loud as she enjoyed his company.

"Aye. Old but solid. Quite a trick, eh?" Archie added, regarding her quietly over his beer mug.

Last call completed, James and Maggie wiped down the counter once again, turned out a bank of lights in the farthest corner where the dart board stood idle. The two nodded good night to the students as they moseyed toward the stone staircase.

His mug drained, Archie stepped surefooted off his stool and gave a good night salute to his friends behind the bar. Diane sensed that Archie played the role of beloved eccentric, and was especially appreciated here, where the sensible rules were set in place for the smooth running of daily life.

Natalie sauntered by with the beefy boys in tow. "Hey, Archie. How about showing us some late-night hot spots in town?" Evidently Natalie had already become acquainted with Trinity's stonemason.

Diane read Archie's response to Natalie with interest. He looked seriously at her roommate, as if formulating the proper words. After a pause he said: "Ah, Natalie. I'd advise you keep away from the shish kabob vendors no matter how tempting a midnight snack may sound. Beyond that, you're on your own, as long as I know you are in the company of these two. Eh, lads?"

"You won't join us?" she offered again.

Some of us work for a living, his face said, Diane seemed to think. She noticed James and Maggie lingering nearby, listening soberly for Archie's reply. "No, thank you. I'm off to find my secret spot to dream peacefully until sunrise. That comes early this part of the summer."

The lads were beginning to jostle Natalie along, evidently impatient for her company and perhaps her other good ideas. Perhaps she knew some late-night spots already.

"Diane, come with us," Natalie commanded rather than asked. Diane bid the staff good night and climbed up the stairs with the small party. Once through the Hall foyer and arched doorway, however, she turned left and disappeared toward Staircase Sixteen as the group wandered through the Durham Quad and toward the front gate.

Everything closes at eleven, James had told her, and even thinking about investigating Oxford after dark only added to the anxiety Diane had about getting lost in it. No. She preferred nice daylight, when perhaps the bad people were sleeping it off and she could look about with additional confidence. She climbed the two flights, slipped her electronic key into her door lock, deciding. Yes, tomorrow would be the day for looking about town.

Sunday, June 30

"Trinity Gate, please." Diane perched herself rather than sat in the wide backseat of the taxi, anticipating a typical speedy, New York-sort of drive. She wedged herself in the best she could, her legs just short of giving her a good anchor. Evidently, British cabs were designed for tall, lanky types who required extra leg room. To Diane's surprise, the cab leisurely pulled away in keeping with the walking pace she had maintained all morning. This pleased Diane, who had walked a good deal farther than she normally would have. Feeling very satisfied with her morning, she peeled off her little jacket and felt free to relax.

"Yank, eh?" the cabby declared in the way that chatty cabbies world-wide do.

"American. Yes."

"Here on holiday?"

"No. I am in school for the summer."

"Ah, I see. Reading English, then?"

"Yes." She let out a brief laugh. The phrase 'reading English' sounded so odd. *Yes,* she thought to herself. *I read it. I speak it. Here I have signed up to* study *it,* but she decided not to point out this differentiation to the driver. At thirty-one, she could certainly take the colloquial comment in stride. Why make a fuss, point out how amusing it was to her ears? Her self-restraint made her feel like a seasoned world traveler. It reminded her of when East Indians told her they had to endure the comment, 'You speak English very well,' and they chose to stop short of pointing out that they had been studying it since the age of five. Ah, humans. Always so amusing, when strangers interact. She settled back a bit more comfortably, feeling empowered by Natalie's right-on-target advice to explore the town then hail a cab.

"Have you been to see the homes of any famous authors?" The driver inquired.

"No, but I did stumble upon Dorothy Sayer's official blue oval plaque this morning."

"Oh, then I have just what you are in the market for. I will swing you by a sight or two on the way back to your College." He sounded so helpful and nice, Diane thought later, as she recounted the wild ride for Natalie.

The cabby made a quick u-turn in the narrow lane just after Diane got in. Now, an endless series of residential turns made it clear the driver's definition of 'on the way' differed greatly from Diane's. She was sorry she'd said *Dorothy Sayers*. That was the moment that seemed to turn her plans on their head. Beginning to feel overly warm, she opened the window.

After a few minutes, they pulled into a quiet lane and stopped. "Now here's the home of JRR Tolkien. A favorite stop for readers from all over the world." Diane thought it odd that he was whispering, but overlooked this detail, hoping for a quick restart back to Trinity. At that moment, some slouchy man in a bathrobe and slippers opened the front door, saw the cab and began shaking his fist. The driver floored it, careened around the corner and didn't slacken speed again. Just like the Races at Ascot, they were off.

Diane's objections held little sway with this cabby, so eager to show her the sights. Like the retired gentlemen in the British Museum, she thought to herself, she couldn't shake him. But she was no longer seventeen and enthralled over an illuminated copy of Chaucer's *Canterbury Tales* in the case in the Manuscripts Room. And unlike the very nice gentlemen who simply *tut-tutted* at the Museum, the cabby would require a fee that Diane didn't have with her, nor would she be willing to invest in this way, even if she had. Her feet were tired and she needed lunch. She watched the meter ticking, and ordered the cab directly again to Trinity Gate. The nonstop sea of famous names and book titles continued, however, from the front seat. Diane's hopes that he was taking her directly home disappeared.

Diane clutched tightly onto her jacket and cursed herself for having been talked into placing herself in such a vulnerable position.

As her panic rose, precise and biting words for Natalie blazed through her mind. One home now seen, the driver took as permission to show the others. All the others.

"No, no!" Diane shouted from the back seat, as politely as possible. "I really need to get back to College."

"No worries, Love. I'll get you there," he assured her at the same time he ignored her.

Think fast, Diane! Should I tell him I'm diabetic? Needed my insulin? Fake a seizure of some sort? Anything to break his insane scheme for running up the fare.

"While we're here you can't miss seeing Lewis Carroll's place, just over that hill." He laid on the speed. The jagged skyline of the golden city faded farther and farther off into the distance. Diane started feeling sick. Panic alternated with heavy waves of resignation. *Everything is fine,* she chanted under her breath. *Everyone speaks English here. Just relax.* The formula did little good. Diane quailed. Was she being kidnaped? Was this some horrible moment when she had been mistaken for some wealthy American tourist or rich Oxford student? Moving too fast for Diane to bolt out the door and into the middle of nowhere, the more she protested, the faster he sped to rush the tour she was loudly resisting. Even the thought that the joke was on him – Diane had exactly five pounds with her – did not diminish the waves of sweating and chills that assailed her as the driver breezed through his well-rehearsed travelogue. She fished the note from her skirt pocket and hid it in her hand, ready to spring at the first opportunity.

The image of coming to the quiet countryside and being kidnaped in some high speed chase finally made her laugh. It reminded her that several of those same Indian friends had told tales of arriving in the United States expecting cloak and dagger danger on every street. They'd seen it in Hollywood movies – and were disappointed to find, instead, sluggish traffic and a complete lack of the exciting glamour they had looked forward to with a mix of trepidation and excited anticipation.

The meter had long passed Diane's resources as they passed several more country cottages and swung back toward town.

"And CS Lewis and his cronies did their drinking right there. Very famous spot." He pointed to a hotel on their right, then swung around the corner, left into Broad Street. "And you see? As promised: the Trinity front gate just ahead."

Diane peered through the front windshield, recognized the Roman heads up ahead and slammed down on the door handle. She thrust the sweaty five pound note through the window slot, leapt to the curb and backed away as fast as she could move, as the cabby made the noisy protests cabbies all around the world make when someone is bolting without paying the entire fee.

"The meter reads fifteen and seventy-five, Miss!" She heard the voice following her as she disappeared through the gate and directly into The Lodge.

"You all right, Miss?" Mr Dickens, asked. "Why, you'd best sit down this minute." He pulled out his chair for the red-faced girl. "What's a matter? You're shaken."

"That cab. I just needed a lift back here and he took me on a tour I didn't want to go on. I thought I was being kidnaped. I kept telling him 'Trinity Gate,' but he just kept going and going. I thought I was toast! I'm not kidding!"

"I'll have a word with him, Miss." The Head Porter frowned and stepped out to the curb. An elderly man in similar uniform and wearing the badge 'Mr Spencer' made an appearance from the other room beyond the counter.

"So much for a quiet Sunday stroll, eh?" she said, hoping her humor might mask her trembling.

Dickens returned immediately. "Was it him?" Mr Spencer asked.

"I got there just in time to see the back-end of the cab pulling away. I got the number. It was Clive all right, just as I expected. It's one thing to take a rich tourist for a ride, I've told him before, but not our students. He had no right, Miss, and I'll tell him as much next time he pulls up to this gate." Mr Spencer returned the desk to Mr Dickens.

Diane rose and insisted Mr Dickens take his chair again, an interesting exercise, something like dancing a courtly quadrille. "He just wouldn't listen," she mewled as she danced. "I told him that I really don't care if I see the home of some famous author, or where what's-his-name did his drinking."

"You don't?"

"No! The same way I don't have a camera," Diane said, as if that would prove the point.

"By 'Bess, you don't. That's odd. Did you lose it? That would be a shame."

"No. I don't carry one. I *don't care* to carry one. I chose *not* to carry one. I like to see things with my own two eyes instead of through the lens of a camera." She'd been through this litany every time she had gone on a vacation with anyone. The simple declaration was usually received as if she had just dropped in from Mars, as if a tourist without a camera is like a robot without a power pack.

"That's very odd, but I must say, I like it. How often does a person pull out the old snaps anyway? Once in a lifetime and then maybe before you die. And such an expense." Mr Dickens folded his hands snugly across his vest. The other guard touched his cap and stepped into the back room again.

"Yes! That's it, exactly," Diane agreed. "That and what a bother! On my first trip to Europe I had everything they told me I'd need – plus the camera – and I had to carry all of it everywhere for three weeks, not to mention having to worry about it being forgotten in a restaurant or ripped off my arm by gypsies. It was crazy. My shoulder was sore for months. I swore, never again."

"Well. That's just extraordinary. I never." They laughed together and Diane felt somewhat relieved of her ordeal.

"And as for photography, a nice postcard has the best shot anyway, wouldn't you say?"

"Postcards. Well, you've certainly brought us a basketful of those already, haven't you, Miss Quinnell?" He looked momentarily rumpled as his brow knit and he reached up to tap his chin. "Now why does that ring a bell?"

"Say, Chucks," the voice called from around the corner. "Is that Miss *Diane* Quinnell?" Spencer returned to the counter. "I've been wanting to meet you; your pigeon hole is full, dear. Here's a stack for you. You must be very much missed." He offered her several letters across the desk, but pulled them back for a final look. "Look at these postmarks, Chucks: Seattle. Miami. Denver. And this one from New Jersey. You must know people all over The States."

"Oh! This is great. Thank you. Yes, I guess I do." Diane glanced through the stack.

"Well, she writes enough to get 'em in return, Spence. Miss Quinnell here is the one I've been telling you about. The one who's been filling our out-going with postcards ever since she landed."

"Pleased to meet you, Miss Quinnell. Always nice to meet a young lady who knows the value of postal correspondence. Though I don't know if I'd want to share my thoughts quite so publicly. Letter writing is more my style."

"I do plenty of that as well, but postcards are special. I use them to practice. There's only the small space. I try to pack it with a good story, just the right words. On the next card, I revise it, make it even better."

"Well. I never thought of that. Like drafts for the perfect paragraph." Mr Dickens smiled.

"Exactly." She was finding that talking was helping to calm her down.

"Well, well. Postal correspondence. Very old fashioned, I must say, but highly commendable. I'll bet you never forget a birthday, either?" Mr Spencer continued.

"Well, no. I guess I don't," Diane flushed pink. "But how could you know?"

"Oh. It goes together, *like the stars with the night* as my old Grams

used to say. Unlike that noisy thing," Mr Spencer said, excusing himself to the next room, to what sounded to Diane like a teletype machine
reeling out several pages. He reappeared holding a fax document
several feet long. "Just as I thought. Another missive for N. Hull. Has
she been by yet today, Chucks?"

"Natalie Hull? She's my roommate," Diane volunteered.

"Well, lucky you. Her mother sends her advice three times a day
like clock-work." Mr Spencer shook his head looking something like he
was shaking off the dust. "Funny, isn't it? Her daughter here, all the
way across the Atlantic, but a mother's apron-strings reach infinitely
wide, I am guessing."

"Perhaps you'll mention it to her if you see her at lunch, Miss
Quinnell?" Mr Dickens added in an official tone. He raised his
eyebrows in Spencer's direction, which Diane interpreted as meaning
to put the conversation back on track. Strictly business at The Lodge.
"Perhaps it's something important. That's usually what the fax
transmissions are for: emergencies."

"Yes, I'll watch for her," Diane added with a wave and turned
toward the door to hide her bemused smile. Picturing the independent,
disaffected Natalie on her mother's leash was an amusing image. She
stepped over the threshold, but ducked her head back in. "Oh, and I
have a lot to tell her. Natalie is the one who suggested the cab ride."

Monday, July 1

Awake again at five, birds singing, Diane was glad to begin her week with her prescribed routine. As she hoisted the window in the Library to full height, she saw Archie across the way. He was walking inch by inch all along the far edge of the Library Quad, just across from where Diane now stood in the window. He took no notice of her, intent on his task, perhaps stalking the elusive mole, that underminer and devastator of old walls. She noticed as he crept along that he used his hands against the stones as if testing their solidity or reading them like braille. Maybe he was divining historic tales through his fingertips – or would that be termed: teledigitally?

Now that she had a chance to watch him working and know that he was employed by the College – not just some eccentric who had wandered in – his preoccupied concentration struck a familiar note. She'd met many fanatical Druids-in-training among the Colorado Renaissance Festival crowd. They resembled Archie in their earthy dress, wild grooming, and love of communing with nature. She was glad, however, that Archie's resemblance to her festival acquaintances stopped there. The Colorado branch – a theatrical party club if Diane had ever seen one – ceaselessly flaunted their thrill of subscribing to the trendy young pagans. Archie, instead, exuded a reflective reserve that would most likely draw the proper company to him.

Her choice words for Natalie had cooled by this morning. She hadn't returned all Sunday, nor Sunday night. Diane hoped to catch up with her advice-giving roommate at breakfast. Processing the cab ride ordeal into story form all Sunday afternoon had also helped quell her frazzled feelings. The hefty wad of postcards that had resulted now landed with a satisfying thud in the belly of the red Royal Mail kiosk across Broad Street. Writing from the relative safety of the defensible outpost she took up in the top window seat of her staircase tower allowed her time to transform the helpless feelings and frustration of the ride into one humorous paragraph. Each successive re-telling moved the story closer to perfection. The pleasant view of rooftops and spires gave her a first taste of wanting to love this beautiful town.

Monday morning after depositing the mail then returning to the Trinity front gate, she watched several elderly couples gliding along at walking pace atop bicycles. This must be rush hour in Oxford, she smiled to herself. The charming sight of old people in cardigan sweaters and women in skirts, pedaling old-style bikes added a comforting note to Diane's morning. It felt like normalcy restored. No more threats from crazy cabbies today. One of the bicycling couples pulled up at the Trinity front gate, dismounted near Diane, and walked their mounts inside past The Lodge.

"Morning, Mary Anne. Hugh. Good morning, Miss Quinnell." Mr Dickens greeted them each in turn as they came through the gate.

Diane smiled and walked next to the woman for a moment. "Mary Ann, would it be possible for me to have an extra blanket? It's gotten rather chilly at night, hasn't it?" She nodded pleasantly to the other two as she addressed her Scout. "Oh, sorry. I'm Diane Quinnell. Sixteen-C. You probably don't recognize me out of my building."

"Yes, of course I do, Diane. And an extra blanket is an easy fix. I'll bring one right along. Anything else you need, do not hesitate to let me know. Any way I can make your stay more comfortable, that's what I'm here for." The grandmotherly figure was in great contrast to the stern Mrs Whappington, the other steel-haired matron in Diane's life at Trinity. "Oh and dear, you don't need to make up your bed each morning; that's my job." She frowned sweetly at the girl. "More pillows, anything at all."

"Well," Diane considered for a moment, "I'm not sure that'll work out. It's a habit for me, you know," she called after them. The concept of having a Scout at all was new for the self-sufficient Diane. The old-age pensioners added a wonderful family feeling to the place. Maybe they even became certain lonely student's confidants, no doubt. For summer, however, Diane pictured little more than the need for a vacuum run over the rug every so often and that was enough. Mary Ann waved to her, as she and Hugh continued toward their duties, Diane to her own. Breakfast.

Diane had enjoyed watching the College coming to life this morning. Aproned cooks had passed her earlier on her way to the post box. She also had a brief chat with Archie about the College's private spearmint patch in the Library Quad which he was tending at the time, an essential ingredient for mixing some popular summer drink using cucumber, ginger ale and a liquor called Pimm's, he had said.

Yes. She very much welcomed the neighborly feeling all morning. She now said hello to the ducklings, who were migrating from the cedars near the clock tower toward a bush just outside The Lodge, mother duck quacking directions quietly. Diane could happily stay behind the Trinity palisade along with the ducklings, and she was sure she was not the first to think so. "Well, off to breakfast. Have a good day, Mr Dickens."

"Right. As you are heading into the Hall, please send Miss N. Hull our way. I believe she has just returned through the back gate." Mr Dickens touched his cap.

Just a few steps around the bend, another worker sat sidesaddle on the concrete container that held the prized grass in Durham Quad. He was now clipping each blade, it seemed, with tiny hand shears about the size of a cuticle scissors.

"Wow. Nice job. This is perfect," Diane greeted him.

"G'morning, Miss," the man replied with an inviting smile and a brief nod to her compliment.

"So, this is something like the putting green on a golf course, isn't it?"

He nodded pleasantly as he continued his pursuit of unruly blades.

"You crush the roots down to compress the growth, I believe."

"Yes, ma'am, that's the idea."

"Yes, I thought so. I studied a little horticulture at Smith, my college back in Massachusetts. So, how often do you have to roll the sod?" she asked.

"Roll the *lawn*, Miss," he looked suddenly flustered and half rose. "What you said isn't polite, Miss."

"Oh?" Diane thought for a moment. Second meaning for the verb: *to roll*. She did remember the street slang from her days at the movie theater in the rough part of town, where homeless people were welcome to buy a ticket at the afternoon rate and stay warm in the theater through the winter evenings. But if they fell asleep planning to camp for the night, or smuggled in liquor and passed out, Big Bill hauled them to the curb, and often *rolled them*, that is: stole any money they had on them. Diane cringed, remembering. Luckily it didn't happen often. Most were just glad to have a warm, dry place available. For the other word, she searched for a Latin declension: *sod, sod – ? Sodomite*? She guessed. "Oh! I'm sorry. I see what you mean," she said, humbled once again by the different meanings words can take on in other settings. "Ah well. I guess I'll leave you to your work. Looks beautiful. Really." Red faced, she trotted off.

She stepped into the Hall entryway, said, "Cheers!" to *The Five Fellows*, then joined Natalie already addressing her toast and tea.

Diane gave the laughing rendition of her cab ride to Natalie, not sure whether she was laughing because she was still angry or whether the absurdity of the entire event wasn't just one more of those moments of irony, stinging whoever is standing nearby.

"Well, I'm glad to hear you got out, finally." Natalie tore open another tea bag. She looked tired, but then she must have had some fun of her own, having disappeared Saturday night and having been seen nowhere until now, a fact which reminded Diane of the awaiting fax at The Lodge.

Natalie received the news with mild disdain. "Ah, so you met Charles Dickens?"

"Pardon me?" Diane was sure she would have remembered that on the cab ride tour. Besides, Dickens belonged in London, didn't he? "Chucks. At The Lodge. That's *Charles* Dickens," she enunciated. "He told me he knew he belonged in a job at a college," she put on the old man's voice: "'as soon as I learned my name has a place in a great book.' Isn't that quaint? He actually ended by saying: 'God bless radio dramas. God bless 'em, every one.' I nearly cried." Her expression remained flat.

Diane wasn't sure at what level Natalie was aiming: poking fun at the very nice old man or perhaps just rattled by Mrs Hull's faxes piling up again, nor did she get to find out. Natalie mumbled something about a shower and excused herself just as Constance and Dr Chandra arrived, punctual as usual.

* * *

After hiding all Monday morning, lingering inside the walls and telling herself she wasn't afraid to go out again, Diane did begin to feel grounded. Her wild ride in the taxi now behind her, she came to grips with her situation. *You know you want to find the Oxford Natural History Museum that you studied in art history class. Just go!* She ordered herself after lunch. So vividly did she remember the dark beige with brown zigzag Moorish brick façade of the Museum, she was certain she could find it on her own. She decided to disappear out the back gate and explore northward, away from the busiest part of town where the crazy taxi driver was probably looking for another unsuspecting tourist to grab.

At the broad iron back gate, however, her key proved incompatible with the lock. To its left, however, a blue wooden door she hadn't noticed before caught her attention. So much did it resemble the drawings of the hidden door in *The Secret Garden* that Diane giggled to herself as she turned the latch, imagining wondrous miracles just beyond. She stepped onto the sidewalk of a shady, tree-lined road, where a French-speaking tourist couple surprised her by asking to enter Trinity by the same door. Diane felt decidedly continental to be able to answer in simple French: "So sorry. This is a private door." It must have made sense to the couple, who smiled and nodded, half-embarrassed at their own boldness, Diane thought. The road continued for a good distance once past the alleyway that disappeared left, behind Trinity Garden wall, toward the west.

Afternoon walking proved different from the early mornings. More people and cars generally, though Parks Road had nothing Diane would describe as traffic. The town felt inhabited rather than deserted, and in knowing that it was peopled with folks who smiled pleasantly and moved about gently, made her feel less vulnerable to additional random, mad taxi drivers.

After each block, Diane glanced over her shoulder to make sure the return route hadn't suddenly been swallowed up. She was also alert for any imperceptible curves that might cause her trouble for getting back. Perhaps a trail of bread crumbs would have been useful, she told herself, the joke meant to prod her out of the pathetic worries she was still feeling.

After about four very long blocks, on the other side of the street, an imposingly tall iron fence enclosed a park of stately old trees. Just up ahead on her side, a glimpse of Moorish brick peeked out through the dense old trees. She held her breath, sensing that the impressive Museum building was about to be revealed.

Instead, the corner sign said: Keble College. Also nice Moorish brick work. Not a complete disappointment. She followed their zigzag brick wall to mid-block and peered discreetly inside the gate.

"We're open Tuesday and Thursday *mornings,*" their stern Porter stepped forward and said in an irritated voice. She then spotted the sign-tent set in their driveway: *Open to public tour Tuesday & Thursday mornings only. One Pound admission.* She hadn't realize that the grounds of each Oxford College were meted out in small chunks to the public. And then you had to pay. This shouldn't have surprised her, but it did. Another way they protected students from being overrun, kept the tourists in check. Yes, if the crowds from Broad Street were allowed to wander freely through Trinity grounds... She made a note to herself to see when Trinity was open to the public.

She continued on her way. The Museum might yet lie farther ahead. At the next major crossroad, however, the traffic convinced her to turn back. She doubled back down Parks Road, only this time on the opposite sidewalk. Across the street from Keble, she stepped tentatively through the park gate.

She rounded a curve along the park's path and stumbled directly upon the Oxford Museum of Natural History. As impressive as any cathedral, this museum was the first permanent iron framework building in England following The Great Exhibition of 1851 where the Crystal Palace demonstrated the new construction method. To Victorian eyes, the exterior said: classic church with long central axis hallway supported by interior columns along parallel side aisles, topped with arching roof vaults. The traditional exterior, however, was designed to disguise the new construction and thereby hide the highly surprising open atrium and glass roof inside.

Diane entered the Museum, familiar with what she would find there, yet astonished to experience it in three dimensions. Most impressive to Diane, and yet easily dismissed in the photographs she had studied: massive stone columns. They complemented the glass ceiling, leading the eye upward, but by no means did they serve to support it. Each one, made of a different stone, showcased the range of geologic forms encompassed within the British Empire, the plaque explained. Diane stood dumbfounded beside the breathtaking beauty of the Malachite column. It must be priceless, if the Malachite hen's egg that her friend from Zaire kept under lock and key was any indication. Diane scarcely believed that this large a piece of the vivid green stone existed.

But the surprises didn't stop there. After enjoying the grandeur of the vast main floor, and walking along the entire balcony, a small sign caught her eye: Pitt-Rivers Collection. An arrow.

Down a darkened ramp at the rear of the building – a complete shift from the airy light of the atrium – Diane found the weirdest oddities, and Diane did not often use the superlative. Oh yes, she'd read about English gentlemen employing scholars to travel, explore and bring home exotic specimens. They strove to concoct collections to rival everyone else's, long before the age of public museums. Here in the dimly lit back rooms, fifty or more squat cases housed every type of bizarre thing from the farthest reaches of the unexplored world. And each item displayed the original yellowed catalogue card, written with India ink and quills of past centuries. Just to see the handwriting on the cards, pulled perhaps from the bottom of knapsacks, native baskets and deep cargo pockets thrilled her. Diane imagined what it would have been like awaiting the expedition's return, then listening to the high-pitched squeaking as crowbars pried the lids from the crates the minute they arrived from their sea voyage. It was all preserved here in this unbelievable display. Truly, Diane's heart jolted in her chest with every new discovery.

* * *

"Blow darts, flint arrowheads, tiny portable oil lamps, tobacco pouches, ceremonial head dresses," she told the tale to her classmates as they waited for Professor Bede to join them in the Dining Hall. "From everywhere: The Americas. The Amazon. Africa, up the Congo. Borneo. You name it. Unbelievable little gadgets and native wares – jewelry, carved pipes from Prince Edward Island in the Northwest. I'm telling you, I never even dreamed of so many ingenious items for daily use. Preserved. And labeled. Maybe that's the most impressive part of it. Every index card tells the location, date of find and a guess at its use. Astonishing."

"If you like that sort of stuff," Jessica thrust in a deflating barb of her own, as she fingered her pearl necklace.

"I think that a collection of moths stuck on pins is depressing," said her roommate, Courtney, equally unimpressed. She flicked her hand through her wispy red hair and stared off into space.

Diane blinked, perhaps more astonished by these nay-sayers than any of the items in the Pitt-Rivers Collection. She was about to launch her counter-attack – sure that there would be one item that would catch their interest – when someone spoke from behind her.

"Do they have the woolly mammoth?"

"Pardon?" Diane turned to see Dr Chandra just over her shoulder with his dinner tray.

"The woolly mammoth. I always wanted to see one. England seems to have everything. Maybe they have one there? I admit to not having visited the Natural History Museum for decades." Chandra set his tray down across from her but did not sit down. He surveyed the group of young women with a broad smile, but focused back on Diane, waiting for more.

Diane frowned and thought a moment. She'd seen so many curiosities, but she was sure they were all under five feet tall. "Well no, Dr Chandra. I don't think so. More like a parchment filled with poison darts. Lesser known nautical pieces, like a solid brick of black tea. You had to chip off pieces, I am guessing," she explained, as the girl with the long dark hair revealed a flicker of interest.

Diane was off in another direction to break through their disaffected attitude. "The identification cards alone. Think of the life of the person who belonged to the hand that wrote those cards. He must have been fascinating, too." Jessica rolled her eyes toward Courtney; Diane countered, taking sudden delight in adding grizzly descriptions: "There were also shrunken heads, tiny oil lamps made from teeth. Human hair bracelets." It was like everything she'd seen in Tarzan movies – but she didn't point out – but even more so. But then, her taste for khaki riding skirts and tall boots also stemmed from watching Jane kick around in similar garb while in the jungle with her anthropologist father. "Very macabre," Diane added in her most seductive tone.

"Oh, lovely," Courtney said, while her face made it clear that macabre was out of fashion in her world.

Diane turned back to Chandra, whose sparkling eyes told her that she had her classmates on the run. His tacit approval made her bolder: "The Pitt-Rivers Collection just became my favorite museum – though it is tough to top Isabella Gardner's collection in Boston. That's old stuff too – have you seen it, Dr Chandra? – ancient mosaics, railing grills from old church confessionals, chunks of architectural artifacts. She hired an architect to build them into her house."

"The Isabella Stewart Gardner Museum? The one with the stolen Rembrandt?" Emily, whom Diane had met at morning coffee, joined in, but was cut off by Superior Girl.

"How can a museum boast having a *stolen* Rembrandt?" Jessica tut-tutted.

"Well, I mean its Rembrandt *was* stolen, along with several other important Dutch paintings," Emily said in apology. Her face fell as the superior girls turned their backs to her. "It was a really big deal in Boston. I live there," Emily mumbled.

"It still is, Emily," Diane charged in. "Those paintings are still missing. There's just tags on the wall where they belong. But think about it; as impressed as I am by Gardner's amazing house, that stuff was being torn out as she bought it. She didn't have to put her life in peril of malaria, wild beasts, or hostile natives the way the collectors for the Pitt-Rivers Museum did when she amassed her collection."

"– or dysentery." Dr Chandra's additional detail created a stir of disgusted shrugs among the ladies.

"Hello, Dr Chandra." At that moment, Professor Bede arrived with a bottle of wine in each hand. Maggie followed with a tray of stemmed glasses. "Please. If you don't mind, my class is gathering in this corner this evening."

"Of course. Just wanted to hear about Miss Quinnell's blow darts. You must promise me more tales, Diane. Perhaps shrunken heads over breakfast." He winked at Courtney who looked suddenly uncomfortable, then carried his tray to join other colleagues nearby. Courtney shot a look of commiseration toward Jessica and slumped off. The others visibly relaxed, but exchanged quizzical looks as if something totally bizarre had just happened.

Diane, still charged up with the recent fray, rolled into her next story: "And yesterday, a cab driver kidnaped me and took me on the wildest ride. Watch out for him. His name is Clive. He'll ask you if you want to see where famous authors lived. Don't get in a taxi here, that's all I can say." The word 'kidnaped' caught the ear of a neatly dressed young man across the aisle, who stepped over to hear the rest, but was instead shooed back to his table by Professor Bede.

The group silently found their places, some trying not to listen to Diane's new rant, others suddenly inhibited by the appearance of their professor or reacting to the tension Diane was trying to dispel with her continued tales.

"Oh, how unfortunate your cab ride, Diane, but I assure all of you that the cabs here in town are perfectly safe." Constance gave Diane a stiff smile that made Diane feel as if she had just done enough to traumatize the already reluctant group for all eternity.

Diane looked around at the stony faces, all eyes now on Professor Bede. Jessica sat with prim posture – yet toying with her pearl strand – ready to make a good impression. Diane wondered at the gulf that seemed to separate her from the others. Surely the ten years passing since graduation hadn't changed her that much? Or had college students become increasingly disengaged? Whatever it was, Diane turned her attention back to Constance as she began.

"Have any of you succeeded in finding any of our missing titles?" Constance asked the silent group. She lifted her eyebrows, surveyed the grim faces, then doubled back. "Ah. Well. How foolish of me." She turned to the student on her right. "Will you please help me fill the glasses, Kate?"

Kate blanched right up to her freckles, then leapt up to obey.

Tuesday, July 2

Tuesday morning, Archie stopped under the Library window just as Diane threw open the sash. "Inspecting," the tiny man said without being asked. The top of his head came just up to the sill.

Standing on her perch high above him, Diane nodded slowly three times feeling a little as if she were counting beats before entering into the next measure, singing. She let the stonemason continue without further comment. *Let the birds accompany him,* she thought, their early morning songs filling the courtyard.

Two hours disappeared in reading and listening to the sounds of another Trinity morning. Just before eight, she crossed to the Sheldonian to post her letters, waved to The Lodge as she returned, then turned toward breakfast.

Bubbling with good feelings, Diane was pleased to find Constance there. So much to tell her that she hadn't gotten to say at dinner with the others last night.

"So sorry about that kidnaped-by-a-taxi story last night. I just didn't want anyone falling for the same bait."

"No, no. I apologize for cutting you off. I sensed some tension there and wanted to rally the forces in a different direction, especially for our first group session. Grueling, wasn't it? And what was Chandra saying? Something about shrunken heads?" Constance asked, about to sacrifice another banana.

"I was crowing about finding the Natural History Museum yesterday. Without a map," Diane added proudly. "The girls showed no interest, so Chandra was joining in." She regarded her dead-looking baked tomato half, and pictured it fitting in, preserved on a shelf at the Pitt-Rivers Collection. "Why exactly do they give us a baked tomato for breakfast?"

"Good for vitamin-C."

"Really? I never would have guessed." She poked at it with a fork.

"Good morning, Connie, Diane," Chandra chirped, as he arrived. "So, is that it then? Part of the long awaited shrunken head story?" He motioned to the action on her plate.

Diane looked up at him with surprise when he added: "I admit to having overheard you just now." Chandra chuckled as he climbed in beside her.

She leaned back and frowned at him, then said, "Good morning, Dyan. I was thinking the same." She contemplated the toast in the toast rack, where it had every chance to grow cold and dry out, and suddenly longed for any of the freshly baked pastries she often indulged in on weekends. "Say, does the Trinity kitchen ever make cinnamon rolls for us?"

"Cinnamon? At breakfast? What a peculiar idea. Sounds horrid," Constance grimaced slightly.

"Cinnamon – outside of Indian food? Unthinkable," Dr Chandra filled in with just enough smoothness to offend no one.

"Are you kidding?" Diane nearly shouted. "Sweet, piping-hot cinnamon rolls covered with icing: I could eat a dozen! I *have* eaten a dozen, straight out of the oven in the morning. Or oatmeal with brown sugar and cinnamon? Don't you even sprinkle it on toast? Cinnamon is the pinnacle of sweetness where I come from. I can't believe you don't have that here."

Chandra's eyes twinkled as he regarded the two women at the opposite ends of the spice spectrum. He cleared his throat and said, "Actually, perhaps a dozen years ago, your Pillsbury Company introduced a barrage of cinnamon-flavored breakfast items here, none of which must have caught on, I gather, since they have now disappeared from the stores. They were a momentary novelty – my auntie in Bristol bought them all, I think – but perhaps without the result in the sales figures needed to sustain them. Indian women prefer baking at home from scratch. Old recipes, you know." He winked at Diane.

The discussion appeared to be giving Constance a bad taste in her mouth. "Coffee anyone?" she said as she rose, nostrils flaring discreetly. Diane and Chandra giggled silently as they watched her go.

"That was interesting," she said to Chandra. "I hadn't linked cinnamon with anything revolting nor with The British Raj. Maybe Constance had a bad experience with curry once? Though I do remember now a friend back in Denver – who used to be a chef in London – he said that any spices beyond salt and pepper are confiscated at Customs." That launched them on a discussion of historical connections which eventually led her back to her own exotic exploring yesterday. "Yes, I was just telling Constance, I had such a great adventure of discovery yesterday, I feel confident that I could find just about anything."

Constance returned at that moment. "Have you found our missing books yet? That would be an excellent mission. Bring me your treasure map for the other girls if you succeed. I'm off!" She gave Diane the same mischievous look from Friday and cleared her tray.

Diane turned to Chandra. "A couple of titles for class I couldn't find in Denver. Oh! I just realized; I should have been looking in London when I was there." She fell into thought.

"Try Blackwell's first, right next door," Chandra coached her as he rose with his tray.

"Isn't that cheating?" she laughed.

"Our little secret. Good luck!" he called as he left for class.

* * *

Confidence spilling over from the successes of yesterday, Diane felt like a native of Oxford, knowing that it was preferable to run errands in the quiet of the morning rather than to press on among the afternoon throng.

Finding the books is part of the course, Professor Bede had told Diane in their first class. Last night at dinner, she had elaborated for the group. "Ten thousand copies of everything Lawrence Sterne or Charles Dickens ever wrote may be purchased everywhere in Oxford, nearly out of every pub, if you asked. But women writers? Still a hidden commodity."

Hunting for assigned books? An unusual system, Diane thought, but it might be fun. At Smith, as at most American colleges, the college bookstore ordered every course book for the classes offered. Sure, it was a painfully long wait in the lines at the beginning of each semester to buy all the books. Equally grueling to drag all ten tons of them home across campus, but Diane remembered the task fondly. Standing in line for over two hours with the same people, creeping forward toward the door of the store was a perfect moment in time to meet other classmates, compare stories, make jokes.

Without that onerous task, would she ever have become friends with Trisha? Over their four years, they'd never had a class together. They didn't live in the same house, the usual place for making friends. Yet getting to know each other thanks to the random arrangement of students waiting to buy books, they'd hit it off enough to meet at the student Kaffee Klatsch nearly every Wednesday and Friday morning between classes. They even managed to catch a few movies in town together when anything good was playing. That took work and devotion. Easier, most of the girls found, to limit friendships to those closest by, like people in the house. Easy to maintain contact that way, sitting at meals each day. Tough work to maintain a friendship across campus, yet worth it. And after graduation, although Trisha couldn't possibly keep up with Diane's ceaseless letter sending, she had made a fair stab at keeping in touch over the years. Ten now. Ten years since Diane stood waiting in front of Seelye Hall, and later, in front of The Quill, when the bookstore moved onto Green Street.

Here – at least for the summer session – Oxford's Colleges relied on individual bookshops. Some of them must be the best in the country and certainly the largest, like Blackwell's, Diane gathered from the series of gymnasium-sized rooms filled with books that she crossed, while looking for her three missing titles. Diane tucked a copy of Bede's book under her arm and presented it triumphantly to Blackwell's cashier. This was Diane's type of scavenger hunt!

But for the rest, Dillon's Booksellers next to Boswell's had nothing.

Yet, in a tiny, one room used-book vendor way down Cornmarket Street, onto Saint Aldates, long past Christ Church entry arch, Diane uncovered the Jeanette Winterson title. They had five copies. But no *Union Street*. Funny that Pat Barker's Booker Prize winner was proving the most elusive. So popular, were all the shops sold out of it? Nope. They didn't carry it. More food for thought.

With renewed confidence, Diane chose an unexplored circuit back to Trinity: down High Street, then up Turl, passing Jesus and Lincoln Colleges. She dropped in at The Lodge where Mr Spencer presented her with another stack of letters, almost like a reward. Then on to lunch, clutching her prizes.

Diane hefted her tray onto the tabletop, set down her books and mail next to it, then climbed over the long wooden bench. Lit by midday light, the hall took on new aspects. The noontime sun darted down through the stained glass windows, bouncing light off the floor in upward shafts that illuminated the upper registers of the huge room. Minor dust motes hung in the air. Multiple baseboards, wainscoting, vertical pilasters, then finally the crown moldings, the decorative elevations in the Hall were an architectural study in themselves. And every surface immaculate. Housekeepers must toil undetected in the night hours like the shoemaker's elves, Diane told herself.

She turned on her bench toward the low balcony that ran the width of the back of the Hall, just above the two main entry doors. A small wooden railing lined with decorative ceramic tiles marked the edge of the space she estimated as perhaps four or five feet deep, just wide enough to accommodate a row of chairs and the sitters' legs. She wondered if it wasn't the College's Minstrel Gallery, where lutes and wooden recorders might have played sweetly during ceremonial dinners centuries ago. Or perhaps they still did, on special occasions. She must remember to ask where the staircase was that led to the loft.

After less than one week into the program, Diane saw that the Dining Hall was nearly deserted during lunch. After seeing the lunchtime crush of tourists on Broad Street last Saturday and again today, Diane easily preferred the quiet of the Hall. To the knowledgeable Natalie, who never yet had appeared for lunch, eating here was probably a sign that you'd found nowhere better to be. Diane was fine with that.

For Diane, the College lunch was what it needed to be: filling. Here you were destined for a slab of meat in thickened sauce, a mountain of potatoes or rice, and a gigantic ladle full of steamed vegetables. This was the hearty midday meal served up for laborers, the type of bountiful repast that homeless people dreamed of. And lots of hard rolls, which Diane couldn't resist. The mound on Diane's plate looked like enough food for a family of six. She protested and begged for less, but the line servers – an uncanny mix of young men in the early twenties and elderly women – insisted that not to fill the plate would imply stinginess. No. Generosity would prevail!

As she buttered a second roll, two young men she didn't recognize approached and nodded to her, then gestured with timid smiles to the tabletop across from her.

"Yes, please join me. I'm Diane Quinnell." She half-rose, then sat again behind her heaping plate.

"Hullo. I am Jan. We admit to watching you each day," said a beautifully dressed, blond lad with some romantic trace of Eastern European accent. The second young man, thin and dark with reluctant posture, smiled meekly and averted his eyes.

"Really? Well, you've been most subtle about it." A candid remark from a gorgeous young man. A nice surprise. How had she missed him here before? Had she been that preoccupied, taking in the artwork? Hadn't Reggie the guard back at the Denver Art Museum said the same, when she went there to draw? *'Stand clear boys! That gal's busy.'* Self-absorbed is good for scholars, she reminded herself, as if to excuse her oversight of these two young men.

"We decided – this is Mark and I, I am Jan – we thought you must be someone very interesting. You are so often sitting with the dons and laughing. You are one yourself, are you? Perhaps a tutor? We have been wondering and so today we find out."

"I am a tutor, yes, but back in Denver, not like the tutors here. I work with students on writing at a prep school. But this summer, I'm a student just like everyone else here." She smiled.

"See, Jan? I told you she must be some genius. Our age and already teaching. See – she already gets her official mail here and everything." Mark's posture slumped in a way that said: we're out-classed. His accent? Some borough of New York and delightfully droning.

"Oh no. Just letters from friends." She shifted her things to the bench next to her, suddenly remembering encountering only scorn from classmates when her letterbox at Emerson filled up so often. "And thank you for the compliment, Mark, but I think I have about ten years on you. I already switched careers." Her eyes twinkled as if needing to launch Plan B was some kind of coup.

"Ten years? Really? Is that what it takes to be able to laugh with professors?" Mark recited the sentence like the punch line to some classic joke. "That's what I do when I'm nervous – laugh. But I'd be petrified having to make small talk with them during a meal. It's tough enough during class."

"Yes! Isn't it great?" Diane burst into laughter. "No way to hide in the back row here if you haven't done your reading assignment. Just plunge right in!"

Jan frowned in her direction, interested.

"You think that's fun?" Mark jerked a little and turned red.

"Yes. And luckily, laughing is the thing I do best, if I do say so myself." Several times already, Diane had been aware of her own laughter reverberating off the vaulted ceiling. Constance had smiled sheepishly at her just this morning, but had refrained from joining in the raising of the roof. British stoicism, perhaps? Diane grinned again, remembering that moment. "Well, I'm glad you decided to join me even though – I know, I know, Jan – Americans are so loud. I try to fit in here and act subdued, but I'm hopeless, I think. What are you two studying?"

"We are with the Masters of Finance program from Georgetown University," Jan continued intently.

"Planning to be stockbrokers?" Diane gave a half smile, accustomed to hearing grand plans from students at fancy colleges. They believed in starting at the top, her Smith classmates included. But Jan must have interpreted Diane's comment differently.

"Yes, but of course you hear my accent. I am at Georgetown as a foreign student from Poland. And now here."

"I'm from Queens," Mark added as if it mattered.

Ah, so that was it, Diane thought. She took the information in stride. "Me too. Here, I'm the exotic foreigner from Denver."

Jan flashed another radiant smile. "Denver. A cowboy town."

"Yes siree, Bob," she drawled and wondered about so many aspects of human perceptions and expectations that she probably couldn't sort them all out in ten years of contemplation. "Georgetown. Ah, yes. Big news there in Washington just as we left, wasn't there? The head of the CIA gone missing? The first headline said, *'Lost canoeing, feared drowned.'* Two days later he was found and dead. Do they think they're fooling anyone?"

The two stared slack jawed at her pronouncement.

She stared straight across at them. "Someone didn't want him available for answering questions. Well, that's what probably happened, don't you think?"

Mark continued to stare as Jan leaned toward her across the wide table. "You are the first American I've ever heard speak this way. It is wonderful. You *know*! Why is it that *you* know and no one else I've met, knows?"

"Do you think that's what happened?" Mark turned to his friend.

"See? Even my friend here." Jan gave her a big smile.

She was just forming a stab at an answer – based perhaps on the superior position her additional decade gave her to observe headlines and compare them to actual happenings – when a chatty furor that had started at the table behind them grew suddenly and engulfed them. Daniel Glasser had entered the hall, red faced and winded, the moment before, saying something emphatically to the table behind her. Now he turned and clapped her on the shoulder.

"You'll never believe it! Salman Rushdie is going to speak tomorrow! Here, at the Oxford Union, just down the street. I'm just running out to get tickets. This is so exciting! You'll want a ticket, Diane? I'll get you one."

"No thanks," Diane replied calmly. Though she recognized that Salman Rushdie suddenly materializing in public was an historic moment, she remained untouched by the electrifying steam of it.

"Omigod, Diane. This is it! Are you joking?" he demanded. "The first time he's come out to speak in public since the *fatwa*!" Daniel leaned closer. "You know he's been in hiding all these years – and now. Wow. It was just announced. I heard about it at the bookshop across the street. I can't believe I'm here at this moment in time! Salman Rushdie! I'll get you a ticket, right?"

Diane remained unruffled. She shook her head slightly while Daniel radiated, bug-eyed. Jan and Mark were riveted on the exchange.

"No? Are you kidding? You'd miss this?" Daniel turned a shade verging on purple, his large watery eyes nearly popping from his head. Something about it seemed familiar. Right: Rodney Dangerfield. She waited for Daniel to start tugging heatedly at his shirt collar.

"You bet I'd miss it," Diane said. "Have you no sense of how dangerous it will be to be there? All tidily squeezed into a lecture hall, all an easy target for a bomb?" Really, how naive Daniel Glasser was, which surprised her. He wasn't just some twenty year old, but a returning graduate student with some living under his belt.

Evidently he hasn't visited his ancestral homeland in the Middle East to get a dose of reality about how militant factions can work, Diane commented to herself. She had never been to the Middle East either, but had met several exchange students in high school, some from Israel, and one in particular, Talia from Beirut, each with upsetting tales to tell.

Talia frequently had lunged at Diane in unexpected situations – to protect her. The first time it had happened, walking down the hallway together after school, Diane had bent down to pick up a stray pen from the floor. In a flash, Talia had kicked Diane's arm aside mid-swoop and then pinned her against the wall, shouting, 'Are you crazy! NEVER pick up a stray item like that! I've seen friends lose fingers that way!' The possible realities of innocent situations came to life for Diane. Talia had remained serious and rarely let down her guard even after a full year in Denver. She never smiled, not even when she won the 100-yard dash at a track meet. Her soberness with everyday life, coupled with tales of mandatory military conscription, made a deep impression on the fifteen year old Diane. Diane began noticing how frivolous and carefree American teenagers were by comparison. This lesson from Talia changed Diane's inner perceptions and added to her own natural inclination to observe and consider more deeply.

She looked up at Jan now, realizing that this might be part of what he'd been seeing in her. A different demeanor.

Aware of Daniel towering over her, waiting, she shifted her focus back to him and said simply, "No, thanks, but you go ahead if you want to."

He was already half way out the door, leaving quite a hubbub behind him.

She turned back to her new friends just as Constance Bede approached, slowed and nodded in her usual manner. Jan and Mark sprang from the table as if they'd been caught trespassing. They pulled their trays with them, and vanished with a wink from Jan and a pale shudder from Mark. Their exit left Professor Bede untouched.

"Diane Quinnell, meet Dr Julian Steele, from across the street." Constance formally introduced the tall blond man she had in tow. The introduction sounded odd to Diane. Constance insisted on the familiar first name basis for herself. Why the formality with Dr Steele? Perhaps it was just a personal quirk. Well. The formal introduction did establish a person's situation, immediately. Diane thought the inconsistency a clever way of observing social protocols while mystifying everyone at the same time. Constance intrigued Diane and if this was just an eccentric glitch, Diane could do with it nicely.

Diane noted Dr Steele: winning smile, impeccable grooming with the glowing bronzed skin tone that Diane associated with spas and expensive facial regimens. She recoiled slightly, recalling other important men she'd met, addicted to appearances, cloaking themselves in every available luxury, the type George Hamilton played so convincingly in made-for-television movies.

"So what was the disturbance that died down just as we entered?" Constance inquired.

"Daniel Glasser said that Salman Rushdie will be giving his first public lecture just down the street from here tomorrow afternoon," Diane filled in, glad to have a reason to divert her gaze from the tall, handsome man.

"Ah. Really. How lovely." Constance raised her beautiful eyebrows slightly, broke her hard roll in half and addressed her attention to minutely buttering every surface of it.

"Ah, yes," said Dr Julian Steele. "Very exciting moment in time, I'd say. Will you be attending, Miss Quinnell?" He spoke in smooth tones and clamped his eyes on her. Diane's opinion of him teetered, then swung readily toward fascination.

The effortless skill some professors had with conversation made them the most pleasant company. Yet how had Steele made attending the event sound so suddenly enticing? Perhaps because he would also be there? Diane wondered what this instant magnetism was that she felt from Steele. She responded in kind, falling into cadence like a tennis match: "I think I wouldn't hear a word of the lecture, fearing the worst for bombs and gunmen, I'm afraid."

"Unique perspective. Is that from your exposure to everyday cloak-and-dagger life in the United States?" Steele parried.

"Perhaps." She smiled, enjoying dropping a mysterious open end, which she suddenly realized wasn't at all like her usual self, ending with a joke. "And you, Dr Steele?"

"Oh, naturally I'll be there. Everyone will be there. You really must consider changing your mind. I assure you it will be perfectly safe. And momentous." She felt his eyes bore into her with an unexpected pleasure, and with it, a warning flag.

"Ah, yes," Constance set down her butter knife, "Now that I think about it, I believe Chandra mentioned something about it."

"Do either of you know Rushdie personally? Was he a scholar here?" Diane asked, more so she could tell her own story of seeing Kurt Vonnegut several times in Northampton than any interest she had in Rushdie. She hadn't read Rushdie, much less anything written after World War I. She was, of course, aware of his situation – unfortunately in hiding a number of years – but his writings, she hadn't explored.

"Oh my, yes," Constance nodded. "We used to see him out and about. Lovely man, actually."

"Yes. How we miss him. Good old Salman," Dr Steele added.

Diane felt that she saw a good deal in his simple comment. Why she chose to doubt Steele's approbation, she wasn't sure. His comment struck her as both glib and overly general. It sounded to her just like the times certain actor friends back in Denver were embellishing facts or acting very with-it in order to appear as though they were fitting in. Could that be? Or maybe Steele just didn't like Salman Rushdie? Diane certainly had never met Rushdie so she was no judge of his character. Maybe Rushdie had an irritating attitude? Perhaps Steele envied Rushdie's success? An academic rivalry, perhaps. That must be the case, Diane decided. She regarded Steele, still searching for further information in his manners, but was interrupted by the arrival of Dr Chandra, followed by Professor Harding.

"Hello, Connie. Dr Steele," Chandra greeted them, then chirped: "Hello, Diane."

"Hello, Dyan!" Diane felt free to respond. *See?* Her face said as she held up the wad of letters just high enough for Chandra to see them, then set them down again. The exchange was not lost on Steele, who eyed each of them in turn but said nothing. "Hello, Professor Harding," she added quickly.

Everyone adjusted seating for the two men, while Diane recapped the news about Rushdie's appearance for the new arrivals.

"Oh yes, Rushdie," Chandra chuckled. "How he used to follow me around, consult me on the smallest occasions. Yes, yes, like a lost lamb looking for a sheepdog, as Thomas Hardy would have said."

Dr Harding shifted noticeably and cleared his throat. Chandra, however, continued without pause. "But then, he came into his own. I noticed the change when his first novel was released to such acclaim. Suddenly, I saw that quiet young man with the twinkle in his eye blossom like a young tour guide as the train pulled into Malgudi, as RK Narayan would have said. Wouldn't you agree, Nick?"

Professor Harding grimaced at this comment as well, which he tried to cover, Diane thought, by biting solidly into his hard roll. Diane was an avid student of dynamics among humans. Little battles occurred wherever humans congregated, Diane knew, and she had observed new vistas of this since she entered the work force. Friction between colleagues was typical stuff. She repositioned herself to observe as subtly as possible the soap opera unfolding.

"Coffee," Constance said, rising. Diane wondered if she was slipping away, sensing a scene? Perhaps she was just tired of repetitious scenarios playing out? Diane tried to gauge Constance's response, all the while under the steady consideration of the immaculate Dr Steele. He chewed quietly, his eyes taking in every nuance, Diane was sure. He had become more attentive since Diane and Chandra's greeting. Diane flashed Steele a polite smile.

"Let me get it, Connie. Anyone else? Dr Steele?" Professor Harding rose and nearly sprinted to the serving area as a noisy group of chatting girls converged on the tea urn. Constance settled again and appeared bored, or perhaps just hungry.

"No, thank you," Dr Steele answered over his shoulder, then dabbed the corners of his mouth. "And, I have a meeting with William

Clarence about my High Table lecture. You'll all excuse me? Nice to meet you, Miss Quinnell. I expect to see you tomorrow for Rushdie. I assure you it will be completely safe and something you can brag about to your grandchildren. An historic moment!"

Diane merely smiled, nodded, then studied his square shoulders and powerful stride as he carried his tray out the door to the dish area. She was convinced he would steal a last glance at the group as he turned and exited. Instead, he came to a halt in the first doorway, in profile, studying something on the wall, deep in thought. Then he passed by the second doorway without turning, which left her feeling slightly deflated.

"What? Diane, you are not attending the significant moment?" Dr Chandra asked.

"Not much of one for circuses," she announced, glad to be recalled to the present moment. She grinned to herself at the irony of that statement, with all her juggler and magician friends these professors knew nothing about. "Say, I noticed you all call him Dr Steele, not Julian. He must be important, then?"

"Oh yes, at the Bodleian, there are shelves full of the books he's written," Constance explained. "Mostly, however, I think Dr Steele is old fashioned, likes the traditional manners."

"We humor him," Dr Chandra added with good nature. "And we send Dr Harding for the coffee." This non-sequitur caused them all to turn to see Dr Harding chatting animatedly with the group of girls around the tea urn.

"Lucky him. He has livelier students than I have this term. How are yours, Dyan?" Constance inquired.

"Oh, very well. Lively, yes, and petrified, by turns. A promising group."

"Excellent. Well," she said, craning her neck longingly toward the coffee that had not yet made its way back to her. "Well, I'll be off. Good afternoon to you both." She hovered a moment then glided effortlessly away, alighting at Dr Harding's elbow, lifting her cup from his hand, and graciously waving off all apologies.

Left at the table together, Chandra volunteered a note on Professor Harding. "Perhaps you noticed Nick chafing at my last comment? Let me explain why. Harding has a claim, a belief in his own distant relationship to Thomas Hardy himself. It is a harmless delusion, augmented by his time at an American college. A full year at Santa Barbara. That is near Hollywood, if you did not know, and I am afraid he returned with the romanticized notion of his own previous incarnation as a silent film star."

"Oh, you're joking, aren't you?" Diane asked. Chandra smiled mildly at her, but allowed her to continue. "Professor Harding has already made an impression on me regarding American movies. He encouraged me to give him any scene from any movie I knew for comparison with our readings. But movies definitely go hand-in-hand with stardom and celebrity." That was an understatement for the actor-types she knew back in Denver.

"Yes, Diane, in the silent film star allusion, I am joking, yet I do take a devilish delight in prodding him. But you see, it is an easy step from the Santa Barbara movie culture to a romanticized connection with historical figures, especially if one is already a Thomas Hardy scholar. Everyone residing in Oxford wants to uncover something new on Thomas Hardy and be the first to publish it."

"And if one's name is so close to sounding like the author's..." Diane chuckled. "Oh! It's hilarious, now that I think about it. Like Tess *Derbyfield* and her *d'Urberville* ancestors."

"Yes, exactly. And that type of connected-to-important-ancestors spiritualism is no stranger to Britain, therefore not the exclusive property of Hollywood. Charlatanism is as old as Vishnu. You know that even Thomas Hardy himself consulted a medium to contact his deceased first wife? Yes, spiritualism was as popular a pastime or parlor game as you may find at the turn of the last century."

"I have plenty of friends back in Denver interested in magic and psychics, but only from the side of showmanship. They're magicians and make a study of humans' capacity to be bamboozled."

"*Bamboozled!* See? You are definitely ready for a game of *Bon Mot*. And your compendium of friends must be fascinating! How interesting you are. But as for Professor Harding's love of movies, I think it may also be fueled by all of this newfound headline-news interest in Salman Rushdie as he reappears before us like magic. Rushdie will also reap the unexpected rewards of his seclusion-fame – his needing to hide these last few years. Such a pity that it seems destined for misleading Harding. But as Rushdie reappears in a flash of celebrity, next thing you know, film makers will be giving Rushdie cameo roles in the movies. I predict that," Chandra added, placing his palm briefly on his forehead with a good natured laugh.

"That's a tough one for me to picture," Diane confessed, thinking of the scholarly writer she'd come to believe must also be a natural recluse. How else could he have withstood such a period of time, remaining out of public view?

"It is my prediction! Everything is interconnected, Diane. And know too that I have a little secret of my own, concerning Thomas Hardy. That's why I have Professor Harding squirming. My thesis on Thomas Hardy's influence on RK Narayan is hush-hush." He leaned closer to whisper: "I will interview Narayan myself in October! Though I have had the privilege of speaking with him briefly on the phone several times over the last few years that I have been developing my study. More on that later. I know you will keep it under your hat, Diane." Chandra smiled at her and added, "Shall we?" then escorted her out of the Dining Hall.

* * *

Diane stepped out of The Lodge into the light drizzle, after a short chat with Mr Spencer over nothing in particular. She was pleased to see Jessica and Emily in the group waiting for Dr Harding, who arrived, glanced at his watch and led them out on their first evening together.

"Tonight we shall become acquainted with Thomas Hardy's

Oxford. As I am sure you know, Hardy set many of his most famous scenes here in Oxford. He knew the city well. Although he never attended college here, his struggles to find recognition for his prodigious talents first as Poet Laureate and later as a controversial novelist, endeared him to this community; he received a number of honorary degrees later in his life from both Cambridge and Oxford, as if to make up for the crushing way they ignored his genius earlier in his life. First stop: just here."

"Hey! Wait for us!" shouted two burly students, barreling toward them. Brandon and Tucker had arrived. Diane instinctively stepped to the far side of the group and stopped next to a personality more her size. "Hi. I'm Diane," she introduced herself to the young man who had listened to her Museum of Curiosities stories last night before dinner.

"Tommy Newton. Pleased to meet you," he nodded politely.

Dr Harding had stopped just a few steps from Trinity's palisade fence and now stood in the middle of Broad Street, an easier trick to perform in the evening than during the midday. Not a vehicle stirred. Even at seven o'clock the misting sky was full of light, here on the second day of July.

Dr Harding frowned at the new arrivals, then motioned to the White Cross painted on the pavement at his feet. "Does anyone know what this is?" he asked the group. When no one ventured a guess, he offered: "The ominous spot Jude Fawley had chosen to meet his cousin, Sue, on their first fateful date. Anything else?" He waited dramatically to unveil the real tidbit of the odious marker: "Three Protestant heretics were burned at the stake on this spot in 1556. Imagine it."

A few faces said, *so what?* but most registered the enormity of the statement. Harding liked the response. Very dramatic. Pretty fun for an old guy who likes movies, too, Diane thought.

"That was a long time ago, but every towns person in Hardy's day knew the history of this mark."

Diane shuddered picturing the event. Everything preserved in historic condition, as Archie said. She couldn't imagine the last time that heretics had been burned on the main street back in Denver, since they never had done that, to her knowledge. Colorado became a state in 1876. A long time ago, Diane reflected, but yesterday compared to this site.

"Nice place to meet for a first date, eh?" Dr Harding said to Tommy Newton, who nodded gravely, while Emily, whom he had been talking with, giggled. "Let us move on." Dr Harding motioned the group to follow toward Cornmarket.

At this moment, Dr Chandra left Trinity's front gate, his umbrella swinging jauntily from his wrist. Chandra, taking in the group then seeing Diane, seemed eager to speak with her. He came up behind for just a moment, pulling at the sleeve of her trench coat. "See the front doors of Balliol, there?" He spoke quietly near her ear. "You can still see where the heretics' pyre scorched the varnish." Diane looked up to the distant doors that perhaps bore slight char marks from the horrible spectacle. The scene took on a deeper reality. The imaginative Diane could have done nicely without that visual detail. *Ah well*, she rallied. *The impact of history, like it or not.*

Dr Harding glanced back, gave Dr Chandra a look that said: *move off!* and added rather loudly: "We shall be walking across town to a special churchyard, then return by way of the Lamb and Flag." Diane imagined that this information, besides summarizing where the group would land, was also an unmistakable suggestion for Chandra to go elsewhere. Sort of like Mr Eager, the English chaplain in Florence, in EM Forster's *A Room With a View*, pointedly excluding the radical thinker, Mr Emerson.

Diane had mixed feelings about this situation between Chandra and Harding. She hoped that she wasn't going to be part of a gossipy pact of confidence that would encumber her all term – though the information Dr Chandra had just given her was pretty irresistible. She smiled and waved as Chandra went his way, then looked again at the

White Cross on the street. Once more she thought of Elm Street and its funeral processions. Death: the humble reminder. Yes, Diane could respect that. She trotted after the group.

Dr Harding, although an older man, showed none of his age tonight, moving them at a clip through the town. From heretics' pyre to graveyard – where the rain began to fall steadily – Harding continued on about Thomas Hardy's relentless interest in expounding upon the morbid topics of life.

Everyone's mood lightened the moment the very wet group entered the Lamb and Flag, the smallest pub Diane had ever been in. Diane had to crouch to get to a table under the low, white-washed ceiling and heavy beamed rafters. Seeing this humbler pub that had existed for centuries, and left in its original simple form, made a deep impression. This place felt ancient to her American eyes. The tiny pub was fueled by a warm glow of firelight and the scent of malty brewer's yeast, exactly the place a laborer would love to come home to at the end of a long rainy day. She felt truly excited for the first time in the grand and colossal Oxford.

"I'd bet my life on that!" someone in another party shouted from behind them, loudly enough for their entire class group to be drawn into the raucous conversation. A group of young men, two that she was sure she recognized from the Trinity kitchen, sat around a table of empty mugs, quite literally rolling on their old wooden chairs, making the place seem as though it was suddenly tossed upon high seas.

"Here, at the Lamb and Flag, I'd bet *my wife* on that," Diane shouted back to the animated crew, watching an absurd look register on their faces, then be quickly replaced by gaping smiles when they saw the young, female challenger. The absurd look spread to her own group as they turned from the boisterous men toward Diane. Dr Harding arrived at that moment to take a place next to her.

"Yes, this is it," Dr Harding confirmed for the group.

"Yes! Where Jude Fawley sold his wife," Diane announced, fully aware that she was mixing two stories together.

"He did?" Tommy Newton asked, looking alternately puzzled and ashamed for how he'd gotten that wrong.

The sour look Dr Harding gave Diane was worth her humorous efforts. "No, Michael *Henchard*, the Mayor of Casterbridge, sold his wife here." Harding began to correct the misinformation, looking at Diane as though she should be the next heretic to be set upon the pyre, and Thomas Hardy, worthy of perpetual adoration.

"*The Mayor of Casterbridge*? Were we supposed to read that?" The young man with the short ponytail between Emily and Jessica looked suddenly pale.

"Yes, Jason." Professor Harding announced with forced composure, then became fully flummoxed as Diane winked at him. She then admitted to stirring up the dust on purpose. She nearly elbowed her professor in the ribs just to rub it in, but restrained herself, he looked so helpless. She chose, instead, the mischievous wink, whose message evidently went awry. Dr Harding blushed deep red.

There was little else to do to explain, so instead, Diane guffawed at her professor's mounting chagrin and lifted her mug to offer a hearty toast to the group: "Here's to Jude Fawley and his two wives! Neither of which did he sell in this pub! Cheers!" She hoped this small confession would appease the Doctor.

Wednesday, July 3

Diane set out carefree into sleepy Oxford, despite the threat of a downpour.

Her long trench coat flapping with her vigorous pace, she turned right toward Balliol and planned for a small circle to the corner, across Broad Street and back again to the Trinity front gate. A nice, quick leg stretch before breakfast.

Along Balliol's face, perhaps one hundred feet before the street corner, a dark gap on her right caused her to pull up short. Within the narrow canyon, an old headstone was wedged. Five feet further on, another, and likewise a third, just into the back of the dark nook. She immediately grasped its relevance, preserving a reverential space. Fascinating, the historical remnants that this town had grown around. Much less than three feet wide, Diane was in no way interested in climbing into the creepy, wet space to see a date or a name on the stones, as soon as she leaned that direction. At that moment, one rain drop arrived on her head, the next splashed on the inside of her glasses. *It's only water,* she reminded herself, though the next larger, colder drop, landed down the back of her neck. She popped up her umbrella as the drops multiplied. She moved on.

Look right, Look left, the crosswalk counseled at Magdalen Street corner. She followed the stenciled directions automatically now, nearly a native, and crossed Broad Street, then halted suddenly as she saw the gaping black hole in the front window before her. What was this? Broken glass littered her path. Dillon's Bookshop. Diane shuddered and glanced about. No cars moved, no crowd stirred there as witnesses. No movement inside the store or beginnings of repair had yet occurred. No alarm blaring. All was tranquil in Broad Street except for the broken window shouting at her. Of course! Rushdie! His name leapt out at her from the sign in the next window. Rushdie would autograph books there following his engagement, it announced.

She shied backward, walked quickly now, almost ran, skirting the sidewalk, a combined dread about stepping on the broken glass and getting too close to exactly one of the unnamed actions she had feared. This was the beginning of a horrible day, she was sure.

Deeply disturbed, she concentrated on her feet, until she saw the toe of her shoe come in contact with the White Cross painted mid-street. She skipped sideways to avoid touching the odious marker of the heretics' pyre. That sight alone darkened the morning.

Overwhelmed, she moved like a skittish horse back through Trinity's front gate and directly to the Dining Hall. She made a beeline to Daniel.

"See? I'm up early to get everything done before the lecture this afternoon," he explained. "Then to the Oxford Union straight from lunch."

"Daniel, you need to know this. Someone threw a brick through the window at the bookstore across the street. I mean, I don't know. It might have been a rock. I didn't stick around to look closer. It's just that – " She realized she was babbling and tried to start again, but Daniel cut her off.

"Yeh, I already heard about it from The Lodge," he said, concentrating on his cereal package.

"Oh, yes. Mr Spencer said it was no big deal," echoed Natalie, suddenly conjured from thin air to join them.

"How can you know that so soon?" Diane said. "I was just out there. On the street. No one around, glass everywhere, no police barricade – yet everyone knows?"

"It was a random car. Nothing too terrible. Small rock." Daniel gave details off-handedly as he continued to shred first one tiny cereal package, then another in an attempt to fill his giant bowl. "Why do they do this? Why do they give us this crazy American snack-pack cereal? Makes me think I'm stuck on a bad camping trip with my family." His exasperation over his breakfast seemed off balance, considering the news from across the street. Hadn't anyone heard what she was saying?

"Daniel. You can't possibly still be going to this Rushdie thing today, can you?"

"Oh, relax, Diane. Mr Spencer said it was no big deal. I wouldn't miss this for anything. Doesn't it make you even more interested to hear Rushdie? Really exciting. I can't believe you're passing up this once in a lifetime experience, Diane. I mean, what did you come all the way to England for if you're not going to take in all the opportunities?"

Natalie didn't say anything, but gave Diane some look. Maybe it said, 'You who would sit on the couch and write letters while... .'

"Sure. I'd fiddle while Rome burns," Diane spoke half to herself.

"Not a valid comparison, Diane." Daniel crushed another box in frustration.

"You're right. I'm not a maniacal emperor, nor did I set the fire. I don't even play the violin." She laughed incredulously. "But have you ever been in a riot? I have. It isn't fun."

"Good morning, everyone. Good morning, Diane." Dr Chandra arrived. "What have we here?" He nodded toward the litter of miniature boxes and crushed flakes that didn't make it into Daniel's bowl.

"Ohhh! I give up! These stupid boxes!" Daniel slopped milk onto what cereal had made it into his enormous bowl and shoved a big spoonful savagely into his mouth.

"Oh, here! Look," Diane grabbed an empty box, stabbed a butter knife into it and deftly sliced open the edges. "It's perforated to open into a bowl. You never have been camping, have you?"

"This looks like origami," Chandra said. "Is this a game you play in The States? Oh, I love learning different cultural traditions."

As the seismic vibrations increased from the Oxford Union, the lunch crowd at Trinity vanished. Nothing more was said of the broken window, as if it had never happened. Instead, everyone was lost in the excitement of the moment. Diane sat at her table and watched people fly past the two doorways to get a good seat for Rushdie. Above the doors, the mystery of the Minstrel Loft caught Diane's attention. On her way to the dish area, she investigated along the wall for a hidden door, then stepped into the foyer to do the same. Left all alone, it was a good day to ask someone. Diane went into the serving area. "Mrs Whappington, where are the stairs to that loft? May I go up there?"

"Oh, that's Lawrence's realm. You'll have to ask him." And good luck with that, the woman's expression added. Diane had seen Lawrence, the head of the dining staff, at the first night banquet. She glanced around the kitchen for him. Mrs Whappington filled in: "You'll have to find him this evening, Miss. He's gone into town for some special something or other. Now excuse me. I'll need to be shutting these doors to keep out late-comers. Enjoy your day."

Diane left the Hall and bumped into Courtney loitering under a sky blue umbrella in the next quad, the one Diane now called the Bowling Green.

"I am so bored," Courtney intoned with languishing posture meant to confirm it.

"Bored? Are you kidding?" Diane said. Less than a week they'd been there and they were about to have a nuclear bomb dropped on Union Hall that afternoon by some fatwa-crazed fanatics. Not exactly what Diane would call boring. "There are about a billion things to do or see. Go hear Rushdie! That ought to be a hoot."

"Who's Rushdie? Who cares?" Ennui threatened to absorb the redhead, but she rallied. "What are you going to do?" Courtney show-ed a small spark of interest that Diane never expected to see from her.

"Probably write some letters. Take a nap. Nice gray day for it."

"What could there possibly be to write about? We just got here and nothing has happened yet. Will it ever?" Courtney rose and wandered off toward the front lawn.

Bored? Unbelievable. *Go play with the ducklings*, Diane thought all of a sudden, picturing Courtney kicking at them if they came anywhere near her. That was laughable. But going out? Diane wanted nothing to do with that today. With my luck of bumping into the unexpected, I'd probably get run over by the getaway car or maybe by the emergency vehicles as they respond to the disaster call from Union Hall.

The campus felt deliciously quiet; Diane preferred it that way. Tranquil. Better for reading and there was plenty of that to be done.

* * *

"Hul-lo?" Diane called into the suite as she gently swung open the tall door from the hallway. No reply. She set her umbrella down. Diane was already getting used to having the place to herself. Wherever Natalie spent her days was classified top-secret. And her nights? Better not mentioned, Diane had concluded from the intense way Natalie smiled at her and replied in tangents to any inquiry. *She likes her privacy. I don't have a problem with that,* Diane had concluded after this week together, meeting vague resistence to common social exchanges.

A pleasant breeze stirred the over-long draperies in the front windows, beginning at the top of the twelve foot ceiling, then spilling out onto the wood flooring. Her treasured copy of Winterson lay on the desk, a major triumph that put Diane one book ahead of the rest. And now to read it. She settled into the corner of their petite couch with the book. Just starting page one, a dark flutter, thumping along the upper window caught her eye. A moth. *Better than a bat,* Diane reminded herself as she swallowed the ugly taste rising in the back of her throat at the sight of the visitor. Maybe it will find its way out, she hoped. Bugs were not among her favorite animal friends. Unfortunately, it continued to bump the pane and buzz pathetically, distracting her concentration. *I suppose I don't want it coming to see me tonight, either.* She involuntarily shuddered at the thought of feeling a flutter on her head or down her neck in the dark tonight. She set down her book on the cushion, grabbed several tissues and dragged a chair over to the window. *Fortitude, Diane. C'mon, just cup it with the tissue and escort it out the window.* Released as quickly as possible, the moth went about its day unperturbed. She watched it flutter across the Quad and attach itself to the building opposite. Diane now felt a little foolish. She glanced around the courtyard to see if anyone had witnessed her squeamish flinging of the moth. Except for those Roman matrons atop the clock tower, no one about. All facing windows quiet. Peace restored. Would have been just the moment for Archie to be working out there, she laughed to herself.

With no one about and the rain soaked view, she left her book where it was and instead brought a sketchbook back to the window. The tiles on the rooftop across from her ran in streams of water. She could see just the top of the weather cock on Balliol's bell tower. She traced the ornate grill work, its arrow pointing west. What a place. The rhythm of the rain, the black and white puffy clouds worked on her like a lovely drug, communicating dreams and breezes to accompany her nap.

She set down her sketchbook and padded to the back of the suite. Her cot groaned as she rolled onto it, adjusting the pillow under her neck. The old world smells of her College bedding were becoming familiar even after just a few days there. Slightly damp, somewhat tangy yet already a scent associated with this charming old place. And a trace of cigarette smoke. Very old world, the scent conjured the image of centuries of professors' pipes and reading by lamplight. She took a deeper breath, caught the scent again. The breeze ruffled the window drape. The hint of cigarettes reminded her of college. Late nights. Papers due. Emerson House back at Smith even called their late night study room The Smoker. Cigarette smoke and drifting off. The lovely breeze transported her thoughts to other late nights, after rehearsals and cast parties following performances. Actors all smoke. *'It's either that or have one's hands fluttering about one's ears while one is supposed to be standing nonchalantly in a scene.'* Who had said it? Oh, yes: Eduardo, back in Denver, who lived to smoke elegantly, stylishly. He was a one-man show, just by his graceful smoking. And he was right. To pretend to smoke on stage was clumsy. A non-smoker could never wield a cigarette convincingly. Her theater friends in Denver were a lively crowd. Talking until dawn. Like the time they all decided to.... .

Cigarettes. Her eyes popped open. Cigarettes being smoked, today, right now. A whiff floated up to her. Two nights ago, the same. It had become intolerable. *'Hello down there,'* she had called out the window that night. *'Could you please take your smoking elsewhere?'* She tried to sound nice about it. Matter of fact. She, the anonymous voice calling from the dense tree. She probably had given someone quite a start. She hoped that it wouldn't become a summer-long annoyance, but now dark thoughts stirred. Would smoke continue to disturb her naps as well as her nights? Just as she rose to say something, a more urgent problem arrived.

A squirrel scrabbled onto the window ledge, its claws scratching unpleasantly on the brick. It skittered to a halt on the inside sill when it spotted Diane, who let out a small shriek and froze. The two stared at each other for a moment, then the squirrel easily reversed paths when Diane bolted up menacingly toward it.

She sat back down and caught her breath. *Are they nuts here?!* She thought not for the first time. *No screens?* She hesitated to get too close to this new entryway, imagining all woodland creatures ready to spring at her. Finally, however, she peeped out and cautiously surveyed the scene. Reason returned. No. This must be unusual. They wouldn't endure animals overrunning the place. Maybe something had happened, something unexpected, that startled that squirrel into making the leap. Impossible to see what it might have been. The ancient tree boughs formed a verdant wall, an effective screen to any activities below or just over the wall that Diane was sure ran the perimeter of the College grounds just behind her building.

She flopped down on the bed again and closed her eyes, trying to convince herself that this had been a chance encounter. Certainly she shouldn't allow herself to become obsessed with the fear that critters were going to be plaguing her at every moment. Her heartbeat eventually slowed and she drifted off.

How long she dozed she couldn't say. She heard the pleasant

quacking of ducks from the front lawn again, then suddenly something happened. Alarming squawks. A dog barking. A flurry. A man shouting in the fray. Repeated whistles. The dog owner? Yet soon enough, all back to normal. Diane's heart raced for a few moments longer, worried about the upset for the ducklings – or worse. It made her feel queasy thinking: one eaten?

* * *

"Are you doing your homework again? I hope you've been out. Why aren't you ready for dinner?" Her roommate materialized in their suite again in late afternoon, evidently to change clothes as was her habit, perhaps to prod Diane into activity as well.

"Just writing a letter. Actually, I just got up from a nice nap. I'll write letters until dinner."

"Dinner? There's the lecture first and it starts in about ten minutes."

"The lecture?"

"Yes, before High Table dinner. What are you wearing?"

"Oh, that's right. Special dinners on Wednesdays," Diane mouthed.

"Yes. *Following* the lecture. Dress up," Natalie called back from her bedroom. Wherever it was Natalie disappeared off to, she seemed to have the agenda memorized, showed up when necessary and in the proper attire. Natalie's challenge hung in the air: '*Catch up or I'll go without you!*' Diane sat up and set her pen down.

Natalie stepped back into the common room wearing a floor length navy blue shift. "Eileen Fischer," she said over her shoulder, taking Diane's reaction in stride. "She's the only designer I wear now," she added, while running a brush through her chin-length hair and donning long silver earrings. "Better hurry up, Diane."

Diane stepped into her room and splashed some water on her face. She threw her traveling dress over her head, tied on a long scarf, stepped into her one pair of high heels and was ready.

"Did you go hear Rushdie?" Diane asked as they clipped down the staircase and burst out into the Quad.

"That's a long story. No, this way," Natalie grabbed Diane by the arm and steered her toward the Library where they found the line proceeding through the front door to the lecture room, young men adjusting their ties and jackets as if dressing up more than once a year was some deadly task.

Diane would have felt foolish to have missed the first half of the evening, and she would have, if Natalie hadn't arrived to fill in the details. Lecture first, then dinner. She was proving a useful information source. Diane pictured Natalie out and about, days and all night, cornering people and grilling them for all the insider tips for a summer in Oxford. Somehow Diane hadn't gotten the full understanding of these Wednesday night High Table dinners. She assumed they must be something like Thursday night candlelight dinners at Smith, when tablecloths were spread in each house's dining room and the meal was served in family style – platters for each table, instead of people passing through the buffet line. Professors and House Fellows were expected. Everybody dressed up, which as term ran on at Smith, meant: don't show up in your pyjamas, as you could for all the other meals. No one at Trinity had mentioned a lecture beforehand nor the posting for formal attire, such as the full-scale makeup, hair and jewelry regimen Natalie breezed through. They had scooted out the door just in time to join the group filing into the lecture room that adjoined the Library lobby.

"Hello, Tommy. You look nice. May I?" Diane slid in next to him without waiting. She leaned into the aisle and nipped at the tail of Daniel's suit coat as he hurried past. "How was it?" she asked, *sotto voce*, the room beginning its preparatory hush as the program director stepped to the podium.

"Amazing!" Daniel replied in classic American shorthand. Knowing him, she trusted that he would expound on that headline later. She watched him bounce into his front row chair chattering quietly with everyone nearby, all excitement and fervor with the thrill of having seen Rushdie. The director cleared his throat and introductions of the guest speaker began.

* * *

Once in the Dining Hall, transformed by candlelight and the elaborate place settings, Daniel waved to her from the High Table and flipped her a delighted smirk as he seated himself next to the guest lecturer, who occupied the place of honor beside the program director. What a day for him: up for breakfast, battling those little cereal boxes, hearing Rushdie speak and now conversing with the guest lecturer.

Diane surveyed the enchanted Hall, chose a place about mid-room, an empty spot beside Dr Harding. The meticulously arranged silver and glassware glimmered before her. She regarded the details with pleasure, feeling they all must have been elevated to the peerage for the night. Sitting regally, perhaps a bit taller than usual, Diane followed the dance of the servers, gliding in and serving each diner from the right, removing from the left, with a deftness that would befit the Bolshoi. In quick succession, her linen serviette had been draped across her lap, soup ladled into the awaiting plate and the feast began. Diane lost track of the courses, but noted Lawrence pausing at her shoulder nearly continually which made her feel supremely cared for. One glance at the content faces up and down the length of the table assured her that everyone was receiving magnificent service. The candlelight quelled conversation and the excellent fare before them stirred little need for talk.

"This is wonderful, Lawrence. Thank you. Your staff is excellent," she whispered to the head waiter as he performed the chopstick-like maneuver with two serving spoons, nestling a stack of thin French green beans next to her fish.

"Thank you for saying so, Miss," he replied. "I work everyone hard to keep things running smoothly."

She turned to her left, content to wait for a break in her dining partner's chat with the student to his left, before posing the question: "No spot for you at High Table, Dr Harding?"

"On Wednesdays we give over our important places to students. Let them sit in with the experts. It's all good experience for developing a rapport, talking with noted scholars."

Diane looked past Harding toward the High Table to see how the students were liking it, this hobnobbing with scholars. She chuckled out loud at the grim faces that stared at their plates, ashen and tortured. Not one was speaking. No one smiled. All sat silently chewing – except Daniel, of course. As a returning student, he felt comfortable with protocol along with being his natural gregarious self. Just then, between his laughs with the lecturer, he noticed Diane and hailed her with lifted glass.

"In fact, which High Table date have you signed up for, Diane?" Harding asked her.

"I didn't realize there's a sign-up sheet," she began, when her breath caught. Above the director's head, the portrait of Anne Boleyn, gone. Had they moved it? Her eye darted all over the far wall. She jerked about suddenly, her search racing around the room. Everyone else supped calmly while the blank spot on the wall preoccupied her. Was she the only one who noticed it? Her mind swam with concern over the priceless piece, and an uncomfortable memory returned of her last scrape with some missing artwork. That discovery had ended her marriage. That too had seemed eons away until this moment. Unexpectedly, her fork clattered onto her plate.

"Everything all right?" her professor asked between bites.

"That woman's portrait, above the High Table, it's gone!"

"Probably those *demned* silly students next door. Excuse my language. An old tradition, kidnaping that portrait and holding it for ransom." He placed a forkload of potatoes in his mouth. "Really excellent repast, isn't this?"

"Oh, I see," Diane felt her initial shock fading. "Oh, there is similar high-jinx at Smith. Each fall, Amherst boys kidnap something from Emerson House and hold it for ransom. A special clock. A plaque." Diane found it an odd mating ritual, but then, she'd never been one to play the damsel in distress as some of those Smith girls enjoyed doing, while negotiating for the return of the item. Besides that, Diane and her friends didn't like their house being broken into, period.

She shuddered slightly, then tried to push aside the creeping worries about the missing painting. She made a stab at recovering the general conversation. "Yes. Nice dinner. Say, by any chance, do you know who the woman in that painting was?"

"Oh, yes. That's Lady Jane Grey. Queen for nine days just as Trinity was opening."

"Lady Jane Grey? So that's who she is. Interesting. That would explain why she's included among the gentlemen scholars. The Monarch. And that explains the Tudor attire. You know, I thought she was Anne Boleyn, for the style of the dress and that telltale necklace she wore high on her throat."

"High on her throat. That's a good line for Anne Boleyn, Miss Quinnell." He glanced over his glasses at her and frowned. "Not to worry. Same pranks every year. You could set your watch by them. The portrait goes missing. A ceremonial candelabrum from the chapel will be next. Just you watch."

"I do hope they're careful with her."

"They usually don't harm her, but then again, a year or two ago, I believe the College removed her for cleaning. Restoration, I should say," Dr Harding recalled. "Or maybe she's out for photographing. The Martínez portrait was gone for weeks that way last year. Insurance photos." At that moment, dessert arrived and Lawrence appeared directly behind with espresso. "Lawrence, you noted the missing – ?" Harding jabbed his fork toward the High Table.

"Yes, sir. My staff noted the missing painting before dinner. Thank you for concerning yourself, sir," Lawrence replied as he poured Diane's after-dinner demitasse with one hand, placed a tiny bowl of nuts between them, then tipped the steaming spout over Dr Harding's miniature cup.

"Out for more cleaning, perhaps?" Harding continued.

"Excuse me, sir. I'm not at liberty to discuss the matter."

Let alone just now, Diane added silently, gathering that Harding seemed not to notice that Lawrence was a little busy. But Lawrence registered no irritation, only calm control and efficiency. Perhaps tonight was not the time to press him about the Minstrel Loft, either.

"How long has Lawrence been here?" Diane asked as the waiter moved swiftly on. "You've probably known him forever. He certainly knows his business."

Harding turned to her. "Oh, Lawrence preceded me and I've been in residence since 1978. You'd think after the years we've both been here, he'd call me by name, wouldn't you? I have asked him to call me Nick. One day last year, I insisted on it.'*As you say, sir,*' he replied, nodding agreeably. '*It's 1996, for God's sake, man,*' I told him." Harding shook his head, baffled.

Diane amused herself by thinking: *Funny that you never asked me to call you Nick.*

Thursday, July 4

Diane stepped through the Trinity front gate at six AM.

To avoid any residual bad vibes from the bookstore on Broad Street, she set off instead in the opposite direction. She tipped a few postcards into the red post box under the eyes of the Roman heads, then rounded the corner at the King's Arms, and traced the east perimeter wall of Trinity that fronted Parks Road.

At Trinity's wide garden gate, she paused and looked in. The flawless green lawn bordered by gardens on each side spread a good open distance leading to her quadrangle, her staircase, just past the lawn. She stepped back, enjoying the change of view with the morning sun setting it ablaze.

A few paces beyond the back gate, Trinity's high wall turned at the edge of the College property, and continued down a narrow walkway that wended somewhere just out of sight.

The quiet of the early morning made her feel as if she had hours and hours. No need to rush. She liked the solitude. It left her free to regard every little detail as she wandered along, pocket a few pretty stones without anyone watching. In fact, while exploring Sunday morning, before the wild taxi ride, she'd come upon the plaque for Dorothy Sayer's birthplace in an alleyway somewhere near the open market. The unexpected discovery thrilled her. She soon began looking for a place to buy a cup of coffee, but nothing opened until nine. The longer she searched and found nothing open, the more she wondered: did she really want coffee? Not really. She just wanted a place to linger, get a feel for early morning Oxford and perhaps have a friendly chat with whoever served her. *Strike that*, she realized now. *I really just want to tell someone about finding Dorothy Sayer's house. They've probably heard it a million times. No wonder tourists seem so pesky.*

Down Parks Road, Keble College again, just ahead. Today a nice morning to see the Natural History Museum in a different light, explore the rest of the park. She stepped across the street to the gate. *Park closes at dark*, the sign declared. Funny. Does it disappear then, once night has fallen? Diane wondered. Or did it become the place of faeries and spooks? More likely a restful spot for homeless people, she thought. How good of the authorities to give them a safe spot for the over-night. No disturbances. Didn't they all have a tough enough day already?

Once inside the park and once she'd viewed the Museum from every angle, Diane investigated the main circle walkway, then all along the Park borders. Some garden patches drew her interest which led her to the far side of the park, bounded by a quiet stream which she guessed was the Cherwell, of punting fame. An unexpected rustling halted her investigations into a patch of holly, just as a bevy of pheasants fluttered out of the underbrush like large missiles. At the farthest point downstream, she noted the well-concealed barbed wire above and just along the undercarriage of the little stone bridge that marked the edge of the park. No one was getting out of the park this way, not without a plunge directly into the murky waters. Diane pictured the very undignified emergence somewhere, perhaps downstream in Christ Church Meadows, soggy and chilled. Again, it made her think of closing times and being locked in. Would a person really need to get out again? Nice benches available here for the night, if it didn't rain.

On her second time around the circular pathway, she passed once again the man with his large dog. The look he gave her over the top of his newspaper both times made Diane feel conspicuous. She decided to return to Trinity.

Just at the alleyway along Trinity's back wall, she peered up and thought more about the history of the immense wall. Just along the rim at the top of the wall, the morning light caught the shards of jagged glass that had been set into the mortar there. It was difficult to see, at her five foot four inches, but it was there, just as the College Historian had said. Necessary, she guessed, and prettier than barbed wire, she thought. New York City was all wrapped up in razor wire while she'd visited there during school. The sight of that never made her feel safer.

She peered up again at the jagged glass.

"Most people don't do that. Peer up, that is." The unexpected voice had a beautiful lilt to it. A pair of goggles under thick, dusty brows peeped over the edge at her, then disappeared.

Diane smiled in half-embarrassment. Caught in the act, she figured she might as well step forward and confess. "Does my key work for this door?" she called over the wall to the worker.

"It should, but you'll have to test it to find out if it does," the voice replied.

She took her electronic key from the kilt pin she had secured at her waistband, and found its tiny receptacle in the stonework next to Trinity's back door. *Click*, said the locking pin. The wood door swung gently inward where she found Archie atop his ladder, a pail of grouting mixture in one hand, a tiny trowel in the other. She stepped through then secured the door.

"Back from the park, I see?" he said from his perch.

"Is everyone a mind-reader here?" She laughed, feeling a little under surveillance, but comfortably so. A nice change from that out-alone feeling of mornings in that town.

"No. It's that sprig of henbane attached to your skirt that is the giveaway. Just in back there. No other place in Oxford has a henbane bush except the park."

"Is it poisonous?" she asked as she did her impersonation of a cat chasing its tail to get a view of the telltale sprig.

"Only if you eat it. Besides reading minds, I've been watching your approach for ages, from the ladder, you know." He patted the rung in front of him to prove he was speaking of the very ladder on which he stood, which made her smile again. To think the first time she'd seen him, she'd mistaken him for some homeless person who had wandered onto the grounds. Not everyone was allowed to sleep under the trees at night. Archie was the exception. Now she was seeing daily how, as stonemason, he literally kept the College preserved.

"Very clever. How did you know it was me? Such a distance." Diane continued catching at the back of her skirt.

"My X-ray vision," he concluded without fanfare.

Diane thought she saw his beard grow slightly wider for a moment. "I don't know many who could keep a straight face while admitting that, Archie. Nice job."

"An appreciative audience is all a man can hope for. Mind your step."

She abruptly halted her elaborate pirouettes near the edge of a crate of broken wine bottles she hadn't noticed in her determination to get at the henbane. The sight of the sharp, erratic edges sent a shudder along with a picture of shredded intruders. Now focused, she saw her simple solution: shift the entire skirt around by the waistband. "What repairs today? *Ouch!*" Diane plucked off the tenacious sprig.

"Nasty stickers, aren't they? But that's what gives them *clin-n-ng.*" She wondered if he meant the plant or himself, by the way his eyes sparkled as he dragged out the word 'cling'.

"Just replacing a bit of the jagged glass up here. I cannot imagine how it's been broken off, but I noticed it this morning on my constitutional." Diane had seen him on his constitutional most mornings. After High Table dinner last night, she'd passed Archie in the quad talking with a handful of students. The words *Tantric* and *transcendental* stood out in his lilting accent and Diane wondered if she was overhearing him telling lovely stories that each morning he chanted while taking the mystic walk, the same way that Druids cleansed their auras long ago. With stories like that, by the end of term, Archie would have an entire cult following him on his morning rounds. Diane guessed that a tradition was playing out, perhaps as old as the origins of Trinity College, which was the second college to exist upon the site, built upon the ruins of the Twelfth Century Durham College. It seemed appropriate.

Stone masonry. How different from home. Surely restoration of the thick walls and ornamental stonework at the College must be an art long cherished here. Not a crack looked older or newer than it should. No patching grout stood out as a close-enough – but wrong – mixture as Diane had often seen in Denver. Every stone here was maintained in its current state, yet its decay was arrested, thanks to the stonemason. That same craftsmanship was absent from similar places in America, whenever mortar has broken loose or historic cobblestones have become disrupted. No Archie-equivalent arrived to mend and blend, preserve. In America, jack-hammers and front-loaders wiped the slate clean instead, ready to pour new concrete. America operated as though *New is better*. Here in Britain, Roman roads still held firm. Diane saw now that a shift of attitude like that in the US might result in deciding to build something worth preserving, for a change.

"The historian said there is a lot of sneaking about, over walls and such, between colleges. Personally, I can't picture it with all this broken glass on the walls."

"Sometimes the wall wins, I'll tell you that," he chuckled as he worked. "But most of that type of damage happens on the wall that fronts with Balliol, the opposite side from this back corner."

College rivalries reminded her of the missing painting. "Is this related to that portrait someone kidnaped?"

"I doubt it. The lads are quite smart and simply hand the painting between the bars in the front palisade, thinking no one is watching, mind you. This garden wall backs all along the alley walkway that leads to Balliol College back wall and then to Magdalen Street, or if you turn at the T, up to St John's. For some reason the St John's students don't go in for such pranks. Not with us, at least."

"So, do you think that is just damage left over from your regular-term students?"

"As for regular term, as you mention, this year, there was an insane – if you ask me – set of funfair rides brought into our gardens for the Commemoration Ball. You can still see the gouges in the lawn from where the party tents stood, if you look for them. But any damage to the wall from the funfair, I would have seen sooner. This is new." He tapped the stone at his chin level.

"Well then. What to do about it." Diane tried turning a phrase in the local syntax. Her ears were growing used to questions that sounded more like statements, by American standards.

"I'll take it up with The Lodge. They'll know what's gone on about here." He said no more, leaving Diane wondering how the Porter could keep an eye on this back corner, while located at the front of the campus, despite its conveniently small proportions. One of those old gents must walk regular rounds, she guessed.

"Say, should I take this comment to The Lodge – or to whom? I had a squirrel in my room yesterday."

"Was he at large or just visiting?"

"Well, he left the minute I saw him land on the windowsill, but what should I do if he comes back?"

"Oh, we train them not to enter, just say hello." He grinned into his pail of grout. "The squirrels here are proper college residents. He won't bother you again."

She was relieved to hear it, even if it was just a guess. Also relieved he didn't say, '*Keep the window closed.*' No. This fresh air loving person never would have suggested that.

As she leaned back to watch Archie's progress with pail and trowel, she saw a tiny camera, trained on the door she'd just come through. It lay hidden in some vines near the top of the wall. Diane had never seen such a small camera, like a super-spy gadget out of a James Bond film. More high-tech than anything she'd seen back home, though her browsing in places like shopping malls and jewelry stores where there would be surveillance cameras was generally limited to bank lobbies. In her usual haunts – thrift shops – she doubted they bothered with security cameras. She couldn't imagine people lining up to steal old junk. This tiny camera was useful and subtle; nor did its situation disturb the quaint, four hundred year old atmosphere.

* * *

Shocking, but the painting was still gone this morning. Diane stared up at the big blank space above High Table. No crime tape. No one in a tizzy over it. Just gone. It made no sense to Diane that the College just went about its business, trusting that the painting would be returned unharmed, as Dr Harding had said last night. Personally, Diane couldn't imagine letting something as old as that painting even exist outside a museum, where it would be properly protected by velvet ropes and guards. A familiar voice interrupted her lamenting the loss of Anne Boleyn.

"Good morning, Diane."

"Good morning, Dyan," she answered him.

"And what role are you playing today?" Dr Chandra bobbed his chin playfully toward her pleated tweed skirt as he took a seat across from her.

"Today I am disguised as a scholar at Oxford," she said saucily.

"Ah, I see. But you have missed an important detail."

"What is that?"

"You need elbow patches on your suit coat. The elbow is where we poor scholars most sorely test our garments." He reached over to check her sleeve. "Say, this is an unusual jacket. One of your own design, perhaps?"

"Actually, it was my dad's. He's six feet tall so I took a seam right up the back, cut out about eight inches of fabric, then shortened the sleeves. That's why it is so long and narrow. Sort of like a morning coat, isn't it?"

"Well, it explains why you were so quick to try to steal my jacket from me upon meeting. Do you make a habit of acquiring other people's clothing, Diane?"

"Actually, yes," she announced, pleased to evade his teasing. "My friend Mario and I used to trade clothes quite often. Costumes, really. We're about the same size and his wife made most of his, so I think I got the better end of the deal. Some really dashing stuff. I'm sorry I didn't bring any. As for you, I meant it as a compliment; that's all. That jacket was really gorgeous. And if you ever did get tired of it, you'll know what to do with it." She smiled her most sparkling smile.

"As for leather elbow patches," she continued, "that's fascinating! I had no idea that was the origin of them. I thought they were just some silly style. But wait a minute." Some associated detail flirted with her just then. "Ah! And it touches on my first theory, you will see. In Spanish there is a saying: 'elbow fix' or 'bar-fix?' Oh, let's see if I can remember it right. I've got it: *Barra fija, levantando pesas*," she pronounced as she demonstrated the hinging, toggle-action of her elbow on the table. "That stress is encountered most often *at the pub*, lifting mug to mouth. It translates something like: *fixed at the bar, lifting weights*. You claim those elbow patches as a hazard of holding open books all day and night. They probably say that up at Salamanca, too. Therefore, however, as I pointed out to you with *The Five Fellows*, I believe that: *A is for Academics – and A is for Alcohol*, as well."

"Excellent, Diane. What a formidable proof. I wish you were in my class." He winked.

"You wish I were in your *claws*?" she laughed. "Sorry. It's just so sweet the way that sounded." This was the second time he had used it. She was sure it must be his signature line.

After a cup of tea and a look around, Diane commented: "No other professors today?"

"Of course not! It is the morning after High Table dinner, Diane. You see, your *A is for Alcohol* theory proves itself once again."

"Ah, yes. I'll make a note of it. But yesterday was quite a day, wasn't it? I took a nap instead of hearing Rushdie, but everyone else had a full day. Funny though, I noticed that no one mentioned it, not even when I asked around last night. Tell me. You went. Was it a complete fizzle?"

"Far from it, Diane. I think, perhaps, however, that the anticipation burned the most sulphur, therefore the event has faded in memory more rapidly than expected. Certainly not for Rushdie, nor for

Her Majesty's government."

"What do you mean?"

"Oh, the ramifications of this *fatwa* spread into Britain's international diplomatic relations, as well. Did you not know that? What will happen next there, we hope will resolve itself." Chandra reflected for a moment, then added: "On your original point, I will not say that Rushdie's reappearance yesterday was just another lecture – we have them nonstop here, as you can imagine – but I will say that perhaps our busy schedules force us all to focus on the current moment and worry about what lies ahead, rather than reviewing what has just occurred," Chandra concluded.

* * *

Eleven o'clock found Diane back in Professor Bede's rooms.

"As for Rushdie, it wasn't as exciting as some imagined, but I was glad to be there considering the occasion. Perhaps that's why no one had much to say about it last night, as you said, Diane." Constance picked up her coffee cup once again, found it empty and set it down again on the side table next to her big chair.

"Did you see Dr Steele there? He seemed all lit up about the occasion."

"Oh, yes. He introduced Rushdie; didn't he tell us that? Oh, perhaps that was before we joined you at the table. Yesterday was it? No, the day before. He even made the front page of the evening paper." Constance scooped up a copy of the *Oxford Mail* from a pile at her feet and handed it to Diane.

Diane clearly remembered the moment, if Professor Bede did not. Steele had regarded her from his height and had said nothing about his role in Salman Rushdie's return to public life. Funny he hadn't mentioned it to Diane.

"All Oxford Stopped as Literary History Soared to New Heights" the headline blared above the photo of Rushdie beaming toward the audience, Dr Steele's outstretched right arm held suspended while surrendering the key spot at the podium. Steele's theatrical gesture and

radiant glow of authority nearly dwarfed Rushdie. She scanned the article. No mention of what concerned her most. "I'm so surprised. They don't have anything about the broken window at Dillon's," Diane said half to herself.

"Broken window? No, I don't recall that." Constance thought a moment. "And I stood on the sidewalk with the queue looking in for rather a long while, considering whether I really wanted to be late for High Table."

"I walked over the broken glass in the morning," Diane nodded solemnly and experienced again a lingering shudder, picturing the jagged black hole in the plate glass.

"Well, I suppose Dillon's must have replaced the window straight away, knowing they would host the signing directly following." Constance pursed her lips a moment. "Baffling, though, isn't it? What is news; what is not?"

Diane studied the photo again. Even the photographer had captured it, Steele's importance pressing down upon even the diminutive Rushdie. So Steele hadn't told her. Maybe he had planned for the surprise it would cause, and had calculated the thrill for her seeing him arrive totally unexpected at the podium. Maybe that was one more reason why Dr Steele had gone out of his way to command her to attend. Diane had a sharp memory of it. He had communicated that he wanted something from her, perhaps to see her moved by his influence. She had mixed feelings about the entire exchange. Diane glanced at the other sensational headlines before handing the paper back to Constance. "When you said there is a shelf full of Dr Steele's books at the Bodleian, I took that to mean he publishes a lot, but no one is reading them."

"You saw right through my comment? How bad of me. My attempts at subtlety will get me in trouble. You are most perceptive, Diane, and I must remember to reform my ways."

Diane smiled sweetly at the fascinating person before her. Constance had a beautiful capacity for understatement that Diane could see reeling off into a comedy routine, perhaps at some tea room. Her comment sounded like an invitation to share candid observations, so Diane let loose. "I found Dr Steele rather good looking, but that tan is too much."

"Yes, he returned from a year at Harvard, the toast of the town, as you Americans say. I believe he also enjoyed a benefactor with a vacation home in Miami. Returned with the tan and that spa-like glow."

Toast of the town. The phrase made Diane wonder; did Steele covet Salman Rushdie's success? That must be the case, Diane decided. Certainly an international literary star, Rushdie. Nice company to keep for Steele. Would make anyone feel important sharing the stage with him.

"Yes, overpowering. Very male. On that subject, Diane, may I ask: are you married?"

"Not at the moment," she said awkwardly, seeing that an obtuse line like that needed explanation. "I was married to an inventor-genius sort of man. We got divorced three years ago." She refrained from adding more details.

"Ah. Inventor-genius, the universal code word for unemployed. Am I right?" Constance laughed lightly with a knowing look that surprised Diane. "Well. You are better off. You deserve an adult who can live up to responsibilities." Constance paused again. "Don't we all?" She allowed the comment to drift off.

Diane thought more deeply about what had been said, then asked: "Are you married?"

"Bravo, and thank you for asking me, the former nun, a normal question." Constance smiled quietly at her pupil. "I am not married, but there is someone lovely for me, yes. A wonderful person. Up at York University. We visit back and forth. Perhaps that's what makes us so compatible. Ideal arrangement, really."

"There was another thing I wanted to ask you, Constance. People are so unconcerned about that woman's painting having been taken."

"You mean the Rosa Martínez? Is it gone already? Well, off to London. Oh, of course you don't know."

Diane stumbled a bit, reorienting, but let Constance continue.

"Yes, off to London for a showing. We are fortunate to have a Rosa Martínez painting. The College was mildly thrilled to secure her for the portrait, then quite recently, her international success has risen. Despite all the historical works here, the Martínez is now our most valuable asset."

"I studied art at Smith. I'm sorry to say, I don't recognize her name," Diane admitted.

"You don't know her work? That surprises me, Diane. I thought everyone in The States was in love with her. Well, the College was fortunate and insightful to invest in Ms Martínez early in her career. Her show in New York a few years ago on exiled French and Russian royalty turned the tide for her. Yes. As a result of that exhibition, a good number of international stars, beginning with whichever Beatle that was – I forget which one was the first – commissioned her to paint his portrait for one million Pounds Sterling. Now she has a string of commissions and the price continues to rise per canvas. In fact, Dr Steele was in New York at the time of that show and astonished us all with the news upon his return. If you ever see him here again, you may catch him stealing a second look at the canvas anytime he is in Hall. He cannot take his eyes off of it."

Diane blinked. "So that's what it was. I saw him pause the other day in the entryway after lunch and I wondered. Of course. *The Five Fellows* painting is right there between those doors."

"Yes, well. Dr Steele, of course, specializes in the Restoration of the Monarchy. I am sure he finds the rise of pop idols right in his line, especially since meeting Bob Dylan that time. How this entire Island still adores Bob, I must say."

Diane's mind flashed back to the DA Pennebaker documentary on Dylan's 1965 tour. The Esquire Theatre in Denver had screened it while Diane was working there. That's right, she said to herself. Dylan captivated England while the Beatles held hands with The States.

"While I am pleased with her accomplishment – the first woman to have a retrospective showing at the Royal Academy of Art – yet even there, the Martínez show is only three weeks long. Most last eight weeks. So even in honoring her, they slight her."

"Why do you suppose that is?" Diane asked and then offered her own answer. "Sounds like a fill-in, between exhibitions, doesn't it? I worked at an art museum for a short while. They often do that, squeeze in someone's work just to fill gallery space."

"Another classic example from a male dominated society, I should say." Constance shook her head sadly. "I do give great credit to Trinity for recognizing the inequity and stepping forward to remedy it here. It is a beginning."

"That's very interesting. I was originally, however, referring to the portrait of the woman above the High Table."

"Ah. So sorry. I didn't quite understand you, Diane, but I took a stab. Sometimes your accent just doesn't come through. Oh, and forgive me for taking you off on that long story! You are very patient with me. Now, what about the High Table portrait?"

"It's gone as of yesterday afternoon. Dr Harding brushed it aside at dinner last night, and I noticed life went on as usual this morning at breakfast. I suppose in the wake of Rushdie yesterday, no one really noticed."

"Oh, that. Yes, well. Gone again, is she? I must have missed that last night. I am afraid that is just one of those seasonal upsets we've all grown accustomed to. 'All in good fun,' that's the College's official word on those kidnapings." Constance stopped for a moment longer, brow furrowed. "You know, you never see female students acting that way, do you?"

* * *

As she arrived for lunch, two workers were wrapping the Martínez painting. Diane stopped to chat with the high-spirited men. They finished that task, then set the bundle on the floor, propped against the wall under its empty hook, happy to follow Diane through the lunch line. Diane asked lots of questions about what they did for the Royal

Academy of Arts, wanting to compare stories of working at an art museum.

As she passed Dr Chandra, however, he called her over. "Ah, Diane. Please join me. There is something I must discuss with you. Gentlemen, excuse us." He dismissed the workers, who took up their own corner table. Diane sat down and lifted her eyebrows, ready for whatever Chandra had to say.

"I have called you here today to say that the shippers are up from London and seemed to me overly friendly, judging by a crude conversation I overheard before you arrived. That is my entire message." He smiled at her kindly as she took in his comment.

"Oh, I didn't realize," she said, suddenly self-conscious. "Was I being too forward, do you think, to join them? I don't want to be rude."

"No, no. Few would find attentions from you as being rude," he chuckled. "No. This was just my wanting to alert you to some vile plans you may not have suspected. Very fatherly, yes?"

"Not at all. I mean, yes, I guess." She looked at him, puzzled. "I mean, I don't think of you as my father, just another human."

"Just another human. What an accolade," he laughed. "No, no. I am understanding you perfectly, I believe."

She stuck around the Hall with Dr Chandra, as the workmen slid the painting into its specially-made shipping crate. They watched as the men carried the crate away through the Durham Quad to a truck parked on the gravel driveway just beyond the clock tower.

"My old friends, off to London. How they still get around," Chandra quipped. "And me? Off to work. Enjoy your afternoon, won't you, Diane."

* * *

Diane didn't quite know what to do with herself after lunch. She'd had enough socializing, enough reading. Didn't really want to explore anywhere. She didn't quite feel like a walk even though the weather was perfection. Funny how the heat wave in London had vanished the moment she boarded the *Oxford Tube* for Trinity.

She climbed the curving steps in Staircase Sixteen pausing at the front window. She scanned the rooftops around her, then lifted her eyes to the spires and towers that made Oxford the most unusual place she'd ever seen. Having grown up in a flat house on the edge of the flat plain that eventually gave way to the Rocky Mountains off in the western distance, Diane could not resist a view. She bolted up every staircase just to have a look. She often surprised her friends by choosing to stroll along the top of any retaining wall rather than remaining on the sidewalk. A new perspective. Mixing up the mundane. Diane excelled at that. Therefore to be living on the second floor was ultimate bliss. And this third floor window here at the top of her staircase, where Sir Christopher Wren used fifteen feet – not ten – for each level, was astoundingly high up.

Modern Denver was nonexistent when Sir Christopher Wren build his buildings. The thickness of the sturdy Seventeenth Century walls featured wide window ledges, a magnificent place to sit and look out. Diane's New England dorm had been old enough to feature window seats. Denver: not one. She fetched her sketchbook and perched it against the perfect elbow height of the third floor windowsill. Enough details to draw all summer and probably not capture them all. The ever-shifting light of these long summer days continually transformed the display. This breezy afternoon, clouds arrived then cleared off completely, twice just since she began sketching.

She placed the Trinity clock tower above the chapel in the center of her page, a curvy Roman matron on each corner, two figures facing north, one of which pointed east. Perhaps all four moved in unison, performing a dance? They formed a nice contrast to the zigzag brick work on the pointed Balliol tower just to their right.

Her solemn concentration made time disappear, until sounds below pulled her attention off her sketch pad. A crew wearing white aprons rolled out several cooking grills to set up a barbeque, it looked like. After another quiet interval, Diane watched Natalie cross the

Garden Quad and enter Staircase Sixteen. She was surprised when Natalie climbed the extra flight directly to Diane's perch.

"Coming down to the barbeque?" Natalie asked after gently pulling Diane's sketch pad toward her.

"So that's what it is."

"Yes, it is meant as a special treat for Americans, since it is Fourth of July and all," she added coolly yet leaned against Diane, scanning the view.

Diane imagined that Natalie the New Yorker probably didn't have the same fond memories of holiday barbeques that Diane did. Grilling in the backyard. Inviting the entire neighborhood. Diane smirked a bit picturing Natalie's cosmopolitan response to one of the classic summer activities in the humble Denver suburbs.

"That's nice of them. Dinner for everyone outside. Should be fun. I'll be down in awhile. The light is just right, you know?"

Natalie soon emerged below, in different attire, as other students began filling the courtyard. The smells of grilling meat soon had Diane stowing her drawing pad and joining them.

The Georgetown students were there as well, but clustered in groups of their own. Diane caught Jan's eye occasionally and they enjoyed smiling at each other, but they kept passing each other, absorbed with their own groups, where – judging by the body language among the graduate students – friendships were rapidly developing. The biggest surprise of all: the nebbish Mark from Queens being chatted up by a pair of intelligent-looking girls.

Diane noticed her professors subtly edging their flock into the garden, while the Georgetown group was prodded through to the front quad, perhaps to catch a motorcoach to some other activity? Who could guess? Diane was pleased to see that, for whatever reason, dons and students were allowed on this back lawn, yet never on the grass by The Lodge. The whole crowd sauntered along and took up places in clusters, like content sheep grazing.

Constance Bede chose a seat from the grouping of chairs nearest

Diane's building, probably as a remedy for the wind that had sprung up. Fortunately, the dark clouds that had swirled above began to clear off by the time the ice cream sundaes were wheeled into the Quad. Daniel ran to fetch several desserts for them all. A welcome bit of chivalry after all that food.

"Yes, Sir Christopher Wren designed your buildings, can you believe it?" Diane overheard Charlotte Ashcroft the College Historian making shop talk with a few students. "Yes, we have a ready supply of historical names here."

Constance called Diane and Daniel's attention to the historian's remark, then added: "Yes. Historical names in abundance. Through no devices of my own, this bronze bust just here on the pedestal happens to be a distant relation of mine. Yes. Venerable Bede himself. How I have been raised to live up to his stature, I cannot begin to tell you." She squinted comfortably into the sunlight.

"A mighty honor, indeed. And will our humble heads be mounted on these walls for centuries after we are gone? Now there is a question for you," Dr Chandra said, joining them.

As far as leaving heads behind, Diane added her own take on the topic: "What a gruesome thought, actually, with the British custom of placing heads on pikes."

"Oh no. That is a custom that originated in Persia, brought here by the Christian Crusaders in the Twelfth Century. Trust me. Though the British have made good use of it for their own, yes," Chandra said.

Diane pictured once again her proposed postcard kittens posing at Madame Tussaud's Chamber of Horrors, but followed Constance's comment instead, wanting to learn more about her.

"So, I wondered that last summer. Did Venerable Bede go to school here, or was he a don at some point?" Daniel asked.

"Oh my, no. Wrong era completely," Constance corrected him. "When was Bede? Oh, we learned it as school children, along with 1066 and 1215. Don't ever tell my mother I've forgotten it."

"Six-seventy-two to 735, I believe," Chandra filled in. Daniel's and

Constance's eyes grew large.

"Wow! I want you on my *Trivial Pursuit* team!" Diane chirped.

"Raised by Anglophiles," Chandra added in clarification.

"The rest I do know," Constance continued. "Venerable Bede's remains are buried at Durham Cathedral, thus the connection with Durham College, which this once was. The documents are sketchy on that point, you know, so no one knows exactly how the bronze came to be here. All I know is that when I came to Trinity to meet the President when I was first being considered for a position, I was stunned to recognize the bust. Do you see the family resemblance around the jaw line?" She turned her head for easier comparison.

"Hmm," Diane studied the two. "Perhaps, a bit."

"I don't see it, either," Constance laughed. "Don't you just love old family lore?"

Through the mild evening, the group chatted, then strolled to another circle of chairs at the far end of the garden. They sat among a small gathering of students and a few professors on the lawn for hours upon hours – even until the hedgehogs came out. The orange tones of sunset lingered in the sky even as someone announced: "Last call for drinks, I'm afraid."

"Half-ten already?" A bearded don Diane hadn't met echoed the announcement. His cowboy boots had caught her eye earlier that afternoon around the barbeque grills. She had not seen them before – and that type of detail she was sure to notice. Perhaps he'd dusted them off them in honor of the American holiday? That pleased Diane for its affable nod to the former Colonies. The boots fit the tall broad fellow. Add a ten gallon hat and he'd make a fine Texan.

Diane held her glass up to the light over the back gate and gazed through the last bit of ruby fluid. Port, the after-dinner beverage of Oxford, Diane had been told. Beautiful to behold, but would she ever prefer its sticky sweetness to a nice pint of Guinness? No, she corrected herself: a *half-pint* of Guinness. *Ladies drank half-pints here*, she remembered Archie's advice. Very ladylike, even if there might be twice as many mugs in front of her as the men. Her laugh must have caught Dr Chandra's attention.

"Nearly empty, Diane? Is that a hint? – Well, it is a good one. Let me get the last round. No, no. It won't take a moment." The elderly gentleman sat across from her, smiled kindly at her raised glass.

Among the general conversation, someone asked Diane: "And where are you from?"

From? Her face clouded for a moment. *I'm from here, aren't I?* She thought, feeling sure that was true. "Denver," she managed to say, while memories of Denver painted a large blank before her. A dream, foggy upon waking. England is here and now. Her world. Seated on a garden bench under the first hint of stars above this college, the northern evening twilight lingered despite the late hour. All the clouds had blown off. Funny to be seated, so tranquilly, so settled-in already. She'd traveled a vast distance to get here. All the way across the thousands of miles from her job tutoring high school students.

"What is it about this place?" Diane asked, looking at the people gathered on the lawn furniture, scattered on the lawn itself, then gazing at the old stone walls lined with lush flowers. "I feel as if I've been transported and amnesia has set in." How long had she actually been here? A week at most. A lifetime?

"It is being surrounded by all this history, Diane." Professor Chandra rose from his chair as he gestured, following her gaze. "Perhaps also it means you are very adaptable. But what surrounds us here is so vivid in our creative and scholarly minds, it works some magic." He stood behind her now, his survey of who-needed-what complete, nodded again at her empty glass, winked and trotted down the gravel path. Diane watched him step into the Garden Quadrangle, pictured the vaulted stone corridor that led back to the College's bar, no: pub. *Get it right, Diane. Pub.*

"That type of magic-induced delirium is often evoked by lingering symptoms of jet lag combined with the rampant romanticism evidenced in American culture by the entertainment industry." Diane turned and found the bored girl, Courtney, who had slipped in un-noticed, interrupting the lovely atmosphere. The redhead now leaned down casually between two students, placed her elbows on the back of the bench she stood behind. She glanced right, then left, ready to challenge any response to her theory. The group stared back in silence.

A quick smile played over Diane's lips as she considered the girl's articulate statement. Diane wondered if Courtney's parents were academics who had raised their daughter to speak in thesis sentences or say nothing at all. She could name several other friends who had been similarly trained. Diane regarded the slim redhead, posed and basking in the impression she'd made. *She certainly knows how to make an entrance,* Diane smiled again, picturing the girl in some stage play about aristocrat's children, set just after the Great War.

When no one took her bait, the redhead stood up and folded her arms across her chest. The pose spelled impatience, American style. Diane's college friend in international business advised Diane to unlearn this particular gesture if she was going to be traveling abroad.

Having now gathered all the attention, Courtney continued: "Books, books and movies. Everything books and movies. Where are our own thrilling, real life adventures?" When no one responded, she shrugged, dragged herself off toward the Laundry Cottage, then disap-peared from view. They all turned and watched as if under hypnosis, until Emily let out an embarrassed giggle which restored the general conversation.

Bored? At Oxford? Diane wondered again at the absurdity of it.

"What an extraordinary view," Professor Harding commented, as he continued to stare behind him in the direction of the girl's depar-ture. Diane saw that no one else had noticed the remark.

"Yes. Very dramatic," Diane quipped, startling the professor, who blinked at Diane, cleared his throat a bit, then returned his attention to the group.

"Did I overhear that you are from Denver?" Professor Dennis Sartorius, the man in the boots, leaned toward her in address. "I once visited Montana for a Neoclassics conference and I admit that I fell in love with the Rocky Mountains." Diane noted that his cowboy boots wiggled as he spoke. "Do you ride horses?"

"Denver. Yes. I'm a tutor there, however, rarely get on horseback anymore." She affected a western drawl. Anticipating his next question, the way his eyebrows had shot up when she said *tutor*; she continued. "Here *tutor* means an assistant professor; back in Denver, well, I try to think of myself as Sherlock Holmes, deducing the mysterious glitches that hold a particular student back... but I am actually more like a Homework Helper." She hoped her schooling this summer would change all that for her return to Denver. Even after this first week among her Oxford dons, however, she began to dread returning to her repetitious routine. All this charged-up brain work would undoubtedly change her, but the ninth graders tended to finish the year unscathed, and a new group – identical to the last – replaced them in the fall.

"You know. I think you'll appreciate this." She eyed his cowboy boots again. "Here's what my students are like. They had an essay set for *Hamlet*, prompt question: *'Describe the man in black.'* I had several students bring in papers on Johnny Cash. I'm not kidding."

The cowboy studied her for a moment, nodding affably until Chandra stepped between them.

"You see? Back in a jiffy." Dr Chandra distributed glasses and brought Diane her drink last, in order to seat himself nearer, she sensed, this time at her feet. Even through the soporific effects of the Port, she felt wary. Diane didn't miss Chandra's clever move, though she protested that his gallantry was misplaced. Girls weren't that fragile, but maybe old men were. She could imagine feeling responsible for his rheumatism coming on, sitting on the ground all evening, though he showed no signs of it. She decided to join him on the lawn to prove her point, the new position gracefully accommodated by her long full skirt.

Her final drink, however, made her feel this was, perhaps, just the right amount of attention. Her admirer was nice to have around, and perhaps his last drink would quiet him down, she hoped. She heard a voice from her past: *'You stand out in a crowd, if you didn't know it, Diane.'* Reggie the old guard at the Art Museum must have been right, judging by Dr Chandra's behavior. Diane looked at Chandra to see what he would come up with next if he meant to monopolize her.*"No one is quite like you,"* his smile said. She could live with that.

"I can't help but point out, you have the most irreverent way of mixing metaphors, Diane... for humorous intent, no doubt. You have a real facility for it. It is the mark of either confidence or foolishness to make such a mockery of your studies." Chandra's black eyes twinkled.

Everyone turned at this point toward the pair. Diane blushed as if she'd been caught doing something wrong, though she wasn't quite sure what it was. Everyone stared. What were they thinking: teacher's pet? Judging by the onlookers' gaping mouths, she was sure they had misunderstood the joking nature of his statement. Most likely, making a mockery of one's studies never had gotten any of them such kudos. Chandra chose to continue.

"The other day you said you don't read anything written after World War One, but you may find Rushdie is right up your humorous alley. He is a delight to read."

"A delight? Then why does he have a price on his head?" Diane asked.

"You see? That's just it. The humor is lost on certain people. Making a delightful mockery of human nature is Rushdie's forte."

"Sort of like the wicked calligrapher monks in *The Name of the Rose* reading all the evil funny books? Laughter cast as Satan's snare?" Diane fell into analytical mode, but retained an ounce of mockery that Chandra didn't miss.

"Oh, Diane. How sorry I am that you are not in my classroom!"

Thank goodness I'm not in his classroom, she thought to herself suddenly and shifted her legs in the other direction under her. This would feel like the unspoken and forbidden pressure for *how to get an A*. Yet he was so attuned to her every word. How could a person not like that? She grimaced slightly thinking how many young women had been duped into thinking they were important to an attentive professor, rather than understanding that they were just a casual and convenient dalliance. But that couldn't be right. She felt muddled. She looked at Chandra's beaming face and hoped he would soon get over his infatuation with her. *Funny how I'm hoping for such a nice man to start ignoring me,* she thought immediately as the last thought occurred to her. *Just enjoy the attention, Diane,* she lectured herself, but shifted her position again, more sluggishly this time, and dwelled on darker thoughts of her own.

"Time to call it a night, for me." She rose.

"Off to write letters, undoubtedly?" Chandra inquired as alert as ever and rising easily to his feet as well.

"Sure," she smiled, deciding not to correct him as they stood eye to eye. She turned and said: "Good-night everyone."

Grateful that Chandra hadn't made everything more awkward by insisting upon the custom of walking a lady to her door, she walked down the path toward her Staircase, noting that it was still quasi-twilight overhead, here above the fifty-first parallel. She paused at the top of her staircase and gazed out at the rooftops from where she had been drawing in the afternoon. A bell rang one o'clock. A distant chime echoed it. The Trinity clock tower above the chapel remained silent, the arm of one Roman matron pointing east, waiting patiently.

Week TWO

Monday, July 8

THE BEAD-COVERED DOORWAY of Raja's Curry Palace gave way to the scent of exotic spices. Diane's mouth watered. Indian food was possibly her current favorite, with certain Japanese dishes, like sukiyaki, running a close second. As she had learned during her choir tour, '*to eat like the Dutch*' meant Chinese food in Amsterdam, she saw little to quibble with in discovering the popularity of Indian cuisine in England. She loved the way incongruence offered surprises.

The Curry Palace host smiled graciously and swept the group to a round table marked with a gold-lettered *reserved* placard. Auspicious animals hailed them from the wall fabric. The colorful decor, ornately embroidered in classical patterns, showed off India's esteemed place as the world's wondrous textile designer.

"Isn't this beautiful?" many of the girls said, quietly studying the elaborate brass plates, goblets and tableware, all arranged on sumptuous silk tablecloths, while one or two scanned the room with a particular scowl they could not mask. Curry was pungent that way. A few jockeyed subtly to get a chair as far from the professor as possible. Seeing this, Professor Bede arranged her seven students. "Won't you sit next to me, Kate?" Bede touched the fair-haired girl on the shoulder. "And your roommate Sarah next to you." The pale two nearly clung together. "Laura, right here," Bede patted the chair to her right for the girl with the amazing cascade of dark hair. "And Jessica, I would like you across, just there, next to Sarah. Then Emily, Diane,

Madeleine just there. Excellent." Gorgeous waiters arrived to fill their water goblets with the magical tinkling of chipped ice.

"Can anyone recommend something they like for the group?" Professor Constance Bede began. Diane beamed and nodded thank you to the young man at her elbow, while the rest of the group obediently opened their menus. The elegantly bejeweled elephants on the draperies raised their trunks in happy salutes that the serious students missed out on. Diane soaked in the delightful atmosphere.

Silence greeted Bede's request, so Diane leapt in. "Perhaps something benign to begin? Dahl and garlic nan – that's the flat bread. And maybe some potato appetizers: Alu Samosa?"

"Oh good, Diane. Thank you for reminding me. Yes, Indian food can be quiet daunting for beginners. Why don't you also bring a large order of the yoghurt with cucumber and the Tamarind sauce. Nice cool things to begin. Yes." She instructed the waiter and folded her menu closed.

"Oh, will this be hot food? I don't like spicy," Sarah said. Her New England pallor might benefit from this visit, Diane imagined. Or she will break out in a rash, she added silently.

Emily looked glum. "I have no idea what any of this is. My dad usually orders for me."

"Well, it's more flavorful than hot, if we order the right things," Diane said. Looking around at the silent young women, she plunged into a story. "We'll have tame stuff. I'll never forget my introduction to Indian food. My friends ordered everything super hot because they were used to it. One bite, my mouth was on fire. I couldn't taste anything for days. I wasn't sure if they were doing it just to be mean – that's how excruciating it was. Don't worry. We won't do that to you!" Some girls smiled, but for Jessica, the story had the reverse effect Diane had intended. Evidently not everyone was sure if they could trust her, she guessed.

When the plates arrived, the group hung back. "Don't be afraid," Diane laughed. "Do this: take a piece of bread and some dahl, or some cucumber yoghurt sauce. Look: just break off a piece and scoop up some sauce. Lovely." Diane demonstrated, placing the steaming bread on her tongue with a broad smile. Warm bread studded with roasted garlic alone could have filled every meal, if it were up to Diane. Her genuine pleasure in the taste must have communicated, as the others followed her lead.

Shy and uncomfortable, the group tittered nervously, like some pack of school girls fearing the worst of initiations, each face set on edge, preparing to encounter the nastiest tastes. Diane therefore found herself overcompensating with an act right out of a comedy pantomime: tearing, dipping and eating with exaggerated delight at every morsel, just trying to ease their reluctance. Only a few of the girls tried more than one bite of anything, though Emily emerged triumphantly, stating: "It's not that bad. Sort of like cheesy pizza bread, without the cheese."

The bowls filled with steaming Jasmine rice, mild chicken curries and vegetable concoctions arrived. Half the girls sniffed at them with appreciation. The others politely reassured everyone that they were fine or enjoying it, when their faces revealed the truer story. The moment made Diane see how much living she'd done. She laughed to herself remembering how Mario and Vonda had devoured their hot curry so enthusiastically that night all those years ago. Had she been such a good actress to have covered her chagrin so well? At least Jessica looked pleased with the dishes, which in turn, pleased Diane. Maybe she'd warm up to Diane a bit. As for the rest, tonight felt just short of a fiasco, several barely touching their plates. The group began to talk a bit more freely as the ordeal drew to a close with soothing Tapioca and Mango puddings.

"And how are you finding your readings?" Professor Bede inquired, evidently hoping to draw on the moment when everyone's guard was relaxing.

Instead, everyone froze. Diane and Constance exchanged a quick look. Diane suppressed a laugh and ended by shaking her head slightly. Absurdity with humans, once again.

"Well!" Diane announced, perhaps a bit too enthusiastically as all eyes darted her direction. The situation triggered an automatic reflex: comedy. "Were we supposed to *read* those books?" Diane burst into laughter as she watched the others catch on. Constance's earnest effort crumbled momentarily, then reasserted itself after a wry glance in Diane's direction.

"I am finding the Jeannette Winterson story very, very odd," Jessica volunteered.

"Is that the *Oranges* title? I couldn't even find a copy of that one," Madeleine joined in.

"Yes. Exactly. The process of locating these books and the challenges therein are meant to improve your understanding of the placement of feminist literature in our society," Constance said as the evening turned into a fledgling book discussion.

Tuesday, July 9

Tuesday night Dr Harding met his class at The Lodge. This second outing struck Diane as hilarious in that they stopped at five pubs – not for drinks, just for a peek inside and a note to connect the setting to a scene in one of Hardy's stories. Diane noted the disgruntled looks from some pub keepers and waitresses as the group hovered for several minutes, intensely in the way, then left without filling the coffers. The encounters gave her a better understanding of how the tourist trade must wear out its welcome.

"Yes, I know, I know how it looks, but please do not write home to your parents that I take you on a pub crawl every Tuesday night," Professor Harding instructed them. "Oh, but look here: The Royal Truffle. Now this is not an official Thomas Hardy site, however, it was chosen as a film location for Winterbottom's soon to be released version of *Jude*."

Several students giggled anytime Harding said Winterbottom, which he said often. A patron who had watched the ungainly group enter The Royal Truffle and had already looked Jessica up and down, made significant eye contact with Diane and said: "Winterbottom. We call him *Frosty Arse* here. Bloody film crews, bollixing up traffic for weeks. Never know where you'll encounter the next blockage. You may as well park it. Buy you a pint, Love?"

"Perhaps another time," Diane smiled, as Jessica decisively turned her back on him. "Official business tonight: mucking up commerce for the waitress," Diane laughed, feeling awkward but enjoying the chance comments.

"No rain tonight. That's a plus," said Emily.

Shawn eyed up the beer selections. "And no beers, either. Great," he added as Dr Harding shifted them all out the door again.

"Before I forget," Harding stopped them just outside the window of The Royal Truffle where they all watched the patrons stare back at them. Which group were the monkeys in the zoo, Diane wondered momentarily, and felt free to wink at the man she had chatted with. "Remember that on Thursday evening we will all meet the motorcoach outside the Trinity front gate at four o'clock sharp that will take us into London where we will then be seeing the Royal Shakespeare Company production of *Julius Caesar*. The Barbican Theatre is a more formal venue than The Swan we visited last Saturday in Stratford, so please remember to dress appropriately and be prompt. All right. This was our last stop, so we now return to Trinity."

Brandon and Tucker gave out a loud hoot at that announcement, grabbed Shawn by the arm and headed for the pub door, nearly knocking down Emily.

Dr Harding turned quickly and called, "Everyone?" He gathered the group into a huddle as Jessica glowered at the two brutes. "It is my job to bring you back to Trinity. Then it is your prerogative to enjoy your evening. So follow me, please."

Diane caught up to Harding's brisk pace. "So, the town is filled with perils after dark, is it?" She glanced back to see if the burly ones were catching any of this. They grumbled not so politely at the back of the group. She was sure Dr Harding could tell her a lot of stories about this town.

* * *

The rest of the week began to fall into a routine of classes, outings and reading. Another interesting High Table lecture was followed by a lovely dinner. Diane traded her first clothing stack with OxFam. A visit to Blenheim Castle and tour of the Bodleian Library rounded out the week.

On her way to get mail following lunch one day, Diane passed under the Trinity clock tower and along the front walkway, stopping to let the ducklings dance just out of reach on the grass. Like an exotic animal in a zoo, Diane stood behind the palisade fencing along Broad Street and watched as the tourists snapped pictures of the students in their natural habitat. Going about her business, she mockingly held her stack of books a little higher in order to play the role of the prim, serious scholar as cameras pointed her way. Imagine the storylines told over family dinners as the photos were passed around the table. Here on her side of the tall fence she felt thoroughly contented.

Week THREE

Friday, July 12

"SO, DID YOU ENJOY the play last night? What did you see?" Constance pointed Diane to the chaise longue.

"*Julius Caesar*. One of my favorites."

"Ah yes. Did it strike you as being as controversial as the paper said it would be, seeing a black in the role of Brutus?" Constance didn't conceal her contempt for the lame marketing angle focusing on race.

"Not really. I'm used to seeing mixed casts. Don't they do that here much? I saw Randall Duk Kim, who is Korean-American, play *Hamlet* one time. That was something new, but that was more than fifteen years ago now that I think about it. The joke last night was the costumer's choice to go with squeaky leather sandals. Totally distracting. Every move: squeak, squeak, squeak."

"Interesting observation." Constance waited for more.

"But Julian Glover as Cassius Caius was wonderful. Without him, the production would have been a real snoozer." Diane could have talked for an hour about the entire experience. From piling onto the coach waiting at their gate, eating a way too large but delicious bag dinner on the way to London, then arriving at the Barbican for the evening theater event. Unfortunately, Diane found the Barbican a confusingly huge and completely ugly place. The theater space staging *Julius Caesar* itself was also broad, bare, and minimal enough that the footwear truly became its own show. Maybe to compensate, all the players had been told to remain stiffly in place, or was that just the classic Royal Shakespearean way, to gesture broadly with one arm only, pivoting at the waist and letting the words tell the tale? Taken together: disappointing. She decided to skip commentary on the concrete bunker of a building, because she really had enjoyed the evening. "It was very exciting to see any play in London. That's a first for me. And The Royal Shakespeare Company is the legendary word, even back in Denver. And how was your evening?"

"Productive, though perhaps not as productive as it might have been. I tried to work in the garden on my laptop and well, my focus fizzled, but one must enjoy the weather when one has it. Next time, I will tie myself to a chair up here in my suite. Maybe even draw the draperies so I am not tempted to wander away again." She cleared her throat slightly. "Speaking of wandering, how are you getting along with Nick Harding? Enjoying his class visits into town?"

"Yes. How Thomas Hardy sprinkled Oxford locations into his books is very interesting. On Tuesday, we stopped at five pubs. He wanted to make sure we saw every filming location used for that new *Jude the Obscure* movie that is coming out."

"Yes, Dr Harding relishes the arrival of every film crew. It was late last winter when Winterbottom's company arrived. We all could understand the need for bleak sets if you wish to film *Jude the Obscure*, but poor Nick nearly caught pneumonia following them about in the cold rain."

"Yes, his discussions often find some way to connect with movies. I'm surprised he doesn't switch departments. Film studies must be the new angle on literature, from the way Professor Harding talks."

"Oh, there's more to it than that, I'm afraid." Constance looked over her glasses at Diane for a moment, glanced left, then leaned forward to study her. Suddenly she sat back in her chair. "Oh, shame on me for gossiping, but..." she leaned forward again, "Nick has developed the belief he is related to Thomas Hardy himself. Based first on his family name: Harding, Hardy – you see what I mean, but then, since he returned a few years ago from his guest semester at Santa

Barbara, he has become convinced of it and driven to prove it."

"You know, Constance, lots of people think they're related to famous people, either historical one or movie stars. I know probably a dozen women who are convinced that they are related to – or are the reincarnation of – Cleopatra. I'm not kidding! I met most of them in theater, probably getting carried away with their own importance on stage, but also, even the gal that counts the coupons at the grocery store told me she's a direct descendant of Guinevere. You know, King Arthur's Guinevere? A lot of people think the word 'legend' is synonymous with factual history. It's usually tied to whatever hit movie just came out. It's a common delusion in America. I think it is a romantic notion that gives people living routine lives some dream to grasp onto. Hollywood thrives on building the illusion, too."

"It isn't easy for anyone to work and live among the august history of this institution without feeling inadequate, especially if you're not in the academic headlines daily," Constance conceded. "But with Nick, I feel partially responsible. I blame myself for being me. *Mea maxima culpa.* You see, I am through no fault of my own, a descendant of Venerable Bede himself." Constance's brow darkened for a moment, then she added, "Did I already mention that?"

"Yes, in the garden the other night. But Venerable Bede: *The Father of English History,*" Diane quoted the phrase she memorized for her British Literature class back in tenth grade. "The only Englishman mentioned in Dante's *Paradiso.* I'd call that noteworthy."

"Forgive me for repeating myself, Diane. So many students over so many years, you know. Yes, well, I think every time Nick sees me in the garden, near the bust of Venerable, it drives him a little further into the pursuit of some documentable connection of his own. Poor man. Like being chased by a gadfly of some sort."

"How about that?" Diane said, feeling mildly amused at first, but then shrugged. "That's right. Dr Chandra mentioned something about that to me."

"Did he?" Constance removed her glasses and studied her, as if hesitating to ask her. "I noticed, Diane, since you bring him up, that Dyan chooses to sit with you. I've never seen him do that before. He isn't being a nuisance, is he? No? I didn't imagine he was. Very curious behavior though, if you were wondering."

Diane hadn't given it much thought, now that she saw that he didn't overstep himself as she had initially feared he might. The thing that struck her just then was that teachers didn't often talk about their colleagues; she'd noticed that reserve while working at the school in Denver. The unusual nature of Constance's comment made her think for a moment longer, then she ventured, playing off a perception she'd felt. "Are you jealous? Did he use to sit with you? I don't mean to rob you of his company. I am, after all, no competition. I'm just the exotic foreigner; that's all."

"Touché, Diane. You used that reference from the Toril Moi article I gave you to advantage. Bravo. And no, I am not at all jealous." She smiled reassuringly. "So, it is Friday. What are your plans?" Constance asked pleasantly.

"Oh, I've discovered tea at four and McVitie's Digestive Biscuits, if that's what you mean," Diane laughed.

"Not joining the pilgrimage to Paris?"

"What do you mean?"

"Oh, several of the girls mentioned that they are going to Paris for Bastille Day on Sunday."

"That's news to me." Diane grinned with a secret inner vision of how Bastille Day would be completely different here, so near Paris. A dazzling thought, but out of her league for this visit.

"Well, this is one of the few weekends with nothing officially scheduled, so definitely use the time to look about." Constance set her book aside and rose.

"Thank you. I will put my mind to it, though my greatest plan is to remain right here in the middle of Oxford until I know every crack in the sidewalk, as we say at home."

* * *

Later that evening, Diane shifted in her seat and looked around. The room was filled. An intimate setting for the lecture by Swami Apu Arjuna. At dinner, Jessica was discussing the event with Emily. "Do you want to come with us, Diane? You have such a taste for things Indian," Jessica had said, which made Diane wonder if the superior Jessica did have a budding respect for her. She was pleased to go out to something unusual with a small group. The ponytailed young man from their Hardy class – Jason – was joining them. The four set off after dinner, Jessica in the lead.

They sauntered past the magnificent rotundity of the Radcliffe Camera, down some twisting stonewalled passages to another college across the way, somewhere behind Magdalen College. "I have no idea where we are," Diane admitted, despite thinking that by now she had learned every step around Trinity. She enjoyed following Jessica, as if they were stumbling through a fun house at a carnival, never guessing what lies around the next corner. An arched bridge linking two buildings that they passed under just before they found the lecture hall made her think she'd emerged in Venice, so like the Bridge of Sighs was the overpass. A magical kind of transmigration in the twilight.

Once seated in the lecture hall, banked in a semicircle of chairs, the well-dressed Swami became the undisputed focal point of the room. Diane settled in her chair, glad to see that the Swami wasn't sporting the long white beard, wrapped in the white windings of costuming that Diane would have expected if this lecture took place anywhere within reach of Hollywood.

Who was this man, this Swami Apu Arjuna? No program notes were given out. Diane would therefore have to make her own calculations. Tidy, silver hair. Perfect grooming. You could tell a lot from people's clothing. She'd learned more details about that divining skill from an interview with Prince Charles's valet in some tabloid her mother subscribed to back in Denver. *'Especially telling, a gentleman's shoes,'* the valet had said. Diane peered at the Swami's immaculate Oxfords. His suit and erect posture contradicted the age evidenced by the deep creases of his face, a face, Diane was sure, in the habit of smiling, as he was now. A nice man. Patient. Not an act. The careworn crinkles at the outside corners of his twinkling eyes told her so.

His long jacket reminded Diane of images from an old calendar page she'd seen at her friend Suzy's in Oceanside, just a short train ride above San Diego. Suzy plastered the guest bathroom walls with eclectic trivia collected from her world travels. Something to study while brushing teeth or fixing hair. Always interesting, like reclaiming idle time. The particular item Diane remembered, *The People of India*, looked like it had been torn from some vintage calendar, the frayed spiral edge still intact, colors faded. Diane studied it anytime she visited Suzy's, which was often now. Being gainfully employed – let alone a faculty member – still felt new and wonderful to her. Her school had actually paid for her to study at Oxford, an unimaginable prospect for her a few years earlier.

Her attention wandered back to the man before her, as he dipped a small bow to the last-minute arrivals who were ushered toward the front row, the universal punishment for arriving late. No unobtrusive slipping into the back of the room for you late-comers, no! Instead: planted directly before the Swami.

She studied his coat again. It was familiar. Was it Parsi? Or what was the other? Gujarati? By the simple examples of perhaps twenty couples in different traditional dress on that calendar, she'd learned a few details that proved that not all Indian men dressed like Gandhi or Nehru. No. Twenty-five distinctive states and additional territories made up India. Then she realized something: it didn't matter if she could identify the right one or not. She'd never even been to India. Plus, she reminded herself, everyone on the planet had her permission to dress as they liked. She certainly chose from the full compendium. The Swami could hail from anywhere.

"Without a receipt, one cannot expect cash back." The Swami Arjuna had spoken.

Diane blinked at the unexpected opening line wondering if she had heard him right. The rest of the audience remained silent, perhaps reverent? The comic intent of his statement seemed obvious to her. He surveyed all the corners of the room, beaming. *Work the crowd.* A standard approach for her stand-up comedian friends back in Denver.

"A wise person would conclude that no news is good news," Arjuna added. Diane couldn't agree more, if he was indeed talking about life philosophies. Keeping one eye locked onto the news at all times, ear turned to the radio, could become a full-time job. One listened and absorbed, but did one observe and think, instead? No. Not exactly.

"When facing the tiger, even the wise person often forgets to reach for his cell phone."

She tried to stifle a laugh. Was this cryptic advice or just plain hilarity? The Swami's entire face glowed with good will, humor, she thought. For a moment, he caught her eye and nodded. She continued smiling, though narrowed her eyes in question, then wondered about the silence in the room. Were the others actually listening or just experiencing the ambient vibrations? Digesting their dinners? She'd seen many an art history student, belly full, snoozing through the after-lunch slide show sessions, in a crowded, darkened room. The effect was tranquilizing. This room was certainly warm enough. Rain fell in a gentle rhythm outside the tall, open windows. The dampness settled a blanket over the incense that pervaded the room.

"Yes. Caller ID makes clairvoyance much simpler," Swami Arjuna was saying next.

Diane laughed aloud while the crowd rendered a reverent pronouncement: "Ahhh..." Jessica stirred and shot an ominous sidelong glance at Diane. Who could not laugh at that? Diane smiled in return. It was a whimsical cross-blend of sooth-saying and high-tech gadgets. *Those expensive gadgets seem to be taking over.* Diane's first look at London this trip, as she passed through customs with a simple wave of the passport – how unlike the scrutiny of security inspections of her high school arrival when the IRA had been so active – was the preponderance of well dressed people walking down the street, nearly half of them talking on small telephones. It was weird. No other word for it. She felt like Alice fallen down the rabbit hole and emerged in some space-age modern place that couldn't possibly be the London she knew. Yet there was the Tower Bridge, Trafalgar Square. All the postcards in the racks she passed on the street said, *Greetings from London*. In Denver, maybe doctors had pagers, but never had she seen a tiny handheld mobile telephone there. The Swami put this new and baffling type of culture shock into beautiful perspective.

"Surely I am a comedian, yet few are laughing." Arjuna spoke directly to Diane, she was certain. Her friends leaned forward abruptly and eyed her, this time with curiosity. Diane laughed at the comment – *a comedian, right*. She felt the frisson of connection, but side-stepped it, alert for what statement would come next. Much of comedy was lost in laughing too soon, thus muffling the follow-up lines, especially anytime she went to see *Three Bobs & A Mario*, her nutty juggler friends. She followed closely the careers of many of her friends, but especially the juggling troupe. Their fast-paced, eclectic repartee was earning *Three Bobs & A Mario* international success.

"A wise person knows that objects in mirror may be closer than they appear." Diane burst a seam laughing. The Swami smiled her way again and raised both eyebrows, with deference, she believed. He then rose from his chair and made a graceful gesture to indicate farewell and left the platform through a side door. The crowd continued to applaud warmly and hovered in their seats, exuding good will and harmony as if they had just stepped out of the most refreshing spa.

Diane stretched a long, catlike stretch, exhaled and turned to find her friends staring at her with disbelief. "Diane! I'll never take you anywhere again!" Jessica said, thrusting her arm into the sleeve of her raincoat. "I am so embarrassed. Laughing? You obviously didn't get him at all."

Diane was taken aback, but rallied playfully. "Well, Jessica, you can pretend that you don't know me on the way out if you like, but certainly you saw he was making jokes all evening? I've rarely heard a funnier comedian."

"Funny? People flock to this man for guidance," Jessica insisted, the only perturbed soul in this sea of tranquility. "C'mon. Let's go." She tried to wedge past Diane into the crowd.

"Yes, yes. It is a troubled world we live in," Diane began with mock condolences for the difficulties of our time.

"I can't believe it." Jason followed Jessica, but turned glowing eyes on Diane as the crowd clogged the aisle. "How did you know all that stuff? Some of those things you said at dinner about life and philosophy? You must have heard Swami Arjuna speak before this?"

"No, I haven't, Jason. Never heard of him. I was just talking in general terms. What did I say that wasn't just common sense?" Diane thought back to her dinner comments. Very general. *Life needs balance. Extreme actions can cause damage and disrupt the balance.* Wasn't it as plain as not hurting yourself? Practical advice. Horse sense. She shrugged a bit and wondered what it was in people that made them cling to the words of others instead of getting a grip on themselves.

"Wow," he said, continuing to glow. Emily just smiled at her as she pressed along behind the other two.

Now two adored her and one stalked off in an exasperated huff. Ah, life with humans, Diane sighed to herself. She turned in her chair to see the three barely inching along yet.

"Wasn't it marvelous, Diane?" a familiar musical voice sounded in her ear. She swivelled the other direction to see who had leaned so near her, as the crowd stood about in the aisles.

"Dr Chandra. I didn't see you there."

"I arrived just after he began. What do you think of him? Swami Arjuna was always a favorite entertainment of my parents. May I show you back to the College or are you all going out? May I join you?" he asked with boyish hesitancy, eyeing the small group.

"Certainly," Diane answered for the group. She turned to seek agreement, but found instead a telltale squirming look on their faces.

Now they must put on their polite best, with a professor joining them. *All fun lost*, their eyes said. Diane smirked a little, feeling half-amused by their plight.

Here it was again. The invisible wall students put up to divide themselves from anyone older. Was it about fear – of what? Or repulsion? Was it about the invisible chasm to be crossed, perhaps from childhood to adulthood, that they so vehemently resisted? Freedom versus authority? Diane didn't understand this automatic negative response to age differences, though she had seen it often enough to speculate upon it. She never felt that distance. Back in high school, so many students, even her best friends, seemed bent on hiding every little thing from parents and teachers as though they were the enemy – and to what end? The bad grade is still the bad grade, even if you got to the mailbox first and hid the letter from your parents. At Smith, she found that lively, carefree girls she knew at the dorm would either clam up or affect a ridiculous, stilted manner once they sat down at the conference table in class. Acting like an adult, but a very bad performance. So stiff. Unnatural. So odd, how people acted. Diane had felt at home with people all her life. Why was that? Perhaps it was the result of being treated like an adult for as long as she could remember. What came first, she often wondered. Was it her parents' theory that if Diane was treated like an adult, she would therefore act like one? Or was it that from birth, she acted with a level sort of self-composure and therefore deserved to be treated as an equal? She highly doubted the latter, recalling numerous times when she rocked the family boat by doing overly energetic things – like cartwheels in the livingroom – that resulted in lots of trouble. No. She wasn't a perfect adult from birth; that was a fact. Yet perhaps it was her parents' way of treating her. By comparison to what she saw when visiting her girlfriends' homes, Dee and Diane's father rarely made a move without Diane weighing her own choices for herself. As far back as she could remember, her parents turned to her saying, '*So what do you make of this? What will you do about that?*' Training her to think, assess and decide. Then make the most of the results, or try another approach. After all, adulthood meant making your own decisions, then taking responsibility for the outcome.

Perhaps that kind of freedom wasn't in everyone's upbringing. Some of Diane's working friends were highly vocal about it, even as they all turned thirty. *"I can't believe your mother actually lives in Denver and leaves you alone,"* one harped repeatedly. *"My mother is still all over me all of the time, even though she moved to Phoenix when I finished high school."* Diane considered herself lucky. Yes, lucky to have those unusual parents who lived to bowl and fought over who would get to work the crossword puzzle in the newspaper each morning. Still buoyant from the Swami Arjuna's spell, she smiled thinking of her harmless parents.

"This will be fun," she prodded Jason gently out the door, speaking encouraging words in his ear. And surely, who couldn't feel lighthearted after the delightful commentary of the Swami Arjuna? She smiled as the three students jostled for position once outside: Emily, Jessica and the boy they were both following.

"Swami Arjuna has a charming way of mixing metaphors," she said over her shoulder to Dr Chandra who placed a gentle pressure on Diane's elbow to link with his, as he joined the exodus. "Hilarious, yet accurate commentary on modern life," Diane bubbled, enjoying being escorted so courteously, though a little surprised by the offer. Her Hindu girl friends had said that men and women don't tend to touch each other in public, not even if they are husband and wife. She took Chandra's arm, relying on this being a very European thing to do.

"Yes, you certainly understood him, Diane. And look: it has stopped raining." Dr Chandra folded his coat over his other arm.

The group of three, generally tranquilized and congenial, wended back toward Trinity's front gate. Chandra and Diane followed a step behind, passing behind the Bodleian and rounding the Sheldonian. The Roman heads eyed the two groups.

Chandra spoke to Diane, who hung at his side: "As for the Swami Arjuna, I hadn't heard him since my youth, when my parents would steal all his good lines, then come home and tell them to us. I am pleased to see he hasn't lost his knack for summing up the absurdities of life among humans. The Swami was very popular with my parents' crowd. A delight. More an amusement than anything. Good clean entertainment – even more amusing when one notices that the crowd of followers he has here are missing several points." He chuckled quietly, lost in thought. "I read an interview with him in the paper many years ago saying that his favorite audiences are college students: *'They are so seriously seeking depth, they miss the easy laughs, which in turn amuses me,'* he said. Yes, I saw that you understood that, as did he."

Did Dr Chandra just say *'the absurdity of life with humans'*? Diane thought to herself, quite surprised. The coincidence was bizarre yet disarmed any resistance she had been planning for Chandra over the summer. "That's exactly what I always say," she blurted to Chandra without thinking. She turned to find him all attention. "I'm working on an essay with that title: *The Absurdity of Life with Humans."*

"Aren't we all, Diane?" he laughed. "Aren't we all."

They had stopped within sight of Trinity's front gate. "Shall we look toward The Turl?" Chandra addressed the group, who acquiesced listlessly, self-absorbed. With a cheery wink at Diane, he led the way down Turl Street. The other three dragged along, shuffling hesitant feet in some form of timid courting dance, Diane thought. They all turned into the little opening.

"Then is Arjuna, as he said himself, a comedian?" Diane picked up the interrupted conversation as she glanced at the sign over the pub door: The Turl. Something about it sounded familiar, more than being named for the short alleyway it occupied. She had passed the tavern, generally on her way to the market, in search of cinnamon items at the bakery there. This was the first time she'd taken the extra steps into the courtyard. Three empty tables occupied the alcove-like outdoor area. A menu board sat propped at the door, the broad window wide open. The interior rang with voices and activity that spilled out to them.

"Oh, yes. Exactly. A comedian. Amusing, isn't it, that he tells everyone so, yet they do not hear it?"

"Very," Diane said, still pondering why this tiny pub, The Turl, meant something to her.

"*Very, very*, as the British say," Dr Chandra seconded her. "Let this be our own little joke, shall we?" he added, glancing at the puzzled faces of the other three as the entire party halted in front of the menu board. The publican stepped out just then, inquiring. Chandra nodded. "Ah, perfect. The rain forced the others inside yet now that it has stopped, leaves us the prime spot in the courtyard. Let us take this corner," he said, shepherding them to it. "We will have an excellent view of passers by. One time as an undergraduate, I caught a glimpse of my hero, RK Narayan, as he exited from Lincoln College, next door. Very exciting." Diane smiled politely, not recognizing the name but pleased that the sighting pleased Chandra. Emily and Jessica flung poorly masked bored looks toward Chandra, but appeared ready to pounce on Jason.

"Why do I know this pub?" Diane said, half to herself, as she took a chair. "I feel as if I'd been here before."

"Thomas Hardy." Dr Chandra answered her. "The famous scene in *The Return of the Native* where –"

"– where the reddle man stops here at night and the locals drop the mutton joint or whatever it was on the ground –" she added.

"And then brush it off and exchange philosophies on the prospects of a little sand in one's dinner." He looked deeply into her eyes as they finished the plot line nearly in unison.

"Yes," she said, still half in reverie, not fully aware of Chandra's ardent gaze.

The other three stared blankly across the table. Suddenly Jason started: "*The Return of the...* what was it? That's not on our assigned list for Hardy class, is it?"

"I don't remember it," Emily chimed in then, in a sudden panic. "They didn't list that one – *did they*?"

"It's not on the list. How do you know it, Diane?" Jessica demanded across the table.

"I read a lot of Hardy one summer, to see what I missed from the advanced placement class I didn't take in highschool. They only read *The Mayor of Casterbridge,* but I liked Hardy so much after the one title, I read everything I could get my hands on."

"You *read* during the summer?" Jason asked, agog.

"I never touch a book that isn't assigned," Jessica agreed. *Why waste my time?* her superior look said.

"How can you have read so much?" Emily had the same question at dinner. "Monday night with Professor Bede, it sounded like you've read everything in print."

"Quit watching television; it opens up a lot of free time," Diane said off-handedly, then immediately sensed two things. The three deadpan faces that looked across the table at her could not even conceive of a normal existence without television – this summer away, a notable exception. Simultaneously, she realized that it had indeed resulted in a huge difference for her reading habits. That hadn't been part of her original decision to turn off the television forever, when she was seventeen. She simply and decisively had understood all at one moment that she couldn't sit still, staring, for one more minute. *Live!* Her being had urged her. She had leapt off the couch, snapped the off-button and never looked back.

"'It opens up a lot of free time,'" Dr Chandra mimicked her. "A good one there, Diane." A look passed between them. Diane wasn't certain, but she wondered if he thought that she had used her television joke to lead the conversation off Thomas Hardy, help divert attention from his secret passion for Professor Harding's curriculum? Their secret.

The group was busy looking alternately concerned, offended and guilty for not having covered all the ancillary materials available for their classes. Emily put on her *I'm so worthless* face, to which Diane added quickly: "Em: I'm thirty-one years old. You're twenty-one. I've had twice as many reading years as you have. Think about it. I started reading real books the year you were born."

"You're thirty-one?!" The three shouted. Diane started laughing, as Jessica's superior look added tacitly: 'held back in school, no doubt?'

"No wonder you're so smart. Man, I thought you were our age, but somehow – now that I think about it – not our age," Jason said.

"No wonder you're so confident," Emily murmured, while Jessica studied her rings intently.

"Oh, how I admire a woman who does not fear numbers. None of that silly pretending, which they tell girls is so attractive," Dr Chandra added for the group.

Puzzlement registered anew, once their ruffled feathers settled. Dr Chandra looked across the table at the three confounded faces and laughed warmly as the publican planted their pints and a brimming pitcher for refills. "Here's to the very well-read Diane." He raised his glass.

"Thank you, Dyan," she felt moved to say. "I yam what I yam!" she added in comic book fashion. In response, she felt a warm hand alight on her knee, bestow a gentle squeeze then withdraw. She turned to Chandra just as Jason reached across the table. The beer pitcher tilted sideways and its contents poured across the table and onto her lap. Everyone leapt up at the same time, as Diane slapped her paper napkins into the wake of the flood. So many surprises at once. As the beer seeped through, she added, "So much for the waterproofing on this coat." Everyone was on their feet, embarrassed, startled and laughing all at once. "And I was told that they served the beer warm in England. Not true!" Diane added.

"It is a modern world, Diane," Chandra said, proving this old historian was living fully in 1996. Running on all cylinders and perhaps turbocharged, Diane thought, considering Chandra's energetic per-sonality. Once again, appearances and assumptions all amount to little when trying to understand people fully.

The immediate uproar settled down, but arguments over who should pay for the dry cleaning occupied them, with nothing being settled. "Accidents happen," Diane protested. "It's only beer." The publican appearing for last call at that moment only prolonged the confusion. To refill or not? They debated while Diane and Dr Chandra mopped up the worst of the spill on the table, then crouched down to wipe off their chairs.

"This is so like the Hardy episode, is it not, Diane?" Professor Chandra chirped through the chair rungs.

Diane laughed too. "Perhaps this exact geographical location has been prone to gravitational shifts for centuries. But please don't say it's built on an ancient Druid mound, OK?"

* * *

"Took a swim in a vat of beer, did you?" Natalie said, as Diane crossed the room and passed by her roommate curled up with a book by the fire, the last thing Diane ever expected to see.

"Oh my, yes. I forgot it would smell stronger as time wore on." She sniffed her left cuff which had taken most of the torrent. The smell vividly recalled the familiar odor of stale beer that assaulted all her juggling friends when they showed up at the rehearsal space they rented from a dance club and bar. Finding a high enough ceiling to toss any kind of throw was the tradeoff for enduring ages worth of beer-soaked carpeting. She slid out of the damp coat and held it aloft. "What should I do with it?"

"Hang it out the window."

"That's crazy. Sir Christopher Wren would turn in his grave."

"It's dark. No one will care and we're not sleeping with that smell in the room." Natalie closed her book and gave Diane a sour look. Diane remembered the stir her choir mates had caused in Nice, believing the same. Why not hang their wash out overnight on the charming wrought iron balcony that faced the seaside? The shouting management came pounding after midnight and made the mistake clear to them – even to those who didn't know any French. Diane knew better now.

"Sleeping? Funny word coming from you who is out every night.

Where do you keep yourself? You're never here. What makes tonight so special?"

"Oh, the rain, I guess. G'Night!" Natalie wandered into her sleeping room and closed the door.

Shortly after they had settled and her light went out, Natalie called: "You're lucky, Diane. I hear that at Cambridge, they would have made you lick that beer off the table."

"You what?" Diane called back, confused.

"Hundreds of years of college-boy pranks, you know?" She sounded sleepy.

"How did you ever –?"

"I'm good at gathering insider secrets. Sweet dreams," she called.

I'll bet you are, Diane thought to herself, but said merely, "Ah," and murmured an echo to Natalie's good night. Unfortunately, sleep eluded her, replaying the evening at The Turl. Should she have discussed it with Natalie? '*I'm sure it was just a fatherly pat of approval,*' Diane pictured herself saying. She doubted Natalie would have agreed.

Neither Diane nor Dr Chandra had spoken of it on the short walk back to the Trinity gate – which was unlike Diane. For whatever reason, she decided not to bring it up, though his hand on her knee occurred to her the minute he offered her his arm again, for the second time that night, for the short stroll home. The squeeze was totally unexpected. Funny yet mildly disconcerting. She couldn't believe Dr Chandra's pat could mean what it so clearly would have meant if it had happened to someone else. There she was: thirty-one, divorced and – well, she had to look at it as she lay there not sleeping – available. Maybe there was a spark there? Or was it just the familiarity of proximity, like sitting by the same people in class every year and getting to know them? Who could tell?

A tiny voice inside her said, '*Hide!*' thinking of Dr Chandra now. She wasn't sure if she should listen to it or to go about normally. She tried to paint the picture as an amusing one. Nothing to worry about.

Yet.

Saturday, July 13

The early midsummer twilight invited early activity the next morning. Diane was awake before the birds and toting her raincoat to the Laundry Cottage. Natalie had been right: even draping the coat halfway out her back window where dense leaves blocked it from view allowed its noxious fumes to intrude upon the room with each breeze. Well after midnight, Diane got up and quietly opened their main door and tucked the coat in the hallway as far from the staircase as possible. She didn't want anyone tripping on it on the way up the staircase to the lavatory in the night, nor did she want anyone to chuck it out the window, thinking they were solving a nasty business.

Everything fell into line Saturday morning as Chandra joined Diane at breakfast, the awkward moment dispelled in the familiar routine of their morning greeting.

"Good morning, Diane. I am so glad you enjoyed the lecture last evening. People chase Swami Arjuna everywhere, looking for advice. It is comical to watch, but I think it must be tiring for him." Chandra scraped butter across his cold toast and with evident enjoyment, pressed the first crispy bite all the way back to his wisdom teeth. Diane smiled watching him, but didn't mention that she'd watched her father perform the same maneuver every morning while she was growing up. She concluded that men must find this very satisfying on some level that she might never fully appreciate.

"Tiring, yes. I don't find that surprising. There are lots of celebrities with throngs of fans living by whatever the newest headline says about them. *Fan* is short for *fanatic*, as you know."

"Is it? I hadn't realized the derivative. How enlightening to place it in that context."

"Well, I worked in movie theaters for many years," Diane said. "All of them, at one time or another, hosted a special showcase of some sort of interest to fans, like *film noir* detective night, or science fiction night. Watching the people who came to those events was educational in understanding – or at least trying to understand – fandom. The science fiction people were the most interesting. The really skinny people wore volumes and volumes of capes and cloaks, and the huge people were all squeezed into tight leotards, playing out fantasy roles of who they wish they were, I guess. It was funny at first, but the more I saw of it, it often struck me as pathetic, to feel so unhappy, stuck being who you are. Well, I'm one to talk. I have often been mistaken for some kind of oddball because I'm out of current fashion. I don't want to be a pirate, or think I'm Audrey Hepburn, but I've been accused of both many times."

"Is that right? How rude Americans must be to each other."

"It's been interesting, but then, I ask for it, I guess. Shopping in used clothing stores. I wasn't aware of how odd I looked to others until a professor passed me one rainy day at Smith and said, '*Basque Resistance, eh?*' That's what my trench coat and beret said to him."

"I see," Chandra said after a sip of tea. "I have not found your attire quite as conspicuous as that. And I did not know you were also interested in film, Diane. That's marvelous."

"Oh! You wouldn't believe how many Americans seek advice from stars or from movie plots." She colored a little, thinking of when she used to run Beatle's lyrics through her head to get through a tough day, believing they had been written with special meaning just for her. "I think that's the biggest influence in people's lives back home, in terms of fantasy. I call it a form of rampant romanticism that most people aren't even aware of. They just know they really like a certain movie or actor in a role and they talk about them obsessively. Thus the uncontrollable popularity of Hollywood films. Even here, Dr Harding nearly begs for someone to compare a plot element of Hardy to a popular film. He nearly rattles he gets so excited, hoping to find another link between great literature and Hollywood. He's jotting down new movie titles all the time."

"Yes, film studies as literature is of growing interest. There is nothing bigger in romantic forces in India, than the movies," Chandra told her.

"Really? So Hollywood reaches even there?"

"Oh, no. In India, film making is tops. We make more movies per year than Hollywood, but differently. Quite differently." He leaned closer. "No sex. No, not even a kiss at the end. But lots of music and the sweetest, saddest songs you ever heard. I used to love watching, and am guilty to say, I still rent a few Indian movies on videotape when I am feeling homesick. Such beautiful sentiments! You've never seen any Indian movies?"

"Satyajit Ray. I've seen one or two of his."

"Ah, the films of Ray. The gritty side of old India. Yes, they have great merit, but the Technicolor-style Indian musicals are much more delightful. Filled with every delicious pang of love you can imagine. In fact, it is this type of cinema worship that provides Salman Rushdie with his hilarious topic for his much-protested book."

"Is it? I didn't know that. I haven't read Rushdie at all. In fact, most of the books I read were written before World War One. This class with Constance is a real stretch for me. Thought I'd try something new. But what does Rushdie's book have to do with movies? I thought his writing was considered high literature."

"As for Rushdie, *The Satanic Verses* is something of the sort, once you look at the devilish nature of celebrity. You must read it, Diane. It is a brilliant, swirling foment presenting modern movie fandom in a hilarious light, all mixed in with ancient and popular mythology. But some factions just didn't follow the humor. For thinking people, Rushdie is another much-appreciated comedian."

Diane thought again of the evening before. The lecture, expected to be some type of guidance for life turning out to be some delightful entertainment instead. And afterward at The Turl, not just some pub – and the beer, she remembered. "Oh! and my coat. Looks like the beer is washing out nicely." She paused and decided this was the moment. No one else had joined them yet. She leaned forward. "Dr Chandra, I need you to clarify something. What was the pat on the knee about, last night?" She felt very brave bringing it up and therefore sat up a little bit taller, waiting for his response.

"So. Yes, yes. It meant: I am most pleased to find a fellow appreciator of the comic Swami Arjuna. Also, you are a person who has an appreciation for Thomas Hardy. So! Two favorites of mine. Nothing more," he placed his gentle eyes upon her and smiled. "Consider me a fan, Diane. One who won't follow you around hoping for an autograph, eh?" He winked and she felt at ease again.

She thought over the moment last night, his quick response to her comment about The Turl feeling familiar. That Thomas Hardy scene, so vividly described. "I wish I could write like that," she said aloud. "Like Hardy's description of the scene outside The Turl. To instantly recognize a place you've been before, but having been there before only in a book." Just then, Jessica with Emily in tow, passed by creating a small breeze by their rapid progress.

Chandra hailed them: "Good morning, ladies!"

The two didn't stop, but seated themselves at a nearby table. Jessica's cold frown was not lost on Diane, nor Emily's sheepish look of distress for being pulled along. Diane smiled knowingly and winked at Emily. She turned to Dr Chandra who said, "I am sure I must be chasing your friends away."

"No problem, really, Dr Chandra," Diane said automatically, then stopped. "Actually, I think you did frighten them away. When you say, '*Good morning, ladies,*' with that British accent, American ears hear something more like, '*Stand up straight, cadets.*'"

"What an extraordinary observation, Diane. That is so lovely. I've never been accused of having a British accent before. But why would that be their interpretation?"

"I'm not sure, but the president of Smith was from Australia. Anytime she passed us on her walk to her office – which she did at quick-march pace – she said, '*Good morning, ladies.*' Something about the accent and the crisp use of the term *ladies* really set us on edge."

Diane laughed, recalling the erect posture of the impeccably dressed Jill Ker Conway. "It felt as if you'd just been caught slouching, though she probably never meant it that way. Oh, and the slouching, that is a joke from the early years at Smith. As a women's college, they used to have classes in deportment, so we'd learn how to carry ourselves as important future wives of important men. Really funny to think about now, but that was the history of it."

"I see. I will make a note of it," Chandra smiled. "You are very wise, I am sure."

Diane looked over again at the pair of young women, pictured them last night, splashed with beer, which reminded her of the interrupted conversation. "You were saying, something about Hardy and The Turl, I believe."

"Yes, Hardy. Powerful prose," Dr Chandra said. "His writing transports you there. Now you see why people agree to study the dour Hardy even during the beautiful summer term."

"Oh! I just thought of this," Diane suddenly interrupted. "That happened to me one other time, a few years ago. Knowing I'd been somewhere before. I was watching *Lolita* – "

"Stanley Kubrick's classic film? Yes."

"Yes. I *knew* that house. I'd been in it before. Obviously it was filmed somewhere in New England so maybe I'd been there before. I doubted it – I didn't get around very much outside of college – but I knew every inch of the place in the film."

"Perhaps you lived there in a previous lifetime?" Chandra offered.

"Funny," Diane said flatly, dismissing his comment. The jocular look on Chandra's face encouraged her, a look she was growing familiar with. "Well, that intense feeling made sitting through the movie almost hair-raising for me, and I wondered about it for years. Then last year, I saw Nabokov's autobiography on the shelf at the library. He said he had written *Lolita* while staying at his friend Mae Sarton's house in New England. Bingo! A cat lover friend of mine had given me a copy of Sarton's *The Fur Person* when we were back in college. It's just a simple children's story told by her gallivanting cat, Tom Jones, but the reader follows the cat all around that house. Nabokov's book went on to say that Kubrick decided to film *Lolita* there at Mae Sarton's home. That just killed me! To feel so disconcerted through coincidences."

"Ah! What a story of discoveries! Thank you for sharing it with me. So you see, back to our theme: film is a powerful medium."

Diane blinked. She'd spent so much attention to downplaying Hollywood as anything more than entertainment, yet there is was. Perhaps. Suddenly she saw a fluttering edge of it: a future when great films stood side by side with literature.

* * *

In the Library that afternoon, Diane was surprised to find a number of students digging in. The ones that hadn't disappeared to Paris seemed to find it a great opportunity to study. She didn't mind sharing what she'd come to think of as her private study room, but a conversation she overheard stopped her from seeking her usual place in the front window.

"Dr Chandra said to her, '*Maybe in a previous life of yours,*' and she laughed at him. Can you believe it? What a cultural *faux pas*! I mean, how unaware can you be? And they both sat there laughing about it. It was too weird. Diane is totally off my list."

Diane had no trouble recognizing Jessica's voice in the next study bay, nor the reference to the conversation at breakfast. Her eyes flew open as she heard her name. Rather than feeling mortified, however, the vision of Jessica keeping a list gave her a good laugh. Girls keeping lists of friends – it was straight out of a woman's magazine. Possible titles for the article flirted through her mind: *How to Select the Best Friends* – or – *How to Get Ahead (While Leaving Heel Marks on Everyone Else's Backs)*. She quashed her smile, in case anyone happened to have overheard Jessica's comment and seen Diane standing there. Funny, too, that the cutting comments of a twenty year old had so little real slash in them for Diane.

Gathering the leading edge of her full skirt, she gracefully pivoted a three-quarter turn right and down the back staircase to the lower level, her hem executing a small flourish behind her. The whimsical exit recharged her spirits for a moment, but stepping into the lower study room, she was surprised to find most of the tables full. *This is news*, she thought to herself, as she settled into the last big chair that was left. The student in the matching arm chair shifted to make room for her, though he was in no one's way. She looked about curiously at the others. Body language answered any questions about the small clusters of people. New friendships, a few new sweethearts, a few exchanging initial high-voltage eye-contact, all of whom could not be apart, chose to flock to the Library under the pretense of studying together. She noted that one member of the couple that had caused the disturbance at the play the other night was now leaning close to some-one new. Diane smiled, spotting starry eyed Sam and Tamara, whom she often saw together bent over their books or sitting in the garden on a blanket, waiting for the hedgehogs to appear. What a cute couple, she thought.

Thoughts of her conversation with Chandra at breakfast returned, as much as she tried to concentrate on the two articles Professor Bede had given her to read. Here was Chandra, trying to talk her into joining the modern world. Read Rushdie? Funny. Her forays into modern literature had left her cold. She remembered flinging a copy of Camus's *The Stranger* across the room after trudging through the first chapter. That first sentence of chapter two had sent the book careening. As for Tolkien and his ilk, she came to the conclusion that if she had to learn more than three new words per page – made-up words for a new world – she could abandon the book without guilt. Her newest rule after trying several mysteries: if the opening scene is a dead prostitute lying on the slab in the morgue – slam the cover.

For Diane, literature needed to be old, established, enduring and preferably with elaborate costumes. And movies? They were bits of modern entertainment, and were great for that, but not much more. Oh sure, there were amazing classic films already. Fritz Lang. Billy Wilder. Werner Herzog. All amazing film makers. But how can you compare *Rebel Without a Cause* to *The Aeneid*? Bother asking which is better: *Casablanca* or *The Tale of Genji? Star Wars* or *Beowulf?* These questions were absurd. Classical references from antiquity should be required, as far as she was concerned.

Then it hit her: here she, the young woman, was arguing for the old things, while the old man who had sat across from her, raised in what Diane thought of as a timeless culture, had been arguing for the merits of modern things. Funny. Everything backwards. Upside down. The most curious part: she felt intrigued.

Oxford Vindaloo

Monday, July 15

Monday night before another Women's Literature class dinner in the Trinity Dining Hall, Diane sat among a gang of chattering girls. Tommy Newton was perched at the edge of the group, the girls' backs to him.

"Oh! Paris for Bastille Day. It took no time to get there through the Channel Tunnel, and it was just so great! Everyone was so friendly," the girl with the long dark hair said. "You should have come, Diane. We had a blast."

"Courtney, did you go?" Diane asked, seeing the redhead among the group yet knowing, of course, that her roommate had stayed for Swami Arjuna. Courtney's eyes slid sideways toward Jessica and back before speaking. "Did I go? Yes. It wasn't much. Paris is just Paris."

"Wasn't much? Are you kidding?" The first girl poured on the tantalizing details. "We even got into the Louvre, despite the crowds. Really thrilling." Diane winced at this detail; she had yet to step through the entryway into the former Palace of Louis de Bourbon, despite her art degree, despite her plans, despite having been married to someone who had two parents who'd studied art in Paris.

"Everywhere we went, people were just handing out amazing food and souvenirs to everyone, no charge." Another girl rattled her *Tricolor* ribbon bracelet; then the three blondes across from her joined in merrily. "And that huge dance troupe danced the minuet in the *Place de la Concorde*, all wearing those elaborate Marie Antoinette costumes and wigs."

"The fireworks at the Eiffel Tower! Unbelievable!" The long-haired girl said and everyone whooped. "My ears are still ringing from that. Diane, you should have come with us."

Diane suddenly felt the full impact of what she had missed.

"Sounds great. Wish I could have." She tried to sound happy about it. That's when she noticed Tommy's expression. "You went too, didn't you Tommy? Was it fun enough for you?" Diane asked, envious.

Tommy, turned a crabby grimace her direction. "You were smart not to go. You didn't miss anything, just a bunch of snobby people. Wish I'd stayed here."

The girl travelers reiterated their social signal to him, forming a closed cluster. Diane wondered how a young man in that vivacious group of cute, smart girls could fail to have a good time on a trip like that, let alone have had such a vastly different take on what sounded like a dream trip for the others. "Really? What kind of things made it so disappointing?" she quizzed him.

"The Parisians were just as arrogant as you'd expect. Pretending they didn't understand English if you wanted anything. Ignoring you as soon as they figured out you were American. A complete waste of time. And the *Mona Lisa* – it's so small! I stood in line for two hours! What a hoax!"

Diane reflected on his tale and tried not to laugh at his unfortunate experience, but by the way he had reeled off this worn-out stereotype about the French, she had to ask: "Maybe you expected them to be rude, so you were acting rude? Maybe they sensed that in you. Had you been to France before?"

"No. And I'd never go there again. No. Being here is the first time I've been out of the US and believe me, I'm thinking foreign travel is completely worthless."

Ah, so that was it. Diane had noticed that American travelers divided easily into two groups: those fascinated by seeing historic places and meeting new people, and the *'they don't even have hot water there'* group. Perhaps Tommy would always feel more comfortable at home where he could read about foreign lands in familiar surroundings that included wall-to-wall carpeting, a refrigerator stocked with Coca-Cola, and a private bathroom.

At the next moment, Professor Bede signaled to them to gather in their private corner.

"Another dinner discussion. Wonderful." Kate looked chagrined.

"I really hate these."

"I liked going to the Indian restaurant," the long-haired girl said. "Maybe we'll go out for Indian food again before term's over?"

"Indian food?" Tommy piped in. "Why would you want to eat that here? This is England."

The girls glanced his way with sour looks.

"Well, the British Empire included India, Tommy, so it does make some sense," Diane said when no one else would answer him.

"This whole trip is turning into *All About India*, isn't it? With that Salman Rushdie person coming out of hiding, taking over the whole semester," Tommy ranted. "Anyone who decides that writing a book about Satan is a good idea gets what he deserves. Why don't we visit Number 10 Downing Street or have tea with someone really important like former Prime Minister Margaret Thatcher, that's what I'd like to know."

Before Diane could even begin to formulate a response, Professor Bede arrived with the wine and gave him a disapproving look over the top of her reading glasses. "Just now, you'll have to excuse us, young man. My class has a discussion group over dinner."

Tommy retreated to a distant table. Several of the others cleared off in the opposite direction.

Going to Bastille Day in Paris was particularly hard for Diane to miss. She had felt left behind all Saturday afternoon as the others had skipped off to catch the train to London. The Channel Tunnel made it a quick trip and at a price that flirted with affordablity. And the cash machine directly across Broad Street from Trinity's front gate beckoned. Connected directly to Diane's bank in Denver, it would have made it easy to grab the cash – automatically dispensed in Pounds Sterling, no less – and go. With her limited funds, however, shelling out that money before even half the term was over wasn't wise, Diane knew from previous experience. Wiring home for more money on her choir trip fifteen years earlier set up a long string of inconveniences she would not look forward to repeating. Still, Diane reminded herself of her plan: return to Denver really having lived in Oxford, not just visited. She found herself chanting it over the weekend, like a mantra: *be here, now*, whenever her thoughts had strayed to the Paris festivities she was missing.

"Why didn't you go with them, Diane? Better than moping about it all weekend." Natalie had said to her Saturday, when she'd brought her trench coat back from the Laundry Cottage. Opportunities. Spontaneous decisions. Diane had weighed them all. She stayed.

Moping about it? Was it that apparent, she wondered at the time, sitting up straighter to combat the sorry feeling of being barred from fun in Paris. Then she remembered the amazing moment Friday night, discovering that particular spot from Thomas Hardy's novel over at The Turl. Now that was singular. Rehashing the Nabokov-writes-*Lolita* story with Chandra, also. The time had memorable high-points. Bastille Day would come again next year.

Constance seated herself. "Welcome back to those of you who popped over to Paris for the festivities. Did you go, Diane?" Constance asked across the table. "Oh no, that's right. I saw you Saturday evening, didn't I?"

Their conversation Saturday had touched on the Swami encounter... but left out the friendly pat on the knee over at The Turl. Constance had been very disconnected, Diane had felt. Bede used her weekends for writing and was quick to apologize that writers go into quite a fog. Hers persisted to Monday dinner, Diane gathered. "That's right. You said you wanted to meet every homeless person in Oxford, instead, didn't you Diane?"

"Meet homeless people?" Jessica repeated, perhaps taking offense for the Swami himself.

Out of context, the comment from Saturday did sound a little bizarre, as Diane recognized at that moment, seeing the puzzled faces turned her direction.

"Yes. I wanted to become familiar with the town, learn every crack in the sidewalk. Get to *know* Oxford. That includes the homeless people." Diane clarified simply.

"Yes, your observations are correct, Diane," Constance continued. "Oxford has quite a population of homeless. Most tourists walk past them as if they're invisible." By the baffled look on the faces around them, this comment included the young women at the table as well. Diane picked up the thread of conversation, yet at the same time, tried not to sound like the teacher's pet.

"Most Americans don't see them at home either, Constance. I worked in a movie theater in an edgy part of town and got to know many homeless people by name. Some have interesting stories; other, just average stuff. But then, maybe with my being unemployed for so many years, I had the time to chat. I had no place to be, usually. The homeless people I know in Denver seem like just more humans to me, though I probably wouldn't invite one to come and live with me. But then, I don't think that's what they want, anyway. Not most of them. Haven't you guys seen the man that lives in that tiny grave area between the walls, next door at Balliol? That's his spot – if it's not raining. His name, I haven't gotten to ask yet, but I will, before I go back to Denver, if I can catch his eye when he's awake."

Silence greeted Diane's chatty confession, so she pressed on. "Even one of the College staff I was talking with in the Beer Cellar one night. He told me that he was a homeless teen here in town. Now he's working the dish job, or do they call it scullery? Good for him."

"Really? You met him in our Beer Cellar?" The dark-haired girl asked.

"Why would anyone spend time talking with the workers?" Jessica cut through Diane's tale.

"Why *wouldn't* you talk to everyone in your path? That's sociology!" Diane smiled.

"I don't do it at all, but yes. Why wouldn't you?" Emily agreed tentatively.

Diane thought back to Saturday dinner, when Dr Chandra too had asked why Diane hadn't gone to Paris. As she had talked about getting to know the town, she had suddenly rethought her plan. In Denver she fit in, knew when to ask someone's name, knew when it was probably intrusive. Maybe it was intrusive here, she suddenly realized. She had said to Chandra: "Is it rude to ask a homeless person his name? Am I crossing a cultural boundary?"

"I think it shows interest. You will know if it is welcome, however, by the way a person responds. Take your impression from there," Chandra had advised her. "And I am sure they believe you are not there to rob them." The sound of his laugh at that piece of the conversation had made her forget about any concerns over pats on the knee.

As she thought that over, Professor Bede turned and asked Diane a question about the reading.

"Sorry. I faded out there for a minute. What was it?" Diane said. All fidgeting ceased around her, every eye on Diane as Constance smiled and repeated the question.

"I was asking if you know why Angela Carter chose to use the words *wild surmise* on the second to last page of *The Magic Toyshop*. Why that particular word choice?" Constance read the passage off an index card.

Diane had no idea, so she said: "I don't know."

Every eye flashed back to their professor, who nodded an agreeable nod to Diane, then simply addressed the person next to her. "Why do you think Carter used *wild surmise*, Kate?" No other name enunciated so precisely could cut a room in half as well as *Kate*, Diane noted.

Not a person breathed as Kate flushed first red then pale green as she stammered, "I... I... think that the umm, was it in the article you gave us on... well. It was an example of... ."

Constance waited another moment in silence, then looked quickly around the group, adding: "Anyone?" More silence. She continued: "I was just wondering if anyone found that scene as inspiring as I did? Apparently not. *Surmise* here derives from Cortez upon seeing the

Pacific Ocean, '*in a wild surmise*,' as John Keats imagined it. Cortez believed he had discovered the passage to India, the Spice Islands they were all seeking, and all the possibilities therein. I was sure you Americans would recognize that allusion. Also, if you look back at page one, you will see Carter's direct reference there to Cortez and the New World." She set her notes down and looked again at Diane.

Diane nodded affably, but had definitely read the unspoken directive, a familiar one from Smith: '*This is exactly the type of close read-ing I will be expecting from you all*.'

"I want to remind you all," Constance continued, "that talking together as a group will help to promote comradeship as well as professional contacts for future use. Studying in a void, perpetually undisturbed, is a blessing for a scholar who has a publishing date to meet, but building scholarly alliances for support is a better balance. When you find yourselves filled with literary insights in the future, you will wish for colleagues to share them with. That begins here."

This beneficent advice registered like torture with most of the group, who waited politely for dismissal into the rainy evening.

* * *

Bede's words hit home for Diane, who loved the tranquil silence of the Trinity Library at dawn. With two weeks of the program past them, she'd had next to no conversations with the other students – with the exception of Jan and Mark that day; she hadn't seen them again since Fourth of July. Only the hilarious evening with Jessica, Emily and Jason at Swami Arjuna stood out, which hadn't exactly resulted in Diane securing a future scholarly alliance. This rainy Monday night offered an opportunity to begin to remedy this, as most of her Women's Lit class left the Dining Hall, brought their trays to the dish window and disappeared directly down the stairs to the Beer Cellar. Diane with her tray said hello to Kent across the stainless steel counter. His smiling face bore the same satisfied message he'd given her in the Beer Cellar: '*another week, another pay packet*.' She wondered if any of the girls ahead of her had noticed him this time. Diane dawdled near the small tag left on the wall between the Dining Hall doors: *Painting on temporary loan to The Royal Academy of Arts*, deciding.

"May I join you?" Diane pulled up with her half pint mug at the edge of the Women's Lit group. Their lively exchange ended abruptly as they turned to stare at her. Not an unfriendly look, but a complete turnaround from the laughing and animated talk that had drawn her to them. "Am I interrupting?"

The group flushed red in unison. Probably discussing which young cook in the kitchen was the cutest, she figured, except for the superior Jessica, who stared directly at her. From there, the response took an unexpected turn.

"You are so brave," the one with the long dark hair said to Diane.

"What do you mean? You're Laura, yes?" Diane ventured a guess at the name.

"You said to Professor Bede: '*I don't know.*' Just like that, at dinner. I can't believe you did that," Laura reiterated.

"Neither can we," the group murmured in agreement, even the Superior One, intent.

"I'll never forget doing that once in ninth grade back at Miss Porter's School. They practically expelled me," Laura continued.

"That happened to me, too. I swore I'd never say those words again, obviously." Poor Kate still looked shaken from that experience – or from the Inquisition at dinner.

"You're joking?" The information caught Diane's interest. She scanned the group as she had before dinner. Jessica's roommate Courtney had rejoined them. Tommy Newton? Nowhere to be seen. Seven girls she should know by name – eight if you counted Natalie, who was preoccupied with two new boys at the other side of the low-vaulted room – and all from New England colleges and prior to that, students at the top prep schools, she'd gathered from different things they had said. Just like being back in the dorm at Smith. In her dorm there, Diane had been one of only two freshmen from public school, and coincidentally, both were from places thousands of miles west of Massachusetts. The other student, Barb, had been from Phoenix. Diane always referred to herself and Barb as the noble experiments, the random contestants for the college to study and see if they were true members of the pack, though unluckily displaced at birth from the Hub of the Universe – New York – by some mysterious occurrence.

This group of young women before her was similar. Monday mornings at breakfast, Diane overheard tales of the weekend in Athens, or day trips to Amsterdam. Diane marveled at their ability to travel so freely, which included visits to Oxford by their parents, as well. Diane's parents had purchased several international rate postage stamps, on the other hand, which had already resulted in one recording of routine sent the day Diane left, the sort of note that corroborated Diane's image of them as steady and content.

"No joke," Laura continued. "And then you just say, '*I don't know,*' just like that and Professor Bede takes it in stride. She even smiled! I couldn't believe it."

"Well," Diane began, casting about for words to explain what seemed natural to her. "I was just being honest. I didn't have anything to say about what she asked."

"Make something up! For heaven's sake. Do it, even if just to spare the rest of us!" Laura led the gaggle in agreement.

"I knew she'd call on me next. She's always calling on me, isn't she? She's chosen me to torture." Kate grimaced, continuing to feel singled out.

"Maybe she likes you, Kate. Maybe that's all there is to it." Diane smiled at her fresh face with its light sprinkling of freckles across her nose.

"These dinners are supposed to be relaxing? I couldn't eat a bite once old Constance started grilling us. Sarah and I didn't get to read that entire Carter book. Did anyone?" Evidently the equally fair Sarah was Kate's roommate, nearly a matched set.

Diane bit her tongue rather than state the obvious: everyone was supposed to arrive at Trinity with the books read. She did some quick math. The Oxford term started the final days of June, and private colleges in New England all ended by May first. That was a reasonable stretch of weeks to cover nearly all the titles for each class. Even the multi-hour flight over from New York or Boston and the wait in the airport at either end would give a person a good crack at one title or put a definite dent in two. And now they were just beginning the third week. *Make use of every minute.* That was the best study tip from three girls Diane had met in art history class at Smith. They had been in British-run boarding schools somewhere in Malawi, though the girls hailed from South Africa and Zimbabwe. The way they could glean ten minutes here and fifteen minutes there repeatedly each day was ingenious. Particularly the trick of going down to meals fifteen minutes late, allowed them to skip standing in the buffet line and gained them a completely silent sanctum up in their rooms for power-studying. They also kept a book in hand and read every moment spent waiting in any line: at the bookstore, at the coffee counter, even if it was just a paragraph or two. And still, Saturday night they reserved for complete fun, and having assuaged most of the panic associated with falling behind, the one night to goof off became a satisfying reward.

"I read them, but I totally don't get that *Mr Wroe's Virgins* book. I mean: did that actually happen? Is that like some Amish community? I was lost from page one," Kate wrinkled her freckled nose with contempt. "And that *Oranges* book, whatever it was, was just too weird. I gave up after the first chapter."

"Kate! I don't want to talk about homework now. I need to relax. Just shut it, will you?" Even her roommate Sarah had picked up on Professor Bede's way of foisting the name forward.

Diane loved the way British idioms were beginning to creep into their language. *Shut it.* So charming as an alternate to the American slap in the face: *shut up.* And so it was true. A photographer friend of Diane's back in Denver had come home with not an accent, she said, as much as with new word choices that were indelibly British.

The group was off on another tack until someone mentioned the time. The flock dispersed with a flutter of voices and clatter of empty drink glasses. "Diane, we're off to The Sheldonian for a concert. Interested?" Laura extracted her tresses from the rain coat she put on while she was speaking.

Diane had seen the selection on the sidewalk tent board this morning when she mailed some cards: Haydn's *Concerto in C Major*. Sedate music she studied to at home, not quite her idea of entertainment to sit quietly through. "Maybe next time," she smiled and said goodbye to the bunch, picturing the superior Jessica's relief that she did not tag along.

Diane rose to join Natalie, now that Tucker and Brandon had found new interests. The two were leading a noisy challenge game of darts, the grumpy Shawn red-faced and concentrating among the jeers. Natalie looked serene sitting among a different set of boys than last week. She gave Diane that steady look that said: *join us.*

As James drew her second half-pint, Diane thought more about the laughable concept of students needing to trick adults into thinking they had everything in hand, homework-wise. These were insights she should bring back to her tutoring in Denver. Diane had said at dinner: *I don't know,* and it had set all the other girls reeling. That's the student's job: learn it! Her ninth graders had a class on world religions that spelled it out. For Hindus, it's *dharma,* one's job. Paying the bills and feeding the family: parents' job. Learning, doing school work: the student's job. She thought of her sweet new arrival, Sarita, starting the ninth grade last fall and struggling with the learning environment. She explained her frustration to Diane one day and from there they became good friends. As a Hindu, Sarita's reverence for learning encompassed a reverence for the tools of learning as well, not just respecting teachers but also the books themselves. To set books on the floor – even in a book bag – was unforgivable behavior. To put your feet up on someone's backpack, unthinkable, yet kids at that school did it everyday. In class, Sarita's inquisitive nature made her a target. "Asking questions, that's how you learn, isn't it? Yet the other kids all laugh and tell me I must be stupid. What exactly is going on with that?" The young woman transplanted to Denver from New Jersey was baffled. Frankly, so was Diane. She now even wondered why she'd chosen a field with so much posturing and free-flying judgments surrounding it. Like stepping back into the worst years of her own life: adolescence. Diane shuddered momentarily, hoping she'd have better tactics for teaching once the summer was over.

Tuesday, July 16 Day trip

"Here we are: Fawley. A tiny hamlet, the one Thomas Hardy drew for the name of his character, Jude Fawley. Let's have a bit of a look." Professor Harding pulled up to an open field.

Diane climbed out of the college van and squinted her eyes in the direction of Oxford.

"You see, off there in the distance?" He motioned.

"What? Past those nuclear power plant cooling towers?" Shawn blustered, which rendered even the brash Brandon and Tucker silent.

"Those aren't nuclear," Dr Harding corrected him a moment too late. The rest of the group fell silent, regarding the stacks. What a queer moment, Diane thought, then snagged a tuft of sheep's wool off the low hedge before her. The students politely remained silent; no one insisted on naming the radioactivity they were all imagining. The comment had, however, already cast its shadow.

"Can you see Oxford, that's the point. This is Jude Fawley's Christminster." Harding read:

> "Some way within the limits of the stretch of landscape, points of light like the topaz gleamed. The air increased in transparency with the lapse of minutes, till the topaz points showed themselves to be the vanes, windows, wet roof slates, and other shining spots upon the spires, domes, freestone-work, and varied outlines that were faintly revealed. It was Christminster, unquestionably; either directly seen, or miraged in the peculiar atmosphere."

"Like the Emerald City," Diane said, "except topaz, instead."

"Oh, right." Jessica dismissed Diane's comment with a brusque snorting sound.

"Well, it's the same era," she clarified.

"*The Wizard of Oz* came out in 1939. Everyone knows that, Diane." The Superior One flexed her superior muscle.

"L. Frank Baum's book came out long before there were movies, Jessica. I was thinking of the book. That came out, oh maybe around 1898 or 99? I'm guessing. Maybe Hardy had an influence on him?" Diane turned to find Professor Harding staring at her, frozen. Was he having a heart attack, she wondered.

"That would be extraordinary," Dr Harding spoke at last. Diane sensed the cogs going around in his head as he became silent for a long moment, brow furrowed.

Diane studied him but couldn't read his expression. Suddenly he glanced up at her. "I just thought of it," she said nonchalantly to brush aside any trace that she might have seen his interest in her comparison. Harding had no idea that his colleagues had named some of his interests. Constance, the Hollywood film connections, which anyone could gather from being around him. Then Dr Chandra's keen awareness of the rivalry among Thomas Hardy scholars, all mining for innovative interpretations.

Next the van stopped at some ancient earthworks. Diane tried to envision the village that had occupied the vast but vague outlines worn upon the hill. The site impressed little upon most of the group, except for Jason and Luke. They studied every angle, walked the lengths and later, when back in the van, they compared role-playing history game groups they enjoyed back home with their friends. Diane had noticed the long haired boys naturally gravitated towards each other their first evening at Trinity. More often now she saw them accompanying Archie, intent on whatever serious topic he shared with them. The two young men's interest in the earliest eras didn't quite light a fire for Jessica or Emily, who had up until now followed Jason everywhere. Instead, the girls took barely three steps from the van, citing the lingering dew in the grass and their new shoes as reasons for hanging back.

During the day's drive, modern Britain unfolded for Diane. Sheep in paddocks. Idyllic landscapes. The Roman highway, still in use. Eventually the baffled Diane had to ask: how can this be 1996? She was in old world England, millennia older than her entire country, yet she was seeing that it aimed at delightful deceptions as it managed its modernizing. While the United States cluttered every panorama and street corner with an ever-increasing jumble of hideous poles and wires, here they concealed modern devices underground. Dr Harding revealed the secret: buried cables. '*Look, Ma: no hands,*' England seemed to be saying, like putting on a magic act with no strings showing. Back at Trinity, the subtle security cameras hidden within the charming stone and ivy edifices was Diane's first glimpse of this nationwide cleverness. Britain fashioned ingenious designs to maintain its aura of quaint villages, venerable old towns and uninterrupted hills and meadows.

For Diane, Britain's respect for its history and landscape culminated at Stonehenge, where the parking area lay artfully hidden beyond a rise, which in turn preserved the singularity of the empty plains around the monoliths.

Finally, the group descended upon the village of Wantage for afternoon tea and a quick lesson on Alfred the Great. Thomas Hardy renamed the town, *Alfredston,* for use in *Jude the Obscure.*

And everywhere he took them that day, Professor Harding moved off at a brisk clip from spot to spot. "Keep walking these next two weeks to get in shape for the Hardy Hike," he reminded them all.

Wednesday, July 17

Diane skipped through the front door of Boswell's, beaming, and chirped a greeting to the cashier. She was becoming a notable regular, lurking about each aisle, picking up nearly every item in the store as if it were some rare artifact. Marjorie, at the cash register, returned an amused smile as she watched Diane climb the stairs for her third visit to the discount loft. Today Diane wanted a few more of the old lord and his lion. She flipped through the box, grabbed the remaining ones, glad to beat the OxFam workers to the stash. But then, with a thoughtful frown, she gently replaced just one back in the box. Let it lie in wait for the next explorer who follows my trail, she said to herself. She stood up straight and turned to her second quest.

Diane sensed that the layers of pendants and tablecloths that hung down from the low ceiling needed further investigating. Thus in her best detective manner, she crouched lower and burrowed deeper, lifting each piece of cloth in succession. She pictured herself being knighted – or damed, or whatever the term was for women – just like the adventurous researchers who had gathered the Pitt-Rivers Collection. Unfortunately, the perfect tea towels she'd envisioned bringing home to her favorite vintage shop in Denver did not materialize. Instead, however, layers of printed matter – calendars and old announcements, dog-eared posters advertising theater and choral performances – covered an old cork board nailed into the wall. Oxford blossomed with special events during the summer months. Many colleges used their garden settings for Shakespearean plays, chamber music, Diane was learning from her classmates Kate and Sarah, who took in a different event in town any night they had free. The old ads themselves were fascinating for Diane, the former graphic designer. Local fairs and special lectures. Not everyone would get a thrill from finding old posters, but Diane was ardent in her pursuit of history in all its forms. She gently shifted and peeked under layers until she saw the edge of an image she instantly recognized.

Her heart pounded seeing it: the name *Mario* in a familiar, hand-lettered style. As she lifted, a sketch of her juggler friends appeared. How odd was that? She'd met the *Three Bobs & A Mario* at the Colorado Renaissance Festival when just out of high school. She'd seen their stage show dozens of times. They traveled all over the world now, but the artwork on this poster was the real shock. Her college friend Alexandra drew it after the *Three Bobs* had invaded Diane's dorm her freshman year. Passing juggling clubs under the Emerson Arch stopped all traffic and turned the entire Quad topsy-turvy. The two girls had been lured to an adventurous 48 hours in Boston, swept up by the spontaneity of it. Not all learning happens inside the classroom; living! was a formidable teacher. Alexandra's small ink sketch immediately became their trademark for their early years. That's right! Diane now remembered as well: her college roommate said she'd seen one of Alexandra's posters while traveling through Ireland one summer. So here was another, waiting years for Diane's arrival, evidently.

The convoluted travel history of the poster explained only half of Diane's emotional shock. Just before she left for Oxford, Diane had read a short note in the *Smith Quarterly* about her friend Alexandra's death. That was the real blow. Taken together, this moment was nearly the definition of *weird*, Diane thought to herself. Suddenly, she felt the blood drain from her face, a feeling she detested. Fainting was just so wimpy. She knew what would come next if she didn't sit down immediately, yet in her muddled state, she decided fresh air would be the better cure. She clutched at the railing, descended the six steps to mezzanine level and moved unsteadily toward the front door.

"Say, Miss. You'll need to pay for those cards before you go," Marjorie's frowning counterpart, the sentinel at the cosmetics counter, called to her.

"Pay? Yes, of course," Diane murmured, turned mechanically and placed her cards on the counter. Lost in thought, she didn't even hear the affronted huff from the older woman who had formed up in line behind her.

"Everything all right?" asked the cashier, noticing the lack of Diane's usual barrage of questions and jokes about each item.

"Yes. I just saw, well, I came across... I wonder? Is it possible that I could have an old poster from the bulletin board up in the loft?"

The customer behind her sputtered: "Bloody tourists! Walking off with everything that isn't bolted down." She folded her arms truculently across her ample bosom.

The complaint barely registered with Diane, who collected her change and stumbled out onto the sidewalk, where she was carried away in the current of people. Deep in private thoughts that weighed upon her, she bumped against everyone in the lunchtime crowd as she automatically walked on the right side of the sidewalk, not the left. She stepped off the curb and into the path of a bicyclist, who simultaneously swerved and swore. Seeing a break, she flattened herself against the wall of shops, the throng outside Morton's sandwich shop stopping all movement.

Dr Chandra exited Blackwell's music shop at that moment. "Hello, Diane! Rough going, eh?" He looked in her staring eyes for a moment, took her by the arm and steered her through the lunch crowd, saying: "Yes, hunger unfortunately reduces even the best of us to irritable specimens on occasion. Just like fussy children!" he commented as he pulled her gently across Turl Street toward a quieter spot near the Sheldonian.

"Are you all right? I saw your progress just now. Your head was somewhere else, as they say. Everything OK?"

"Umm, yes. I think so. I just..." she began, but slowed to a halt and studied her shoes while standing beneath the disapproving frowns of the Roman heads.

Dr Chandra looked up at them for a moment then suggested, "Perhaps you need some air. Follow me." He led her up five small steps, through the gate and into the Sheldonian Theatre. In one move he deposited two coins at the entry desk and guided her across the circular wood flooring to the observation deck staircase. Diane offered no resistence and little comment, still detached from all around her. They climbed to the cupola, Chandra narrating, "Not many climb these stairs. Perhaps the whirlwind tours do not allow time for enjoying the view." Quiet and high above the town, Oxford spread out around them like a fancy crinoline skirt, bathed in sunlight and studded with gilded trinkets. Ornamentation glittered on every possible surface, yet made up a soothing whole that invited contemplation. Breathtaking, one may call it, at the same time arresting. One could pause here. Here one could sense both the weight and the effervescence of history, displayed for centuries to anyone who would take a moment to look outside their books and observe the world around them. Diane's senses benefitted from the quiet breezes.

"You see, Diane, we have only crossed one street and yet have stepped into a different world. I am pleased to share with you my favorite spot." His eyes rested upon her for several long moments. With quiet manners he said nothing more, turning his attention to the view of Trinity College before them.

"I didn't realize you could come up here," she said, slowly becoming reattached to the present, after staring blankly into the vast panorama for what seemed to her like a lifetime or a moment.

She pointed out Trinity's garden in the foreground, its far wall and beyond. "I had no idea what was beyond my window. See that big tree behind my building? It blocks the view completely." She scanned into the distance as college wall after college wall progressed to the northern limits of the town. Thirty-five – or twenty-nine? – small colleges intimately nestled together, occupied more space than she had imagined. She wasn't sure of the number.

"Thirty-five," Chandra spoke aloud. "Thirty-five Oxford Colleges and half of them are just behind us."

She turned and looked at his profile as he continued to search the horizon. She knew she hadn't spoken her last thought aloud, not wanting to reveal her woefully inaccurate memory for numbers, but perhaps she had said it? She studied his face, so peaceful and absorbed in his own thoughts. Up until this moment, Chandra had focused completely upon her anytime they met, and smiled without stopping. That was nice attention for a first cheery greeting, but too much of that kind of intensity Diane found tiring. Back in high school, each time some new boy had suddenly noticed that she had interesting things to say, it resulted in her being forced into dinner at a fancy restaurant. The expense, the formality and that intense focus on her every movement made for stiff, unpleasant evenings. At Trinity, she had hoped that Chandra would soon relax and treat her normally, like a brother or a cousin. And now, here they stood in companionable silence, high above the town.

Tourists directly below distracted her thoughts. Most groups bunched tightly together as if afraid to be left behind if they strayed. "Oh, look," Diane pointed out to Chandra the one or two who were stepping away from their group, actually looking around and not darting about to get a better photo. Diane enjoyed thinking of the special impressions they were going to take with them.

"Yes! Wonderful. And the others? Soon they will all hop back into their motorcoach and squeeze in one or two more stops before dinner. Extraordinary, isn't it?" Chandra said.

"And all as seen through the lens of their cameras. That's what they will remember," Diane added as if she were talking to herself. She stepped back from the window ledge, turned and leaned back on it, remaining by Chandra's side. Looking now across the observation space and out the farther windows, the top of the Radcliffe Camera was visible above the far window ledge. They were alone. The room felt warmed from the sun yet a pleasant breeze ruffled across her face. She leaned closer to him. "You know. This is exactly the kind of place I'd look for when I went on choir tour a long time ago. Everyone else would step off the bus and directly into a souvenir shop. I'd turn the opposite direction and look for a park or a place just to look around.

I could never get anyone to go with me, either. What a relief to get away from a group you've been stuck sitting with on a bus day after day! But everyone else needed to get that darned souvenir spoon from that particular city for their spoon collection or that darned charm for that darned charm bracelet." She grew animated, though her laugh was tinged with fatigue. "Oh, I would buy a lot of postcards. They're better shots than I'd ever take! But I also liked to record an impression of something I saw and sent it to a friend interested in the same thing.

"People don't write letters much any more." She stood there putting two thoughts together that had never occurred to her before: "Maybe that's why I like to read old books. Everyone always sending notes, receiving letters. Expressing themselves in writing. It takes time and thought. You know, people love to get mail, but don't write back very often." She grew quiet thinking just then of the two letters Alexandra had sent her. Just two in response to the dozens Diane had written to her. Feeling suddenly wistful, she turned that over in her mind. A bird flew by.

"And what do you have here?" he gently took the postcards she was still clutching in her fist. "Ah! Very nice. And the lord domesticates the little lion cub, which used to represent the conquering of foreign lands. Also, of course, it grows into the emblem of Great Britain. You see it on the Royal Seal. Fascinating, is it not?"

"I hadn't thought of that; I just liked the craziness of having a wild animal in the house. Must be murder on the upholstery." Diane took the cards back. "You'll never believe what else I found at Boswell's," she found herself saying. "I still can't believe the coincidence." Her words trailed off. "Excuse me, won't you? I am usually in a big hurry to explain, but I don't have the words right now."

"More time to reflect is a good thing." His white beard, his black eyelashes and brows. The lines around his eyes, the sparkling youth within them. Age and energy. Chandra seemed to possess some form of timelessness.

No pressure. *Amazing*, Diane thought, then continued. "I had a very good friend back at Smith. An artist, like me. Wanting to side-step the mundane, I guess that's the interest we shared. I was a freshman, she a senior, so she was doubly tired of the routine, plus she knew all the fun spots. But one weekend I had a great plan. Some theater friends of mine were making their first trip to the East Coast. They're from Denver, like me, and – do you understand how far that is to go? About two thousand miles by car. So I dragged Alexandra into Boston that weekend with me. The friends are jugglers and so amazing! They were just street performers then – though they do stage shows all over the place now. But we met them in Harvard Yard and spent the day with them there. Well, the point is: Alexandra was so impressed with their act, she did a drawing of them that they started using on all their posters. They used it for quite awhile until they had the money to have professional logos designed. But here's the part you won't believe – I don't believe: I just found one of Alexandra's posters buried under a bunch of old ones on a bulletin board upstairs at Boswell's."

"How delightful that must be for you. How long has it been waiting for you to find it?"

"Really exciting, yes! It didn't have the year on it, but I remember they came back from England and Ireland before I finished college, so more than ten years maybe."

"My, oh my, how strange and lovely."

"But Dyan, there's more." She paused. She was never one for sharing sorrow, nor for doing anything with it but trying to get back to business. This tough training had come from being raised by a strong, capable mother. '*The crying child gets sent to her room,*' Dee Quinnell had often told the tiny Diane if she was acting troublesome. It worked. Diane had learned to swallow those tears and move on rather than be banished from her most beloved playmate: her mother. The lesson had especially stuck the day at the bowling alley when Dee had carried through on the aphorism and had placed the crying child into the very separate daycare area. Banned from league play? Diane never again made a peep of displeasure. And lived her life as a little adult in all situations.

"But you see, the timing is so strange," she went on. "Just before I left to come here, I learned that Alexandra recently got sick and died suddenly, just like that. I wouldn't have seen the notice if a friend hadn't called me. And what are we? She was thirty-two or thirty-three. Sheesh! I didn't really even have time to digest the news in the rush of leaving for England. And getting here wasn't exactly as easy as I had pictured. I've never planned a trip of my own before, I mean not to a different country and well... you know... things can just be so much harder than you expect." She burst into tears and began sputtering apologies simultaneously. "Sorry! So sorry. I..." She put her hand over her eyes, yet struggled to find a tissue in her pocket at the same time.

"Convenient," she commented as she held up the tissue as evidence for her next statement. "I always carry a tissue. In case someone needs one. Like a good mom." Her voice broke again, seeing the pathetic irony of what she was saying. *A tissue in case someone else needed one!* Funny. Sort of. She must have held it all in until this moment. Everything. Her having to take on college alone. Her disappointment in not getting established after school in a good career. Her divorce after the shock of finding out her husband's hidden financial arrangements. Not to mention, she realized that minute, that he'd taken the only photo she had of Alexandra along with some of her other artwork. Of all things to remember at this moment! It seemed endless. Everything tumbled onto her. She had no idea how she was going to live this down, crying high above Oxford with a kindly old professor standing there watching. And now she definitely was out of tissue.

Gently he rustled in his pocket and withdrew a tissue from a small packet. "I too keep tissues, just in case."

"In case a student needs one... when she sees the grade you gave her?" She half-chuckled, half-choked.

His mild eyes rested upon her. "Yes. Perhaps."

This small joke restored some balance for Diane and allowed her to relax enough to collect herself. When she thought about it, she couldn't believe it. Dr Chandra just stood by her. Not grabbing her, yet not ignoring her, nor asking questions, nor insisting everything would be OK. Platitudes! She really hated those!

Once she got her wind back, she glanced up between puffy eyelids to see the sweet look of concern on Chandra's face. His grim smile was full of understanding.

"I never cry," she mumbled, without ever explaining why. *More confessions!* She thought to herself suddenly. *Funny how I feel so understood right now.*

"I'll bet that is true," he said simply. "Evidently today is the perfect moment for it."

She looked at him again. His eyes were glistening. At that moment she gave up every plan of explaining. Instead, she smiled and let out a short burst of laughter, patted him on the shoulder and assured him, "Please, please. I'm fine." And with that, she felt totally calm.

"I am pleased to see animation returning, Diane. When I saw your progress, bumping into people all along the walk, I knew something was not right. How unlike you to be jostled by a crowd instead of leading it!"

"That's sweet," Diane said with a sad smile, choosing to ignore the exaggeration.

"Sadness at losing a friend is completely natural. But what a powerful reminder, at this moment!"

"Usually I love coincidences, but this one really walloped me."

"Well, well. I will say something here intended to restore perspective: '*Time heals all wounds.*' That is a universal aphorism, I believe. We hear it so many times without listening, but it is true and can be soothing advice."

Diane winced comically, after fearing the worst in platitudes. "My mom says: '*Time wounds all heels.*'" She watched his reaction.

"The mysteries of the Universe revealed! Perhaps your mother's version is a more accurate understanding of the infinite?"

"Or just plain silliness, which is perhaps the same thing when comparing cultural references." She managed a sorry grin.

"What an interesting image I am forming of your mother." He laughed with delight.

"Oh, she was a comic book artist and therefore has a sort of warped sense of puns," Diane said feeling a new sort of giddiness that must have registered on her face.

"Have you eaten, Diane?" He placed a caring hand on hers and touched her cheek lightly. "I think lunch will restore you. Allow me to take you, as it has been my fault to hold you captive here. We have missed the menu at Trinity. Perhaps a blessing? I am also a senior and know all the good places." He winked. "Just one moment. I will alert my scout." He pulled a tiny cell phone from his breast pocket, pushed two buttons and spoke: "Alden, yes. Chandra here. Would you please post a note on my door that I am running a little late? I will see my afternoon students on a one-half hour delay. Yes. Thank you."

"Can you do that? Be late for class?" Diane tried to protest.

"Oh, yes. Stephan and Tamara will secretly thank me. They will be pleased to have a little extra time to prepare. They have never yet caught up with their reading."

"Scouts have cell phones?" she blurted without thinking.

"Of course. How else could we order them about?" he smiled at her and wrapped her hand over his arm.

Thursday, July 18

"Are you ready, Diane? You have a very odd look on your face."

Diane had arrived for her morning session with Constance well prepared, but had bumped into a disconcerting glitch on her way up to the suite. "It was just so strange to see Dr Chandra just now with his toothbrush," Diane began, feeling a little foolish. She left out the part that he was also in his bathrobe, towel around his neck, in the hallway. Decently wrapped up and with wet hair, returning from his shower at some shared location, just as on her staircase. And he'd surprised her in the act of placing a thank you card under his door for lunch yesterday.

'Ah, Diane. Sliding a note under my door?' Chandra had said, catching her completely off guard. 'I hope not in a state similar to poor Tess, confessing to Angel Clare her iniquities. Do you have something important to confess?' He had smiled sweetly at her, the toothbrush suspended casually from his hand, elbow propped on his hip as if seeing students with mussed up wet hair and in this attire were a daily occurrence. Diane wished he had come to breakfast as usual. Then she would never have had to resort to writing the note in the first place.

"Yes, Diane," Constance pronounced with an amused look, "we professors are mere humans and tooth brushing must therefore follow."

"I know that of course – and wouldn't have it any other way, the tooth brushing, that is," Diane paused to smirk at her own joke.

"Oh! Even more amusing – or disconcerting – in winter when we learn who still resorts to wearing night caps." Constance grimaced over her reading glasses.

Diane chuckled at the image. "I guess I just now realize that I've always lived at a segregated distance from my professors. Never actually stepped into their homes – though the choir director did have us in for a Christmas celebration that one time. We actually met his wife. Otherwise, students and teachers stay very separate in the United States. Even with the students I tutor. Yes, I make sure I don't take my walks in their neighborhoods. The school makes a point of it in their policies, too."

"Maybe that's the difference there, Diane. You Americans classify teaching as a job. Perhaps we consider it a vocation. Ironic word coming from a former nun, I know, yet still a poignant word choice. A small residential college operates as a community in that way."

"Yes, of course," Diane reiterated, still not sure what about the encounter with Chandra was still bothering her. The pause gave Constance a moment to reflect as well.

"But as you mention the living arrangements and tight quarters here, it requires a perhaps more subtle or more vigilant form of discreet living. After living here within the College walls for even one year, one comes to understand the boundaries within the walls." Constance's cheeks colored for just a moment. She looked squarely at Diane. "You can hear everything. The stone walls and brick buildings afford no privacy. Intimacy. A row. It's all public here, echoing off the walls, especially in summer term with all the windows thrown open. One summer a very uncomfortable bond formed between a don and a student. I'll never forget it. I was astonished when the don... even at the far end of the garden." She did not elaborate and Diane didn't need her to. "Yes. Discretion is definitely in order, especially during summer. And that professor is no longer here, I'm sure you can guess. But then again, as a man, he could easily have continued as if nothing had happened and no one would have mentioned it. Secrecy among men, as usual. I'm afraid to say that we all looked the other way. Appalling, but still true."

Constance's story made her think of the trick ceiling in the Emerson House dining room, barrel-vaulted and therefore affording certain secret listening spots, directly cross-corner from the sitter's location. Alternately interesting and mundane commentary could easily be gathered there, if one remained silently sipping tea at the receiving end. The ceiling revealed many truths, mostly confirming who were spreading gossip about others, thinking they were speaking in private.

"Yes, and what have you for me today, Diane?"

"I've been doing some thinking about that phrase you called to our attention at dinner on Monday: *a wild surmise*. Speaking of Angela Carter's Melanie, who was poised on exploring her own New World, choosing Cortez's sighting of the Pacific as an allusion put me in mind of oceans and sailing. That made me aware of an obvious yet over-looked point: England is an island, sitting in the middle of a body of water.

"I studied some Japanese literary criticism at Smith, and maybe it would apply here also?" Diane cleared her throat. "For the Japanese, Japan – as an island – stands as a metaphor for the embryo floating in a mother's womb. If you used that non-Western interpretation here, wouldn't England be a similar place of creation and birth, literarily speaking? I see that would be a way to get at more meaning in Carter's New World possibilities for her characters. What do you think?"

Professor Bede's eyebrows shot up as she said, "Diane! That's ex-actly the cog that is missing in Daniel's article on Mediaeval Female Archetypes. My graduate student – Daniel. Would you mind having a chat with him? His article would definitely benefit from that idea. He will, of course, properly credit you as a reference for your insight."

"Credit me as a reference?" Diane's lips moved over the words, though little sound came out.

"It's so exciting to see how you link together existing theories in ways I've never heard of before. With ideas like that, Diane, you really should consider PhD work. I would love to see what you could do with Jane Rogers or Faye Weldon. We feminists are still in need of salient articles on our craft. Honestly, Diane, you have the makings of a new voice in literary criticism."

The ring of Constance's pronouncement faded in the room, as Diane sat wide-eyed and silent.

Week FOUR

BACK FROM BREAKFAST, Diane was delighted to find Natalie in residence.

"Ah, Natalie. Nice to see you! Where have you been keeping yourself?" With faxes arriving from her mother each day, Natalie probably didn't appreciate another pair of eyes watching her every move, but Diane wanted her to know she did like having her around.

Sidestepping the question, Natalie surprised her by beginning: "Dr Chandra mentioned you yesterday."

"Really? Where did you see him?"

"In class," she added casually.

Diane stopped what she was doing. "I didn't know you were taking a class with him. I thought you were Constance's student exclusively, like Daniel."

"Nope." Natalie's laser-like gaze clung to Diane as Natalie folded herself onto the love seat and burrowed down until the armrest became her neck rest. All the while, her eyes remained locked on Diane until only her eyes were visible around the side of the couch.

Diane laughed at the classic spy pose, yet the green eyes continued silently to probe her for some playful purpose. Who would make the first move, Diane wondered, as she froze, ready to play.

"What?" Diane finally asked after several tense seconds, agreeing to let her roommate play out whatever it was she wanted to spring on her. Maybe some pleasant surprise? Then what Natalie had said hit her, beyond the teasing. What had Chandra said? Was he going to be a nuisance after all? Constance had suggested it, and Diane had shrugged off the comment. Maybe there was more to it that she was aware. She dreaded that, when people are pesky. Her brow furrowed. "Does he usually talk about me to you? I mean, he knows you're my roommate."

Natalie turned her profile to Diane as if she wished to read her book, but said: "That's the only time he's ever done it, which surprised me." The corner of her mouth curled slowly upward, like a cat who just pinned a mouse under her paw. "But by the way he said your name, I could tell you've been on his mind." She addressed her pages.

"Oh, nonsense." Diane scoffed at the remark, but needed more information. In fact, as she stood there waiting, she became aware of the thup-thup-thupping in her left ear, accompanying the voice in her head that kept demanding: '*What did he say?! What did he say?!*'

"Well, that's just the way it seemed. That he'd been thinking about you." Natalie purred, turning the pages in a theatrical slow motion that signaled more to come. The velvet barb came flying at Diane: "I wouldn't blame you if you found him attractive." She spoke casually to her book.

Found him attractive? Diane's mind shouted. She squirmed at the gossipy tone, which felt like stepping into quicksand. She disliked being wheedled like that, so she turned the conversation by asking a practical question. "What are you studying with Chandra? I didn't think your feminist studies would ever find you taking a class from a male professor."

"Dyan is the Edwardian scholar."

Diane winced as her roommate used his first name. Natalie evidently got the response she wanted because she looked gratified, then continued in the same vein: "The Edwardian era was a decisive moment in the growth of feminist authors and philosophy."

"Ah," Diane acquiesced, hoping the teasing was over, now that Natalie seemed to have gotten what she wanted, but for what mysterious purpose? *Collecting research?* – perhaps that's the way Natalie defined this episode in her head. Diane started toward her bedroom door, but pulled up short when Natalie continued.

"Dyan's a lot more insightful than these rich white boys in the program."

"Well, *duh!*" Diane choked. She jerked around, feeling as if she'd been punched in the stomach. "He's a professor," she said perhaps a little too forcefully, trying to put the conversation back on track, while at the same time trying to resist launching a defensive counterattack, perhaps on whichever rich white boys were keeping Natalie away from the room all night. Funny how that came to mind just then! Then suddenly Diane saw the crazy humor in it: *'Insights from rich white boys in the program.'* That concept alone was worth the price of admission to this comical exchange. Feeling she'd had enough taunting, Diane spotted her sketchbook nearby, scooped it up along with the pencil bag and called goodbye over her shoulder as she sailed out the door. "See you later on the bus for Stratford, Nat."

* * *

Stratford-Upon-Avon. A poetic name for the little town that was probably one of the most visited spots in England. A holy pilgrimage for all theater lovers. Her Renaissance Festival friends back home were rabid with envy when word spread that Diane would be seeing four Royal Shakespeare Company productions during her stay. Even her mother, the biggest Vivien Leigh fan in Denver, told her daughter to make sure to visit Sir Laurence Olivier's grave, if possible.

On pulling in for their first visit to Stratford to see '*The Comedy of Errors'* two weeks earlier, Diane had expected many things of the town. And most naturally, a replica of an Elizabethan style Globe Theater. The town had been abuzz with tourists, yet the feeling along every street was one of tranquility. Perhaps the brimming baskets of amazing flowers hanging from every building and lamppost was the reason for its charm. More flowers in one basket than Diane had ever seen, as if bursting forth for visitors by special command of the Queen or someone from the Royal Academy of British History. More likely – Diane reminded herself to curb her romantic imagination – by decree of the Stratford tourism council. A glance through the windows of the shops she had strolled past displayed local items to buy, most of which bore the famous ink etching of The Bard of Avon or the famous signature from the famous Folio. Diane had to admit it: Shakespeare really was incomparable to anyone else in the West, with the exception, perhaps, of Napoleon. The town felt nicely under control. The birthplace of Shakespeare. The grammar school of Shakespeare. The graveyard where he was buried – and yet stopping short of signs announcing: *Shakespeare slept here.* All lovely.

And there it was: Anne Hathaway's cottage. Easy to spot from having seen a photo of it in every British literature book and Shakespeare paperback she'd ever picked up.

On that first visit, Diane had offered the extras from her box lunch to ravenous boys on the Trinity motorcoach, then pitched the remainder in the trash at the curb. She had made straight for the white swans that lolled majestically nearby, her student companions left far behind in the shops. While walking a strip of grassy park along the Avon, away from the pavement of the town proper, that's when she had noticed a few people digging through the open bin of trash where they'd been let off.

Having had this first visit experience, Diane had a new plan for today. She studied the movements of a solitary homeless man while she visited the swans, then wandered along just ahead of him. She sat momentarily on a bench, casually setting her box lunch beside her. It now contained: half the sandwich cut neatly in halves, the second apple, a giant brownie, a sealed bag of garlic potato crisps and a tetra-box of apple juice. She looked all about casually, stood up and then wandered downstream to allow her man to claim his lunch.

Her motorcoach driver had carried his lunch a few steps farther downstream.

"Hi, Steven," She smiled. "Nice to be out of the driver's seat for awhile, I'll bet."

"Yes. Nice of you to say so, Miss." He tried to rise, but she waved him back.

"May I?" She sat down while speaking. "What a lunch, eh?"

"Yes. Our kitchens take good care of us. May I?" He asked, lifting his sandwich.

"By all means," she encouraged him to continue. "Customs are interesting, aren't they? But lunch is lunch; eat up!" She allowed him to chew his next bite undisturbed. Over her shoulder she saw her man alight next to her lunch as planned. She tried to repress a very pleased look as she turned back to Steven. "I always wonder what the driver does once we stop. You don't have to stay with the bus?"

"Oh no. Stratford is one of my favorite destinations. The town's coach park – you can see it from here – allows us to stretch our legs. There's an attendant who keeps an eye on everything."

Diane looked across the Avon. In the distance, a sea of motorcoach roofs glinted back the noontime sunshine. "So that's what makes this town so palatable! It felt different in some way, but I just couldn't name it." Like the cleverly concealed parking lot at Stonehenge, she again appreciated the care with which the English preserved the landscape.

"You see, with a coach park, motor traffic doesn't clutter the town. I wish Oxford would implement the same system. The town council brings it up for a vote, but it hasn't passed yet," Steven told her between bites.

"Really? Hmm. That would be a nice improvement, wouldn't it? There's enough foot traffic – you couldn't get rid of that – but take away the buses and it would quiet things down a lot, wouldn't it? I don't even go out anymore during the day. Feels like I'm going to get run over," she admitted.

"It would be a vast improvement for us who live there. I don't know what is holding up the change." Nor did Diane. They watched the stream gurgle by for a few minutes.

"So, do you have a ticket for the play today?" She asked, double-checking her watch.

"That is always an option, yes, but today I have chosen to enjoy the beautiful weather instead."

"This is a nice spot." She looked up into the broad tree that shaded them, wondered how old it must be, how many people had enjoyed a rest on this bench. "I was thinking, as I visited the memorial grave of Shakespeare on our last visit, this whole town is a lot of hubbub for a man who may have been just the pen name for a collective of playwrights, eh?" Shock registered on Steven's face, quickly replaced by a furrowed brow. But before he could reply, the homeless man passed by them, saluted Diane with a broad grin and a nod. She smiled back and nodded.

'Interesting exchange,' the coach driver's face said.

Diane explained: "Oh, I saw him coming, so I left my box lunch for him. He evidently saw through my plan. Nice of him to say so."

"Why, I never," the coach driver said, to include both her comment and the man's greeting, Diane gathered. "Perhaps you would enjoy visiting a real historic site. An old English inn, The Dirty Duck. It has been the haunt of theater goers – Shakespeare or not – for centuries. It's right up there across from the theater on Waterside."

"Sounds like just the ticket." She thanked him and said, "See you later. Have a nice afternoon." Making a detour back to her first bench, she plucked the empty lunch box and wrappers, then deposited them in a trash bin at the curb on Waterside.

Tuesday, July 23 Day trip

Their scholarly expedition through Dorset resembled a thinly veiled tourist excursion, but not for want of planning on Professor Harding's part. Each time the van stopped, eight of the nine students unloaded, stretched and wandered off in search of snacks or trinkets. Diane subsequently spent a good deal of time at Professor Harding's elbow, for moral support. The man was in his element.

In the morning at Thomas Hardy's grave side, Dr Harding revealed Hardy's unorthodox burial, beginning with his refusal to be interred in Poet's Corner at Westminster Abbey, but finally acquiescing to a compromise. Their professor pulled them all through the tale to its thrilling conclusion: "Thomas Hardy's body lies here in this quiet churchyard, while his heart was removed, on the kitchen table, mind you," bubbled Harding, "and sent on to London in a tin... if indeed the cat didn't actually eat half of it, as legend holds." That got the attention of the eight. They drew closer, evidently hoping for more. A first.

Diane listened at a distance, as she wandered down the sidewalk, and as the others finally gave Harding his due. Fewer than ten headstones on, a name leapt out at her: *CECIL DAY LEWIS. Died 1972.* Could this possibly be Daniel Day Lewis's father? Let alone, the father of the actor in her favorite film, *A Room With A View*, playing Cecil Vyse? What a good laugh for him, answering to his father's name throughout the production. They certainly shouted: 'Cecil!' as often as Constance invoked the name: 'Kate!' Perhaps that is what inspired the actor's spiky, suppressed smirks? He probably stood right here on this sidewalk, too. Unbelievable. She wanted to shout for everyone to see it, confirm what she was thinking. Thoughts flew through Diane's head, relating this bizarre discovery to friends she had in theater and film – and trying to put some reality on it. As much as people thrilled over movie actors, sometimes it just destroyed the mood of a movie, when one of her friends suddenly appeared on the screen. Like that

Schwarzenegger film, where Peter had shown up with two lines half-way through the movie. Ruined! as her attention was yanked out of the building fiction. She bubbled deliciously to herself now, however, standing there roving through multiple friends-in-movies incidents and enjoying them once again.

"Something, Miss Quinnell?" Dr Harding joined her with the group at his heels.

"Is this person related to Daniel Day Lewis, the actor?" she asked, indicating the gravestone.

"Who is the actor?" Emily asked.

"What film is he in?" Jessica chimed in.

Diane gave them all the information, which did not register with the others. How could that be? she wondered, watching Brandon and Tucker light up cigarettes. She remembered going to see *A Room With A View* at a regular theater, so it had been in major distribution, not hidden in independent film venues only. Well, of course the others don't know it! She realized. It was not a Hollywood blockbuster film. Nothing blew up. No one being chased by the police. No graphic sex. A quiet film, the story hinging on one spontaneous kiss. Naturally, it must have been off their radar.

"Yes. The actor's father. That film is a classic, though more appropriate to Dr Chandra's studies." Dr Harding cut her off, guarding his scholarly boundaries, perhaps. "It leads to a fascinating Thomas Hardy story, however. Cecil Day Lewis, also a Poet Laureate, followed Hardy's unconventional lead and insisted he be buried here near Hardy. That is the calibre of Hardy's influence," he concluded with a flourish. Tommy Newton nodded enthusiastically to that.

"Cecil Day Lewis, Poet Laureate? That's what I get for not reading movie gossip magazines, I guess," Diane laughed.

What was it that makes me see these things others just walk by as if on autopilot? She pondered as the others hung in a group and chatted as if they were meeting up in some social room, not visiting a cemetery. A better sense of history? The art training? Seeing details, thrashing them out, comparing this to that. Even the visual side of art, apart from the analysis, gave her a distinct difference.

In Dorchester, they paused at the royal blue historical plaque on the face of Barclay's bank on South Street. "Here's a good one," The professor commented on the official blue oval plaque. He read:

'This house is reputed to have been lived in by the Mayor of Casterbridge, in Thomas Hardy's story by that name written in 1885.'

Several students nodded politely, the point lost.

Diane chirped a supportive comment: "Ah. A historical plaque for a fictional character. Funny!"

Dr Harding nodded her way stiffly. She wasn't sure if he wanted her help. The others shuffled their feet under them, perhaps impatient for lunch.

"Well, perhaps we all should be thankful that people still read the book and therefore show interest in this plaque, erroneous as it is," sniffed Professor Harding. "Perhaps reading Thomas Hardy will disappear one day."

"Ah, but the movie people will do another remake, won't they?" Diane added with verve, knowing the professor's appreciation for Hollywood.

"Yes, well. Perhaps we should find some lunch next. I know a café on High Street." He led them there and held the door. Diane lingered near the back of the group, peeked inside the quaint café, remembering the disaster of their last day trip together.

"I'll be right back," she notified Dr Harding, who had no choice but to watch her slip down the block.

Marks & Spencer. She went straight to the neatly packaged takeaway food section, whisked a salad through the cashier and established herself on the bench opposite the café. The group was still ordering. Diane chuckled, remembering Wantage. Once they had parked in the shadow of Alfred the Great, the group descended upon a very small tea shop and overtaxed the wait staff of one. The dilemma was written on the woman's face as she stepped up to the first of the group that had invaded the shop. Accustomed to speeding a crowd of movie-goers through the candy counter at The Esquire in Denver, Diane made quick work of the situation. Ready to streamline and serve, she stepped forward to place the order: five Horlick's hot chocolates, three lemonades, paid in one transaction. The look on the matron's face was either relief or chagrin – Diane wasn't sure which – as Diane then assisted in distributing the libations, as well. An efficient, helpful gesture can look like a rescue or like American pushiness. Diane decided to opt out on a repeat performance today.

In Dorchester, her salad finished, she watched the waitress serve the last of the group inside the café. Diane deposited her empty wrappers in the bin beside her bench and strolled in the other direction until the OxFam sign caught her eye.

Diane climbed back into the college van clad in black. The Russian-style tunic's perimeter of buttons topped a similar broadcloth A-line skirt with nine-button naval-style closure. It appeared to have been tailored for her. Professor Harding eyed her warily. Jessica let out a guarded squawk.

"Yes, I traded for this Soviet spy outfit, circa 1964, while y'all finished lunch," Diane volunteered. She buckled in and winked at Emily. She felt supremely clever, probably the only one ever to change costumes mid-way through a Thomas Hardy excursion.

Wednesday, July 24

"I never expected Dennis Sartorius to be the Neoclassical poetry scholar." Diane let the cowboy boots remained unmentioned.

Diane followed Constance from the Wednesday night lecture toward the Dining Hall. The cowboy had read out many of his favorite Seventeenth Century poems, which worked magic on Diane, still so keenly aware of residing in Seventeenth Century housing. But something more about the lecture had kept her leaping around in her seat and now caused her to prance along the path, waiting to pounce on someone who would listen, who would understand.

"Did you happen to look around the room, Connie? I don't mean to laugh, but it was nearly a joke. Not one of the other students has studied Latin, I'll bet. I asked Jessica, Emily, Jason – even Daniel. They were all completely lost. Rather sad, isn't it? I must be the only one who knew what Dennis was getting at. Personally, I loved it!"

"Is that why you gave Dennis that standing ovation? Oh Diane, you really are refreshing." She watched Diane, whose spontaneous nature seemed irrepressible tonight. "You don't wear makeup, do you?" Constance asked out of the blue. Perhaps the afternoon light or Diane's animation had triggered the question.

"No," Diane said as a matter of fact. "Only if I'm in a theater production. Even then, it seems like too much work. And what a bother cleaning it off."

"How I envy you your young skin. It really glows. Lucky. You'd be terrified to see what I look like without my makeup." Constance seemed to ponder more on that image, grimacing slightly as they entered the cool stone foyer to the Dining Hall. "I do think Wednesday night candlelight serves us all well."

It was Diane's turn to tut-tut. "Yes. Very forgiving." She nodded with mock sentiment, then squeezed Constance's arm affectionately. As they passed by the empty spot for *The Five Fellows*, she wondered how Constance could ever feel mournful about her classic features? Certainly she wasn't begging for a compliment, was she? Another thought occurred to Diane. Was her comment about beauty or was it about age? As they chose a table, Diane asked: "Do you have a big birthday coming up or something?"

"No, no. Nothing like that," Constance said studying Diane's face, evidently enjoying what she had come to know of her lively student. She took her place across from Diane.

To say '*you are so beautiful*' to a feminist was asking for a fight, Diane knew. Many beautiful women grew weary of superficial compliments, and finally grew angry. Was there any wonder about it, once you laid out the scenario? Like her amazing friend Lily, back in Denver. After giving a full day presentation at a professional conference, a man came over to compliment her – not on her intelligence, her professional demeanor nor on the presentation itself – he complimented her on her looks. '*I nearly belted him in the jaw,*' she had told Diane. In that way, Diane learned that to dismiss all else for beauty was insulting to intelligent women. Yet it was a typical, initial reaction from many, Diane began to notice. After college, for herself, Diane had begun to add, "I'm also very intelligent," anytime someone mentioned how cute she was. If her parents were nearby on those occasions, they usually buried their heads, mortified.

So to stop herself from gushing all over Constance to assure her of how thoroughly attractive she was – attractive in truly valuable ways – Diane diverted instead. "No makeup – but costumes! I'm big on costumes for everyday wear."

"And what play is this dress from?" Dr Chandra entered as if on cue. "May I join you?"

He took a seat beside her after receiving her nod.

"Isn't this great?" She ruffled the Peter Pan collar on her print dress. The starched cotton fabric still held its colors, watercolor washes of pastel pinks, lavenders and grays. Bold triangular brush marks of India ink defined beatnik kittens, some with dark glasses, others sporting berets. "If this came in only grays, I could picture it on Betty in *Father Knows Best*. Do you know that show? Wait a minute; this pink probably came out gray on black and white broadcast television. No matter. I found it yesterday at an OxFam shop in Dorchester when we stopped for lunch."

"Along with the spy costume you were wearing when you returned? Yes, I noticed that you left in one outfit and returned in another. Interesting trips, those Hardy excursions," Dr Chandra said in a skeptical tone.

She turned and smiled, enjoying the teasing, which reminded her of the fun she'd had before dinner. "Oh say, I was just telling Connie. Wasn't Dennis's lecture great? It finally made sense of all the Roman poets I studied in high school. The point was – Connie, I didn't quite get to this – finally! Hearing Roman-style poems read aloud in English, the formulas of Horace I had studied so long made sense to me. *Spring, Love, Death. Fame, Love, Death.* I knew exactly where the poems were going next. Too bad no one else did! It was wonderful though, wasn't it?" She gave Chandra a wink.

"Ah! So that was your Urdu poetry training, then. I see it now."

"Yes!" Diane saw it also. "It's just like you said. The thrill of knowing how the poem ends. The same thing but in a different form. How funny!"

Constance stood up suddenly, saying, "What am I doing? Look at the time. I must fly. My editor said she would be calling me this evening. Nearly forgot that. Good night, Diane. Dyan." Constance stepped away. They watched her signal to Lawrence, have a word with him at the door with much pointing toward her rooms, followed by knowing nods from Lawrence – to have dinner brought up to her, they guessed.

"Did I interrupt some girl talk?" Chandra asked Diane just after Constance left.

"Maybe." Diane too was surprised by Constance's sudden exit. "Just as you arrived, we were talking – believe it or not – about beautiful women and – I cringe to say it – makeup. Not my usual conversation, but there it is." She smiled sideways at him and gave over to a mild temptation that formed in her head. "So. I like sociological studies," she began. She busied herself with buttering a roll while he waited for her to complete her thought. "Do you find makeup on women attractive? Necessary? Threatening?" She wondered for a moment how this bit of silliness had seized her, but riding a wave of enthusiastic energy was an irresistible delight for her.

"Ah. I am to be your guinea pig?" he flashed his dimple at her, but paused to consider. "Agreed, but just for this moment."

"I can see you hesitate, so I will lead the way," she charged back in. "I have always thought that Hindu women are the most beautiful women in the world." Diane stated it with finality. She did believe that. Why not tell him?

"*Do* you?" Chandra turned to get a better look at her. "Well, yes. *Beautiful* Hindu women are very beautiful –" which sounded to Diane like a much wiser rearrangement of her larger statement.

He continued: "Despite seven millennia of adornment customs in my country, pardon my irreverence, but I find elaborate jewelry and makeup trivial. '*They make for pretty packages.*' That is what my grand-father always said, and I must agree. I think that one should not have to work so hard to be beautiful."

"Ah! You are an ascetic, then?" Diane said in a bold and challenging way. Just as she said it, she realized how ironic it was that it was Constance, who had been the nun, who was worrying about her looks. Funny, funny world, Diane thought. So many things upside down. Another observation for her essay.

"You are very lit up tonight, Miss Quinnell. Perhaps you are drawing some playfulness from these kittens?" he remarked.

Thursday, July 25

"Perhaps this will be a theme for our summer together," Diane heard Dr Chandra announce to a few professor friends at breakfast the next morning.

"What will be?" Diane asked, taking a seat next to Dr Harding.

Professor Bede looked tired as she mashed her baked beans into her plate with her fork. Diane wondered if she'd already grown weary of whatever this topic was.

"Oh, good morning, Diane. I was postulating that at this august moment, heralded by Salman Rushdie's returning from retirement, shall we say, we may see a theme play out over our time together. Perhaps Rushdie's appearance will mark a turning point in the way scholars communicate."

Diane followed Dr Chandra's idea; she felt half-embarrassed, however, to say she too had forgotten all about Rushdie. When had that happened? She also remembered now that right after the event, no one had had anything insightful to add, barely any comment at all, even though she had asked around. Why was that? Interest in the event had disappeared almost immediately.

"Who else will come out to speak, is the question – or – who else has been forbidden to speak?" Chandra regarded his colleagues, then turned to Diane with a twinkle in his eye. "Perhaps you, Diane? I hope you never feel a need to remain silent in the company of such humble academics as ourselves."

Constance and Dennis turned in her direction, missing the frown Professor Harding shot at Chandra. Threatened by Chandra's easy rapport with *his* student? Whatever was between those two, Diane decided to ignore. Dr Harding shifted impatiently in his seat. That said a lot, she thought. He had the same way of squirming through their sessions anytime she presented a theory. She couldn't imagine that her nutty ideas could cause him to leap about the room, or cut her off in the group, but he often did. Now Harding craned his head around, checked the opposite direction and suddenly rose from the table as if in a hurry to catch a departing train. "Excuse me, won't you?" he mumbled over his shoulder and was gone through the dish return.

Diane brushed aside Dr Chandra's playful compliment and tried to add something salient. "It seems ages ago, already, doesn't it, since Rushdie spoke? Time passing can be so deceptive."

"Yes, yes. Who else will come out to speak, is the question." Chandra turned to Diane. "We must keep our eyes open."

* * *

Diane returned from breakfast to find that Mary Ann had already been there. Yet on her freshly made bed, three photos sat upon her pillow.

Natalie entered from the hallway at that moment in a thick bathrobe, patting her wet hair with a bright green bath towel.

"Did you put these photos here?" Diane stepped into the main room, sat down on the love seat while looking at them.

"Yes. There's a nice one of you with Dyan." Natalie disappeared into her room.

Diane held up the picture. There they were, she and Chandra seated side by side in the Dining Hall, engaged in conversation with whoever was across the table from them. The candlelight made it easy to identify as taken during a High Table dinner. Diane had just worn the pink kitten print dress with the Peter Pan collar last night. Then she noticed the date printed in the corner. Sure enough. Last night. "How did you take this? I don't remember ever seeing you with a camera."

"Oh, I'm very good at capturing candid shots. My camera has an amazing zoom lens."

"This was just last night. And then you had it printed today?" In Diane's world, tourists brought home rolls and rolls of film at the end of their vacations and had them developed there. Diane laughed at her own limited understanding of what could be done in a modern

Oxford. "But you can do that, can't you? I've never stayed in one spot before. This isn't a tour, is it?"

She handed the snapshots back to Natalie, who shrugged her shoulder, saying: "Keep them. I noticed you don't have a camera, so I had two sets printed."

Diane laughed to herself at the irony of not carrying a camera and then ending up with a bunch of photos anyway. She didn't care much about photos, and she loathed the concept that they must all be put into albums and shown to friends – or tossed into a drawer and forgotten. *Some are born taking photos, some have photos thrust upon them,* she thought to herself. Like Shakespeare's Malvolio. Funny, in that light. But, Diane had to admit, it was nice to have this one of Chandra. And this one with Constance. Diane normally would have tried to meet someone new for each Wednesday dinner, grab someone who looked left out or was too shy to join anyone. Constance, however, tended to gravitate toward Diane on these evenings, then Chandra would arrive. Diane liked that. Here they were, professors, nearly twice her age, yet just like any kids who wanted to sit with their friends in the lunchroom. The gregarious nature of humans. Yes, it felt good to be a part of a group.

"Thank you. That was very thoughtful," Diane said, surprised at her own warm response to a commodity she usually didn't value.

Diane looked more closely at each image. A digital date was printed in bright orange in the corner of each. The digital date must be a new feature. Probably very useful after years had gone by, but in Diane's estimation, it marred the picture. Her art training weighed the visual composition of everything she came across.

Natalie had judiciously chosen only the photos Diane was in, except for this last one: Natalie standing on a sidewalk, smiling mischievously at the camera, pointing impishly to a group of three boys next to a car. Two were loading something bulky into the backseat – sun reflecting off the back window – while the third was looking right at Natalie, his mouth gaping open in surprise. A larger man in a beige suit coat was behind the open car door. The classic Oxford College crest patch on his pocket was over-printed with the digital date: July 3. Diane recognized that date immediately, the day Rushdie spoke.

"What's this one? You, with these prep school boys on the sidewalk." Diane flashed the picture of the slim, uniformed young men at her, now dressed.

"Oh, I wanted you to see what you miss by not coming out with me. There are cute guys everywhere in this town."

"Those are local boys? They look pretty dashing in those nice school jackets," Diane commented, then looked at the date again. "You mean you didn't go to hear Rushdie?" Diane asked. "I take it the dates on the pictures are when they're taken, or are they when they're printed?"

"I never said I *did* go to hear Rushdie." Natalie brushed off the comment.

Diane studied Natalie as she wandered over to the front windows and looked out, rearranged the notepads on the table as she passed it, crossed back to her room, made a rustling commotion there and reappeared with a hair brush. With Diane thinking all the while, piecing together a number of details that were coursing through her brain, Natalie faded from her attention, but the restless motions drew Diane back to the moment.

"You're right. You never mentioned it. I was just surprised, that's all, when I saw the date on this photo. Where did you take this?"

"Oh, I met those guys a few nights before that picture, in fact the first night we were here. Classic idle young men, probably up to something. I've seen enough of those in New York to recognize the type. You know, it's funny. Now that you mention Rushdie – boy, that was last week's news, wasn't it? – they asked me that too. 'Why aren't you at Rushdie? Did everyone else go to it?' It surprised me that they even knew the name. They just aren't literary types, you know? But they were kind of attractive in the *my parents would just hate it if I knew them* way that can be so irresistible. To catch them out in the afternoon for a good picture was a real treat." Natalie stared absently past the photo in Diane's hand, then down at her toes.

Diane had seen the same look on the faces of the New York debutantes at Emerson House her freshman year, when they had flocked to meet her juggler friends who visited. *'Circus performers!'* a few of them had squealed. *'How mother and father would disapprove of me talking to them!'* they had declared as they rushed forward to meet the young men. Diane stifled a chuckle, thinking back.

Diane looked at the photo again, remembered the July third afternoon vividly. The rest of the Dining Hall had emptied immediately from lunch to go to the Rushdie event. Courtney had been bored! Diane took a nap. That's right! There were smokers under her window, so she wasn't the only one who had missed Rushdie's appearance. Yet Dr Steele had made such a forceful statement, like using the power of suggestion, commanding Diane to join them. She hadn't fallen for that.

"Where was this taken?" Diane asked, studying the picture.

"Oh, way across town. You've never been there. That disco is open all night. A real shady place after dark, but that afternoon it was busy and normal. You know, a typical touristy stop for tea and late lunch. I was so glad to meet up with these three again, that I got Brandon to snap the shot when they weren't looking. I was hoping to bump into them again – the accent on this tall one is gorgeous – but they must have gotten hauled off for some infraction. Fighting on the street after bar close or robbing a tourist in the restroom at a pub. Yeh, they were very edgy."

So, it was Brandon she was hanging around with. That's right, Brandon and Tucker for the first week of the program. They had all moved on to others now, evidently.

The dreamy look in her roommate's eyes hinted at more intrigue of the romantic sort, something Diane recognized from her own undergraduate days among rockers. Attractive, exciting times – or so it seems when you're caught up in the moment. The memory familiar, yet tinged now with little interest in the thrill of marauding after dark, she moved on.

These several and long sentences from Natalie filled in more than Diane needed to know to identify where her suite mate kept herself most nights. This room – Sixteen-C – serving as just a storage place for her vast wardrobe. Like a dressing room for quick costume changes. Natalie, such a puzzle of calming and thoughtful comments, backed with a very different sort of life away from Diane. Interesting.

* * *

Unbelievable. That was the word for it. Trips to England carry with them expectations of castles and Anglo-Saxon history encounters. Diane enjoyed every detail of those, but never fit the mold for what most would stumble across. Now this: bump into the Dalai Lama.

That evening, the Trinity motorcoach approached the massive Barbican, a concrete bunker with a pleasant lakeside terrace and view of St Paul's Cathedral dome. As the coach crept through arrival traffic, Diane caught a glimpse of an orange robe. A Buddhist monk or two, not an unusual sight anywhere these days. The wave of robes, however, swelled as the Trinity students unloaded and ambled with the crowd toward the theater entrance. Something unexpected was going on. This was confirmed for Diane when she caught a glimpse of two white women with shaved heads dressed in Buddhist robes. She'd never seen that before. Whispers began circulating with the words: the Dalai Lama. "What's he doing here?" everyone was saying at once. The electricity crackled as they entered the multilevel lobby and wended upward toward the space presenting *Richard III*.

Rising above the ground floor gathering of heads, Diane raked the crowd from the balcony. Orange and yellow robes. Shaved heads. And sure enough, there across the lobby stood the chief of the Tibetan Buddhists. Just then, tasteful recorded trumpets heralded curtain time.

Once all were aboard the motorcoach for home, a boy and his

mother climbed on board: the young actor had played one of the murdered young Princes in the production. Diane delighted in it! Another vote for British sensibilities, as the mother explained that nightly they checked the line of departing coaches looking for a lift to their car park, just this side of Oxford. "It just makes sense to share a ride, doesn't it?" the woman said.

By the jocular reactions of the Trinity students as they made room for the young boy, Diane sensed that this must be the first time they'd ever spoken with an actor. Never gone backstage to meet friends, as Diane did by habit. It looked to Diane that the ten year old boy – half the age of those college kids – fit right in, perched on the arm of a seat, entertaining a new crowd as the motorcoach pulled away.

Diane sank back into her seat and savored the memory of the ginger ice cream she'd bought during intermission. How refreshing, exotic! That thought brought her back to the beginning of the evening. The Dalai Lama. Not a trace of his gathering remained when *Richard III* let out. She'd already lost sight of her thrill at spotting him there in the crowd. She had felt transfixed for a moment, as if she'd been clouted by the spiritual heavens at seeing such a wondrous sight completely by chance.

So much excitement. She wasn't aware of the Dalai Lama visiting anywhere in the West. Must have been a really big deal for London, as well as for her. He'd remained a ghostly filament of a person, more just a concept, until she was so suddenly face to face with him. Diane wondered if it meant something auspicious for her future. She liked to take advice from fortune cookies and random happenstance, if the message felt uplifting. This did.

Suddenly energized, she turned and faced her seat mate, Shawn. "Did you see him? The Dalai Lama?"

"The Dolly–who?" replied the sleepy theater goer.

"The Dalai Lama. The head of the Tibetan Buddhists. Didn't you see all those people in orange robes?"

"Yeh, but I didn't think much about it." Shawn remained an inert lumpage next to her.

Daniel's face popped over the top of her seat: "Oh sure, Diane. Be all nuts over seeing the Dalai Lama, but when I said, *Salman Rushdie*, you said, *So what?*"

"Diane did not say, '*So what?*' She said that she wasn't going. Too scary. I was there when she said it." Diane's roommate stepped in from nowhere and wedged Shawn's sleepy lump right into the aisle. The unpredictable, bold moves from her nearly invisible roommate gave Diane a laugh.

Natalie's interruption gave Diane a minute to consider what to say to Daniel. Sometimes agreeing with someone makes a person consider the other side of things, she reflected. That's when she saw his complaint for perhaps what it really was. Diane turned all the way around now. "Daniel. That's sweet. You really wanted me to go to Rushdie. I'm sorry I disappointed you." They exchanged a look as the motor way lights pulsed by in a regular rhythm as the coach pulled onto the M40 and caught up to cruising speed. She could see he was thinking that over.

"Well, you missed it." Daniel slumped back into his seat and remained silent.

"Wonder why that lama guy was there?" Shawn leaned across the aisle now.

"Well, I'm sure he was seeing *Richard III* just like us. It's a classic!" Diane tried not to laugh as she pronounced this absurd combination. Nothing like taking the world leader for passivity to London and then buy him a ticket to one of Shakespeare's bloodiest plays.

"If he's the highest holy man in Tibet," Shawn traced his logic out loud, "I don't think he was seeing that play. That's like saying, like saying," he fished around for a comparison, "that the Pope goes ball-room dancing. Ridiculous."

"The Pope. Hmm," Diane began formulating. "He's from Poland, right? You think he's Polish and doesn't enjoy the Polka? I don't think he took a vow against that," Diane concluded in as matter-of-fact a tone as possible. She studied Shawn's confusion as she shifted into high comedy mode. "I'll ask Jan when I see him. That's a student from Poland at Trinity in the other program. I'm sure he'll know. And I'm sure the Pope's just a regular guy, Shawn."

"That's ridiculous. He's the head of an entire religion. Show some respect," Shawn half muttered.

"Hey! This Pope: what's the first thing he did?" She quizzed him. "He had Marvel Comics make a comic book about his life. Popes usually don't do that, either." Shawn glared at her, not willing to budge an inch. She continued: "He also invited The Ramones to give a concert in Vatican City. See? He wanted to look into what modern youths were interested in. That's why he picked a comic book and a punk rock band to start with." Shawn rolled his eyes. Diane had more news. "And what were his first travel plans?"

"No idea," Shawn said through clamped teeth. "The Moon?" he ventured.

"He went directly to Japan."

"No way."

"Yes, way. Not only is there a big population of Catholics there – that's a surprise, isn't it? – he wanted to get a better idea of what was going on in the world. Modernize. And the coolest thing happened on that visit," Diane was pulling this information from her friend Miyoko, whom she'd met in design class back in Denver. Diane had totally forgotten it until this moment. "My friend Miyoko said that the Pope passed a man begging there in Japan and stopped to talk to him. He saw something in his eyes. On the spot, he hired the beggar to become his translator and liaison officer. Took him back to Rome because he wanted to improve his understandings and the Church's relationship with Japan and Asia. In fact, my friend Miyoko spends Christmas with the Pope every year at The Vatican. Her mother flies in from Osaka, Miyoko from New York, now."

"Give me a break. That's crazy." A crowd of hecklers had formed around Diane.

"Nope! I thought she was mixed up or I wasn't understanding her accent. When she showed me a picture of herself with John Paul II, I said, *'Oh, that's nice,'* thinking he just stopped for a picture when she was there as a tourist, but no. That Japanese beggar the Pope hired went on to run a program for young Japanese girls to study at a Catholic school in Texas – of all places. Miyoko was a student there, and that's how she met the Pope, touring the Vatican with her classmates. From there, she started visiting him every Christmas. Just a regular guy, see?"

"How do you know all of this?!" Daniel's head had appeared hovering over her again, about the time she said: The Ramones.

"I don't know! I just like to talk to people!" Diane concluded, wondering how it was that she so often looked up and found herself in the middle of an audience.

At that moment, the intercom crackled a message: "C'mon up here, Loren. Your stop." The young actor bade goodbye to his listeners and squeezed past Diane's gathering. Everyone turned to hear his mother saying to the driver: "Wheatley, yes. We're just over in Wheatley. A simple drive from here. Ah, there's our car. Thank you so much. Cheers, everyone!"

Week FIVE

Friday, July 26

WITH A TWISTED SMILE, Diane saluted Dyan the next morning. *"'Who else will come out to speak?'* you said. You're so funny! You must have read it in the paper, didn't you?"

"I must admit, yes, being born on the sub-continent, I receive advance notice for such momentous occasions as a visit from the Dalai Lama. I knew you were heading that direction last night, but I didn't want to spoil the surprise for you, Miss Diane."

* * *

"Any ideas for a final paper topic?" Dr Harding concluded their session looking alert and ready to check Diane's name off his list.

"I want to write about Hardy's poems to his dead wife. They are love poems, but I am sensing something in them that seems just – off."

"What do you mean? Perhaps the making of ghoulish delights?" He grinned, though Diane didn't quite follow his point.

"No, not at all. Do you remember how you said he hadn't really even spoken to her, though he remained solely devoted to her all those years? You mentioned that when we visited their cottage, I believe."

"Yes? And?"

"Well, I think I have an interesting take on the poems and their marriage."

"Well," Professor Harding seemed to grow suddenly overheated and shifted in his chair. He looked eager to close the conversation, for he rushed to close her file and stand up, the signal that their meeting was over. "I have rarely had a student want to delve into the dark psyche of Thomas Hardy's poems to his first wife, but as Poet Laureate of England, they certainly are worth studying. I look forward to reading your attempt." Dr Hardy smiled stiffly, stepped toward the door, and opened it.

"Yes, as Poet Laureate he must have had something going for him," Diane said innocently as she gathered her few items. "Do you know, did Queen Victoria really like his poems?"

He looked at her as if she had just asked him to loan her a million dollars. "I don't quite know what you are getting at. She must have. The Queen chooses the poet."

"Well, maybe these poems will bear some scrutiny under the reign of the mourning Queen Victoria, as well," she said, just thinking of that aspect of the era.

"Fascinating," he said curtly and added: "Remember the guidelines. Handwritten, every other line and in my box here by the final Tuesday morning. I will of course see you again next Friday for our last session together."

Diane stepped out into the hallway. "I'll try to resist the urge to include illustrations, though it will be hard. Once I have that quill in my hand, sometimes I just can't stop myself."

Dr Harding stared at her, swallowed hard and didn't seem to enjoy the joke. "Do not forget, of course, the Hardy Hike on Tuesday morning. Seven o'clock sharp at The Lodge. The Dining Hall will be open for breakfast at half-six."

"Half-six. Right," she enunciated with enthusiasm. "Is that half an hour *before* six, or half an hour *after* six?" Her query seemed to accelerate his rush.

"Half an hour *after* six. How peculiar to clarify." His face thought over something serious. He closed his door, saying: "Cheers, then. Good luck."

* * *

"Yes, I'm afraid that as we come down to the wire, we will all have to share the last two books. We came up scarce on the Pat Barker and Jane Rogers titles, but if we stick to this plan, we can get everyone a chance to read." Constance handed a typed list across to Diane. "Two hours per session, then hand off to next person. The exchange will be the Dining Hall foyer, a nice, easy spot for everyone to access."

Diane leaned back and looked at the list of names. Their staircase and room numbers were also listed.

Connie saw her smiling and added mildly: "Along with the room number, yes. Just in case. I expect a few of the girls will lose track of the time."

"And hog the book?"

"Yes, you caught my drift," Connie laughed but looked concerned, perhaps over Diane's choice of word for *monopolize*.

"You are not only beautiful, but also very wise." Diane joined in, finding at last the right compliment.

"Experience with students," Connie confirmed modestly after weighing Diane's statement for a moment. "Say, I hear you had an experience yourself at the Barbican last night. I must say that seeing the Dalai Lama would be a memorable occasion, if only glimpsed from across the room. What did you think?"

"Yes, it was pretty surprising. There he was." Diane recapped the hints, the whispers and the moment, spotting him from the balcony.

Connie picked up on the moment. "Yes. Such a paragon of peace. I am sure he was there to share his message."

"Nonsense. I'm sure he was there to see *Richard III*, just like the rest of us," Diane said with a straight face.

Connie's flabbergasted look turned into a peal of laughter. "Very funny, Diane."

"More surprising, but not quite so funny, was how many of our group noticed the orange robes everywhere, but really had no idea who the Dalai Lama is."

"That is incredible, isn't it?" Connie removed her glasses and tapped one bow against her lips, thinking, then looked Diane in the eye. "While reflecting on peaceful life choices, I must tell you that a tiny bit of a story came back to me about your last visit to Stratford. You gave your lunch to a homeless man? That was very kind of you. What ever possessed you?"

"They give us so much food, can you really just throw the extras away? When I saw a few homeless men digging in the trash, I figured why not give it to one of them?"

"Again, I must tell you that your perceptions of your surroundings are far beyond your classmates. Now, now, don't give me the *because I am ten years older I speech*, I want to pay you the compliment you deserve. Hearing of it certainly touched my heart. Perhaps you know that I was a Carmelite nun? My work was mainly in a street mission, actually in a soup kitchen, in a rather run down part of a depressed industrial town."

"That's interesting! I had pictured you..." Diane began.

Constance cut her off with a kind smile. "You pictured me in Twelfth Century garb, silent and cloistered in the French countryside, didn't you? That's our modern romanticized notion for nuns. Peaceful, idyllic and staged in elaborate costumes."

Diane nodded and smiled, reorienting her former picture of the beautiful Sister Mary Constance. She had no idea what modern nuns do. "Serving soup? Well, when I was fourteen, I tried to join Mother Teresa's group in Calcutta. I wanted to carry dying people off the streets. I guess some of that inclination has stayed with me, even though they wouldn't take me. Couldn't speak Hindu, I mean Hindi. I was useless to them. But I can hand out a sandwich and bag of crisps."

"Ah yes, Mother Teresa's work is so beneficial. Joining her sisters is a notion many girls have." She became thoughtful again, then she peered at Diane over her reading glasses. "But let me tell you, in Nun Training 101, we learned to discourage talented young girls from choosing the convent. Face it: well-off white girls have powerful parents with plans for their daughters' futures."

"That explains it!" Diane nearly shouted. "Sister Mary Aloysius had said *'You're too pretty to be a nun.'* I always wondered where a crack like that came from, let alone what it said about how she thought of herself. How funny." Diane laughed harder.

"I'm sure there are more hilarious details. Escape stories are like that." Constance paused again, lost in thought. "Well, my parents' plans for my future didn't deter me. I was determined to set my own path and join. And that alone was telling. Afterwards, I learned that obedience was not my strong suit. I think now that I could have joined the Royal British Army and come to the same conclusions, as well as having been out again in four years' time." She laughed. "And maybe I was looking for the romanticism. Writing secretly at night by candlelight behind a great fortress. Something like a castle, isn't it? Good thing I rescued myself! I never thought nunhood would be a job in social work."

"Shows how realities can be far different from daydreams," Diane added, sobering. Like her own art degree. She'd pictured herself leaping forward, engaged in interesting work, beautifying her surroundings. Where had that gotten her? The thought drifted away as she regarded Connie, whose efforts thwarted her own first steps into adulthood as well.

"I'm glad you feel comfortable enough with me to share that personal story, Diane. Had you told me this upon first meeting, I would have doubted your sincerity. It is easy, and I suppose natural, to hear the word 'nun' and tell a stranger your story. For whatever reason, people get very edgy around nuns. Vicars say the same. People want to confess to relative strangers. Easy to tell and run. Makes them feel better. As for nun stories, it seems most girls have given some thought to what it might be like to live in the convent. Away from men. Someone making all their decisions for them. Sounds very attractive at certain times in life. I could collect 'How I escaped becoming a nun' stories and publish them as a study, or a warning." She chuckled to herself without explaining exactly why that amused her. "One moment." She made a note in a black leather bound notebook from the table at her side, looked guilty, then added: "If indeed I collect escape stories, I'll contact you for yours. Perhaps it could be a collaborative work? I find collaboration an excellent way to motivate students to publish."

Publish?! Diane's face must have shouted it, because Bede simply smiled and said, "Yes. Diane. You show signs of brilliance. I hope you know that."

"A few professors at Smith might die of shock hearing that. They weren't impressed with my writing."

"I find that hard to believe. In what way?"

"Well, they often – often! – said my arguments were not substantiated enough. I needed to prove it using the theories we studied, and that may have been very true. Sometimes, however, I thought they were being overly cautious. I wondered what they meant: prove it to whom? It started to feel to me as if they were looking for the nod of approval from some august institution – maybe like Oxford or Cambridge – before proceeding. It seemed to me like they were afraid to step forward and innovate."

"I find that astonishing since I usually think of Americans as mavericks, wanting to break new ground. And that is what I sense in your discussions."

"Well, trust me, Smith professors didn't care much for my theories."

"Well, I look forward to your final written work, capturing the marvelous interconnections from such diverse sources. And Diane," Connie added, "most people are capable of serving soup to the needy. Not everyone can think and write as you do."

Saturday, July 27. London

"You see?" Natalie said when they came out of the Royal Academy of Art. "No big banner for the Rosa Martínez Retrospective like the other shows have. Just the temporary sign in a kiosk in the lobby. That's not exactly fair, is it?" Constance had given Natalie the assignment to get to London for this show. Natalie had made a point of bringing her art historian roommate with her.

A retrospective. A life's work. Retrospectives happened once, and occasionally twice, during the life of an artist; therefore, by design, it constituted a definitive moment in time.

One hundred and seven major canvases had arrived for the Martínez show, all on loan. About two-thirds of her entire oeuvre, the short biography said. The main works were magnificent, monumental. They dwarfed Trinity's canvas, which Diane could only get a glimpse of over the crowd. Chandra had been right; *The Five Fellows* portrait possessed an intimacy the others lacked.

Natalie – a true New Yorker – grabbed Diane's arm at that viewing impasse and had burrowed them forward through the people blocking their view. She had also pulled Diane through to another smaller canvas. "The Dalai Lama, see? From the *Exiled Royalty* show in New York." The concept surprised Diane; she couldn't imagine him commissioning his own portrait. The wall tag informed her: *On loan from the artist's personal collection.* That made more sense.

Diane was glad to leave the overstuffed galleries and disappear into a quieter side room of Rosa Martínez's early works. Diane usually found these aspects more revealing. An artist may have prodigy status from the crib, spinning out masterful or inventive genius, clearly superior to their toddler cohorts – but not often. Diane loved seeing the fledgling efforts – shaky and tentative – that, through continued study and practice, grew into masterful and often inventive iterations that then developed into a style or themes immediately identifiable with the artist. From what Diane saw, the young Martínez girl arrived at the drawing pad with an innate sense of inner personalities. That talent radiated from the first animals she drew at the Central Park Zoo near her childhood home, that then extended into portraits of grandparents and elderly neighbors – a momentous shift seen at age twelve. Her family's return to London in 1958 facilitated her studies at the Royal Academy of Art in The Hague, and her nomination to the Royal Academy of Art, London, in 1990.

Diane paused at the sidewalk, full of things to say. "I wanted to see that one Beatle portrait in person, since I'll never see a Beatle. Too bad it wasn't there."

"Perhaps he could be parted from it?" Natalie said, sliding her eyes sideways at Diane.

"Funny. Well, nice turnout for Rosa. That crowd in there reminded me of that big Picasso show that came through Denver. *'Your one chance to see Picasso's work,'* the brochure said, and people believed it! As if people in the middle of the country are incapable of traveling anywhere? We're not a herd of cows." She broke into laughter, seeing the irony just then: "It actually packed the museum so you *couldn't* see a Picasso."

Natalie winced. "I can relate, actually. Being lumped into a group. I'll tell you what it's like to be me, sometime," but she didn't complete the thought, having already chosen their next stop. "Have you seen this? The West End is the theater district. Though of course, the Barbican, monstrosity that it is, is across town. You said you take in a lot of theater in Denver so I thought you might like to stroll through here." They turned left down the street. "Have you seen many shows in New York?" Natalie asked as they walked toward Piccadilly Circus and finally arrived at Regency Street.

"No. Not at those prices," Diane scoffed despite herself.

Waiting for the signal to cross again, they stood awash in noisy traffic, sidewalks vibrant with people who moved as though they all had somewhere important to be.

Across the street, through all the traffic, Diane eyed the splashy marquee for the Criterion Theatre. Under it, a Hawaiian shirt caught her attention. You don't see many of those in London, she thought to herself. The man wearing it was standing peacefully, watching the crowd. The bold black lettering above him stated: *Three Bobs & A Mario in: "Counting on Monte Cristo."*

"Unbelievable!" Diane said out loud. It must be Mario. She and Natalie crossed with the crowd and continued with them past the ticket kiosk toward the theater. From there Diane could make out the distinctive scar on the man's right cheek. That's when Diane gasped.

"Mario?!" she shouted to him now just a few paces off, not trusting her eyes. He turned. At the same time, Diane knew that no one but Mario wore a heart-shaped pin on the lapel of a Hawaiian shirt. "Oh my gosh!!" she yelped. At that moment, a tall, slim man stepped out of the restaurant next door and joined Mario. "You guys!" She called and grabbed David and Mario by the arm, thrilled to see both of them.

"Oh hi, Diane. Imagine meeting you here," David said from his superior height. Always matter-of-fact. Such world travelers, she thought. Hasn't seen me in four or five years and yet, they must have gotten used to every kind of strange coincidence that could possibly happen.

"We've got to stop meeting like this," Mario said coyly, and planted a little kiss on her cheek. Just then, the other two *Bobs* came out of the restaurant and stopped when they saw her.

Her heart felt like it jolted to a stop as she remembered the other thing. "Kevin! Rick! I found an old poster of you guys in the drugstore, on the bulletin board! Up in Oxford, where I'm in school." She grabbed Mario and gave him another big squeeze. "I can't believe this. Why didn't I know you'd be here?"

"Not here for long, though. We close tonight. Hey," said Mario, thinking aloud.

"Great to see you!" Kevin gave her a big squeeze. "You must come to the show tonight. Closing night. You haven't seen this show yet, have you? We're looking for a Denver booking but maybe next year.

"After the Kennedy Center run," said David.

"Then The Helen Hayes," said Mario.

"And that movie filming. Another movie. I'm still worn out from the last one," Rick added. She turned to him, the one she had found most attractive, the one she used to follow around. He looked like he'd aged a good deal as he leaned back against the building.

"Well, you're in for a real treat tonight," Kevin continued, always the leader.

"It's sold out, but we can squeeze you into the lighting booth," Mario added.

"It's thrilling to be playing in London's famous theater district, but..." Kevin broke off.

"Honestly, we feel uncomfortable in such a fancy theater," David continued. "The arty people who usually come to our shows can't possibly afford the tickets. It's a completely different audience from the one we're used to."

"We're not sure if we like it," Kevin added, "but hey –"

"That's show biz!" they concluded in unison. She had forgotten their tag-team style of speaking, a holdover from their act. They hadn't outgrown it. Everything became a comedy routine with stylized delivery. She also noted the tired look in their eyes, something she hadn't seen when they'd first met over ten years ago in Denver. They played the renaissance festival circuit and had gotten their first stage booking in Denver. Diane went to the show every night. Here in 1996 London, no longer were stray pieces of straw lodged in their long hair, either. They looked clean, satisfied, relaxed – or was it worn out?

So there they were. All four of them. Denver audiences went crazy over their fast-paced physical comedy from the start. They suddenly had bookings all over the globe, yet remained in touch with Diane until fairly recently. Yet all standing here, out of their trademark yellow tuxedo tailcoats and silk jockey caps, they resembled any other four young men. They could be from Amsterdam, Cairo or California in their comfortable casual clothes.

None of *The Three Bobs* was actually named Bob, but they enjoyed blurring their identities. The shared, generic name worked, in addition to all of them looking alike: slim as panthers and each about six feet tall. It all added up to moments of well-planned confusion in their act, something like the Marx Brothers, who with the addition of the black mustache and eyebrow-bearing glasses or blond fright wig readily interchanged roles as well early in their stage careers. As for Mario, the miniature one, he had short hair and wore round wire-rimmed glasses. He reveled in his unique appearance as well as the undivided attention he received as the one and only Mario. And so, Kevin and David – who were Bobs – and Rick – the third Bob – had not only developed into a cohesive unit for their extraordinary stage act, but because of their travels, were rarely apart for more than a few minutes each day, especially in the days when they traveled by bus, playing a different college every night. This lament had been a recurrent theme in Rick's cards.

"Look, Diane," sparkled Kevin, "come to the show tonight, after that we'll climb into the coach for Edinburgh. We're going to catch up with a few old friends setting up for the theater festival there. You should come with us."

"Come with us. Like the old days." They all grinned, even Rick.

"I can't. I have school work. *This* is my day off." Diane laughed, caught up in the easy rapport, as usual.

"Skip it!" they again spoke in unison, watching her like a Greek chorus.

What a magnetic group. Yet Rick was leaning back again, against a bit of wall, stand-offish in a way she saw only once back in Colorado, but remembered from Boston. Moody. Sullen. Not really cut out for the life of travel. Like Travis, really. Back in Denver. They had left Travis there, along with a new wife, along with three-year-old twins who were probably destined for showbiz as well, considering their blazing orange hair and their training in gymnastic tumbling skills. Travis and his wife must have set this all in motion while Rita taught yoga upside down during every day of her pregnancy. Prodigy tumblers they were. Not convenient for hitting the road, however.

Rick's sullenness had been enough to send her thoughts off in other directions. Old boyfriends, she thought now. In lonely times, how much we long to see them and then we do! This old boyfriend was proving fun for about two minutes, then the clarity of why she'd lost interest set in. Even the late hours of theater coupled with matinees and tech rehearsals set Rick in a disoriented world of his own. How miserable he'd been during that long run in Boston; she remembered that. That was only a hint of the weary sadness she saw in him today.

Diane noted the sidelong looks from the newest groupies, who had wandered out of the restaurant after Rick and Kevin, but remained at a distance, eyeing her suspiciously. Waiting and glaring mildly at the new arrival who might afford them some competition. Oh, these talented, attractive men! Diane thought to herself. Always in demand.

And look at them: selling out this huge theater. She studied their poster in the case. The photo showed *Three Bobs & A Mario* in real tuxedos – with dry cleaning! She laughed to herself recalling the characteristic scent of sweat and travel that lingered in their first, rag-tag costumes. She wondered how these new gals would have liked them back then. Look how far they'd come in the last few years. Their meteoric rise was legend among Denver theater-types. Diane had suffered through a number of other local acts who tried to mimic *The Three Bobs'* style the minute the troupe went away on tour. The others, performing with admiration mixed with rivalry, fell flat without the originators behind the scripts. Just cheap copies.

"Impossible, I'm afraid," Diane gritted her teeth and said it. "Today was one of the only idle moments in the program schedule." Program! She thought. She had forgotten Natalie completely, waiting quietly at her side. "Oh! Sorry! This is my roommate from Trinity. Natalie."

Natalie's normal nonchalant look put on a calm and natural smile as the boys all turned their attention to her for a split second, also in unison, a duplicate experience for Diane, when she had introduced Alexandra to them in Boston. She rushed to tell them the news.

"Oh! Did you know? Alexandra, my friend from Smith who drew your picture – the one you used to have on all your posters?" she filled in when no one seemed to recognize the reference. "She died recently. I just found out."

"No kidding?" Mario said, while the other two murmured generally sad sounds, but kept the corner of their eyes on the four women waiting for them. Rick just stared at her blankly. Diane was shocked. This tremendous news was not registering with them. She felt terribly disappointed. And there was Rick, still removed. How things changed.

A mixture of bittersweet memories assailed her. So much of her education at Smith happened in adventures outside the classroom, beyond the campus, outside the books. A great time for exploring and learning. *The Bobs* had been a bit of that.

"That time, when we all met up in Boston at Harvard Yard," Diane told them now, "and I skipped class to see you, well! I can still remember the result." She vividly recalled the fun weekend in Boston, but also remembered the mess it had caused, with a larger penalty than she had expected. She'd missed a chamber choir rehearsal, thinking it wouldn't be a big deal. It was. The director never gave her another solo piece, probably convinced she'd just begun on a reckless and possibly escalating set of adventures. That ramification hadn't occurred to her as she and Alexandra had hopped on the Trailways bus to Boston, filled with anticipation and excitement. But you couldn't have an expert chorale if members cut rehearsals, Diane understood later, after the *how unfair!* stage wore off. That lesson showed her that even her beloved spontaneity must find a balance with responsibility. A promise made, then broken, could undo a lot of respect. It was her decision not to burn herself again. Here in England, she'd set aside the time to study; therefore she would study.

"Priorities, boys!" she enunciated upward into their familiar faces. "You don't skip class at Oxford, because you're the only student in it. Did you know that?"

"The other kids will fill in for..." Mario began.

"No! There *are* no other kids. That's the point. One student, one professor. That's the superiority of the education there." She held her ground as she watched their responses.

They looked at her with a mixture of wanting her company – perhaps the chance to hear another voice from home – and respecting her enviable situation.

"Wow! We knew you had superior gray matter," David said patting her on the head, "but – *that's* a program." She saw a light in their eyes she'd never seen before. Maybe up until this moment, just now, when she clarified her reasoning, she'd been just another cute girl at the stage door to them? Maybe. Dating theater people. Well, Diane had had enough of that.

"Yep." She smiled up at David and felt a need to wrap up this unexpected encounter, get back to life as she knew it right now. "Sorry, but I must be off. I bid you a wonderful time without me," she added with a queenly wave of the arm.

As Diane and Natalie rode the subway back to Victoria Station and got on the *Oxford Tube* back to school, Natalie said little. Diane was lost in her own thoughts. Once the coach reached cruising speed toward Oxford, Natalie said, "I'm so surprised you didn't go with them. I've seen them in New York, of course. They were the big ticket last year. And weren't they in that one movie, too? With Brad Pitt?" Natalie waited for Diane to confirm. "I didn't know you knew them. You should have gone."

Diane frowned. So much had been communicated in that random meeting with *The Bobs*. For Diane, getting into London on a little adventure outside the program was good enough. Then to bump into her old friends! Really amazing. And yet –

"You know, Natalie, seeing them out of context and so suddenly like that, I just didn't click back in. It felt like the time apart has divided us, which surprises me."

"Time and distance can be like that," Natalie agreed blandly, then ventured: "Are they old sweethearts?"

"No. Well... maybe that's it. Everything is different from what it was like when they were getting started." Diane paused for a long while, putting it into order and seeing that it stretched far wider for her than just *The Bobs*. "You know, it's probably not that interesting."

"No, go ahead," Natalie cooed.

"I used to have a big group of theater friends in Denver. *The Three Bobs* were part of that. And no, we really weren't sweethearts – ever – sorry to disappoint you! Just pals, like all my guy friends. When I married, all those guy friends disappeared. Suddenly. Fine, I thought. Maybe that's the way it would be when you're married. I did want to be hanging around with Max then, naturally. But then, I got divorced four years later and looked up my old friends." She paused again, putting more pieces into place after today's encounter. "So those great friends, total pals, who never made a move on me, never even engaged in meaningful eye contact, turned out, the minute I was free, they all sprang forward and tossed their nets over me."

"Sure! What a catch you'd be," Natalie smiled at her. "So, you've broken a lot of hearts?"

"Turned down a lot of proposals? Yes." Diane didn't want to admit how many. She wasn't trying to show off, but that's the way others in the past had received the information. Diane decided to risk it, if only in the name of human comedy. "Eight in two weeks' time," she said, knowing she was lying. It had been twelve. The minute news of her divorce hit the street, her phone began ringing.

"That's insane," Natalie agreed. "You're so funny." Her roommate looked for the first time as if she didn't know exactly what to think regarding Diane, who looked more chagrined than pleased. "How could you get so many offers and turn them all down? Were they real proposals or just jokes? Bachelor uncles? The drunk old neighbor from down the block?"

"Oh, they were sincere, all right. My pals!" Diane paused, infuriated anew, then laughed. "And what does never making the slightest inference about their feelings say about their communication skills? I totally scoffed at each one in turn, well – after the first two or three. Can you picture anything as absurd as that?" The scowl on her face just now showed little amusement as she lapsed into reverie. "Luckily only one or two hounded me with flowers and stupid gifts after I said I wasn't interested. I really hated that! So, they asked; I said no; they vanished. I lost all my lifelong friends. It made me so mad. Never befriend men!" she concluded.

"Fascinating." Natalie said, but continued to study her. Diane saw that her look said that she hoped there was more, so she continued. These tales could stretch on late into the night. She watched the edges of the city flying by the window.

"The weirdest part of it was that not one of them asked me how I felt about *them*. Did *I* want to marry them? They all just decided, swooped in, declared how I exactly fit the bill for who would make them the perfect wife. None of them had even kissed me. I'm not kidding!" she added.

Natalie let out an amused snort, adding, "Very honorable."

"It was completely laughable! I mean, would you ever agree to marry someone who had never even kissed you?" Diane laughed for a long time over that.

Finally Natalie said, "Oh, you'd be surprised what it is to be a Hull." Diane opened her eyes a little wider, listening.

"You haven't heard of Hull, Massachusetts?"

"Oh," Diane said, knowing Hull was early in the colonial settlement and therefore of historic note.

"Yes. Oh," she continued quietly. "Here in England they have the

Hons. The Honorables, the daughters of minor noble families. At home, when someone hears my last name, they practically bow like I'm royalty. Do I deserve it? Do I like it? What a burden." She stared out the window past Diane for a long time. "And they all want to date you. Marry you. Then divorce you and take half your money. It's a cumbersome existence, being a Hull."

Diane was used to debutantes, if you could call it 'used to.' She had had some exposure to them at college. One or two told her dark, personal things when winter pressed down upon them all in the dorms, but generally, they didn't mix with the girl from Denver.

"And you talk about that Beatle portrait you hoped to see? My mother kept her Rosa Martínez at home, as well."

Diane's response momentarily stalled as she grasped the second level of it: the dollar signs.

"Yes. My mother spent months trying to decide. Was it better to show off her empty wall to friends and say *'London'* a lot, or was it better to invite people over and say that she refused to risk the shipment? She likes being thought of as *'the one who got away.'*"

They both leaned back in silent understanding.

Outside the coach window, the city's expanses finally gave way to countryside. Diane continued to mull over her day. Juggler friends in London. Amazing. But not really. Their casual response to the death of the mutual friend stunned her the most, she added to herself. The weight of it returned. Diane told Natalie briefly about her dead friend, the bizarre afternoon finding *The Three Bobs* poster at Boswell's. She left out the part about crying her eyes out in the Sheldonian cupola with Dr Chandra by her side.

Natalie listened in her silent, serious way. Sitting together, speaking in the hushed tone one uses to discuss private matters in public, Natalie surprised Diane by asking several questions about Alexandra, the artist friend, gone. What Natalie had to add was a deep understanding, a quiet wisdom and exactly the type of soothing concern Diane had heard in her voice the first night when she had bidden her, '*Sweet dreams.*' Maybe this trip would be the pivotal moment, a lasting friendship forming. The prospect was tantalizing.

Diane started recognizing landmarks as they approached the town. She thought about why *The Three Bobs* experience had fallen short of feeling fun, didn't linger with a thrill. She'd just randomly bumped into old friends five thousand miles away from home! She had enjoyed thoughts of them for years. Yet here she was. Not in Denver. Not just finishing college and moving home. She suddenly understood the difference the ten years had made on her. She wasn't feeling any kind of regret for missing the offer of a new adventure either; she, instead, reveled in choosing her own plan – classes at Oxford – and sticking with that focus. Steady commitment felt good. Accomplishing a major task of her own. And once she got her head back to the moment, while walking with Natalie past the gorgeous Radcliffe Camera, under the impressive Roman heads meant to intimidate her, and over to Trinity's front gate, she realized that she couldn't wait to tell Dyan about her meeting with the jugglers.

Monday, July 29

Diane opened her notebook and reviewed the outline she had put together on Sunday. Love poems Thomas Hardy had written to his late wife. Point one: he wrote these poems after she died. There are no poems for her while she lived with him for decades. In the poems he wishes for a farewell, a word of blessing from her for his future, but says no word of remorse for having lived in the same house, yet estranged from her, for over forty years. The physical person is noted as missing. Emma's spirit, however – who she was, what presence she had contributed to his home – is absent from the texts. Did he even know her spirit, the inner Emma? That became Diane's thesis. Now she was ready to flesh out the ideas.

Throughout the morning, therefore, she contemplated grief and absence. Diane's former marriage – her invisible ex-husband – came to mind. He had not intruded on her until that moment. There Thomas Hardy had been, living well-acquainted with solitude, yet missing the silent someone's company. How different had Diane's short marriage been? She asked herself, would my marriage have been like Hardy's if I'd allowed the four years to continue on the same path to forty? The sentiment had brushed against her own and set her up with an eye for minute details in Hardy's poems. Diane searched all morning for answers, perhaps to more than Hardy's own loveless existence with Emma.

Picking up on these thoughts after lunch, she was ready to write her first draft. The buzz of talking around her, however, made concentration difficult. She cleared her throat in the direction of Brandon and Tucker and held her two fingers against her lips when they glanced up. She caught herself thinking with grim humor: *Man, I would have made a great witch of a librarian, wouldn't I?* Finally, she collected her books and moved to the lower level, hoping for a quieter spot there.

Here too, the room was all animation, everyone operating in get-friendly mode. Despite the grimacing looks Diane shot at the noisier pairs, and their quick replies of, "Sorry!" Diane soon closed her notebook in surrender. Getting to know people is a wonderful thing; she tried to think happy thoughts. Deciding to apply yourselves to your studies is admirable. But it's the last week to do it, *so be quiet!* she added with inner vexation. Flexing her jaw muscles slightly, she stepped out into the lower hallway, wound up the back stairs, then stood in the Library entryway. Now where would she plant herself?

The Library Quad was filled with bird song. A few students had taken to the benches to read outdoors. One student, one bench: too territorial to intrude. Diane knew she didn't want to write in her room, although it was probably available. Her body would go into automatic after-lunch-nap mode if she tried to work there. The Dining Hall? She imagined her presence there would draw conversation from whoever wandered by, and that would be hard to resist. Maybe she could drag a lawn chair to the shade, face her back to anyone else and get back to it? Drag a wrought iron chair? She imagined it, tearing up the lawn all the way. Not an option. With Archie nowhere in sight, she gave up on that idea. She stepped into the garden, spotted Chandra sitting on a blanket under a tree with a book.

She went directly to him. "Hi, Dyan."

"Hello, Diane." He moved to rise to his feet as Diane sank down onto the lawn next to him. "Oh! You don't mind the grass?"

"Nope. Just like Jane in the *Tarzan* movies, I can do anything in a skirt." She let her books drop in an untidy pile next to her.

"Everything OK? What was that scowl on your face? You look like one of the barbered Roman heads. Worried about your class work?"

"No, actually. Both papers are in good shape. Just need some tightening up, then re-copying."

"As I expected. I couldn't imagine you leaving it for the last minute. Personally, this last week before the final moment is my most pleasurable time. The place becomes like a tomb for several days, the tension palpable! Then the knocks at my door, begging for extensions, which of course are out of the question with everyone jetting off." He chuckled.

"Tell them: *Sink or Swim*," she said, still disgruntled at being displaced from the Library.

"Excuse me? I am not familiar with – oh, oh. I see, I see," he began to giggle. "That's quite vindictive of you. Thinking back to your students in Denver, perhaps?"

"Oh, maybe!" Diane laughed. "It's an old Navy trick. My dad told me, they quite literally throw any sailor off the pier and walk away if he says that he can't swim. Decide to learn to swim, or drown. You signed up for the Navy."

"Be a man! How I love the American sense of rugged individualism. It is quite Spartan, isn't it?"

"It's harsh, but puts things in perspective. Your responsibility is your responsibility." *And that's how I was raised*, she added to herself, seeing that clearly for the first time.

Constance Bede passed them about this time. The usually quiet Madeleine hung at her elbow, the strains of her pleas easily recognizable. Constance greeted Diane and Chandra with a slight roll of her eyes. "Pleasant day," she nodded genially to them, then continued listening to her distraught student, possibly waiting for the storm to burn itself out.

"No, honestly. What's troubling you, Diane? Do you have a headache, perhaps?"

"Oh, I don't know. I just feel like I got chased out of the Library. Everyone is chatting merrily." Diane plucked at a piece of grass. "I wanted to write my paper and, well, I should just relax and enjoy the afternoon, I guess."

"I have a theory about all that; I've seen it often enough. What would you think if we enjoyed a piece of chocolate cake at The King's Arms and I enlighten you?" He laughed. "I have been told by several experts that chocolate is the perfect complement to Guinness. Shall we test the theory?"

"You hit me in my weak spot! Let's go."

They disappeared out the front gate and around the corner. She caught an image of them side by side in the window of Blackwell's Bookshop as they strolled along the street. The bright rays had illuminated them in a most pleasant manner, a golden glow radiating all around them like some Byzantine icon.

"I am so pleased that you never asked me where I am from," Chandra said to Diane without preface.

"Really? Well," Diane wondered for a moment at this non-sequitur. "People usually do ask, don't they? That's polite social conversation. It's not that I wasn't interested, Dyan, but after asking a few people that over the years, I've learned that it's an empty question. In your case, especially, since I've never been to India, I have no frame of reference. You can name your town and I wouldn't know you any better. It's polite, I guess, but pretty meaningless when you think about it. I'd rather ask you what you're reading now."

"Good show!" Chandra cheered. "You have such a refreshing attitude, Diane. Perhaps you already know that? Ah, here we are. Inside or out, do you think?" he asked as they crossed Parks Road to The King's Arms tavern.

"So you are widowed, I am guessing," Diane asked him, regarding his close cropped white beard and how it accentuated the deep dimples that played above his square jaw line. A man as personable as Chandra could not have gone through life alone. They fell into easy rapport. Their exchanges were pleasant and natural. Diane balked only momentarily at the concept of being attracted to the older man when Natalie had sprung it on her – when was that? Eons ago.

"Or hiding a wife back in India?" Chandra leaned slightly her way tilting his head playfully. "No, I don't mind your asking," he chuckled, reading her face.

"I've been contemplating widowers all day. Thomas Hardy's poems to his dead wife."

"Ah, I see." He nodded for her to go on.

"Everyone has their story, I find, if a person gives the time to listen. I hope yours is a good one."

"And as most are more than willing to talk about themselves, you shall have mine! But first!" He held up his fork ceremoniously. They clicked forks together and dove into their dark chocolate cake.

"My story is no secret, Diane, but perhaps more off the traditional path than you may have pictured for me. I was, in the traditional way, bound to a young girl from her childhood, awaiting the auspicious moment. These things are elaborately planned, as I am sure you know. Well, a minor disagreement befell our families during the in-between time, as I was completing my Bachelor of Arts here, ready to return to Bombay and marry. A member of my family quarreled with a member of my bride-to-be's family, over exactly what, I've never been sure. Perhaps an interpretation of Narayan's work? Who knows? Humans can be so amusing! But the subject didn't matter. As plans moved forward, an auspicious date for the marriage could not be found. That sealed it. The delays led to even greater stresses and finally, my fiancée's family broke off the arrangement. *Shameful*, my parents said! I would like to say I was devastated, but I confess, it did not affect me one way or the other. I only read of it in letters sent to me here, thus I was nearly completely removed from the emotional trauma my parents had to face.

"I had my studies and became lost in them. Perhaps I gave myself permission to disappear that way. I have rarely regretted it." He smiled at her, perhaps a little sadly, she thought. "So you learn my secret shame! I have never married. Shocking, I know," he said in mock horror.

Diane took his hand and pressed it briefly.

"Poor you," Diane found herself saying, picturing the traces of some long gone sadness. "But you're pretty cute – and smart," she added with a laugh. "Surely your parents immediately wished to attach you to someone else?"

"Such things are not done as lightly as you imagine, Diane." He looked at her in an assuring way. "When I emerged from my doctoral program several years later, I simply continued in my position here. Publishing papers gained me a satisfaction I felt most comfortable with, along with a rich life among fascinating minds and caring colleagues. A rich inner life is nothing to regret, Diane. The traditional path of marriage and children isn't for everyone. And fate is fate, which my elderly and wise parents found out. They eventually wrote to me that despite the history for it, they realized that they couldn't picture the next suitable infant as a useful match, with me more than thirty years her elder. The matter was allowed to come to a rest. I cannot say I have been unhappy with the outcome." His eyes twinkled. "Understanding woman, my mother."

Diane easily believed his tale, having come to know him as upbeat and contented. She wanted more story, however, so she asked: "Your theory about enjoying the afternoon? You were going to tell me that as well."

"Actually, the theory is about your noisy library that so unhinged you. Here's the theory. The last week of classes is here, so now we come to the desperate stage."

Diane's question must have registered on her face, for he said: "So easy to read you, Diane. Think of your term here like storytelling in literature, or in films, if you like. When people are thrown together for a set amount of time – even for six weeks of summer term – associations follow a strict development. First, the getting acquainted and exchanging of trivial facts stage. The quick development of intimacies about halfway through the experience stage."

"Then!" she stepped in, "the breaking off of connections and reforming with new friends – for those who have told too much! Like musical chairs: switch! Yes! I saw that at college, but even more intensely on the two weeks of choir tour I went on through Europe."

"You are a singer, as well?"

"Yes. I'm perfect," she frowned at him, then continued. "As I was saying, each singer came from different parts of Colorado, and despite a few rehearsals, we had only begun to know each other once we had our seats on the plane. One week into the tour – that's half way – our guide in Lucerne abruptly ended our history walk. No one was listening to her. Pairs were busy gazing into each other's eyes. No interest in history. She was incensed! None of the other kids seemed aware of her anger, or noticed that the tour had ended suddenly." She laughed merrily. "And! I just remembered this: for the trip home, you were seated next to the person you met on the way there. You should have seen the chagrin for those who had already dumped that person and moved on."

"Yes. The Switch, half-way," he laughed. "Too true. Then for those who continue more steadily, the last day brings the moment of desperate truth! The parting, imminent. Decisions made! And – poof! The goodbye and disappearance, as final as death."

"Or, if it's a film: the sudden marriage and off into the sunset," Diane added.

"And in most of Western literature, it plays out for the female character with a choice: *marry or die.* That's the ending. Oh, yes. I have observed this pattern over many, many terms here at Trinity," Chandra said. They returned to their last bite of cake, each wrapped in their own thoughts.

"My former husband," Diane began.

"And so! You were married. How fascinating." He looked at her differently, perhaps, but added, "I love it as stories unfold."

"No secret, either, though it seems like a different lifetime. Certainly a different place." Diane was increasingly aware that here in Oxford, Denver didn't exist. Her past marriage; had there even been one? "My husband was invisible. Very busy with projects. Actually, I think I have spent more time in your company, Dyan, than with my husband over the four years we were married. Really strange, but true nonetheless." She felt rather stunned to put it in those blunt terms, yet undeniable. "Then, in his absences and silences, I learned that he..."

She paused to think. How to put it? Just spit it out, Diane: *He was involved in criminal activities.*

"Was he seeing another woman?" Chandra prompted her.

"Ha! Maybe!" Diane nearly shouted, picturing Cherise Vander-Lyden, Max's boss who had her hand in all the Glampers' family affairs. Diane laughed at the absurdity of coming all the way to England for someone to state a – perhaps obvious – piece of her divorce puzzle. "I hadn't thought of that, but he hid a lot of things from me. Some of them criminal. Once I finally figured that out, I wanted nothing to do with him. That kind of behavior doesn't change." *And certainly doesn't go away if you ignore it*, she added to herself, shaking her head, remembering months upon months of pretending everything would right itself. It hadn't. And then the stolen art prints appeared. She shuddered.

"Unfortunately so," Chandra agreed. "Congratulations, Diane, for not enduring in silence. Think of the pitiable Mrs Hardy!" He burst into laughter. "And tomorrow, the big day. The Hardy Hike."

"I'm ready for it!" Diane raised her mug to that.

* * *

"What exactly are those?" Emily asked, looking intently at Diane's trousers before dinner.

"Riding jodhpurs. I've always wondered what they would be like. Don't they make you think of silent film directors? '*All ready on the set, CB.*'" She spoke through the megaphone of her fist, then turned to show them off from all angles. Emily seemed to enjoy them in that different light.

"Diane, did you bring ten trunks of clothing with you?" Laura asked, not able to contain her admiration for pulling that off.

"No, not at all. I trade about once a week at the OxFam shop across the street. You should go have a look. Cool, one-of-a-kind stuff." Just then, Jessica arrived without Courtney, for once. She took one glance at Diane's outfit and winced.

"Why on earth did you drag those old things with you? Hoping for a polo invitation?" Jessica's barb didn't quite hit the mark, but the next comment did. "I gave up an entire summer of riding to be here. Funny how I'd forgotten that until now." She sat down next to Diane, an unusual move.

Perhaps the Superior One's icy façade was melting? Perhaps she had forgiven Diane for all the many odd and challenging comments, and the embarrassing moments around Swamis?

Halfway through the dinner, Constance signaled for more wine and the Women's Lit final session gathered speed.

"I didn't like that *She Devil* book. Ruth is such a monster," Kate spoke up candidly, which registered as shock on her own face, two seconds after the utterance.

"All that surgery? Yuck!" Emily agreed.

"That's easy to see," Jessica negated those comments for her own superior insight. "My objection: Ruth knows everything. It's completely contrived." She was in good form tonight. All of them were, perhaps understanding that it was their last moment to impress. Diane joined in with gusto.

"Yes!" Diane nearly shouted. "That's the best point. Weldon presents Ruth with seemingly superhuman abilities, but look at it: *I* know all those things too, when I really stopped to think about it. Nothing was a surprise."

The faces registered confusion, shock, incredulous disbelief. Diane elaborated, counting the examples off on her fingers: "Look. Anyone can see that nursing homes sedate their patients because it's more convenient for the staff to care for them that way, right? You could get in there and salvage one resident. Then, think about it: I know where subversives hang out. I could buy forged documents and fake IDs through them. Write misleading official-looking business letters? A snap! Use costumes and makeup, take on a different persona at work? That can be done." Diane looked into each of the shocked faces in turn. "Just because I don't have the dire need to use those forbidden tactics to carry out a plan doesn't mean it's outside my abilities to do it successfully."

"What she did was totally impossible," Jessica insisted with a scoff of dismissal.

"Impossible? Why? Because we are women? We all know those things if we gave it some thought! Therefore, aren't we all super-women?" Diane rested her case.

The others chewed on Diane's confession with various reactions. Jessica continued the challenge: "You know where subversives hang out? Oh, right. We all know that."

"Yes, you do! Think about it," Diane pressed her. "If you live in a big city – or even a small town – you've seen them, identified them in a split second, and avoided them. The gas station. The bowling alley. The sleazy corner bar. Driving by in the nasty car. They're living with us every day, if we just notice them. Something akin to the invisibility of lesbians and homeless people."

That capped the dead silence at the table.

"Maybe that is true – some of it," Emily acquiesced. "In town, I always go to the deli by the route that sidesteps the most people asking for money." The admission impressed Diane, recalling that Emily was the one whose father always ordered for her.

Is it from my ten extra years of living that I learned all that? Diane asked herself and considered. She saw herself keeping her eye peeled on family driving trips, on her choir trip in high school, taking in every detail anytime she left the house, talking late into the night with all the very friendly people – and often with complete strangers – at the Renaissance Festival, chatting with the bus driver anytime she took the bus. She even struck up conversations with whoever she bumped into in the public restroom. It was just the way she was. So, no. She'd seen most of that stuff by the time she headed to college. *Does that mean I'm smarter? Or just more observant?* she wondered. The thought left her rather stunned.

At that moment Constance said thank you and good night to

everyone. The group disappeared in a hurry. Constance stepped over to Diane. "Fascinating places you've been, the things you've seen. It has been insightful getting to know you and I don't often find myself saying that to a student."

Diane, completely carried away with the discussion, realized at that moment that Constance had been there the entire time, just listening. She felt suddenly as if she had taken over someone else's class. "I'm not sure, Connie. I get the feeling the other girls either tune me out or see me as some alien dropped in from the Caleb Galaxy."

"Well, a few of the girls may shun you for the rest of the program as a complete criminal, most likely hiding a prison record, but other than that, it was a brilliant observation, Diane, really. Perhaps beyond belief for some, but you certainly have raised their awareness – however they treat you from here."

Tuesday, July 30 Hardy Hike

Diane arrived at The Lodge, seven AM sharp, to traverse Dorset's country paths with the other nineteen brave souls that would make up this year's Hardy Hike. She turned up, sporting a tropical print skirt that placed her in Honolulu, circa 1942, or perhaps cast her as a chorister from the musical *South Pacific*. Her plans to wear the beige tweed skirt with the generous pleats that allowed for easy climbing over fences had been foiled. The classic skirt had lost five percent of its classic size in the wash. Diane, unfortunately, had acquired an additional three percent on her part, as those McVitie's Digestive Biscuits continued to be served bounteously each day at ten and again at four. Thus she set forth in tropical print and hiking boots, an eyesore that Jessica could barely overlook. Jessica stayed near Professor Harding at the head of the pack, while Diane dawdled behind, picking up every little twig and interesting rock.

Diane had a grand but arduous day, traversing seventeen miles of rolling hills, stepping into a centuries-old sheep shearing barn built like a fortress cathedral, encountering a variety of staircase-like stiles for getting over enclosures without opening and closing gates, catching first sight of the chalk drawing of the Giant at Cerne Abbas on the same hillside he had occupied for millennia. The group continuing walking toward him for over an hour, every step making him more profoundly enormous as well as puzzling. And did the very naked Giant complain of her tropical costume? She laughed to herself, after the Superior One also avoided her through lunch in Cerne Abbas. No. *He may, in fact, benefit from a similar foliage-covered wrap*, Diane concluded, surveying the wild expanse of his ungirded loins. She did not bother Jessica with this observation.

At one point during the afternoon, Dr Harding called them together. "All right, everyone. Come place your hand on the handprint indented on this ancient stone pillar, as Tess and countless pilgrims before her have done." Diane observed the ritual for a moment or two, but preferred watching the clouds moving swiftly across the great expanse of sky she was enjoying on the hilltop meadow.

"C'mon Diane. It's an interesting sensation," Emily encouraged her, straightening up from the crouch it took to get at the hand-print.

"No thanks," Diane said, scanning the view, then added: "Doing so didn't bring Tess Derbyfield much luck." Dr Harding frowned. Perhaps she would discuss the relative powers of ancient upright stones with Archie upon their return to Oxford.

Once arriving back at the Oxford train depot – long after the doubling-back, slightly-lost part, reserved for the end of the day when spirits were flagging – Diane crawled into a cab, too exhausted to worry about where it might take her.

Diane's feet had never felt as burned, beat up and blistered. What she found once she peeled off her socks in her room would have made a fine scene in a horror movie. She pulled a chair over to her bedroom dresser and climbed up on it to soak her feet in the sink for an hour, while reevaluating her plans to go on that walking tour in The Cotswolds following the end of term.

Postcard: Ancient Dorset countryside.

> *July 30. Hardy Hike, Dorset. Seventeen miles. That's as the crow flies, maybe. Seventeen miles once you got there, and there was a lot of getting there to get there. Resisted the wisdom of refusing to stand up again after lunch at a sweet little café, and instead wait for the group's return. Would have made for a long and throbbing-footed wait, but could have drawn! I'm sure my big toenails will grow back by Christmas. I didn't know they could detach like that. Unwilling to admit defeat. (A painful pun.)*

Wednesday, July 31

Approximately twenty hours later, Diane eased her blistered feet into her good shoes and hobbled over to the sign-in board outside the Dining Hall. Instructions said: "Wednesday High Table Receptions: Four O'clock, Junior Common Room." No further directions.

Natalie had said: the Durham Quad. Diane peered around the corner, the octagon of rolled turf as perfect as ever. No one there. No sign. She knew that the farthest door was the Chapel. She therefore entered the only other door on the courtyard and ventured inside. Eventually, the hallway led her up a staircase and into a large lounge that contained about twenty well-dressed people and, incongruously, a television. Seeing it, the only one she'd come across in all of England, reminded her that these windows must be the ones the shouts of soccer fans had poured through the day she'd arrived. Now that she thought back to it, their cheers had been the only actual noise Diane had heard at Trinity all summer. Surprising, really. Usually, when a bunch of American kids gathered, it's a noisy affair. But not here. Maybe the grand architecture intimidated after all? Pages turning in books, pens scratching on notebook paper, few other sounds had emanated from Trinity, outside the ducklings quacking. Oh, that dog barked that one day. She guessed that scholarship – whoever was doing it – made few audible waves. Never even blaring stereos, now that Diane thought about it, just as she spotted the hors d'oeuvres and drinks table. Typical for colleges to have music broadcast into the common areas, like the Smith Quad: non-stop newest hits. Great stuff. Here, even the hubbub on the other side of the front palisade, where tourists thronged the sidewalks and tour buses choked Broad Street between mid-morning and mid-afternoon, even that noise rarely penetrated. No, this place was ideal for someone like Diane.

And so, Diane entered the quiet room full of perhaps a dozen students, several of the program's dons and the guest speaker: Dr

Julian Steele. He turned his perfectly groomed head her direction, and beamed. Diane broke into a grin, seeing him in his broad-shouldered majesty, especially as she realized at that same moment that she'd completely forgotten he existed. An eon must have passed since he urged her to go hear Rushdie.

It felt like a special treat to chat with the dons under different circumstances. Unusual too, to mingle with students one didn't sit with at meals or on the coach to and from theater events. Who was here? Dr Steele in the center of a group, naturally. She knew half the students by name, but they stood about like a scattering of lambs, first time out on their own. That made Steele the wolf, didn't it? Diane giggled as she scooped up a tiny glass of red wine, scanning the room while taking a sip. The powerful liquid clobbered her palate.

"So, you are a not sherry drinker?" Constance Bede greeted her. "Delightful though, isn't it? Once you get used to it. A true Oxford tradition."

Diane tried to swallow her grimace and act as casually as possible, an attempt at decorum in the face of the unexpected siege. "That's what this is? Sherry? You're right, I've never had it before." She scowled at the tiny stemmed glass.

"That was evident from the face you made, though I must say, you didn't spit it out as one of your classmates did just before you arrived. Ah, yes. Madeleine. There she is. Quite recovered now, I see," Constance added *sotto voce*. They turned to see Maddy, more flushed than usual, bobbing near Daniel as if he were a lifeline in a turbulent ocean.

Once everyone had assembled at the Library, Dr Steele's lecture, a history tour of Restoration London, included the ravages of the Plague Years and Great Fire of 1666. The speaker vindicated Diane's correct pronunciation of Pepys. Boldly through the past decade she'd said *PEEPS* – just like chicks at Easter time – and she dashed it off with authority. Unabashed, unafraid of sounding foolish. So what if someone laughed? Her comedian friends said sillier things just to get laughs. Her unrestrained pronunciation always created an embarrassed hush immediately afterward. And that from the best of the intellectual theater-types in Denver? Diane found their offstage fears quite surprising.

She was riveted on Steele from the moment he began. His mannerisms were identical to Marco the Magnificent's, a magician friend back in Denver, who had an electrifying ability to spring stupendous effects on his trusting audiences. Steele shared Marco's style: the scowling face to draw the audience into believing he was sharing intimate secrets with them alone. Creating that type of rapport was the first step to gaining their confidence and then – *wham*! Some horrible, unexpected disclosure or ghastly image shot a shockwave through the crowd. Thus did Dr Steele leap upon his audience. He was completely fabulous.

Diane chortled through the first half of the lecture, on the edge of her chair, willing to follow Steele wherever he led. But during the last half of the hour, she fought to stay focused. The libations at the reception combined devilishly with the warmth in the lecture room. Then Steele dimmed the lights for his slide presentation.

Once the lights came on, she sauntered with the dazed crowd back to the Dining Hall. Dr Chandra hovered just out of reach chatting with his students. As they entered the stone foyer, Diane stole over to Chandra to say: "Steele is just like a comic magician friend of mine back home. I can't wait to tell him!"

"Oh, I am sure he will love to hear that news, Diane." Chandra's eyes twinkled in the dim passageway. "And look here. My five old friends. Welcome back!" Chandra addressed the newly returned Martínez portrait. "Did you enjoy your holiday in London?" At that moment, Dr Steele swept by them. "Grab your chance to speak with Steele, Diane. I believe he is leaving town very soon. Summer holiday time for dons, you know."

Excited to tell Steele her news, she tripped after him, and yet finding herself unsteady on her feet, she decided to save her story for dessert. She circled the High Table twice before finding her place card. *Diane Quinnell* appeared, written in a delicate flourish, sitting prettily next to a tiny drawing of a two-headed dragon.

Diane sat down feeling blissfully relaxed. To her right sat Tommy, the student who hated Parisians, always hung back on the Hardy evenings in town and had declined joining the Hardy Hike. *Smart decision*, she granted him now, still suffering with every step the bandages on her heels and toes. To Diane's left, Professor Morrison of the Trinity economics department introduced himself succinctly.

The High Table diners settled with a few obligatory pleasantries and redundant commentary on the vast number of forks, spoons and stemmed glasses set out before each of them. Small talk. Seeing others do likewise, Madeleine reached forward toward her serviette just as Lawrence, the head waiter, gracefully captured it, gently snapped it and draped it over her lap. He then filled the right-most of her three stemmed glasses, and proceeded around the table with a deft hand. Diane vowed to taste each concoction, but leave the rest.

Diners fell upon their first course, as if to forestall speaking to strangers, Diane guessed. She spotted Daniel at the far end of the table, highly animated as usual. How had he managed to be up here again, she wondered. Maybe grad students got to sign up twice? Her gaze wandered across the table, over to the seminar director, Dr Steele seated next to him, then to the painting on the wall directly behind them. While they all had been hiking the Dorset countryside, the school's Foundress portrait had been returned, or rather, had been found by dining staff, hiding in the staircase to the Minstrel Loft. Mrs Whappington had told Diane the details after she had limped over to breakfast. The return of the portrait signaled a good omen for the end of term, Diane was certain. A doubly-auspicious moment, considering that it was recovered at the same time they reinstalled the Rosa Martínez *Five Fellows*, returned from The Royal Academy of Art.

Diane tried the next delicacy and a sip of the proper wine for it, as she smiled a squinty smile up at the Foundress, happy that she had come to no harm. In her tranquilized state, Diane felt boldly sure that it was, indeed, Anne Boleyn who looked back at her. The discovery felt like an excellent conversation starter at the overly quiet table.

"You must know," she asked Professor Morrison, who looked like he'd been at Trinity for a hundred years himself, "about that woman's portrait? How is it that everyone I've asked has a different identity for this woman?" Diane hoped for a definitive explanation. None came. She turned to Professor Morrison, who continued chewing politely, but motioned with his fork for her to go on.

She looked again at that necklace, set high on the throat. Perhaps it was a well-established fashion from the era. Did everybody have one? Diane began babbling merrily about costume fashions, trusting that all Englishmen must possess an innate knowledge of their country's historical details. "As you know, Professor Morrison, by the mid-Sixteenth Century, when that painting was painted, Anne Boleyn's French court styles were replaced by Mary Tudor's Spanish fashions. As for who that woman in the painting is, with the tight-fitting initialed necklace on her bare throat, which seems a duplicate of the initialed necklace that Holbein used to identify his sitters, I am sure it is Anne Boleyn. Yet I wondered: why would Anne Boleyn, King Henry VIII's second wife, beheaded in infamy – why would she be preserved here in the place of honor in an Oxford college dining hall?"

The professor on her left listened with undivided attention. He now swallowed, nodded, took a sip of water, and then concluded: "Couldn't tell you."

Diane's head felt muddled, especially after concocting such a recital. She surveyed her goblets, finding them emptier than she had planned.

After ages of eating, the tiny cup of espresso awaited the after dinner mints and nuts. Diane struggled to rise from the table. "These heavy chairs. No wonder you need a servant to pull them out for you," she told Professor Morrison when he attempted to assist her. Once standing, she leaned back over the table and grabbed her place card to add to her small treasures.

"Where's everyone going now?" Diane felt uncommonly friendly as the diners all rose and bumped their way out into the foyer. Once there, Diane grabbed Daniel's arm. "So! Usurping a spot at Head Table, eh? Hobnobbing with the head nobs?"

"No one else signed up and since it is the last one, I filled in." His cheeks were flushed red.

"And what about these gents? Did you notice them? All drinking." She made Daniel stop at the portrait of *The Five Fellows*. "Funny, isn't it? And what is it they drink? Port? Oh, no. Not for those gents. They go for the hard stuff. Whaddisit?" Diane's nose nearly touched the painting as she read the label. "Well, lookit, here. I'm not too drunk to read. Wait a minute. It's a good joke, Daniel. What's that? Whisky? That's strange." She tried to get a better focus on the glass decanter, made of classic cut glass, stopper in top, with no label of any kind. "No, no. The Fellows drink Glenlivet. I remember that clearly."

"How about that," Daniel humored her. "Are you coming out to the garden?"

Diane continued lecturing. "I remember it because it sounded like it has liver in it. Get it? Glen-livet: goes right to the liv-er." She tugged on Daniel's lapel urgently. "That's right, and Chandra also said he was wondering when humble senior tutors like him will have a budget for such delicacies. Where's Chandra anyway?" Diane stood up straighter and wheeled around to find Jessica leaning surprisingly close to her. The paw of the Superior One landed on Diane's shoulder.

"Say, Diane!" Jessica said, "Diane, you do know, don't you? You may think I don't like you, but actually you have been very entertaining." Courtney stood just behind her roommate and grinned sloppily over at Diane, as well.

"Well! That's great news! I live to entertain, so – Jolly good!" Diane felt wonderful. Just then, Dr Steele stepped into the foyer with the program director, and into Diane's colorful world. "Hey, Dr Steele: great lecture. And looky! Glad to see your favorite painting back in its proper spot, eh?" Diane accosted him with enthusiasm.

Without stopping, Dr Steele walked past her. "Good night, everyone," he said loudly, with a general backhanded flourish over his shoulder, and exited with Dr Clarence.

Once out of the Dining Hall, the fresh air cooled Diane's cheeks. As she wandered toward the garden with her new best friends, Jessica and Courtney – one under each arm – vivid images of her under-graduate years swam through her mind. She drew in a deep breath as they all stepped onto the lawn. The scent brought back images of magical moments, when warm spring rains in Northampton transformed the walk to classes into a surprising delight of budding trees or when frost encased every twig, every blade of grass with dazzling crystals. Being out in nature every day on the Smith campus had been a life-altering boon for the studious Diane. And here within Trinity's walls, the world was all congeniality, perpetual twilight and gentle breezes.

In the garden, Diane drank water and watched Courtney. An attractive young woman, Diane believed her to be, despite her affected ennui. She moved like a dancer, her erect posture and graceful placement of footsteps upon the lawn allowed her hair – a wispy mop, much like Twyla Tharp's signature 'do – to bob and sway with each movement, yet never block the view of the stage edge. Courtney, liberated from her ennui, or emboldened by whatever she'd been drinking at dinner, tried a different tack to ease her boredom. She sat down much too close to Dennis Sartorius. He stood abruptly, however, bowed, and moved to a different location. Courtney looked ready to hunt down a man like a *femme fatale* in a silent film. The opposite type to Sarah and Kate, who sat together and chatted nearby but not within speaking distance of any men. Diane wondered if they had ever been alone in the same room with a boy in their lives.

Diane's freshman roommate was something like these two, and foreign to Diane. Erin had been sent to girls' schools all her life, arriving at college with no idea of what boys were like or how to act around them. And act was the operative word, Diane found, as she watched encounters at mixers, when college boys traveled from Harvard, Yale – sometimes as far away as Duke in North Carolina – to meet Smith girls. Those legendary cocktail parties were the chance to find a man and secure an engagement before graduation, each man also fishing for a wife. Diane wondered why those capable, independent women would want to sign on to a man's future instead of making their own way. She believed the right time to look for a partner was once you'd entered your career field. She'd found Max in graphic design in Denver. And, well, maybe that hadn't worked out so well, but being in the same field had given them a shared interest to begin.

OK. Maybe she had the move-order all wrong, but marriage wasn't a chess game. Or was it?

That was the biggest point with her freshman roommate: no brothers. Diane didn't have any either, but had been raised by a down-to-earth, capable, tomboy mother. Definitely athletic. Dee's strong, accurate pitching arm, the best on the block, had every boy between five and twenty begging for Mrs Quinnell to come out and join their side in neighborhood street-ball games. She made sure her daughters could field a pop fly as well as throw a runner out at home. In that way Diane and her older sister had earned the respect of the other kids, along with self-respect for their own abilities.

Erin hadn't been as lucky; her mother focused on the girly virtues of being tidy, punctual and suitably agreeable whenever men spoke. She looked over at Sarah and Kate and wondered if their mothers had given them the same advice.

"So, Diane," Daniel asked. "Do you have any brothers or sisters?" Considering they had spent a good deal of time discussing everything from Rushdie to Japan, she found it interesting to hear this line from him in the garden. Perhaps the wine had warmed him up to try that first-date type of opening line.

"An older sister. My college roommate still occasionally reminds me of how I fell down on that score, not having a brother for her to marry." Diane laughed, still feeling the effects of the wine from dinner. "A quick and clever way to meet the right type of boy, actually. Each roommate's brother already had been pre-screened, as it were." *Now what on earth did I just tell him that for?*

She sobered for a moment, and regarded Daniel, his hair sticking up in back as usual. *Maybe I am just as sorry that she didn't have a brother for me either,* she found herself thinking for the first time. Diane didn't often slip into a maudlin state over her life, but just now, it landed on her like a large rock. She looked about her. The garden. The amazingly lovely evening. She felt her view drawn away and upward into the starry sky, as though she could look down from above and see herself seated there. Surrounded by a group of interesting students, several professors. Daniel, however, wasn't striking her as the one to discover, just as term ended. She turned to find Dr Chandra approaching.

"Ah. We meet again," he said, easily seating himself at her feet.

"Where have you been hiding? I wanted to ask you something, but now I forget what it was." Diane looked at Chandra, her mind half-occupied elsewhere. Daniel drifted from view. "Ah, this is that jacket I like so much." She reached over to feel the fabric on the sleeve. "Why haven't you added a crested patch to it, I wonder?"

"Oh, do you?" he smiled.

"Yes. I thought all professors and princes have those stitched onto their suit coats. Like Dr Steele," she added, remembering his crested patch that she'd been staring at all evening during the lecture. What did it represent? A lion? A dragon? A shield? She wasn't sure, due to his habit of bobbing forward to emphasize points. The image blurred for her, on top of the sherry and the semidarkness of the room. *Note to self, Diane: no sherry before dinner,* she reminded herself, a headache beginning to set in.

"Oh, Dr Steele's patch is a special one he has appended to each of his jackets. An honorary distinction from Harvard. I am sure if I had received such an honor, I would stitch them to my jackets as well,

Miss Diane." Diane was sure he batted his eye lashes at her with that last phrase.

That patch, that jacket... so she had seen it before. It aroused some familiar yet vague sensation. Had Steele been wearing that jacket at lunch the day she met him? The day they announced that Rushdie would speak. Perhaps. She recalled only the well-tailored cut of the back plackets of his navy blue blazer, as he rose and walked away from the table. That impression hadn't faded. At that first meeting, she had been sorry her mother hadn't been there to see Steele turn and stride away. Dee was always a sucker for a pair of broad shoulders and a trim waist, or so she said anytime they watched a Cary Grant movie together on late night television.

"So, Diane. Jessica said you are a teacher." Courtney made a stop at her best friend Diane's chair.

"A tutor at a prep school," Diane clarified. Her mounting headache triggered a candidness that urged her beyond a short, polite response. "A tutor is treated like the hired help, just like a century ago. Over the summer when I work with kids at their homes, I'm instructed to use the servants' entrance." She looked around the garden. Some of these kids probably had homes with servants' entrances, though there was a lack of them in Diane's neighborhood. Did she really want to return to that life, she suddenly wondered.

"Oh my. I hadn't pictured it. Like a caste system." Chandra said, picking up as Courtney drifted to the next intriguing person.

"A rigid class system, yes, though people pretend they don't see it and deny that it exists if you bring it up. I seem to be one of the few who mention it." Diane agreed. "That's always puzzled me: how and why Americans started acting like the aristocracy when we had set up the country to get rid of royal privilege. Ironic, yes?"

"Human nature? *My arrangement is better than your arrangement, simply because it is MINE?*" Chandra offered.

"I suppose. My romantic visions of grandeur that place me at the top? Or is it fragile egos with a need to make onlookers think they are superior? The pose points out instead inner feelings of inadequacy, perhaps." *I could be Courtney's thesis-saying sister, spouting philosophies like that,* she thought. But Chandra looked interested and no one else seemed to be listening to them, so she continued.

"I am already tired of the posturing at the school I teach at, and its larger form: fanaticism over winning sports events. And why wouldn't they win? They have financial resources in their district and more money in every family to start sports lessons as soon as their kids can walk. Now that's superiority, isn't it? *'We're better than you are!'* All those trophies prove it, don't they?" She gave in to bitter feelings that multiplied, once given free rein. "Professional sports teams, the same. *We win!* And is nationalism any different? *'We're better than you are!'"* she repeated.

Chandra's face lit up. He looked up at her in a singular way that seemed to say: *Aha! I have found her. The one who understands the Universe the way I understand it.* He cleared his throat and said quietly: "Diane. Will you join me for coffee?"

"Now?" she bellowed. Long past midnight, Diane's love of a good night's sleep easily outweighed this bizarre invitation to talk all night, even if it was only talk he was talking about, which she highly doubted by the way he was looking at her so steadily.

"Yes. Come to my room; I'll make coffee."

She was stunned by his transparent intentions, but rallied quickly. "Dr Chandra. No, thank you. I have some correspondence to catch up on." True. She felt a great need to be writing letters at this moment. An invitation for coffee in a professor's room after midnight? It was a classic setup for a joke. Perfect way to start a letter.

She rose immediately, wishing to be clear. Yet not wanting to offend the dear old man, she leaned very close to him, and she said: "I am old enough to know what *coffee* means, Dyan. Good night." With a laugh on her lips – she'd seen that graceful exit motif in Noel Coward plays – she stood full height and walked away, leaving him to sort it out for himself.

Near the iron fence to the Garden Quad, half-hidden in the dark, Archie and three students sat on the lawn in a line facing the Laundry Cottage. Diane shot them an inquiring look; Archie replied by placing his forefinger against his lips, then motioning her silently closer. "Hedgehogs," he said in a stage whisper. "Just about to pay a visit." Luke, Sam and Tamara glanced her way, ecstatic at the prospect.

Diane's world had just turned on its ear, and normal life went on with hedgehogs. It was the perfect reminder to just get over it.

With a graceful, single action, Diane spun the narrow door of Staircase Sixteen on its hinge and stepped inside before it snapped shut. She returned to her rooms half-amused but also surprisingly shaken. And why, she wondered. *Nothing wrong with being admired, Diane*, she told herself. As she walked up the uneven wooden staircase to her door, she laughed quietly. *'Catch up on some correspondence.'* What a silly excuse. I could have said: *'Wash out some sweaters.'* She laughed to herself, but wondered what the consequences would have been – coffee with Chandra? She unlocked her door and found that she again had the suite to herself.

'More letters to write?' Chandra's voice came back to her from the first night she left the garden. Maybe that's where she had pulled the excuse from, unbidden. She toyed with the idea, sat down with pen and paper for a few moments, set them down. She wasn't ready to tell anyone about this evening. And what would she do about it tomorrow? Would Chandra be waiting for her at breakfast as usual? Now that he had found his soul mate – she laughed to herself – would he begin dogging her everywhere? A battle raged in her mind, the conflict centering on what exactly did he want? And how would his increased attentions – oh, Diane was convinced of that – inflict themselves on her for the last week? She didn't want to have to speak harshly to chase him away, then spend the final week snubbing him or hiding.

And what did she want?

A moth fluttered through the open window and headed directly to the overhead light. Suddenly self-conscious, realizing her front window was visible to those who remained in the garden, she snapped off the light and groped her way back to her bedroom. What a bother! She mumbled, irritated that things were turning out this way. She plunked down on her bed and kicked off her shoes. And the worst part was, she really liked Chandra. His company had been so pleasant, the memory of his light laughter often accompanying her through the day.

Just this afternoon she had hoped he would pop his head into the Library, though she'd never seen him in the Library. Maybe today he'd arrive to get a book from the reserve closet, she had imagined, and then would find her, tell her a little joke.

Oh, why did he have to get that stupid idea into his head to ask her up to his room, let alone with everyone listening? *Men can be so annoying when they suddenly think they want something*, she cursed under her breath. Her thoughts raced as she lay there alone in the dark.

And Constance's comment came to mind as she wasn't falling asleep, even though her eyelids drooped like heavy velvet stage curtains. *'I notice Dyan chooses to sit with you.'*

Diane wasn't sure how she felt about any of this, as the breeze gently stirred the drapes, and set the leaves tapping lightly on her windowsill.

Thursday, August 1

Diane woke up early as usual, though walking slower after the late night in the garden. Now the real stiffness set in from Tuesday's all-day hike. Creaking down her staircase this morning, she decided to skip the Library visit, to wake up instead with a quiet stroll to the end of the garden and back. As she neared the chairs by the back gate where they'd all been last night, she decided to sit down and just be. The leaves in the old trees ruffled gently in the quiet morning breezes.

She dwelled on the first of two things: Dr Chandra's invitation to his room. Her head still groggy from a rotten night's sleep, she stared out at Parks Road and disengaged. Time passed. She decided that she should compare notes with Connie in class at eleven. And thinking of Connie, coffee started sounding very good to her. She took the long route past the President's Lodgings and through Durham Quad, allowing herself to perhaps put off seeing Chandra, just this time.

The second thing: that painting. It hadn't entered her mind again until she walked into the foyer of the Dining Hall for breakfast. She looked again: cut glass decanter. No label. And Chandra's voice from her first week of classes: '*The Glenlivet? When will we humble senior tutors have a budget for such delicacies?'*

She passed through the serving line and into the Hall.

"Too bad you missed it, Diane." Natalie called her over to her spot. "I saw you talking with Archie, but then you disappeared. Anyway, once Courtney had identified her prey, she assailed him directly and relentlessly. I stood there watching her: '*Here, have the rest of my drink,'* she said, and pressed her glass on Dr Harding."

"No!" Diane's mouth dropped open, recalling some vague image of Courtney making her dramatic, pouting exit several weeks ago, and Dr Harding, saying: '*What an extraordinary view.'*

"Yes!" Natalie filled in the details. "With the added steady pressure of leaning against him, she pressed him into the corner of the bench they shared, but he pulled a beautiful reversal, by saying, '*Have you spoken with Daniel?*' I don't know how he hit the mark so accurately, but Courtney must have found Daniel completely amusing, because they were still entwined on that bench at the far end of the garden hours later when I got in. Good thing the moon had set so I could slide by them without notice. How embarrassing! I'm surprised you couldn't hear them up in the room here. You should have been there when she pinned Harding, though; everyone exited, pronto."

So Daniel actually had been scouting for a friend. Diane recalled his silly '*any brothers or sisters?*' line. "Well, I hope we don't encounter Courtney twining herself around Daniel for the rest of term."

"Well, thankfully, that's only a few days now." Natalie tore open another tea packet.

Diane's concerns over Chandra had been trumped. Natalie had no idea of Diane's challenging night; Diane silently bless Courtney's ennui, totally knocking Diane and Chandra out of the spotlight.

Constance's earlier advice about how sounds travel, especially in summer, came back to Diane just then, confirming her plan. She must ask Constance: was Chandra one of those to find a new interest every term? She couldn't think that he did, but her mind raced with fear. *Wait a minute*, she corrected herself. *Fear over what?*

Diane grabbed up her tray and skipped a second cup of coffee, wanting to step out before Chandra showed up. Perhaps she could hide in the Library, then go for a walk through town, all the while convincing herself that she wasn't avoiding him.

Unfortunately, as she turned from the dish window, he had pulled up in front of *The Five Fellows*. Chandra skipped his usual greeting when he saw her face.

"Dyan, look at this." She forgot everything else and pointed to the decanter in the painting.

"Oh yes, look at that. That is not good."

"I noticed it last night but hoped I was mistaken. That's what I wanted to ask you." She took a deep breath and let it out. "Well. Who do I report it to? The Lodge?"

"Do you want me to come along with you, to corroborate what you have seen?"

"No. I'll do it." Diane said, believing it was her job. "I'll just pop up to The Lodge and tell them."

She walked directly through Durham Quad and passed under the clock tower, telling herself that everything would be fine. This wasn't going to be a repeat of her previous brush with stolen art. Stolen art wasn't going to be pursuing her everywhere she went. This discovery was sheer accident, a consequence of her paying attention to details that no one else bothered with, but a remembered dread had gripped her heart already. Deep in dark thoughts of her own, she nearly tripped over the teenage ducks as they crossed the path to greet her. "Quack-quack," they said now. No longer: *'Peep, peep, peep.'* Seeing them gave her a nice excuse to stop and think a little longer.

The clock tower chimed the half hour directly above her, making her jump. What time was it? She glanced up. Half-eight, as they said so quaintly here. It reminded her that she needed to be with Connie at ten, no, eleven. An hour later, the day following High Table. And papers due next Tuesday. Suddenly a long list of things needing to be completed flooded her mind. And she hadn't made a productive move this morning, had wasted time just staring out the back gate. That wasn't like her. And now, she was supposed to just walk in there and tell the Porter: *'a forgery of* The Five Fellows *is hanging in the Dining Hall.'* How much would that mess up the last days of her term? She began to panic, thinking about not finishing her work. *'No extensions.'* Chandra had said it. So had Constance. What would happen to all her plans for using this summer's credit to boost her position back in Denver if she was prevented from completing her work? Suddenly everything she had planned felt threatened.

Her mind raced: *My Thomas Hardy paper! It's nearly done. All I need to do is recopy it. All twelve pages, by hand. I've got until eleven to see*

Constance. I could easily get that taken care of. Then at least, if all the police investigations hold me up, I could probably manage to get Connie's paper done in between interrogations. I have no idea what the police are going to expect from me, but if I can just get Harding's paper done and turned in, I could then report the problem. Yes. That's it. I'll just skip along to the Library, finish that up and tell them after class. Or right after lunch. That painting isn't going anywhere.

And thus, she walked directly past The Lodge. At that moment, Mr Spencer stepped out to greet her. "Ah, Miss Quinnell. Any sign of N. Hull this morning?"

"Yes, yes. She is still at breakfast, if you hurry," Diane called over her shoulder, not to be delayed.

"I have a stack of letters for you, if you hold on – "

"Must run just now. I'll get them later!" she shouted now, feeling that obstacles were springing up like dragon's teeth to stop her from getting to the Library, and back to her work.

Archie cornered her as she turned into the Library Quad, chattier than she'd ever seen him. "Hello, Diane. Sorry you didn't stay to meet Eloise and Harold. They trundled out of the hedge just a few moments after you left us last night. Cute little beasties!"

"Maybe next time," she cut him off, as she kept to her pressing mission and disappeared through the Trinity Library doors.

Yes, time to get serious about that Hardy paper, she repeated under her breath. I'll have this done for tomorrow. Imagine the surprise in handing it to Dr Harding tomorrow instead of Tuesday! She giggled nervously at the triumph she pictured.

Unfortunately, the Library was packed with cooing couples. How could you get anything done here? She tried the lower floor. No luck there either. Jessica glared at her from her table. Back to normal. The place was useless to her. How would anyone get her work done? She shot out the lower door into the basement hallway where she paused to think what to do next. She peered down the hallway. Maybe a small meeting room would be open that she could invade?

The first door, no luck, but then she came upon an open door halfway down the hallway. There sat the College Historian busy at her desk, surrounded by filing cabinets. Diane hadn't seen her again since the start of term, but had thought of her often, wanting to settle the question about the painting above High Table. The need for an answer pressed upon her suddenly. She'd also forgotten the name. *Charlotte Ashcroft, Archivist* the plate on the open door stated. She looked up as Diane paused to knock.

"Oh hello, Charlotte. I'm Diane Quinnell. I was hoping to find a quiet spot to write out a paper – the Library is teeming with chat today." Diane tried to read the Archivist to see if this was a good time, then continued. "But while I'm here, I have had a question I've been wanting to ask you."

"By all means," Charlotte smiled pleasantly and set down her pen.

"Who is the woman in that portrait above the High Table, the one that has been missing the last couple of weeks. Is it, by any chance, Anne Boleyn?"

"No," Charlotte shook her head slightly, "though many visitors who see it assume it is Queen Mary Tudor or Queen Elizabeth I, probably due to the fashion of the dress. The woman is Lady Elizabeth Pope, the second or third wife – we're not sure which, due to divorce laws of the time – of Sir Thomas Pope, the Trinity College founder."

"And yet the initial on her necklace is a "B" and is in the style Holbein used for his portraits of Boleyn," Diane was quick to add.

"Ah," the Archivist paused for a moment, studying Diane and thinking before she continued. "It may appear that way to you, and to tourists, now that you mention it." Charlotte smiled and rose, towering over Diane as she did. She stepped around to Diane, then parked herself more casually on the edge of her desk as she continued. "If you were, however, to pull a chair over and climb slightly higher, you would be able to see that the necklace is a "P" for Pope. Unfortunately some damage to the painting during the Protestant Civil War was imperfectly repaired. A sword thrust through the neck, given to the painting by Cromwell's Army about 1651. Angry about the Fellows hiding the College's silver serving plates before the army could confiscate them, melt them down for coin, we believe. It is this flaw in the canvas from that clumsy repair that you see catching the light."

"No kidding!" Diane blurted. "So that's it. I've seen many paintings at antique stores with both eyes poked through, then repaired. Same game. Someone with a sword in a foul humor. How interesting, but what a shame."

"Ah well. We inherit the works as Time has preserved them," Charlotte said. "Though I am so glad you stumbled upon my office here and brought it up. I hadn't fully noted that particular detail. It explains a good deal of the confusion. Just a moment." She rose and opened a file drawer behind her desk and duly pulled out a file. "Yes. See here. The photograph of Lady Elizabeth's portrait."

Once at eye level as the camera had been, the "P" on the necklace was easy to make out. Diane waved away the offered magnifying glass. "No. I can see it clearly. Really interesting. Thank you."

"Glad to be of service, Diane." Charlotte closed the file. "Is there's something else?" she asked as she turned to find Diane stock still and staring at nothing.

"Yes, actually. Do you have photographs of *The Five Fellows* painting as well? There's just something I'd like to check."

"The Martínez? Yes. We're glad to have it back from London. You know it was in a show there at the Royal Academy of Arts? First retrospective of a woman artist. We're very proud." She pulled another file and a photograph from it, then handed it to Diane.

"Yes, Constance Bede mentioned that to me." Diane applied herself directly to the lower right corner of the photograph. "May I use the magnifying glass?"

"Here it is. That's interesting. Nice to know our staff is talking about our notable effects." Charlotte said. "And nice that you have taken an interest in – what is it?"

Diane stood up straight, feeling a little sick. There could be no mistake. Glenlivet. "Charlotte. I think you need to have a look at the painting with me." Diane felt the pulse in her throat rocketing upward as she grasped the enormity of what she had stumbled across.

* * *

Facing one fear and getting it cleared out of the way gave Diane some confidence for her next task: Constance.

"Sorry I'm late. I was delayed on an errand," she lied, not wanting to pull the entire session out of whack over what she had just set in motion back in the Trinity Dining Hall. Charlotte Ashcroft – after nearly fainting herself – had assured her the matter would be taken care of without disrupting Diane's studies. Relieved over finally telling the right person, Diane felt inclined to trust Charlotte's prediction.

In the most normal voice she could muster, Diane put her question to Connie. "Does Dr Chandra often invite students to his room for coffee in the evening? Say around midnight?"

"Chandra? Coffee in his rooms?" Constance let her hand fall limp over the side of her arm chair, then regarded her student who remained perched on the edge of a chair rather than sinking into her familiar corner of the chaise longue. "Oh. I see your concern, Diane. No. He has never in all the years I have known him been involved with a student, or with anyone. And I have traveled with him to a number of conferences, as well. He isn't one to indulge in wild behavior even outside his usual setting. No, actually. I am pleased to hear this. He is such a lovely man. Truly, Diane, I think you have nothing to fear from Chandra."

Except another marriage proposal, Diane filled in with a dour expression. Haven't I had more than my fair share of being fitted into someone else's plans?

"You are, after all, the exotic American, Diane, and bring with you many fascinating tales for us all." Constance smiled in a motherly way. Or perhaps in the way a best friend does when saying: *take a chance.*

* * *

By lunchtime Thursday, authorities had seized the Rosa Martínez forgery. Diane walked swiftly through the empty corridor, looking straight ahead, and went through the serving line, sure that every eye in the kitchen was trained upon her.

Diane sat with a random group of students, full of introductory social questions, bubbling through lunch on pure adrenalin. All her energy played out about the time she wound up Staircase Sixteen. She crumpled onto her bed. When she awoke near four, she took herself off to a cup of tea in the Dining Hall with the plan to jump back into her Thomas Hardy paper. Mr Spencer, however, casually brought her mail to her along with an official request. "I am also delivering an invitation to see President Jeffreys. Before dinner is served, please," he said quietly and waited for her acknowledgment.

Diane knew the President's rose-covered residence. The door opened for her as she arrived. She expected to see police everywhere.

"Miss Quinnell. Pleased to meet you." President Merton Jeffreys shook her hand warmly and invited her to step inside his tranquil – and unoccupied – drawing room. Diane was struck by his resemblance to the five men in Rosa Martínez's painting. In a word: emeritus.

"First, I want to thank you for reporting your findings – not everyone would have – and second, I want to assure you that you need not alarm yourself on account of this incident. The College and the authorities will be directly on top of the followup. The evening newspaper will use the phrase 'a student' to identify the person who uncovered the situation, which I hope will set your mind at ease.

"Your discovery, I must add, attests to the brains of the scholars who attend Trinity, Miss Quinnell," he added with a pleased chuckle, "and I like it when we are able to remind everyone of that fact in print. You have rendered a service to the College by being observant as well as conscientious. An admirable combination." President Jeffreys rose and extended his hand to her again. "I am only sorry that I was not here earlier in term to have had the chance to meet such a perceptive and charming American student."

She rose. A tinkling of fine crystal was heard from the next room. Was a champagne toast part of this visit? As she turned her head, taking in the room for the first time, she saw that she was probably standing in the exact spot where the original Five Fellows had posed for their portraits all those years ago. The thought stalled her exit.

"Now you must excuse me, as my guests will be arriving for dinner. Thank you again and carry on!"

Diane walked in the direction of the Dining Hall, mulling over what had been said. President Jeffreys' great pleasure in boosting Trinity's public profile amused her. That couldn't balance against losing their most valuable asset, could it? She accepted it, however, as stoicism mixed with a bit of fancy in order to put her at ease. Very sweet of him. Yes. Just the man to head up this community.

She sobered, passing by the empty wall, now that she had stood where they had stood. That irony struck her again. No little card, this time, announcing where *The Five Fellows* had gone visiting. And how long had it been sitting there, the forgery? Out of habit, Diane felt responsible to figure it out. Mrs Whappington and Lawrence – who must have noted the police inspector's arrival and removal of the painting – barely looked her way as she came through the serving line.

She welcomed Dr Chandra and Constance's company over dinner. No one spoke of the missing painting, not even Constance, who was so fond of it. Diane couldn't be sure Connie had even noticed its absence. Chandra acted his old self, something Diane also felt grateful for. He held her secret comfortably, giving no indication that they were suddenly bonded by it or any other rubbish that might mean: '*Ha! Now I have you in my clutches!*' Just as with the day in the Sheldonian cupola, time and life moved on for them in a natural flow. The staff remained busy with setting up Thursday High Table dinner for the Georgetown students, the moment the rest of them were done eating. They seemed unaware of Diane's part in the removal of the painting.

The three left together. Constance returned to her rooms. Chandra waved Diane to her staircase, allowing her to return to her studies, undisturbed.

Week SIX

WHAT A MOMENT to concentrate on Thomas Hardy's dead first wife. Yet she'd done it. She recopied the paper Thursday evening and would present it to Dr Harding Friday morning at ten. Sitting down at her favorite spot in the empty Library at five AM for the final proofread felt like a delicious triumph. Good thing President Jeffreys hadn't broken out the champagne after all, she concluded, as she added the finishing touches.

Archie arrived, looking as if he'd had a restful night, with well-mannered hedgehogs scampering yet never intruding on his slumbers. "You might find it interesting to know," he said, stepping closer under the Library window, "The Lodge saw on camera the boys moving the Martínez painting out the front fence in the usual manner and thought little of it, assuming it was the Foundress portrait. They're nearly the same size. They kept the painted side to the wall. An interesting point, however: the Royal Academy of Art took photos of all the Martínez pieces as they arrived. The painting they displayed was already the forgery. Good thing insurance insists on photographs all around."

For a man of few words, these were choice ones for Diane, who was glad to talk about it with someone, especially someone as knowledgeable and connected as Archie. She hoped her anonymity would be preserved among the larger College population. She would gladly skip being the center of attention for something like this.

"Perhaps you recall the broken glass at the back gate the morning following the kidnaping of the Foundress? Now the inspectors are thinking it was a decoy, just as you had thought."

* * *

"I almost lost hope for finishing this paper, with all the trouble about the painting and the police, but here it is. One less to wait for." She handed it to Dr Harding at ten. President Jeffreys and Charlotte Ashcroft had assured her: '*Not for you to worry over. We'll take it from here*' – then had sent her, with the tap of some magic wand, back into her idyllic life as a summer student in the gardens of Oxford. So far, it was working out as they had said.

Harding couldn't mask his surprise as he received her paper. "I'm not sure what delays you are referring to, but this is a first, I believe. And I will therefore be able to give it the time it deserves, I am sure." It disappeared into a folder without a glance.

Suddenly Diane pictured the scene she had missed in the garden: Courtney landing on his knee. All credit to Dr Harding: he clearly and publicly had not been the instigator, rather a hapless victim caught in the combined trap of the late hours, spirits and the romantic notions those produce in certain personalities. Everyone in earshot also had been spared the audacious scene Courtney had planned. Daniel could be overlooked; Professor Harding, never. That he was keeping his composure so level this morning must mean he had brushed aside the incident already. Diane took this as a lesson.

An awkward silence grew. She felt she had little to tell him about her paper – he must read it – but knew that this was the moment for her to offer some thanks and some good words about the entire course, in her estimation. After she did, she turned the conversation to movies, an easy topic.

"Did you get to see that new film, *Fargo*? Wasn't it hilarious?!"

"*Fargo*? Thoroughly gruesome! You found it amusing?" Harding's face registered complete shock, which set Diane laughing uproariously, thinking again of the unrestrained laughter in the theater. The audience in Denver immediately recognized the sound of the wood chipper and had exploded at the kidnaper's inevitable fate.

When she stopped laughing, she suddenly put the two things together. "Perhaps that's what drew me to study Thomas Hardy this summer? A wry appreciation for life's little tragedies."

Class with Connie at two was not quite so raucous an affair. Constance hovered like a mother hen, making sure all the elements for success had been provided. "Are you getting the books all right? Are the other girls sticking to the schedule? Have you come up with your thesis yet?" Diane nodded politely and assured her lovely professor that it was now time for each student to show what they knew, all of their own volition.

With one paper completed, Diane was full of confidence that she could knock down the second without a problem and perhaps even squeeze in an original joke or two. That was always her favorite goal: surprise the teacher with a good laugh along with a salient discussion. She thought then of EB White's writing advice to limit the use of exclamation points to one per year. Diane started chuckling, thinking of it. Though she did not share her insight with Constance, she would definitely mention it to her comic book artist mother in the next postcard.

"Yes, I'm expanding that superwoman theme, beyond Weldon's *She Devil*, as you suggested. I'm having a lot of fun with it."

"Excellent, Diane. I look forward to reading it."

Diane attended tea straight from Connie's, promptly at four, ready to celebrate her last class by indulging in too many McVitie's. She was therefore stunned to find only a small plate of meager Danish butter cookies set out for the largest crowd of students Diane had ever encountered at afternoon tea.

A buoyant atmosphere filled the Hall, the crowd friendly, chatty, bubbling with the last sprint just ahead of them. "Tomorrow," she heard them promising themselves. "First thing tomorrow, I'll get going on that paper." The planning stages continued through dinner, she noticed. This final Friday night marked the great divide. From this moment, the pressure would be on to complete readings, compose the final papers; everything due Tuesday morning.

The moment the kitchen worker appeared to check the tea urn, Diane pounced upon her. "Daphne, may we have some McVitie's, please?"

"I am sorry. No more can be brought out, ma'am. The allotment for the term has been consumed."

Diane tried not to overreact to the news, but disappointment registered on her face.

Daphne looked sheepish. "I'm sorry, but you have all enjoyed them so much that Kent admitted to putting out more than he should have, nearly every day. Thus we discover, they are now all gone. I am sorry."

Diane walked slowly back to her cup and saucer and plunked herself down on the bench, trying not to think badly of the generous Kent. That's when she noticed that the animated talk all around her was indeed all around her – and not including her. What she had seen the beginnings of on Monday in the Library had intensified. There was Daniel with his arm around Courtney, sure enough, as they wedged together over some picture book and giggled as they turned the pages and sipped their tea. Near them, Madeleine leaned all her weight on Jason's shoulders, standing behind him, yet nearly on his shoulders, and participating in the lively conversation over the table filled with the students she had seen flocking together during intermissions at Stratford. It was a room full of best friends and sweethearts. The lack of McVitie's never touched them.

Now that she thought about it, the blank wall also did not touch them. *The Five Fellows* painting was removed yesterday afternoon. Diane had her radar on for any word of it in the Hall. Not one student had mentioned it. Well, she considered: it had been gone for four weeks, then it was back, then it was gone again. Yet she remembered watching many students literally stepping over the workmen that day, as they packed the painting to leave for London. Not a word from anyone then either. Did they notice? Just not worth commenting on? Something like Rushdie's day, wasn't it?

Feeling very distant from this group of pals, Diane spotted The Foundress, returned. She moved closer and gave Lady Elizabeth Pope her rightful attention. Over a good long while, a new thought struck her. Every college had a Founder or Foundress portrait, most likely, here at Oxford, with its large number of colleges. Certainly every house at Smith had some dedicatory item, a bronze plaque or framed portrait of their namesake. Long after her tea cup sat emptied, she realized that her own infatuation with British history was probably responsible for leading her to think that she'd discovered something exciting and unique in the Tudor portrait. Suddenly she became aware of the hundreds of students who had sat here in the company of this painting. Hundreds? No, three hundred students *each year* now – and for how long? Over four hundred years? Add in all the visitors and tourists who had viewed her, and Diane couldn't have been the only one to have found a thrill in contemplating the intriguing Lady Elizabeth Pope.

Being suddenly reduced from amazing art history analyst to just one more in a long line of admirers, Diane laughed out loud, then glanced back self-consciously. She sank a little lower, thinking she must look to others like some solitary nut or self-amused loser, sitting there laughing by herself. No one had looked over, though.

Suddenly she felt entirely worn out. The sore muscles from the Hardy hike. The added emotional bump of Chandra and his coffee invitation. The intense amount of last-minute reading. At that precise moment, all the agitation over the forgery, as well – trounced her spirits. Weariness set in and a host of other anticlimactic feelings – that possibly a good dinner would help to dispel, since the McVitie's could not work the charm.

Saturday, August 3

The book lay on the table. Pat Barker, *Union Street.* The sole copy. It had been sitting there since one PM. Diane checked the list. It was slated for Madeleine at three. That was forty-five minutes from now.

"Go ahead and read it if you want to." Natalie swept into the room, wet hair in a towel. "I need to pop into town for a minute," she called from her bedroom, changed quickly and then dashed out the door with a simple: "Ta!"

Diane eyed the book several times while working through her expanding pile of notes, at war with the image of Madeleine waiting in the Dining Hall foyer. At two minutes past three, she scooped up her notes and Natalie's book, then transported them to the first seat inside the door of the Dining Hall. No Madeleine. Eventually, Daphne began setting up for tea at four, wheeling in the urn, cups and saucers.

"That is so funny," Diane said to Daphne, pointing to the large plate of McVitie's.

"Someone ran to the grocery and brought back several packets. I think it was Lawrence, but please don't say I said so," Daphne filled in quietly.

"Well, tell whoever it was *thank you* from me!" She dove into the plate.

Despite glancing up at every sound in the foyer, Diane had the table to herself until nearly five, when three stray students she didn't know wandered in for a snack. They glanced at Diane and her sheaf of notes, and left soon thereafter, without comment.

"I think I've had enough of these," she said to herself as she set down the last bite of her McVitie's biscuit. She let out a big sigh and shook her head. Madeleine had not appeared.

Diane gathered her things and wandered out of the Dining Hall into a perfect afternoon. A flight of mischievous birds swooped through the courtyard at that moment, their frenzied tweeting adding to the cheery scene. Students wandered in idle pairs, a few lounging at the edge of the bowling green in the Durham Quad. Reminded that these were her last days here, last chances to look around, a walk was in order.

She wandered in the direction of the front gate, but on a whim, decided to turn into the Chapel for a moment. She hadn't been in there since her first evening; perhaps it needed one more look before saying goodbye to Trinity. Diane sauntered through the stone doorway and took a place just inside on the first pew that ran along the north wall. The darkened dampness remained a constant. Not exactly the place to spend long hours sitting quietly in meditation, she thought. Actually, though, as she settled and listened to the silence, it seemed a nice out-of-the-way spot to just relax. The Laundry Cottage was another one of those, though more palatable with its warm, fragrant tumbling of drying laundry. And the Chapel's painted ceiling overhead was quite impressive.

Just then, she became aware of a certain rustling in the far corner diagonal from her position. Mice. Definitely mice. She hated those. Diane rose to leave just as two heads pressed together popped up from that same corner. She heard the familiar *klonk* sound of knees hitting against the kneeler and a muffled giggle that clarified everything. She slipped away as quietly as she'd come in, although certainly more animatedly, thinking about the comic scene that could have ensued with less restraint on everyone's part.

She passed the President's Lodgings, its doorway a profusion of roses. Just before The Lodge, something was missing. "Where are the ducklings?" she asked as she stepped out of The Lodge into the front quad and scanned the lawn for her little buddies.

"Gone to the river." Mr Spencer stepped outside with her. "The mother duck takes them on a walk to the Cherwell from here, every year about this time."

"Oh, what a nice picture." *I hope they left early in the day*, she thought suddenly to herself, picturing them flattened by a fleet of cars and motorcoaches. "Oh! Are they safe doing that?"

"No worries. She left just before the Scouts arrived. Plenty of time to get there. She knows the way." Mr Spencer rocked back on his heels looking comfortable and content.

Other threatening dangers sprang to mind. "Say, that reminds me. One day I heard a lot of quacking and barking. Did a dog wander in?"

"That's right. Chucks chased that dog out of here before any harm was done. Crazy thing. Set everything off. We don't often get a dog stirring up a ruckus – not to mention what they can do to our lawn."

"Right, right. Now I remember," she said.

She went down the back passage to the Library Quad. Once there, the open windows made it easy to see that the place was packed with students, some sitting on the windowsills chatting, not quite ready to surrender the Saturday to study. She smiled at everyone getting along so congenially, and yet with the encounter in the Chapel still fresh in her mind, she pictured a few sneaking kisses in the book loft or a quick, forbidden squeeze into the reserve closet together.

In the distance, under the row of trees that fronted the garden lawn – The Wilderness, as Archie called it – couples sat close together or lounged on blankets in varying degrees of proximity, books in varying states of disregard. By the sheer number of bodies, even the Georgetown students must be enjoying the day. Yes, there was Jan squinting into the sun, on a blanket next to a girl with long dark hair. My goodness. It was Laura, wasn't it?

Taken all together, these chummy sights served to drain the remaining life from Diane. A nap was exactly what she needed.

She clicked the electronic lock on the door to her suite and found Natalie with friends everywhere in their room. A wall of noise greeted her. "Yes! Here it is!" The gleeful crowd said. "The last Saturday. Time to party!" Natalie gestured broadly to Diane with her glass, which caused the burly Brandon to grab Natalie around the waist and lift her shoulder high. In the far corner, Madeleine had come out of her shell, half-wrapped around Jason, and took no notice when Diane flashed

the Pat Barker book her direction. Diane laughed, but secretly wondered when they planned to get serious. This would be her chance to
find out. The words "Papers all done?" formed on her lips as Tucker
strode over to her and draped his beefy arm over her shoulder. "Hello.
Come here often?" he said and pressed his cold beer bottle against her
bare arm. Suddenly, her interest in this research project evaporated.

Diane stepped out into the Garden Quad and stood still, rather
dazzled by the bright sunlight. She tried to laugh about the state of her
rooms. How long had she longed for company there?

As the term rolled into its final weekend, Diane felt completely
isolated, which surprised and wounded her. Her roommate had
disappeared almost after their first morning and remained generally
unavailable for the whole of the term. She'd gotten used to that. Sure,
they had chatted a bit as Natalie had returned to shower and change
clothing sporadically, and they did have their day in London. Their
return from London on the bus, sitting next to each other talking in
quiet tones had made Diane understand that she wished they had
been closer this whole summer. But the program would end in just a
few days' time. Natalie would probably disappear into study mode –
after tonight's revelries – and then that would be that.

There were definite advantages to having an entire suite to
oneself, Diane consoled herself as she contemplated the chalk drawing
of crew oars on the building across from hers. On your own, you could
read uninterrupted, write those essays uninterrupted and spend many
uninterrupted hours sitting in the wide window seat, sketching views
of their Seventeenth Century quadrangle, contemplating history. Yet
now that they were in the last few days together, Diane wished she
and Natalie could have established a regular bond with memorable
habits. Evening chats over a cup of hot tea in front of their fireplace
would have been a nice memory to take home.

With nowhere to land, and the end of her time in Oxford
approaching, Diane saw an opportunity to go visiting. Perhaps she
could pick up Constance on her way to dinner?

Diane knocked on Connie's door, then saw the note: '*Shall return Sunday evening.*'

Just then, a door opened down the hall and Chandra stepped out looking his usual energetic self. "Ah! Looking for an escort to dinner, or are we too early?" He motioned for Diane to step down the hall ahead of him.

"Looking for Constance, to no avail." She pulled open the door for both of them at the end of the hallway, and they continued out into the courtyard.

"Yes. She has deserted us for York this weekend."

"That's right. She has a sweetheart there. Well, Love is in the air, I guess. Kissers in every corner everywhere I went today."

"Right on schedule, are they not Diane? Just as I said. And yes, like flames for moths, dark corners attract young lovers. And the funniest part," he laughed out loud and stopped her with his hand on her arm. "They are unaware of the numerous security cameras in every secluded spot, especially."

"Yes! I discovered many of those tiny cameras while following Archie around my first week." They had walked as far as the Dining Hall foyer.

"The College made sure to tell all the tutors and dons as they were installed. Let me quote President Jeffreys on that occasion: '*The Lodge knows all. Be advised.*' Yes, yes," he chuckled gleefully. "A cautionary tale, Diane." He wagged a finger at her then patted her arm again like a doting grandfather admonishing a new puppy.

"Oh, don't worry about me. I don't need the warning. From what I've encountered today, I'm the only one *not* getting kissed on this campus." She laughed sadly and then looked carefully at him, thinking. "OK. You *and* me," she said, then planted a tiny kiss on his cheek. "There. Now we fit right in."

At that moment, Natalie and her merry crew flooded into the stone archway, nothing stopping them from pressing noisily into the front of the serving line. For herself, Natalie spotted her professor and her roommate, and came up between them, taking one on each arm. "You two are so cute! I must kiss you," she said half-stumbling, and grazing Chandra's cheek with her lips. She pivoted unsteadily to Diane, enveloped her in smooches for a moment, then moved on.

The Cute Two watched her rejoin her friends, then turned to each other and burst out laughing. "Ah! That was a classic moment!" Dr Chandra spouted.

"*A is for Alcohol*! Huzzah!" Diane added. "And to think, I thought I was going to get myself in trouble, guided by *my* spontaneous act."

"Sorry my old friends were not here to witness that." He smiled at the blank wall between the doorways.

Diane stopped laughing and stared at the empty spot where the painting belonged. "Isn't it enough that Salman Rushdie came out of seclusion," she mewled suddenly, "The Dalai Lama spoke to his first Western audience? But no. The Foundress portrait vanishes, then is found in the Loft – and I was always asking to go up there. Then add in this art forgery. It feels like it's all on my shoulders."

They carried their trays into the Dining Hall. "You are a very exciting woman, Diane. Is your daily life back home filled with such adventures or must you travel internationally for the Good Things to find you?" He chuckled as he spoke.

"I'll bet you say that to all the girls," she said automatically but tinged with pathos, then caught herself. *I didn't mean that. That isn't at all what I meant to say.*

"I assure you not." He smiled at her in a particular manner from behind his long, dark lashes. The look gave her the feeling he had intended some private joke with the comment.

They looked into each other's eyes for a long moment, but she couldn't detect anything more in the exchange, though she sensed that something had changed between them. "Do random art thefts follow me everywhere? It feels like it." And there was something else hanging just on the periphery, she said to herself, something that felt creepy and threatening like a sinister shadow pressing towards her.

"That's not quite what I meant."

She looked at him, puzzled, but side-stepped any clarifying he might add. "You know, Dyan, this feels all too familiar. I just wanted to get my papers done, you know? But instead, I have to notice that a painting is a forgery. And now, I need to finish my paper for Connie. I would like to just focus on that." She buttered her second hard roll and chewed thoughtfully for a long time. At the next table, Natalie and her noisy party had a race, bolting their food down and making a big show of taking all their plates to the dish return. Even that detail didn't escape Diane, who started feeling very, very sleepy, thoughts churning.

"This must be very complicated for you, Diane, considering what you have told me about your ex-husband's actions. It must have very unpleasant overtones for you. And as you said, all this just as final papers are due. No wonder you are in a muddle. I often believe that when in a muddle, go for a walk."

Go for a walk. That sounded familiar as well. "Is that what I'm in? A muddle?" She stared at the open archway in the direction Natalie's group had disappeared. "I thought I just needed a nap."

"Oh, I see. Perhaps you are right. Have a nap, then. I'll see you in the morning, I am sure."

* * *

Natalie and company did not return after dinner, but had left behind a room full of empty bottles, neatly stacked on the table corner. Diane could respect that. As she sat down to write, she wondered what Mary Anne would make of them in the morning. Many hours later, after putting a Herculean effort into pulling together the complete outline for Connie's paper, she dragged herself into her bedroom. She picked up Connie and Chandra's pictures off the bureau for a moment, then tossed them back down on the third: Natalie and her wild young men. Diane switched off the light.

A mash of thoughts tumbled through her head. Here she was,

thirty-one years old. A high school tutor, having embarked on a grand new adventure that would actually improve her teaching credentials. The trip felt like a reward for three years of helping young students, plus surviving a divorce after four disconnected years waiting for her husband to finish a project and spend some time with her, or finish his degree and actually find a home together. Yet now she chose to turn in at a normal hour on a Saturday night. It made her think: *maybe I have been alone too long.*

As a tutor, the noise and bustle of the hallways and especially the lunchroom caught Diane in a daily routine that made her quiet evenings seem a blessing. But when weekends and vacations arrived, Diane wished for fun friends, or better, meaningful conversations featuring a more balanced give-and-take than the average teenaged students could engage in. After her divorce, she'd swung back to what she'd known: lots of theater outings to see friends perform. Lovely when they fell during vacation time, but after a school day and frequent evenings of school activities, late nights weren't as easily enjoyed as they used to be. Lately, for lack of energy, Diane had acquiesced, allowed lack of planning to give her permission to read quietly at night, retire early. Yet under all of it, her true self still desired to grab a suitcase and go! Her friends, however, were busy now with young families on top of careers, so any trip featured Diane climbing onto a plane alone. She visited friends who sent her off sight-seeing during work hours, then tried to keep up with her in the evenings. And so she had begun to follow a more solitary routine.

She lay there now with all her books read, her last essay nearly written. Saturday night.

Yes, she was alone too much. Maybe she was turning into a pragmatic, spinster school teacher.

Sunday, August 4

Late Sunday afternoon, Diane tucked her final paper into the wall slot outside Connie's door. Done. It felt great. She thought momentarily of Chandra, halfway down the hall. The image of him in his robe, holding his toothbrush that day in this very hallway, fluttered somewhere inside her blurry brain. Unconsciously she rubbed her aching hand. The pain amused her, considering that she had been so excited to write out her papers longhand. No computers. What a joy to get back to basics, she had thought at the time. She'd forgotten that moving even one paragraph was devilishly complicated with pen on paper if it had to look presentable. Well, if she'd learned one thing at Oxford, it was the true value of a computer's CUT and PASTE commands. It made her look back at Smith a dozen years ago, when her freshman papers had all been typed with liberal use of correction tape. How suddenly these basic things had changed.

She stepped back through the doorway into the afternoon sunlight in the Sir Christopher Wren Quadrangle and thought for the first time: *Now I can have some fun.*

And so she headed to four o'clock tea with a skip in her step.

The Hall was crowded and churning with stress. There, the procrastinators had begun pecking at each other, even over the selection of cookies. Diane had the full report on this crew, having watched every detail as the semester unfolded. Generally, students had milled about morning coffee and afternoon tea. Once the large plate of McVitie's Digestive Biscuits was bare, most students would wander off, languidly saying they really should study. Meeting again at dinner, Diane found that their original admirable plans often had dissolved the moment they stepped out of the Dining Hall. Sun sent them to the garden to chat. Rain sent them to their rooms for a nap. And there was always shopping. Thus, in these last three days of the term, everyone would knuckle down at once.

Diane was content with tea. She sauntered about the room, sampling conversations, sidestepping the woeful or panicking ones. She joined a group reflecting on the end of their time there. A woman she hadn't spoken with before was saying, "I wish I'd gotten to know the town a little better. I asked at the tea room over on Cornmarket Street if I could work a shift or two, you know, even just clear tables, just to get a feel for the local people. That would have been nice."

"You mean: take someone else's job," Diane broke in and immediately drew the group's attention. "Marjorie at Boswell's said that happens a lot. American students want a little job, not understanding that there aren't enough for the locals. The economy's in a pinch but we, just visiting, don't see it. There are no jobs. Mick at OxFam said most of the clerks there just volunteer for something to do. There's only the one actual paid position there. Mr Spencer at The Lodge said his son's been laid off for more than two years now and there's nothing to apply for. Archie also said several times that... ."

Shawn who had kept his distance since they argued on the bus announced: "You are just the oddest person, Diane. When did you get to know the people at OxFam and the cashier at Boswell's? Or did your Japanese friend of the Pope introduce you?"

Diane shook her head and laughed. "Not to mention the pub keeper next door at the White Swan," just to bait him.

"I never got past the bartender and his wife in our Beer Cellar," Kate joined in.

"Who has time for more than just the two professors?" Tamara, who preferred spending time with hedgehogs, added.

"Professors?" Diane laughed. "Sit with them at a meal, chat with them at the reception before lecture. They're not exactly the enemy."

"I wouldn't know what to say to my professor outside class time," Emily said while Jessica smirked. "Actually, I hardly know what to say to them during the session. This program has been brutal." A very quiet Asian girl made a sour face, listening from her distant position, then walked back to the other side of the room for more tea.

Diane laughed as they all murmured agreement. Fun for her to hear the actual responses to the scenes she had envisioned the day she had discovered the Oxford tutorial tradition.

Sensing their distress, Diane said: "Well, I'm free until the Wednesday night farewell banquet. Anyone up for a tour of the Pitt-River's Collection tomorrow? I tell you, it's amazing." The crowd exploded. "No takers? That's fine. Well, off I go." She must have been half delirious to make that offer to such a volatile crowd, she realized as she brought her cup and saucer to Kent.

She spread her blanket in the sun on the garden lawn for an hour, tucked her arms behind her head and looked up at the sky. She mostly wanted to rest her eyes, her head. Think about nothing. Her brain felt cross-eyed, putting in that last bit in her Women's Lit paper. Had she been thinking straight? It all started to look like a mess, the threads of logic lost in all the rehashing. She hoped it would fly with Connie. In the margin Diane had written in tiny letters: '*Does this make sense?*' If she had completely mixed up the order in the final draft, why not note it? If she made it clear that she too questioned that particular spot, Connie would add a suggestion. She had been very helpful in those ways before.

This was Sunday afternoon before Thursday morning when they would all leave. Watching the clouds drift by, she closed her eyes only to find her eyelids fluttering at every tiny sound. This was not relaxing.

Could you turn your brain off, just like that? This weariness reminded her of the crushing weight on her entire being following her first finals at Smith. What an unpleasant memory. Finishing the fourth, grueling final exam, she went in search of a reward: espresso. Real espresso, not easy to find then. She discovered the bakery with the espresso machine at the farthest end of Main Street. Finding it, filled with adult faces, real live adults that coexisted in Northampton, was like stumbling upon a hidden, parallel universe. Like here, really, when she'd doubled back to get her umbrella before getting on the coach to the Barbican one evening, and bumped into the Georgetown students dressed in their suits and ties, filing in for their Thursday High Table dinner. Why did she never see any of those students regularly in the Library, she wondered at the time.

Now. Late Sunday afternoon. All her obligations fulfilled. And here was Diane's reward: no playmates. She had already taken two walking tours through campus, hoping to bump into people somewhere on the grounds. So far she'd met the two Porters, several cooks and waiters taking a break under a row of trees near the Library, the six Scouts just heading out to their bicycles at the end of their duties, and the man who rolled the lawn, all done for the day. Even Archie remained invisible somewhere. Maybe he had gone into town.

Here was the perfect spot to review the events of the summer herself, but it all came out a jumble of snippets. Blow darts and Malachite columns. A beer-soaked coat. A comedian Swami. Rushdie. Roman heads. Random photographs. Broken glass. The Dalai Lama. Jugglers and dead friends. That taxi ride! How could anyone pack that much action into one summer, yet feel as if she'd spent the entire time safe behind the Trinity gate, enjoying the pursuit of quiet mornings in the Library, or drawing from her perch at the top of her staircase? Especially the last unexpected discovery. Diane's heart still raced, thinking about how she ended up in the middle of another art theft. And the College had taken it in stride. That completely surprised her. Efficient and making sure no one's summer visit was ruined. Really gracious and professional. *They're right: I had nothing to do with it, just happened to stumble upon some random evidence. Glad to have as little as possible to do with it.* So much action, then suddenly nothing. Yet every nerve vibrated.

A voice came to her as she drifted off for a moment: *'When you find yourself in the laundry at five AM, no wonder you don't have any playmates, Diane.'* A raindrop landed on her forehead. Another on her arm.

Monday, August 5

Monday morning, Diane took a long, hot shower to counteract the effects of a lingering dreadful evening. She had eventually slept, but had awakened feeling beat-up, instead of refreshed. She sat alone through breakfast, the sole person in the cavernous hall. Sipping her tea, she tried to feel happy about a chance to study the paintings around her, but the emptiness of the place carried through the bleak feelings of the past evening.

"Good morning, Diane," Chandra greeted her over his breakfast tray.

"Good morning, Dyan," she chirped, taken by surprise, her back to the serving area. The classic routine felt particularly welcoming, following the heavy-hearted loneliness that had ended the previous day.

"You were lost in thought just then. Would you like some company or solitude?"

"Oh, please join me." Diane heard the neediness in her own voice and looked up quickly to see if it had registered with Chandra as well. "Yes, lots to think about, as we near the last moment," she said with a grim smile.

"Papers all turned in?" He paused for confirmation and added, "I thought so." He nodded approvingly and seated himself across from her. "Where is everyone?"

"Working on their papers?" She meant it as a joke, but paused to reconsider. "Maybe they are? I didn't see the Library this morning. They were getting pretty surly yesterday afternoon at tea," she shook her head remembering. "I'm sure lots of students are totally on top of their work, but why is it that the ones not working always make the impression?"

"Visibility. Different people catch on differently, and few wish to believe that socializing is antithetical to producing actual work." He studied her for a long moment while she idly braided four tea bag strings together. "Are you sorry to be done here?"

"No. Done is good. That was a lot! I'm just sort of... fried. My brain feels like mush. I don't see how anyone could start the next term straight from here. When is it?"

"Michaelmas."

"And that is when?"

"September 29."

"Oh, that's not so bad. What's today? August fourth? Fifth? So that's a real break. In Denver, we'll begin again before the month is out. I just can't picture it. So, a few more days here, then I go on a walking tour in the Cotswolds for a week. Then a week after that, I'll be back in the classroom."

"How will you like that?"

"Oh, it'll be fine. I'm glad to have the job. And I don't have any new material to cover before we start again. It's just so... I'm not sure. I just feel tired now."

"Yes, of course." He took a big bite of toast. They sat quietly for a few moments. "Diane, perhaps since you find your hands free and I must disappear into grading papers, perhaps you would like a look at this book. It is right up your RENaissance alley," he enunciated carefully. He handed her a well-thumbed copy of *The Moor's Last Sigh*.

"I knew you'd find a way to put a Salman Rushdie book into my hands," she said the minute she saw the cover. *How did I know that?* she asked herself the next moment, not quite knowing why she had said that to him. She looked up to find him smiling comfortably. Then what he had said registered: he'd be incommunicado for the next few days. Diane wilted, not realizing until then that even this person would be cut off from her. She continued: "I meant: thank you. I don't know any of Rushdie's titles. What's the connection here for my Renaissance interests?"

"This book is set in the newly united Spain, approaching 1492 and the beginning of–"

"The Spanish Inquisition," they said together.

"Really?" Diane gawped. "I don't know a thing about this book, I must admit. I don't read anything..."

"...anything written after World War One," they said in unison.

"Wow. I must sound like a broken record," Diane studied the book in her hand to mask her self-consciousness.

"Not at all. I wanted you to know that I have been paying attention. Give this a try."

She opened to the first page of text. Chandra's elegant handwriting crowded the margins with arrows and neat underlining. This was a well-loved book. She read the first sentence aloud.

"'I have lost count of the days that have passed
since I fled the horrors of Vasco Miranda's mad fortress
in the Andalusian mountain-village of Benengeli; ran
from death under cover of darkness and left a message
nailed to the door.'

"Exciting. Spooky," she said in theatrical tones, then glanced at the cover blurb and burst out laughing. "Looks like this story has a lot to live up to. I'll have a look and tell you what I think," she added playfully.

She studied the cover art. A dark-haired woman's beautiful face. A mustachioed man dressed in elaborate attire on a rampant Arabian steed. The woman's dark, almond eyes resembled art from the Coptic Christians who had inhabited the Mediterranean coast of Egypt in Late Roman Antiquity. They left behind soulful grave portraits much like this one. Set in Spain? Rushdie wrote this? She found the concoction irresistible.

* * *

Two students showed up for Monday morning coffee at ten.

"Where is everyone? Sleeping in, now that they're done?" Diane said to Vivien, a quiet, self-contained Asian girl who had seated herself with her coffee in an out-of-the-way spot. "Maybe they have already determined that the supply of McVitie's has run out. Not worth coming down?"

"No. They're all busy writing papers. You should see the Library." Vivien said in a strong, clear voice that Diane hadn't expected from her withdrawn posture all term.

"And you? Just taking a break?"

"No. I'm done." Vivien surprised her again.

"That's good. Me too." Diane felt better recovered after even one morning of reading for pleasure. Rushdie's writing had pulled her interests in new directions.

The silence between them filled up the high vault as they sat quietly for a long while. Sensing something, Diane began, "How has the term been for you?"

"OK."

Diane recalled seeing Vivien at the edge of the group yesterday at the frenzied afternoon tea. She'd made that wounded face when Emily had called the program *brutal*. But look at Vivien: she's done and in one piece. Seems to be in better shape than I was even a few hours ago. And what do I have to add, Diane asked herself, trying to rise out of her preoccupation with Rushdie's book.

"The only thing I've been disappointed with being here is that my roommate is never around,"Diane volunteered. Lucky that Natalie hadn't been dragging boys through the place all term, now that she thought about it. It could have been one nonstop party, like Saturday. The thought didn't quite soothe her feelings. She continued: "OK, that is kind of nice if you like your privacy, but I mean she's NEVER around. I wish I'd had someone to hang around with a little bit."

"I wish you'd come knocking on my door," Vivien spoke up. "I've been sitting alone up there at the top of my staircase wishing I had someone to do something with. You can't read all the time. Up there, no one even passed by my door. I'm at the end of the hall."

"Really? Why didn't you say something at morning coffee or at tea? You were usually there." She smiled at Vivien, who was often included, but rarely had spoken.

"Oh, I don't know. I guess it takes me time to get to know people. And you were always laughing with the professors. How could I possibly have anything interesting to add?" She slumped down even more. "And now that I have three free days, everyone else is busy with papers. Mine are done. What else was there to do but study? That's all I've done here."

Diane wanted to grab the opportunity, but moderated, seeing her Rushdie book sitting there. Her budget wouldn't cover dinner out, either. "OK. Let's do something – tonight after dinner. I'd go right now, but I need to finish this and return it," she tapped the book. "What do you think? I could show you a charming, tiny pub – the Lamb and Flag – just around the corner. Do you like dark beer?"

"Oh no. Beer tastes terrible."

"Have you tried any since you've been here?"

"No. I never liked beer." Vivien's grimace reiterated the statement. Diane pictured the childhood sip, meant to discourage future consumption, and laughed.

"Then you've never tried a smooth, creamy stout? I know what we'll do. I'll order one and you can try it. I bet you'll like it; if not, I'll drink it. Beer can be nasty stuff, you're right, but I think you'll be quite surprised at what different flavors they serve here."

'*I'm not sure,*' Vivien's face said. Diane tried to gauge whether the girl wanted encouragement or truly wanted none of this plan.

"Look. Even if you don't like it, you'll get to see a new place with me in tow. No one will bother us. Trust me. We'll have fun."

"OK." The hesitant grin told Diane she'd make her best attempt to try to enjoy the proposed plan.

Vivien, prepared to hate the thick black brew, but trying to please a new friend, was seized by some sort of new-found bravery. She quaffed not a tiny sip but rather, a big gulp. She sputtered then licked her lips as her eyes grew wide. "I thought it would be like medicine," she laughed shyly, "so I figured: get it over with. It really wasn't that bad. Hey – the taste is different now. Sort of like burned chocolate. But not bitter at all." She studied the foamy glass with surprise and ventured another sip. "Now what did you say happened here again?" Vivien came to life. She touched the ceiling timbers just above their heads. "People must have been shorter back then, eh? Even as a small Asian person, this low ceiling is pretty funny. Like a Hobbit hole. You've read that, haven't you?"

Diane immediately pictured the child Vivien having read everything in the school library before she was twelve. So unlike Diane's childhood at the bowling alley. "*The Hobbit*? Actually, no, but I know a lot about it. I knew a guy who lived in a real Hobbit hole at a renaissance festival. Near Denver. I can't imagine how he could stand living in a hole, but," she suddenly remembered more of the story, "he'd also dress as Darth Vader and would go striding up and down in front of any line waiting to see *Star Wars*. Maybe that's what living in a snow-covered hole all winter does to you."

"You know that tall boy in our group with the ponytail? He said he's named after Luke Skywalker from *Star Wars*. How can parents do that to their child?"

"Only in America," Diane nodded with a bemused grin. She spotted the dishwasher from Trinity, smiled and nodded to him. Vivien turned to look. "You know Kent, from the Dining Hall?"

"Oh, I guess so," Vivien agreed. "He looks different out of his kitchen uniform."

Diane nodded and continued their conversation. "Well, I had an artistic mom, but I guess I was lucky; she didn't try to give me some unique art name like some of her friends did to their kids. Alizarine Crimson Johnson," Diane enunciated with smug theatricality, then seeing Vivien smile, made up another: "Burnt Sienna Larson, Raw Umber Schmidt. I like 'Diane' just fine." As she said it, she chuckled to herself, thinking just now of Chandra's seven-syllabled first name. "Names are always interesting. Why did your parents name you Vivien? A family name?"

"I grew up in Portland, but was born in Hong Kong. Because of that, I'm actually British, by nationality. By race, Chinese, of course. So it's a British name. You know: Merlin's nemesis. My parents are big Anglophiles. That's why I'm here. Well, that's why I was signed up for this program."

"That's interesting. So what's your full name?"

"Vivien Li. That's spelled *L-I* but pronounced like Bruce Lee."

Diane looked at her without blinking and repeated as politely as possible: "Excuse me. Did you say Vivien Li?"

"Yes."

"Like the actress, Vivien Leigh?"

"Sorry. I don't know her."

Diane tipped her head back and laughed the way a person can only when sitting in a famous pub in a tiny corner of Oxford, England, with a sweet Chinese-American girl named after Diane's mother's favorite actress. Once she finished laughing, Diane clarified. "Vivien Leigh played Scarlet O'Hara in *Gone With the Wind*. She was married to Sir Laurence Olivier, the Shakespearean actor. He's buried in Westminster Abbey." She decided to leave out the part about Margaret Mitchell having gone to Smith College and the part about Dee Quinnell wearing her hair like Scarlet's on any occasion when she had to tidy herself up to go out, like to a funeral or a wedding once every five years. Diane loved it when she did that.

"Really? That's some old movie, isn't it? I've never seen it." Vivien sipped her beer, liking it almost enough to order a second one, Diane thought. It took her awhile to get over the fact that Vivien had never seen *Gone With the Wind*. That was a first. But then again, many of the undergrads hadn't heard of the Dalai Lama. Diane let the thought rest there, as Kent smiled over at her. Then she remembered that she'd seen him here her first week when the Hardy class had stopped in. It felt like a lifetime ago, and yet a familiar happening.

As they finished their pints and Diane recognized that sleepy look in Vivien's eyes, Kent appeared at their table.

"So, back to The States for the two of you, then?" He asked and the girls nodded.

"Yes, in two days we'll all be gone and you guys can relax for awhile, eh?" Diane kidded him. "Should we head back, Vivien?" They gathered themselves to leave.

"Are you leaving? Let me walk you back. It'll be safer that way." The two looked at him with curiosity. Kent went on: "Haven't you noticed that if you're out after dark there's always someone to come along and bother you? Happens to me all the time."

"No, not really," Diane replied, but then realized that staying out all night in New York and Denver didn't translate into knowing everything about Oxford. Now that she thought about it, when she had been out after dark, it was with professors. *They seem to frighten everyone away*, she laughed to herself as she cinched her trench coat.

"Well, believe me, the streets can get rough this time of night. Shall we?" To Diane, Kent's report sounded more an echo of his former tough times living on the streets than anything Diane had sensed. She, however, was glad for the company as they stepped out into a night rendered moonless by mounting storm clouds.

They fell in with him easily, chatting freely. When he took them on a quick turn down a dark passageway, however, Diane balked. Kent replied: "This is the back way over to Parks Road. Don't you know it? Quicker. Then we enter Trinity through the garden."

Not totally dark, but on unfamiliar ground, Diane bowed to his local knowledge. The beer had made Vivien completely trusting. The three proceeded between tall stone walls, tree branches often spreading over them. "See, this here is Balliol's back wall and right here, this small cranny marks the beginning of Trinity's. We'll pass right behind your rooms. Sure enough. Smell that smoke? This is where workers stop for a fag at the end of shift."

"Stop for a what?" Vivien asked, suddenly confused.

"Sorry. A cigarette."

Diane couldn't see any of the buildings over the wall, but gauging from the density of trees and the distance to the street light seen at the end of the passage at Parks Road, she guessed: "So this is what my tree looks like from the other side? My room is right up there, I think." Under her feet, she felt the litter of cigarette butts just as the three passed under the densest tree coverage. She laughed picturing the responsible kitchen workers pitching them over the wall rather than leaving a mess on their own grounds, but also had a sudden vivid memory of smoke drifting up to her window. "Kent," she said quietly in the stillness, "I haven't enjoyed the smokers gathering here, especially just after lunch. Could you tell them that, next time?"

"Oh, after lunch? No, that wouldn't have been us. First shift ends at five, but I'll mention it to the lads, yes. No idea this rubbish had piled up here. May as well mention that as well," he added, flicking the toe of his shoe through the stubs.

That's a long day, Diane was thinking, but was distracted by a distinct scraping and the tinkling of broken glass on the pavement. Kent stopped as well. "Now that wasn't us. We would never chuck a bottle over the wall."

Diane wondered if he was being honest about that or just wanting to keep up a good impression. She didn't give it another thought as rain began to fall.

Kent left them quietly in the Garden Quad. Diane walked Vivien up to her room at the very back of her professors' building, just to see her end-of-the-hall arrangement. As she passed back down the closed-in hallways, Diane again felt her luck, having the airy view she enjoyed on Staircase Sixteen.

A folded copy of the *Oxford Mail* lay in front of Dr Harding's door, neglected. The front headline caught her eye: *"Oxford Authorities Solicit Additional Clues in Trinity Painting Forgery."* *Oh great*, she thought. *Now everyone will start talking about it. – Or maybe not.* She looked again at the wordy headline and laughed. If Harding had missed the first three days of shocking coverage, she was probably safe from having to dodge anyone asking compelling questions about the situation. Come to think of it, this was not the time in term for anyone to be using up precious time reading headlines. Certainly not students.

She wished a silent good night to Chandra as she passed his door, and sent congenial thoughts to Connie's door as well.

Arriving in her own rooms, empty as usual, Diane lay in bed thinking how funny life in this town was. Everyone circulated in their own little sphere, focused on intense and demanding research, or engaged in putting in their regular effort to keep the daily works functioning. This grand town where everything was built to dwarf humans. Yet just down the street, Diane had spent the evening in an old pub where everyone had to duck under the beams not to hit their heads. Curious. Nothing standard, and in those oddities lay the real charm. Yet deceptively rustic, with its well-hidden infrastructure and security cameras.

Tuesday, August 6

Diane awakened to a rainy Tuesday morning and an entire day to relax. She made herself a cup of tea, then burrowed back under the covers with *The Moor's Last Sigh* propped on her knees until breakfast time arrived.

Diane returned from lunch to find Natalie seated behind a laptop computer.

"Where did that come from?" Diane blurted, completely confused. She stood with her umbrella dripping on the carpet.

"I just bought it," Natalie answered smoothly, as if it were the most normal thing in the world to buy a new computer on the last day of term, a term at historic Oxford, where summer students were told to handwrite their papers.

"Interesting," was all Diane could come up with, so incongruous was it to see the thing here in her rooms. Diane glanced at the clock as if she had suddenly forgotten that she had just finished eating lunch and to double check that it was no longer Tuesday morning, the time at which all papers were due. To cover such blatant shock, she stepped out into the hall with her umbrella.

"I can work faster on a laptop," Natalie said through the open door, stating a fact Diane felt was intended to deflect any criticism. Natalie, however, proved her wrong by exhibiting no signs of stress. "Chandra will accept my paper when it's done. He can't exactly refuse it." Natalie's logic in the face of realities truly impressed Diane. She wished for some of her roommate's moxie, interpretations and simple, sensible conclusions – if they always resulted in such a calm disposition. Diane's brain switched to full speed to compare Natalie's earlier simple advice: '*Yes! Go get lost, then call a taxi,*' with this new deadline logic. Diane wondered about exactly where she had gone wrong with that cabby who hadn't been privy to Natalie's rule book.

"Oh," Diane felt a bit relieved. "So you already have Connie's paper done?"

"It'll happen. All in good time," she purred to Diane without a trace of concern.

"Will I disturb you if I just go in here and read?" Diane said, nodding toward her own room. She had hoped for a quiet dry spot in a cozy library chair. Unfortunately, when she checked after lunch, bad vibes were spilling over from the remaining desperate, disheveled and irritable students there. Closing her door, she plumped up her pillows and propped her book on her knees. The rain picked up a pace. Diane got up to adjust the window, leaving it open just a crack, loving the sound and the fresh cool air. *Maybe we'll have a real thunderstorm*, Diane hoped. She loved a good bout of thunder and lightning. She snuggled again under the blanket ready to get back into the fascinating story that filled her with a longing for the spices of Bombay and Cochin.

Having fallen directly under the spell of *The Moor's Last Sigh*, she disappeared into her own thoroughly enjoyable experience that touched on memories of reading Sir Richard Burton's *Thousand Arabian Nights and a Night*, as well as Washington Irving's hilarious *Tales of the Alhambra*, a tattered, gold-embossed, tiny red leather copy of which she had found for a dollar at some flea market back in Denver. But her best guides through Rushdie's book were the insights from her perceptive and exacting English professor at Smith, who had called out all the slapstick, bawdy, incendiary – *picaresque* – references in *Don Quixote*, which had puzzled the freshman Diane, but made complete sense today.

When she opened her eyes, the room was dark. The sound of pounding rain came through the windowpane. She must have fallen asleep. Diane peeked over the edge of her mattress to find her book splayed on the floor where it had landed. She fished for it in the darkness, came up empty-handed, so she swung her leg over the edge and nearly fell, as the book crushed and slid under her foot, the bookmark photos she had tucked in, permanently ruined. She looked again at the dim images of Connie, Chandra and herself, Natalie and the Wild Boys. Such a shame. Creased right through.

The bent edge thrust the date into her face: July 3. It blazed at her like an orange laser beam. She heard Natalie's voice saying at the time: *"They asked me that, too. 'Why aren't you at Rushdie? Did everyone else go to it?'"* And the man standing behind the car.

Diane leapt up and flipped on the light. That jacket. That crest.

She flung open her door. The room stood deserted.

She sat down on the bed again to let her head clear.

It was evident what she needed to do.

* * *

Diane felt totally ill as she approached The Lodge. Mr Dickens took her to the side room filled with small video monitors – the first she'd seen of them – and asked his assistant to step outside for awhile. She pulled out the photograph, pointed glumly to the date, and asked: "Were these the boys you saw taking the painting that day?"

"I dunno," Mr Dickens studied the photo. "I started out of The Lodge to stop them, but that bloody dog – excuse my language – ran in and threw off my getting a better look. I'm still angry about that." His face went suddenly rigid, then he cleared his throat gruffly. "Well. The inspectors have our Lodge's security tapes. This may prove very helpful." He tapped the photograph against his left palm.

She felt the corners of her mouth droop downwards and tears welling up in her eyes. "Here's the larger point," she said, her voice breaking, barely audible. "I'm not sure, but... Would you tell them that I think this man at the car here – see that crest on his jacket? Oh, I hate to say it, but they should check somehow – I think this man may be Dr Steele, from across the street." She burst into silent tears.

"There, there, Miss Quinnell. Sit down, sit down." He pushed a chair under her as her chin quivered pitifully. She didn't see Mr Dickens's eyes grow large as he grasped the severity of her declaration. He responded to her distress with an encouraging pat on her shoulder. "None of this is your fault, my dear girl, but I must insist that you stay right here, while I get someone from town on the line. They may need to take your statement. I am so sorry that this is something that I cannot just jot a note or two for, and let you go. I'm sure you understand. They made it clear to us to call them with any additional information. Courage, my girl. This won't take a moment and then you're free. Promise."

Mr Spencer put his head in, took in the chagrin on both faces. "Everything all right in here, Chucks?"

"One phone call will set things straight. One moment." Mr Dickens dialed. Diane sat sweating until his brief conversation ended with: "The information is clear to me. All right then. Will you need to take a statement? No? All right then for me to allow this student to get back to it? Good. Right. Yes, yes. Goodbye."

Diane was escorted kindly to The Lodge door where the threshold stood between her and the downpour. "Our ducklings are probably loving this rain, eh?" she said to the two, trying not to let her voice quaver.

"That's the spirit, Miss," Mr Dickens said.

As she paused to open her umbrella, she heard Mr Spencer over her shoulder say to his friend: "Such a sweet girl. So chipper and bright. I'll truly miss her daily visits as she returns home."

Wednesday, August 7

"This must be the quietest day of the summer," Diane said to Archie when she found him on his morning rounds near the back gate. The emotional storm of yesterday had eventually blown over. A hearty dinner of Shepherd's Pie had helped anchor her. Luckily, many students had followed the dining-out trend that left few in Hall to note her swollen eyelids or uncharacteristically quiet manner. Dyan had told her not to expect to see him until the Wednesday evening banquet. Natalie had disappeared again. Vivien had waved to her as she joined Laura, Kate and Emily for what Laura had called their last chance for Indian food. The quiet dinner had given Diane a chance to sort through her feelings.

"So, everyone is sleeping in, professors madly reading final papers all day, don't you think?" Diane offered.

Archie gave his shaggy head a shake. "With a few exceptions of all-night efforts still at it in the Library," he informed her.

"No!" Diane shouted. "You're joking?"

"Same every year. Have a look if you like, but I warn you; it is not a proper sight for a young lady to witness."

Diane suddenly wondered: "Natalie?"

"No, no. Just two burly lads who could benefit from opening the windows. I obliged them, not seeing your mark there. Let's say it helped." His eye twinkled. "I may like earthy smells and therefore sleep out of doors, but I also know when to have a bathe," he added. "Speaking of that, it looks that Dr Steele and those lads have taken the bath. You'll see it in the evening news. That photograph of yours sorted it out in no time, an exact match with the photograph of Steele introducing Rushdie that appeared on the front page of the *Oxford Mail* at the time. Steele's arrest was a simple thing after that."

"I'm relieved to hear it. I guess." Diane turned glum for a moment. "No. I am glad to hear it. And especially from you, Archie.

Thank you." She clapped her hand on his dusty shoulder.

"Oh, don't continue to fret over any of this, Diane. You're a hero! For one hundred thousand Pounds Sterling, you couldn't buy this much publicity for the College and its collections. There's more," he said with a broadening grin. "If you'd like to hear it."

"If we can sit down," Diane said, a momentary sinking feeling settling in her legs. She moved the few steps to a garden bench without pausing. Once there, she sat back, stunned by this *We-make-the-best-of-it!* revelation, meant to transform her role.

Archie perched next to her, his vibrant spirits barely allowing him to touch the seat of the bench, wanting to catch her up on every detail before she left Trinity. "The inspectors figured that Steele must have backed off the stage and out a side door. You see, the crowd rose to its feet cheering Rushdie for a long while before they allowed him to speak. And sure enough, once the press photographer's full set of prints was collected, Steele's movements were visible on the edge of several shots."

"How did you learn all this? Do you know the photographer at the newspaper?"

"No. This is straight from The Lodge, who have it straight from the Inspector. Actually, President Jeffreys, when he was consulted, gave word to Chucks to make sure that I brought you all the details. Pretty clever, isn't it?" He grinned proudly. "But as I was saying, immediately last night, they collected those shards of broken glass just behind your building. Did you not know that? Kent told us that you had discovered them, along with your complaint of smelling cigarette smoke on the afternoon in question. All these pieces work together, as you see."

"Well," she began, wanting to deny that she had discovered the broken glass, but hurried him on instead. So, Kent had carried through. Good for him, she thought.

"So, once they found that the broken glass was from the top of our wall – that damage, hidden by the densest part of that large tree – they suggested that the forgery was lifted over the wall there following lunch, and carried behind the buildings to the Dining Hall's back door near the dish room. Then, an easy switch with the real Martínez painting – place the Foundress in the staircase to the Loft – and out through the front fencing with the Martínez, keeping the back of the canvas toward The Lodge."

"I'd say this is all thanks to that squirrel waking me up," Diane admitted. "That totally freaked me out when it jumped into my room. It must have been frightened by the painting going over the wall. Maybe I wouldn't have heard them otherwise? I could have easily slept through the cigarette smoke." She paused to consider. "No. I take that back. Both things probably woke me up."

"Aye. We can chalk that up to Nature's inscrutable ways." He trilled. "Caught by the squirrel – and your nose."

"Trusting that everyone would be at Rushdie's event, that really was a clever plan," Diane acknowledged. "But then, they also had that dog. That couldn't have been a coincidence."

"I was just getting to that," Archie cut her off. "You are right, and were right, when you told me the broken glass at the back gate had something to do with the Foundress disappearing. But thinking it was just a prank, we all overlooked it. This plan included several ingenious diversions. But then, making off with the Martínez, even if you only received half its value, that would be worth planning properly. The dog is the only piece missing. The security cameras didn't get a good image of the owner's face. They must have known the camera's range limits. Dog and owner have not reappeared. But they'll turn up. Plus the most important person has been sacked. Steele."

Diane wondered if that was a rugby term, but suddenly thought of another thing. "Did they talk to Natalie, then?" Diane asked, falling into Archie's speaking rhythm.

"And just why would they do that?"

"She took the photo of those boys that day. She didn't go to hear Rushdie either and it really mixed them up to have their picture snapped on the street like that. Oh, you didn't get to see the actual photo?" she guessed as his brow furrowed.

"No, just a darkish photocopy that Chucks pulled of it before the Inspector arrived. So that is Natalie in the photo?" His face went through several expressions. "Well, I'll mention that, but I'm sure they already have what they need. Those lads have quite a history with the law all across Oxfordshire. And Steele, I'm sure he won't be able to wiggle out of this."

* * *

Diane dumped an armload of clothing with Mick at OxFam and waved off his attempts to interest her in a few new items. "Thanks, but no thanks," she said in her best American accent. "I'm leaving tomorrow and the less I have to carry, the better. Say, charge a definitely higher price for that jacket I brought in last week. It's Saks Fifth Avenue. Very exotic here. Someone will snap it up. Are you sure no one will want this kilt?" She pulled at the accordion pleats and rattled the leather buckle.

"Kilts are best taken back to The States. We have plenty here to go round," Mick assured her with a straight face. "Perhaps one day you'll find just the right pair of jack boots to make it work. Those sandals I saw you walk by in the other day are a real insult to a kilt."

"OK! Good advice. I'll keep my eyes peeled." She draped the kilt over her arm once again. "Really nice to have met you all, and thanks for swapping all summer. Bye-bye, now." The clerk waved her out of the shop.

She walked swiftly toward Cornmarket Street to find the grocery store. Rounding the corner from Dillon's, as Mr Dickens had instructed her, Diane bumped straight into two women in smocks, one, the cosmetics cashier from Boswell's. Diane gave them a quick apology.

"Oh, that one. A fixture in the sales bins," Diane overheard the woman explaining to her new assistant as Diane disappeared down the street.

Diane watched for a broad set of plate glass windows and clear view of brightly lit grocery shelving. Finding none, she doubled back from High Street, then remembered that Mr Dickens had said, lower level. A small sign along the antique-looking storefronts said *grocery*. She stepped into a doorway, rode the escalator down to a well-stocked modern market and marveled again at Oxford's ability to hide everything behind its historical wrapper. Brands were similar to those at home, even in the candy aisle, which disappointed her sense of adventure. She'd either expanded her knowledge of where to get imported goods in Denver, or the world was getting smaller. She bought a small bag of *Cheeky Little Monkeys*, just to show Natalie.

Next stop: the card shop several steps further down Cornmarket Street. Diane carried away several cards featuring mice in Wellington boots gone in search of 'chocs,' border collies chasing 'woolly buggers.' At the post office, she requested the most beautiful airmail postage stamps available. This would be a grand afternoon for recording parting thoughts. Last stop: choose the perfect Oxford sweatshirt for Dee to show off at the bowling alley, though the twenty dollars the Quinnells had given her for it didn't quiet cover it.

She climbed Staircase Sixteen with her small bags.

"I see you're all packed," Natalie called from behind her half-closed bedroom door.

"Yep. I've got everything I need to head home, now," she laughed as she tucked the two packets of Chocolate Covered McVitie's into her suitcase. "Did you get everything you needed to do done?" Diane called delicately, seeing Natalie's workspace properly packed up.

"Oh, yes. Chandra is ultimately happy and Constance gave me a week's extension."

"Really?" Diane thought more than said, remembering Bede's finality: '*and then they leave.*' "How does that work?"

"I presented a logical case, based on lack of access to books."

"Any chance your dad is a lawyer?"

"My mother," Natalie clarified then continued. "Then I'll stay in guest lodging here at the College. Oh, and Greg has arrived from New York. He'll just have to explore town without me. Then we'll head off on a driving trip."

Diane took the unexpected news in stride. "Say, what are we supposed to do with our books? I certainly don't want to drag them with me." Diane said, confronting her last duty, stacked on her desk.

"You sell them back to Blackwell's, next door."

"How do you know that?" Diane called to her, amazed anew at her roommate's vast knowledge.

"Mary Ann told me. She wanted to make sure we didn't leave anything of value behind. They'll probably think our Scouts stole them, otherwise."

"You're kidding?" Diane called again, thinking her roommate must be dressing or napping; otherwise she'd have come out already.

"No. That's the way it is with servants. Not that they steal things, but that they get blamed for it if anything is out of place."

Diane started breathing again as soon as Natalie clarified. She'd just hate to think of Natalie as a snobby rich girl who blames the servants for everything. *Servants*, Diane laughed under her breath. *Not exactly my term for our Scout.*

"Oh, and remember to take your Trinity ID to Blackwell's, otherwise they'll think you're selling stolen books," she called, still remaining in her room.

Diane went into her own room to wash up, wondering what had put stealing things into Natalie's mind. Had she seen the local papers? Did she know any of Diane's ordeal? There on her bed she found the old *Three Bobs & A Mario* poster. "Oh!" she cried, picking it up and running her thumb over the places the tacks had held it for a decade.

"Thought you might like to have that," Natalie said, popping her head around the corner.

"How on earth did you get this?"

"Oh. It was simple. I just tucked it under my raincoat yesterday."

"You didn't!" Diane said with mixed horror and amusement.

"Yes, I did. Go ahead. Turn me in," she purred.

* * *

Their final Wednesday night was for celebrating: a gathering in the garden for cocktails and photos, followed by dinner, then dancing. Diane was surprised when Constance handed her a final grade sheet along with the return of her paper. Grades hadn't even crossed her mind. She assumed credit would be calculated and mailed to the official institutions, then a carbonless copy would arrive at her door in Denver in perhaps four to six weeks.

"It has been a great pleasure getting to know you, Diane. I hope you will seriously consider my offer to work with you on that PhD you should have." Diane beamed, feeling steps closer to that reality, but rather tired of intense thinking for now. She'd put herself into the last analysis and honestly – thinking of school lying ahead of her in just three weeks' time – she really just wanted to have a break.

"Thank you, Connie. I'm not sure. There is so much criticism I haven't even looked into yet. I can't imagine being able to study it all and come up with something useful."

"Well, that's the beauty of your approach, Diane. You already have put forward perhaps a dozen ideas I'd love to see you develop. Stay in contact and I'll make sure to give you the jot list I made as you were talking all term."

"Thank you. That list will probably be the best evaluation of my abilities I'll ever see, so I look forward to seeing it." Connie's paper comments were her biggest interest just now. She turned directly to them.

"Make sure to join our group at dinner once we go in." Constance motioned toward Hall with her reading glasses, then walked toward Venerable Bede's bust, where Daniel stood waiting, without Courtney for the first time since their pairing.

Diane bent her head to decipher Connie's flowing handwriting, when another sheet fluttered into view, attached to Dr Harding's hand.

"Your grade sheet, Miss Quinnell. Thank you for your hard work," he said, bowed, then stepped away to distribute the rest of his small pile of papers. His brusque style, so different from Connie's, gave Diane a smile. The proverbial stiff upper lip delivery. Diane glanced at his single sentence, under the A she received for the course. "See paper for comments," he had typewritten, making copies with the simple statement to save time. She flipped through her attached paper until she found his only comment on the back of the final sheet. *'Your interpretation of Hardy's marriage is unique; however, with the current abundance of Hardy scholars about, extensive additional reading and developments would be necessary to prove this new angle to experts. Thank you for your contributions... etc. Sincerely yours, Dr Nicolas A. Harding.'*

Diane laughed at the irony of having Dr Harding echo her own words to Constance from just the moment before. She looked up to watch Harding's progress across the courtyard. Last page delivered, he made a beeline into the garden, sidestepping the bored redhead who stood just at the blue gates.

Another professor appeared with a sheaf of papers. "Did you pass, Miss Diane?" Dr Chandra spoke to her ear as he brushed past her shoulder. She enjoyed the way he pronounced the low *ah* sound: *'Did you paws?'* He disappeared into the cluster of students shuffling their feet while waiting, not yet released from their obligations to act politely to adults. Even Natalie, who had lounged comfortably at a distance in the grouping of lawn furniture just outside the gathering, peeled herself away from her group of young men as Chandra joined his students. As Natalie stepped into the courtyard, Diane caught Connie's eyes watching Natalie. *'How did I ever let her get by with an extension?'* the professor's face seemed to say.

Diane glanced about wondering what grading day at Oxford looked like for the other students. Would it be anything like her high schoolers: glance and fling? All the work teachers put into their comments, dismissed.

Brandon and Tucker stood in a compact huddle with their grading sheets, brows forming the scowling V not necessarily associated with Victory. Tommy Newton, his grading sheet rolled into a neat scroll like a relay runner's baton, seemed to be enjoying a serious conversation with Dennis Sartorius. Nice to see he had found a sympathetic mentor in the group. Neoclassicism might be just the topic for that young man, who wanted more weight to his studies. Courtney joined Jessica and Emily the moment Harding had done his work. They set their papers down on the beverage table, picked up glasses and glanced about, poufing their hair nervously, adjusting necklaces like contestants in a talent show. Then the ringleader appeared. Laura stepped into the Quad, her long dark hair swept up formally. All heads turned. The pale green off-the-shoulder gown she wore featured generous layers of crinoline that shushed as she crossed the courtyard toward her friends. Diane gave her kudos for knowing how to navigate in such a stately costume. Once Laura had landed on her mark, she smiled serenely, then tipped a cheery nod to Diane, perhaps to acknowledge her comments on finding vintage wear in town. Diane turned, wanting to see Natalie's reaction; her roommate stood preoccupied studying her shoes while Dr Chandra chatted with her visiting boyfriend. Off in a corner, Diane saw Vivien standing alone with her brother who had arrived to escort her back to Portland. Diane made her way to them to introduce herself, curious to see if he might also have a famous literary name.

Dr Clarence officially gathered everyone on the lawn for a group photograph just before dinner. The party mood of the occasion overpowered the rewards of a summer of scholarship, as the group herded to the Dining Hall. Diane took a moment to tuck her papers just inside her staircase door. As she crossed the courtyard at the rear of the pack, she watched several papers set casually on table edges fall to the pavement, as the last breezes of afternoon quelled into early evening.

Constance's class gathered in their usual spot, her two graduate students joining the group. Daniel Glasser brought new levity to the table. Natalie hovered at the far end, her New York boyfriend nearly an outcast from the sudden warm affections inspired by this parting evening.

Lawrence approached with a silver tray. Upon it, a bottle of champagne and one champagne flute. "Miss Quinnell?" he inquired quietly, handing her a small envelope. Diane couldn't conceal her surprise – and confusion. Her first instinct was to find Chandra. He seemed the type to do something sweet like this as a good-bye. But from his distance, he lifted his eyebrows, conveying his own puzzlement. Lawrence poured a glass and placed it near her, along with the bottle resting in its ice bucket.

She opened the envelope. '*For services rendered to the College,*' stated the official embossed card, signed by President Merton Jeffreys. Diane stared at her lap, very aware of everyone watching her.

Constance, to her left, smiled quietly, then lifted her glass and clinked it against Diane's. "Yes, Diane," she said just loudly enough. "Nice work on that additional art history research for the College Archivist." The information spread around the table, but was quickly overlooked as soup arrived.

"So you did know?" Diane said quietly to Connie.

"Yes. I saw the headline on my way to York." She smiled quietly at her pupil. "When I returned, I made a few discreet inquiries, along with the promise not to disturb you."

Dinner wound to a close. Dancing in the Beer Cellar would cap the night. Diane passed through the foyer just as Courtney was telling a group: "Daniel and I will be in Greece for a week. I haven't been there, so at least that will be interesting." If there had been even one hint of self-directed happiness in that girl, Diane would have wished her well. Unfortunately the redhead's characteristic boredom stamped doom over their future together, Diane was sure.

Down in the Beer Cellar, Diane's newly discovered security assistant from The Lodge doubled as DJ for the evening. His collection of vinyl 45s he presented half-proudly, half-apologetically. "The music selections tonight end abruptly in 1984," he spoke into a microphone. "But it is all good dance music and that's what you Americans all seem to like."

Diane joined the students on the dance floor, turning to this girlfriend, that nameless classmate, everyone smiling gleefully. Diane noticed that despite the initial complaints, everyone knew the words to the outdated tunes. Slow numbers allowed for last minute declarations between couples who clung closely to each other. Diane felt euphoric; she loved dancing! And with her soft spot for wallflowers, she scooped up several in turn. Even the College Archivist was pressed into service. "I'm done for, now!" Charlotte shouted into Diane's ear, as the swelling group crowded them under one of the low-hanging arches halfway through *Rock the Casbah*.

Diane crossed to a nearby table of professors and took Chandra by the hand. "I thought you would never ask," he shouted in her ear as she pulled him to his feet without much resistance. Chandra bobbed gently through the song looking both amused and pleased, then stood smiling intensely at her as the next song started, preempting her plan to switch partners. Even the stodgy Tommy Newton over in the corner, with his prickly feelings toward everything foreign, was on her dance card. But Chandra's gaze held her tight.

The opening guitar chords for *All Day and All of the Night*, slashed through the room. "Ah! I love this song!" she shouted in Chandra's ear. "Ray Davies! He's so great! So old now, but he skips all over the stage all night. I've seen him twice in Denver. What a performer!"

"Yes, and those high-top tennis shoes and those skinny legs in those tight jeans!" Chandra shouted. "Amazing how he always stirs the crowd!"

"You've seen The Kinks?" She clung to his shoulder in order to hear him.

"Oh, yes! You are looking at a man who has lived in many eras! I knew how to close the books sometimes, as well, Diane. Ray played the small clubs back then, before his celebrity grew." His comment shot through her like an electric jolt. Was he trying to impress her, she wondered, or being playful to make her envious?

Chandra grinned gleefully; he knew how to dance to this 1964 hit. She, a natural clown raised on *Beach Party* movies reruns, did *The Jerk*, while the other students looked sideways at her antiquated convulsions. Chandra joined her, then they did *The Twist* – to the floor and back up several times – through the Middle-Eight. Students around them looked on with mixed reactions, as they continued bouncing up and down, with little idea of how this song was meant to be danced.

A natural impulse to squeeze this sweet and surprising old gentleman caused Diane to lean forward as the song ended, and bestow a quick kiss. She aimed for the spot just above his jaw line where the mischievous dimple played. Bull's-eye. She detached herself from him, and grabbed Emily, then Vivien and her brother, Gawain.

Courtney dragged Daniel from table to table, but did not dance. Natalie appeared momentarily on the dance floor with her American boyfriend, as Diane was negotiating her way around Laura's swaying crinoline. "This is my roommate, Diane. Here's Greg. Have a dance," Natalie said and stepped off through the crowd. Greg smiled affably and fell into step.

Frivolity mixed with melancholy, as the basement room grew louder and hotter. Sloppy declarations in the classic American style: 'I'll call you,' were heard everywhere. Last-minute friendly gestures gave the evening a superlative glow. Diane sidestepped several groups of maudlin well-wishers, preferring to round up her own thoughts in private. The last song played, the lights turned up. She headed upstairs and out into the night air.

This was the last night of an amazing summer. Dancing, a rousing workout. Comments from Constance on her writing pulsed through Diane's head along with the echoes of the heart-beating rhythms. Thinking in new directions. Exhilarated and relaxed.

Lingering good-byes and last chance embraces multiplied as the students flooded into the Garden Quad, many heading directly for the lawn furniture near the back gate. Diane planned a pit stop, but found her feet tripping awkwardly up the uneven wooden stairs that wound up to the lavatory at the top of Staircase Sixteen. Her shaky return descent convinced her to head for bed rather than fall asleep with the rest of them in the Gardens under the stars.

Thursday, August 8

Diane stopped at the window at the top of Staircase Sixteen for a final look at the view before her. The distant towers of Oxford appeared dimmer now in the predawn light, the approach of autumn apparent. Trinity's Roman matron pointed toward the dawn through all seasons, Diane understood. Today they would have to wait a little longer for their Rosy-fingered friend to appear.

Just beyond the tall blue fence, a dozen students formed a ring on the Trinity lawn. Their slow, graceful movements looked to Diane like a warmup stretching session, though related, perhaps, to some form of ages-old sunrise dance.

She descended and stepped out into the courtyard to watch them. Archie nodded in her direction as they all raised their arms full over their heads, drew in deep breaths then held positions with arms pointing east. Diane exhaled with them, feeling really pleased for Archie, having gathered to him these kindred souls.

"Good morning, Dyan." She was also glad to bump into Chandra as usual on this final morning. "Do you wait in the doorway until you see me?" she asked playfully as they fell into step. "I will miss my breakfast companion – who is also an amazing dancer." She squeezed his arm affectionately.

"Good morning, Diane." He looked at her differently she thought, though he smiled.

"Are you all right?" she asked.

"Yes, yes." He assured her, though in a manner quieter than his usual self.

"Come look at this." She led him over to the tall palisade gate to the Garden. The dancing students had seated themselves in a tight-knit circle in the sun, mid-lawn. "Look at that lengthening shadow the morning sun casts across the Trinity lawn. See how they are sitting right at the edge of it? Has the sun changed angles so suddenly in the past week? I guess I had other things to think about. I didn't notice it until today."

He smiled quietly for a moment, then said, "Perhaps breakfast is in order?"

He was moving slower than usual. Maybe he is just tired, she thought to herself, watching the dappled morning light play across his silver hair as they walked back across the courtyard. The morning light also brought out traces of shadows under his eyes. All those papers he graded, probably. And all that dancing. A moment of motherly concern swept over her. "Soon you get a break, don't you? August off, once we all leave?"

"Yes, August is a joyous time," Chandra replied. "Plans? Oh, I was going to go to the Costa del Sol of Spain for some sun." He seemed to brighten at this thought. Diane, ready to say in their easy rapport, *'Reminds you of home?'* She thought better of it for some intuitive reason. Naturally, anyone might like some summer sunshine, with the gray English winter approaching. And she also would head back to another school year. Denver would be its typical self: continual sunshine. She looked again at Chandra. "But now I am not sure," he trailed off.

Diane felt surprised by his demeanor. "No, really, Dyan. Are you all right? Have you had some bad news?" she asked again, puzzled by his lack of effervescence.

"No, no. Nothing like that, I assure you," he patted her arm and flashed her a tired smile.

The kitchen staff all stood in their places, each smiling at the two.

"Well, well. Here they are. Glad to see someone still keeps decent hours," Mrs Whappington greeted them as they entered the serving line. "You see, Chester? I knew we could count on these two for keeping to a sensible schedule. You two are our only diners. We wagered on it. I've seen enough final weeks when we cook and no one arrives to eat, but Chester here didn't believe me. Then the last morning, like clockwork: no one. I told Lawrence it was a mistake to over-prepare. Well. You have first choice for seating, that's for certain." Mrs Whappington's voice echoed after them into the empty Hall.

"Shall we sit at Head Table?" Diane prodded Dr Chandra, hoping to lighten his mood.

"If you like."

They pulled up under the Foundress painting.

The sight of it seemed to revive Chandra. He then looked about, as if finally awake, glanced back at the empty room and smiled. "Yes, this would be excellent."

"That's more like it!" Diane teased him. She pulled his chair out for him with a flourish, since here, on the raised dais, chairs were set for the fellows and dons. "My mother raised me to be a gentleman, I think. Very theatrical. Maybe that's why I always step forward to open doors. That really bugs Dr Harding. Did I tell you that? He walked me out of your building one day, I grabbed the door pull when we got to the door. He didn't know what to do. *'You American girls!'* He said, *'So unusual.'* So I told him: look, we're both walking through the door. I am a step ahead. Why would I stop and wait for you to open the door? I can open the door." She laughed, remembering his dismay. "I suppose I robbed him of a chance to be polite, but really!" The sound of her laughter returned to them from the distant Minstrel Loft.

"Have a cup of tea, Dyan. That should fix you up." Diane tore open her own tea bag wrapper and merrily plopped it in her own cup all the while studying Chandra. She continued smiling at her own silliness, wondering at the same time what exactly he had done to bring out this nurturing side of her personality.

"Seeing Lady Elizabeth Pope here on the wall brings me to another subject. I have brought you something, though you are probably not one for mementos, Diane." He pulled a plain envelope out of his breast pocket and placed it on the table between them.

Diane loathed mushy cards. She put on her best smile, nevertheless, and hoped for the best. The envelope contained several newspaper clippings tracing the Trinity art forgery.

"I wasn't sure you wanted to be reminded of this aspect of your summer here, but I also thought that perhaps you would like to show them to friends in Denver. Have you seen these?"

"Connie showed me this one – but no. I haven't seen the rest. Here's the one Archie said to watch for." She tapped on the headline from last night's paper: *"Sensational Arrest of Oxford Professor."*

"You know, I myself, preoccupied with grading, had not been aware of this final development involving Dr Steele. I guessed that it must have been you who supplied the missing details, connected the dots for them. Connie confirmed it when we crossed paths in our hallway late last night." He watched Diane gravely as she nodded. "I discovered the article after the dance, seeking some light reading while winding down from the loud music. I have been concerned about you ever since. I went straight to the garden, but you were not there."

"I knew something was bothering you," Diane said half to herself, sobered by his recital. In the celebrations last night, she had evidently thrown off all concerns for her part in sealing Steele's fate. And now the situation had upset another person's night. When would all this finally be done, she wondered.

"The other night in the garden, there was something I wanted to say to you privately. The circumstances, however, did not allow for it." His dark eyes looked directly into hers.

Diane froze. *Sentiment. He wants to express it. That's pretty normal,* she told herself, but it still raised a question for her: *Why am I feeling all stressed out about it?*

He broke off with a small laugh: "Ah! Where are my parents when I need them?"

Diane blinked twice and cocked her chin sideways at his non-sequitur. She noticed, however, that he was holding his breath. *He must have something big to tell me. Oh, I hope no one has died,* she thought suddenly, frowning.

"What I wanted to say to you, privately – but foolishly chose the wrong way to say it. *'Coffee in my room?'* You left me sitting there, laughing at my own foolishness. Even in that, you were right to leave me in the garden. Your sense of wisdom about being in this world," he gestured about him, "your understanding of Trinity was more attuned than mine at that moment. And you, a newcomer by comparison to my years here, arrive here and understand my world often better than I do myself."

It was a palatable compliment, but Diane wondered if old people often wandered around like this, rambling to get to the point? Chandra's confusion communicated itself to Diane, but the source of it still lay unnamed. Was he just apologizing for an awkward phrase that he thought had insulted her? A bashful, boyish look suffused his face. He took a deep breath in preparation to say whatever it was that was bothering him.

"I simply wonder, Diane: what do you think of me? Would you like to stay here and marry me? And I do mean marry," he added, looking at her steadily. "Not simply stay and – well, whatever you would want to call that. I mean, would you consider having me as your husband?"

Diane, completely caught off guard by his question, froze, trying to take it in.

"I apologize for waiting until the last moment, but if I'd said this much earlier, you would have dismissed me as crazy."

Perhaps she remained staring silently for a long time, because Chandra, who usually possessed such a calm and patient demeanor, began adding information hurriedly into the silence.

"You could of course continue your studies. It would be a simple matter to transfer into a program here and complete a PhD, for instance." He cleared his throat, having regained a more logical tone. "Connie has been praising your discussions and written work ever since you arrived. Even Dr Harding has let slip a comment on your insights which, frankly, have rattled his radar, so to speak. But it all depends on your opinion of me, I believe, Diane."

Diane progressively passed through varying shades of pink and purple, she was sure. First hot then cold and hot again. So much to think about, all at once and yet – hadn't thoughts about their friendship been constantly in her mind since – when? She thought back to the moment they had met, his initiating the same-name ritual. And that night at The Turl?

Now Diane put Chandra's demeanor in context. Still she hadn't said anything. Instead, she started to laugh. "*Where are my parents when I need them?*" She said his words back to him, copying his accent, then squeezed his arm.

"I told you before, Miss Diane. That kind of irreverent mockery will lead you into trouble," he scolded her like the most adoring grandfather – or the sweetest lover.

"I'm just speechless, Dyan. I have a million things to say." She set down the toast she had held suspended through this last bit.

"Oh! Of that I am sure. Your wonderful face; so easy to read. What a whirlwind you have come through in these last few moments." And with that magic phrase, they fell back into their normal rapport. His eyes too had lost the sadness, but the serious mood remained, as he awaited her answer.

"Perhaps you want some additional time to think about this? But, no. I believe you will know now, yes or no. It will be clear, if I know you, Diane."

"Wow. You really do know me, don't you? This is really, really... great. I mean the you and me part. I think you're right. I love your company. I think you're a real foil for my jokes, if nothing else. – Oh, I'm sorry. I always trivialize when things get serious, but listen. I've never told you this, but this proposal is something like number twenty-eight for me. Oh! Oh! Don't worry!" she saw his face fall. "I don't mean I'm saying: *So what. Just another one.* No, no. Not that. The thing I can't believe you said, and no one else ever did say was, what do *I* want? All those other proposals focused on what a prize I was for them, how they decided I must become their wife. And don't think I'm quoting EM Forster's character, Lucy Honeychurch, either. You'd never believe it: those men all actually said it, unaware they were trying to claim a possession. You're the only one to ask me what I want. I am amazed by you."

"So, am I lucky twenty-eight?" he asked with gleaming eyes.

She leaned forward and planted a kiss on his cheek. Just the right kiss. "There's a lot to talk about, Dyan."

"Oh! Perhaps you are not sure about living here? I could easily seek a professorship in Chicago, Syracuse. Something near Denver so you could be close to your family whom you will miss, I am sure."

Diane laughed louder than she ought to have at his grasp on geography, but then, what was 2000 miles in an age of jets? As for home-sickness, she pointed out: "I've never missed my family yet. Well, maybe about for three minutes at Smith when I was feeling frustrated with the personalities there, but my parents couldn't exactly do much about it, anyway. My family unit is probably not as close-knit as yours, Dyan, which is fine. We don't hate each other or anything. I was raised to operate independently so my parents could get on with what they wanted to do, that's all. Plus, I really do love it here."

"Ah, there is that as well. You will meet my family. I hope you wanted to go to Bombay. Did you know the city's real name is Mumbai? There's a nice fact for your trivia list. My mother wouldn't possibly come here. So, you must meet her there."

Diane saw herself there. "Will I get to wear a sari?" the question popped out of her mouth all on its own.

Chandra hooted: "More chances to wear costumes! Naturally."

Picturing herself there, wound up in yards of embroidered silks, she remembered something her Big Sister at Smith had told her. Katari – the Santa Barbara girl – had ordered a sari while she visited her relatives in India, but when it arrived at school, she never put it on. She had been sure she wanted one while she was there, but seeing it in Massachusetts, she felt foolish that she had ever had it made. Perhaps Diane would also? Her Hawaiian muumuu never quite felt right in Denver, either.

"I mean," she backtracked, "me in a sari? I'm not so sure."

"Oh, my sister also!" Chandra lit up. "The first time I saw her in blue jeans, I had a shock as well, but that has worn off now. What are clothes, after all, but costumes?" He leaned closer. "Diane, as you have said, your family is not the academic type – yet you took yourself to college anyway. Mine is not the traveling type – yet I came here and remained. Not having married years ago also sets me aside. So you see again how similar we are: we both choose the unusual path. Mine may look more traditional to you, though the more you learn of it, the more you'll see what I mean. I hope this factor alone will speak to you to join me here."

Traditional. She stuck on the word. That was it. This aspect was an unknown commodity when coming from different lands, families and their sets of assumed expectations. "So, what is the traditional role of wife for me in your mind? What do you picture?"

He thought a moment then spoke. "I never had a slave before, so I do not think I will suddenly need one, if that is your worry."

"Part of it. But will you be making all of my decisions for me? Will your word be law in our house?"

"That is a sticky question on the surface, but not deep down, Diane."

"Yes, but you have been making all of the decisions for yourself for how many years, Dyan?"

"Since I came to England, not yet forty years ago," he answered steadily. "And you, Miss Quinnell? You have been making all of your own for as long as I can tell, from what you have told me of your upbringing and your adventures. Who will prove the more headstrong?" He smiled at her, satisfied that he had made his point, as well. "Will I need to e-mail your colleagues in Denver? You may certainly ask mine, here." He had handled the very serious question with a levelheadedness and grace that reassured Diane of his equanimity.

The musical murmur of his voice lulled her racing thoughts, like the tranquilizing effect of a purring cat. *Everything's all right, everything's all right*, it gently insisted. *Just relax and listen to my purring*, it said. She felt rather wonderful. And she'd noticed that before now. She'd thought it nearly every time they were together.

Yet, the clock was ticking! That rush exaggerated the experience, made it into an exciting opportunity with only a small window to grab it. And then what? Did it disappear, the thrill? She wondered.

"What is on your mind?" Chandra asked.

"Is it too much? Out of balance, do you think, Dyan? I feel so good around you and you certainly glow. But what is this? The exaggerated joy that is heightened unnaturally – beyond reality – only by our circumstances? I've got an airline ticket to leave England in five days. I'm supposed to vacate my room here by lunchtime. The moment of decision. *Speak or part*, as we have talked about before. I'm glad we didn't disappear into your rooms, then wake up and feel completely awkward about the situation. It's easy to operate that way in an exciting moment. Well, listen Dyan, I know enough about dating to know that the exciting tension of a moment like this is not a good time for making sound decisions."

"My! What a skeptic you are at thirty-one years of age, Diane Quinnell," Chandra said. "What if instead of skepticism, what if, as they say: *this is it?* The moment you've been waiting for? The person you belong with, if you think in those terms? Oh-ho! That look alone just told me a great deal about your own feelings: logic must prevail!

I can only speak for myself. This is not some glittering moment for me, but a comfortable, familiar, solid warmth that has been steadily growing since we met. You're right. It has only been six weeks, however, and today the last day."

Diane's thoughts flew as her logical self struggled with her spontaneous nature. An entire list of things left unfinished back in Denver appeared before her. All trivialities, she quickly assessed. At the end of the imagined list, she saw the truth. Her personal understanding.

"Dyan, I hesitate because I know what it is to make a quick decision based on a flash of insight into the future, and then spend years puzzled as to how to get out of it. You don't know this, but I married my ex-husband within three months of meeting him, focused only on the amazing things ahead for both of us. I jumped into a bigger commitment than I had estimated, and a lot faster than made sense." *But this is different today, isn't it, Diane?* a voice in her head argued. *Look at this man: is he a mystery to you? Does he hide everything from you? He's been open and communicative. He's answered every query you've given him. Constance – without being asked – gave him rave reviews in terms of respectability and history of behavior.*

She had to agree with Connie's assertions. A highly expressive person sat before her. No mystery. No guessing. No building future plans on illusions. No. Dr Chandra is what he is. *How existential,* Diane thought with a flash of understanding. *And! He doesn't live with his mother,* she laughed to herself. She'd been through that grind before.

"Look, Diane. I hear your high-hearted laugh, but you are building a wall of highly reasonable objections based on your own experiences, I can see it on your face. I encourage you to look at all of them. And if this is your style of academic debate, you are a formidable scholar! That is another aspect that I admire about you. But for a moment, please lean against that wall you are constructing and ask yourself one question: how do you feel inside about yourself at this moment? As you sit here, today. There is the wall. You are safe. All the other considerations aside for a moment." He gave her the moment.

She listened and sat very still, trying to strip away all the worries. She immediately realized that this man was not trying to manipulate her or even force an answer. He invited her just to be. The same way he had allowed her to compose herself in the Sheldonian cupola. This was a rare form of torture. She liked it very much.

"Now please, just peek over that wall for a moment and think about what you see here." He pressed his palm against his chest. "I am not here to push your wall over. I am standing and waiting for you. I feel we have enjoyed a familiar yet delightful camaraderie. I feel as though I have known you forever, although that is not to be misconstrued as a romantic convention," he warned her. "I am hoping you experience similar feelings in my company."

This is totally different, Diane's head told her. *Look at him. You know more about him, how he will respond, than you ever did about Max. Mysterious, silent, always absent Max. Here is Dyan, who has spent time with you, not followed you around in any annoying way as you feared he might when he seemed so interested in you the first few days. He hasn't tried to grab you or monopolize you. He isn't just playing around.* Yet this is all happening so fast, Diane reminded herself.

'*Dyan,*' she was about to say, '*let me sleep on it,*' but suddenly she saw the unwarranted distress of that delay, the wasted time, besides her own disturbed sleep. He was right; she knew already. But there was one more matter.

"Dyan," she looked at him squarely, "I would never be so foolish as to marry someone I have never even kissed. Could we...?" Despite herself, she blushed.

"You have already kissed me three times. Didn't you notice? See how natural it was? Oh – not *that* kind of kiss? I see. I see." His eyes twinkled. His deep dimple re-appeared.

"OK, OK," Diane felt mildly foolish, but bore it well. "I want that kind of kiss that tells me everything I want to know."

"Gladly," he grinned warmly. "But not here, of course." They both glanced toward the kitchen area.

"I like to keep private life private, as well. In that way, I'm not very modern, am I?" she said with a crooked grin, keenly aware that her modesty was a contradiction to much of her other boldness, particularly her demand for a kiss.

"You see. Another proof we think alike," he purred.

They laughed and rose a bit timidly, then disappeared out of the Dining Hall together.

And where will he take me for this exciting moment, she wondered only for a moment, feeling free to be led by him to wherever necessary. The Park perhaps? No, no. A potential for colleagues everywhere. This was kind of fun, like solving a puzzle together. And as they meandered without destination, she was glad to understand that none of this had been planned. He hadn't led her directly to some well-used, secret spot. This was good. The situation was unfolding naturally, honestly.

"Diane, I also have one rather contradictory request. As I have said, no kissing is allowed in Hindu musicals, but I agree to this kiss, since neither one of us is a virgin. Oh, I do not mean to shock you," he laughed easily, "but as a younger man, I certainly learned about romance. I will gladly kiss you in some secluded corner, if we can find one, but the rest must wait until the wedding night. I insist! Why ruin all the thrilling anticipation of the auspicious moment? Humor me in this, will you?" They stopped just east of The Lodge.

"As long as I get my kiss – which will tell me everything I want to know," she reiterated like a lawyer, "your plan sounds like a good one. Where I come from, anticipation is a vanishing art form. That must be true here as well, since you name it so clearly."

"This is the Graduate's Garden. And now, I think you see our difficulty." They both looked around with diminishing ideas.

"Discretion is important. And it is another reason I praise you for not accepting that bold invitation to coffee in my room the other night. What was I thinking? Actually, your refusal helped me see what needed to happen. I would never take you into my room, I concluded that night, unless you were my wife. No. Otherwise your reputation is compromised, and that I would never wish for. So you see? It is your correct understanding that has brought all this about."

"You know, Dyan. I've learned a thing or two about discretion from theater, believe it or not. For instance, actors often need to change costumes backstage, or behind a tree, or in the parking lot, when necessary. You change clothes in public, and then you're done." She snapped off the last phrase and smiled, safely under cover of proper clothing just now. "People don't look around much, I can assure you of that. If you just operate without fanfare, many things can slip by unnoticed. Couldn't we just assume that the most average, open place may be the most unobserved place, if we don't call attention to ourselves by skulking about?" She laughed.

"Excellent advice." Chandra looked at her for a long moment, and then stared over her shoulder, thinking. "Well then, I have it. Look." He gestured with a subtle rise of his chin.

She turned to see it, just beyond them, rising above the Trinity cottages that front Broad Street. "Ah, The Sheldonian Theatre cupola. A most public spot," she enunciated as though reading from the tourist brochure. They made way toward the front gate.

"Try not to look so eager," she teased him as they walked very separately past The Lodge and turned east into the morning light. She passed under the Roman heads without a thought of how their features had created such a foreboding atmosphere that first evening she had arrived in Oxford. She wanted to fix this moment in her mind, record every detail of their fateful progress toward that first kiss. Within a moment, however, Chandra spoke of other matters.

"How are you liking the Rushdie book? Did you find time to pick it up while I was away?"

"Oh, I forgot to say: Wow! '*A hilarious, whirling frolic,*' just as the cover said." She looked askance at him, grinning. "No, really; I love it. But that is another reason I dislike these new books; I always distrust those cover blurbs. Why? Maybe because most of my friends studied under PT Barnum. You don't know him? He said: '*There's a sucker born every minute.*' That's his contribution to skepticism! But you proved me wrong on this one, even in review blurbs. *The Moor's Last Sigh* is *fabulous.*" She chose the word purposely – the book being a mash of fables – just to watch his reaction. He nodded, but arched one eyebrow, knowingly. That's when she realized that the whole town could wait; this moment was Dyan's. He was the real territory to explore and to record in her mind.

"So, you're an Edwardian scholar?" she began, with an interest in finding out everything about him that she had overlooked until now. He nodded and smiled, but said nothing. "That's before World War One, isn't it?" Diane asked as innocently as possible. "I guess I could get used to that."

"That's right! I forgot to list that as an asset: I have a good job," he added, not knowing the sweet irony his statement held for Diane. "You see, the practical side of basic living goes hand-in-hand with happy marriage arrangements. That is one part of the superior method of centuries of Hindu parents making wise choices for their children."

It might be a stretch for Chandra to believe it of this young American, but Diane already knew this to be true. It had gone through her head enough times after she divorced Max. Looking for a good job, waiting for Max to finish school, find a job, so they could get out of his mother's attic. But he had no interest in that direction. A fatal blow to their marriage, not putting their own independent unit together. Her practical parents, however, had they a tradition of choosing husbands for their daughters, would never have chosen a marriage with that young man.

Chandra clinked two coins into the observation fee box. As they climbed the stairs he continued, turning back to her with nearly each step: "And yes, definitely a PhD for you, Diane. The world can easily welcome another Dr Chandra."

"Like a law firm: Chandra, Chandra & Chandra? Or more like adding up to our own comedy act, something akin to *Three Bobs & A Mario?* " She laughed and tugged his sleeve. "Well, Dyan. Maybe the world needs a Dr Quinnell? Oh, Dyan. I hadn't even thought about that!" But she saw he looked not at all crushed by her statement. Would she take his name? Right now it sounded like an added attraction to being joined with him. Start a new life with a new name, though of course all the while retaining the best aspects of her own quirky self.

She followed closely behind him, up the stairway to the observation cupola. Her nose wrinkled suddenly. She tugged at his sleeve. "Did I just get a big whiff of cinnamon?" She looked at him, puzzled.

"Ah! My personal aftershave. Actually, it is cardamom scented. I use it to exert subtle influence on American girls." He paused to watch her reaction, then continued. "Well, the question of names will settle itself in time. And as for children?"

She stopped dead in her tracks. "I hadn't even thought of that." They reached the observation platform, laughing like teenagers.

"Well," he looked at her seriously. "You may not know it yet, but writing a book is often compared to giving birth to a child. Will that suffice?"

"That's a lot of latitude," she admitted. "Thank you."

"From hearing only some of the stories you tell, I believe you have many novels in you, as well. You are surprised when I say *novels*, I see, but a PhD can take many forms. Diane, you may do as you like, however – put your feet up, draw in the park. We shall get along fine if we both have purpose in life by pursuing our projects. I have enough income for both of us, I am sure."

"With my new interpretations of Thomas Hardy's love poems to his dead wife," Diane fell right in stride with his thoughts, "with those alone, I believe we can anticipate our many offspring in the form of collaborative works, m'dear."

AFTER WORD

"Dear Robyn: You have brilliantly captured the romance of Oxford, for it is a very romantic place. I am not sure why it should be so, perhaps because it is such a small, concentrated city, where students live very full and intense lives during their extremely short terms. You have also captured the spirit of summer schools, where everybody lives very much in the present, and has a great curiosity and energy, which seems very different from the normal lives of regular term inhabitants. Trinity is instantly recognizable in your description, which I very much enjoyed."
– Clare Hopkins, Trinity College Archivist, 9 May, 2011

When in November of 2010, I contacted Sir Ivor Roberts, President of Trinity College, Oxford University, with news of my project, I had little idea of his gracious reception for the proposed novel. He immediately placed his staff at my disposal and through this, I became reacquainted with Trinity College Archivist, Clare Hopkins. Looking into the theme for her history, *Trinity: 450 years of an Oxford college community*,(OUP2005), struck me as serendipitous. My own impressions of the place, during the University of Massachusetts at Amherst's Summer Seminar 1996, also formed around daily interactions with the collection of individuals that make up that quiet enclave behind Trinity's palisade fence and stone walls.

Several specific items spurred this project: a desire to tout the modern fellows painting by June Mendoza, to share with history lovers the contemplation time I spent with Lady Elizabeth Pope, along with a wish to weave an enjoyable story of the unending string of historic events that occurred while I lived on Staircase Sixteen of Sir Christopher Wren's Trinity Garden Quad Building.

Foremost, however, my crunching across the broken glass that littered the sidewalk in the silence of the early morning is what most compelled me to write this book. This minor, overlooked detail – which was dwarfed by the enormity of the success for Rushdie reappearing at last, freely and unmolested – haunted me. Why had that broken window not appeared in the headline news? No one seemed aware of it, as if it hadn't happened. Beyond that, I found it unbelievable that no one had yet written a story about that precise moment in time. And so I put that oversight to rights with this volume.

The movie-version tag line *"based on a true story"* taunted me all through the writing of *Oxford Vindaloo*, and the factual elements of the story certainly give it deeper meaning. Here's a short list of specifics. The date is correct. It was summer term1996, Oxford. Salman Rushdie did reappear nearly unannounced just after term began. The Dalai Lama did speak to his first Western audience at London's Barbican Theatre, though the actual date was July 18; I moved the date for plot convenience. The Royal Shakespeare Company did produce the plays discussed, in squeaky sandals as noted. The physical descriptions of the setting I kept as accurate as possible, with the exception of moving the Lamb and Flag Passage a bit farther south.

Some of the incidental details are also true. My friend from design class did go to that private girls' school in Texas and then, after meeting Pope John Paul II, spent many Christmas dinners with him at the Vatican, along with her mother, flying in from Japan. I do have the Marvel Comics version of that Pope's life, and yes, The Ramones did play by invitation in Vatican City (1980), as well.

As for the celebrated jugglers, magicians, clowns and artists that Diane Quinnell knows, I drew upon a large supply of my own talented acquaintances, combining their random details with pure fantasy for this story. To all them I say: "Thus are you fictionalized!" To that, Mario Lorenz – who was in the juggling troupe *Sideshow Productions*, as was I, briefly – asked, "Which Bob am I?"

At the time, I did find that watching Christopher Ricks' High

Table lecture on WH Auden was like meeting a shorter, blonder version of Penn Jillette's stage persona. The amazing magic Ricks found in the verses of *A Shropshire Lad* was not lost on me either, despite my having been dumbfounded by Ricks' familiar, spectacular intensity. I hope Ricks will enjoy the compliment. This declaration made does not mean, however, that Marco the Magnificent's actions in *Returning to Denver* are related to Penn in any reality. That story snippet is a collage of other performer friends.

My late friend Anne Wells Clark, who I spent one year with at Smith College and who died suddenly in 1993, did sketch the Flying Karamazov Brothers when they drove for the first time from San Francisco to the Atlantic Ocean, the spring of 1979. Gasoline prices soared to a dollar a gallon for the first time in history that week, another memorable occasion. Another friend of mine did actually discover a FKB poster featuring Anne's sketch while traveling through Ireland in 1981. Everything beyond that is tailored to fit the tale.

At Trinity College, the late Alistair McLay, born in Glasgow and very proud of his Scottish heritage and who died unexpectedly in 2003, was the general model for my character Archie, who admitted freely, "Yes. I sleep under the night sky when the weather is fine." Aly's actual job title was 'general handyman' but I liked using the term 'stonemason' in order to link Archie with Thomas Hardy's character, Jude Fawley.

Aly's ubiquitous presence continues to occupy a beloved spot at Trinity, now in the college's history. An olive tree was dedicated as a memorial for him in the Fellows' Garden, where Aly had done a great deal of work on the stone walls there. Also 'Aly's stone' – an alabaster one given to him by Marcelle Quinton, sculptress wife of former President Tony Quinton, when they left Trinity in 1987 – now engraved, lies in just the right spot near the Laundry Cottage.

More dead friends! I am saddened to learn that Victorian Scholar Robin Gilmour, University of St Andrews, and my Thomas Hardy tutor, Dr Martin Ray of the University of Aberdeen, have since passed away. For the record, neither of them stole any of my literary insights, squeezed my knee, nor asked me to marry him.

Jenny Newman retired last spring from Liverpool John Moores University. She did her best to convince me to pursue a PhD. After much thought, I chose to write the Diane Quinnell novels, instead.

Anyone who studies art history in any depth comes away with a set of skills for digging into visual details. Add that training onto a life as keenly observed as Diane's has been, and boundless opportunities for discovery arise. Diane's primary tool is art analysis; she uses it anytime she contemplates her own life, whether in Oxford or at home in *Returning to Denver*. And art and artists deserve their due; here are the correct titles for the works discussed in this book.

Lady Elizabeth Pope, artist or copyist unknown.

Clare Hopkins adds: "Lady Elizabeth styled herself as the foundress, and was an active patron of the college between the death of Thomas in 1559 and her own in 1593. The fellows purchased the portraits of Thomas (hanging above) and her as a pair in the late Sixteenth Century."

Arts and Sciences at Trinity, 1976, is by June Mendoza, who graciously allows me to recast the title of her original painting for use in this novel. The affable portrait remains on display in the entry to the Trinity College Dining Hall. The five distinguished men in the painting are from left to right:

Kenneth Lord Clark, Slade Professor of art history, 1946-1950.

Alexander (Sandy) Ogston, biochemist & Trinity President

Sir Hans Krebs FRS (seated), biochemist Nobel Laureate

Sir Ronald Syme, ancient historian

Professor Rodney Porter, biochemist Nobel Laureate.

To read more than these few reflections on summer term in Oxford, visit my website: returningtodenver.com.

* * *

Trinity College President, Sir Ivor Roberts enthusiastically agreed to review my work in progress, perhaps due in part to his diplomatic involvement in relation to Political Islam, both at the time of Rushdie's prolonged *fatwa* ordeal, and continuing most recently, even as this manuscript crossed his desk. For that support and interest, I owe him a debt of gratitude.

About the author

RD McHattie has spent thirty years
as an actor, artist, writer and teacher.
She holds degrees from Smith College and the
University of Minnesota and has also studied literature
at Trinity College, Oxford University. She lives in Minneapolis
with her husband Don McHattie, who writes books on
reading improvement.

Oxford Vindaloo is RD McHattie's second Diane Quinnell novel.

Visit
RD McHattie's website

returningtodenver.com

Contact the author at

rdmchattie@returningtodenver.com

Oxford Vindaloo by RD McHattie

Reading discussion questions

ART HISTORY and MUSEUMS

Diane revels in visiting art museums. Have you been to any of the museums Diane names? What are the favorite impressions you came away with?

How does Diane's expedition to and through the Pitt-Rivers Collection parallel her trips to Boswell's sales bins? In what other instances does the metaphor of exploring new worlds play out through the story?

Art fosters many interpretations. Rosa Martínez's work, *The Five Fellows*, holds different interests for Diane, Natalie Hull, Dr Chandra, Professor Bede and Dr Steele. What are they?

Trace the foreshadowing of mystery that suggests that Diane Quinnell is actually in Oxford to solve a crime. What other themes do you see introduced while she is initially in London?

OXFORD and EDUCATION

Diane's first big jolt is learning about the demanding Oxford tutorial tradition. Do you sense further consequences/rewards of that educational system that extend beyond Diane's first reactions? How does such an arrangement compare to your own educational settings?

Name several reasons that Diane gives for writing & sending postcards.

Have you ever been kidnaped on a simple cab ride? Where? Certain steps lead Diane to befriend Oxford, the "daunting fortress of a town." What are some turning points for her to begin warming to her new surroundings?

Have you traveled much or lived abroad for a time? What factors, beyond Diane's initial sense of being lost, come to the fore when trying to feel a part of a new community? How does social isolation affect the summer students?

Oxford Vindaloo by RD McHattie

Women authors: are their titles still as difficult to get a hold of as Professor Bede described in her 1996 Oxford setting? In your own experience, have you noticed a marked change in the availability of titles written by women?

Interdepartmental studies were newly developing in the era Diane traveled to Oxford (1996). How do you feel about her contemplations on placing movies-as-storytelling on equal footing with literature? As video-streaming becomes more readily accessible worldwide, do you think written works will continue to be read? Required for school assignments?

Diane's own interests in Latin are thrilled by Oxford, "a town with Latin at nose level." She then goes on to bemoan the lack of it for the Neoclassical lecturer. Clare Hopkins, Trinity College Archivist and consultant on this book, confirms that Latin is also no longer a requirement for schools in Britain, and voices a concern for historians in the future, since Latin was the official form of record until the Eighteenth Century. Do you find the lack of Latin requirements in schools a loss or an advantage? What parts of the issue would make for a call to reinstate Latin requirements?

Diane frames part of her interest in traveling to Oxford as a comparative study between her American women's college experience, and the British men's college. What elements become apparent in the story? What other kinds of comparisons develop as the story unfolds, beyond the readily identifiable gender lines? In terms of culture limitations or expectations?

Diane's ability to say, "I don't know" in situations shocks and irritates many of her classmates. What reasons/examples does Diane give for choosing to live so candidly? How does her quizzical nature function in the educational setting? In social positioning? How is it educational to live in this self-revealing manner?

After reading of Diane's Summer Term, what new learning/study ideas would you employ as you head off to college? Why aren't these learning skills taught early on in schools?

CHARACTERS
Diane meets a new cast of characters that she must get to know. How do

Oxford Vindaloo by RD McHattie

her first impressions of some of them change over time? How do the other students change as the summer progresses?

What personal challenges does Diane bring with her as she arrives for Summer Term? What does she learn over the summer about her capacity for solving all her own problems? Were her capable parents good teachers?

On what levels does Natalie serve as a counterpoint to Diane? Of the two, which character type interests you more? In a book? In life?

Do you know people who have made choices to stop watching television, never carry a camera? What reasons did they give?

History and Nature appear as characters in this story. Where do you see them? What functions does each serve to enhance the meaning of the novel?

Diane enjoyed weighing the tales of the Bastille Day trip. Do you find that travelers divide into groups, as Diane does? What forms each group?

*** Diane's ability to value humans as humans, challenges some character's belief in an obligatory reverence toward established traditions. See the conversation on the motorcoach concerning two world religious leaders, or talk concerning the social order of students and servants. In what ways does Diane's ability to declassify social rankings allow her to explore unthinkable or taboo territories? In what ways do the characters near her respond to her unusual attitude? What about college staff? Townspeople? Homeless?

*** Through friendships with the theater crowd and her own cultural social observations, what revealing insights does Diane bring to her own under-standings of the merits of celebrity? How does meeting Constance Bede and Nick Harding add to this understanding?

Reading tip for young readers (more ideas at: returningtodenver.com)
Re-reading a novel's first page once you've finished it is an excellent way to learn more about the writer's craft. What did you miss on a first reading?

Find Diane Quinnell in the literary date book: **The Book of Fictional Days.**

Lightning Source UK Ltd.
Milton Keynes UK
UKOW051135220812

197895UK00001B/8/P